The

Son

Silas Rising

A Novel By

Doug Dahlgren

Ridge House Publishing
Decatur, Georgia USA

D1158629

ISBN: 0-578-05624-0
EAN-13: 978-0-578-05624-1
Printed in the United States of America

Cover Art and Photo refined by Memory Magic
memorymagic@mindspring.com

This is a work of pure fiction. Names, characters, places and incidents are

either the product of the author's imagination or used fictitiously.

Any resemblance to persons living or dead, locales or events is purely

coincidental.

Dedication in Memorium

To my brother, Dale

Gone too soon

Acknowledgments

Where does one start? So many have shown support in ways
that have surprised me. Neighbors of many years, friends I see now
and then, family members who I tended to wear out with the topic of
my "new work" and then, a group of folks I never would have met had I
not started this.

My rock and compass, through all, has been my wife of over 42 years,
Donna. I know she must have gotten tired of my constantly talking
about this book, but she seldom complained. Her reads and rereads of
the sections, and then the entire book, had to be a work way beyond
love. But she was there with encouragement and much needed
corrections.

My, oh so talented, daughter-in–law, Linda.
Few have her schedule and patience. She stepped up with a smile. Her
edits and corrections were critical, her help with the cover design
invaluable.

A few other names that must be mentioned, Don, Alan in Tenn, Ruth,
Susan, Mrs. Lewis, Chuck in Virginia, Jan in the great northeast, Dr.
Doug, Tina and Bryon. Also offering support were Wig, Roy, Peggy and
the many good folks at PDB and of course, Susan W.
You know who you are, now know that I appreciate you.

Thank you, all.

Also

By Doug Dahlgren

It Was Thursday

dougdahlgren.com

The

SON

Book One

Silas Rising

begins now..........

Prologue

The wire would normally shine from the moonlight. This night there was barely a sliver of moon, so they rode with caution as they neared the fence. A shrill whistle from the left carried well in their direction. Three horsemen pulled up sharply and looked to the south where now emerged the flickering beams from a flashlight. Their leader glanced around; assuring himself that the others had also heard it, then all three recklessly spurred their mounts down the fence line in the direction of the light.

They had found what they sought, the missing patriarch of the family, but not at all as they expected. The body was clearly that of the senator and it draped limply from the top strands of barbed wire fencing. Its hands touched the ground, as did the legs below the knee, but nothing else. The face, now ashen, clearly reflected both shock and fear.

The whistler, a Hispanic ranch hand, had lowered his light and stood in silence over the body. He looked up at the approaching riders and shook his head. Dust rose from the dried ground and swirled around the body as the riders stopped abruptly at the scene. Two of them stayed mounted and shone their lights on the scene. The third, another hired hand, jumped down and began looking around in silence, for what he did not say.

No one spoke. The rescue party appeared struck dumb by inward reflection at what they had found. Within a minute, all but their leader had their hat in hand as they stared at the corpse. The scene became a strange silhouette, two on foot, two on horseback and a body in the wire.

They stayed as they were until the headlights of a vehicle approaching from behind stirred them into action. They knew who that had to be.

"Stop 'em back there," the head of the rescue party ordered as he twisted around in his saddle to point at the oncoming vehicle. "Mom doesn't need to see this. Not this way."

The other man who was still mounted, pulled hard left on his reins and kicked his horse into motion. He rode directly into the oncoming lights, waving his hat for them to stop.

The group's leader steadied his horse with one hand and reached into a vest pocket with the other. He flipped open a cell phone and punched in 911.

"Yeah," he told the operator, "this is Murray Bilstock." He paused for the operator to acknowledge him while adjusting the front of his hatband high on his forehead. "I need the sheriff and the coroner out here right away," he continued.

"We're," he paused again as he thought for a second, looking around, "about three miles southwest of the house. It's along the fence line."

He listened to the person on the other end for a couple of minutes and then added,

"Tell Wilbury it's the old man." There was no real emotion in his voice. "Yeah, the senator. Get 'em out here, quick," he concluded and pushed the end-call button.

The caller put his phone away and momentarily looked back at the Jeep. It was now stopped yet continued to flood the area with its headlights. Crossing his arms over the horn of his saddle, he stayed where he was, opting to neither dismount, nor approach the vehicle. He could hear wailing and sobbing coming from behind the headlights, but that soon subsided.

Sheriff Wilbury was on the scene within an hour. He was a tall, heavyset man with a large hat and a quiet demeanor. Stepping out of his vehicle, he glanced toward the man on the horse, walked around the scene in a wide path, and said very little to anyone. The county coroner arrived shortly after that with a small entourage of investigators and then, of course, came the FBI, the Homeland Security people and a reporter from the local newspaper. They looked at the scene from every angle, made notes and took pictures. They gathered in pairs and then small groups to discuss their theories all before interviewing any of the witnesses. The sheriff stayed to himself.

Then, as Wilbury finished his tour of the area, he walked up to the man who had called for him. Though on foot, the sheriff was nearly eye-to-eye with the other man who was still astride his horse.

"You boys see anything unusual when you got here?" the sheriff asked.

The man he addressed leaned back hard in his saddle, turned his head away and spit.

"Naw," he replied as he sat back forward, never really looking directly at the sheriff. "Charo found him," he continued as he nodded his head towards one of the Hispanic ranch hands, "we were spread out north along the fence line. Got here pretty quick when he signaled." There was a pause as he shifted in the saddle. "This is what it was," he raised his arm slightly and pointed to the body in the wire, "nothing else."

The sheriff dipped his hat in silence and turned to walk away. After two steps he glanced back at the unimpassioned cowboy.

"Sorry 'bout yer loss, son," he offered. He did not receive a reply.

Agents from the different authorities approached the cowboy as others began firing questions at the two Hispanics. The other man from the rescue party stayed at the Jeep with the widow. An FBI agent found him there and they spoke briefly. The story was consistent.

3

There really was no story.

The coroner established the time of death at approximately 5:00PM and issued his opinion of "asphyxiation due to self-induced strangulation. Death by accidental causes." No one on site disagreed or offered any other opinion. Within twenty minutes of their arrival the body was cut loose and loaded in the ambulance.

There were handshakes and nods as the assembled dispersed. That was that.

The scene of the death though, was not at all as it appeared and that was no accident.

The man responsible was very good at what he does. So good, that no one yet understood any crime existed.

1

"All that is necessary for the triumph of evil is that good men do nothing."
Edmund Burke

He took four days to get there. The job itself was another full day. He considered going back through Dallas, but that was the route he used to get to the job. Rules were rules and one ironclad number was "do not use the same path twice." This was his fourth job and so far, everything had gone just fine. The rules seemed to work.

The killer was long gone from the west Texas cattle ranch before the body was discovered. Authorities accepted the evidence and declared the case closed despite the status and ranking of the victim. That victim was indeed a sitting United States Senator.

He was found mostly suspended by two strands of barbed wire, his body on the far side of the fence with the wires tightly around and cutting into his neck. A dead calf, also tangled in the lower wires, lay nearby.

Careless riders have been known to lose their balance and fall into the wire. This scene had all the markings of such an accident, including the motivation for a rider to lean into the fence. It looked as though the senator had struggled to free himself at least for a short time. The marks on his neck were in a complete circle indicating he had twisted trying to free himself. But evidence can be deceitful.

The responsible assassin was a loner who was not from Texas. First drawn there by a need to confirm suspicions of unspeakable acts by this powerful public official. While doing so, the loner had devised three possible ways to carry out the kill. Each would appear to be an accident or natural causes. He would determine which to use on his return trip as the circumstances presented themselves.

This hunter went to great lengths in assuring both the guilt of his quarry and that his own identity would not be discovered. The absolute guilt of this senator had been established on the killer's first trip to the area, a few weeks prior.

Among other things, the senator was a man of habit and strong will. The ranch was vast, covering thousands of acres and the senator enjoyed checking the fence line in the afternoons. Against the objections of his protection detail, he always rode alone. The path he used was the same every day, leaving the barn heading north till he reached the fence, then following it west to the edge of the property. There the fence line would turn south and the senator would check for broken wires or other problems as he rode for miles in that direction. His trek never varied and would take hours, returning him to the ranch house just before dark. So predictable was this ride that it had not gone unnoticed by the assassin on that first trip to the area.

The return visit to the ranch did not take long. The killer's plan was carefully mapped out. He had "borrowed" a horse from a neighboring ranch and rode north onto the senator's property. The assassin brought with him the supplies he would need to carry out his scheme, including a replacement lock for the entry gate he had just broken. Finding the dead calf resolved the *how* and having already picked the *where* it was simply a matter of pulling the carcass under

6

the lower strand of wire and then dragging the calf to the location. That spot was about six hundred yards north but still along the fence line. Placing the calf carcass near the fence, he entangled one rear leg in the lower fence wires. Then hiding his device, a wire-throwing sling, under a large dried out pile of brush; he took the horse back several hundred yards down the fence line to be out of view.

The assassin had rules, which he followed to the letter. Rules, though concocted by him, that had served their purpose well thus far. One of the rules required him to think of himself in the third person while on a mission. This worked for the loner by keeping him focused on this other identity, the one that inspired him. A student of the American Revolution and its heroes, he picked a relatively unknown revolutionary figure as his surrogate model. The alter ego he created was Silas, Silas the Patriot.

The influence for his Silas was Silas Downer, a man who had lived over two and a half centuries before. Known as the "forgotten patriot," Silas Downer had been a member of the Sons of Liberty. A small band, whose acts of patriotism were considered by some to be radical crimes. While a few of this revolutionary band gained notoriety, Silas Downer and others remained in the shadows of history. The modern day Silas saw his missions as acts of patriotism that also required anonymity and complete secrecy with no awareness of his actions, only the results. Those results were to cleanse congress of its most vile members. Unfortunately, there was much work to be done in that area.

Obscuring his and the horse's tracks with a piece of brush on his walk back to the dead calf, this assassin, Silas, then added it to the pile that would be his cover. He wore desert camouflage and a tan sock hat. Silas checked the mechanism of the wire sling then settled down in the brush pile some ten yards away from the fence and waited.

He would wait just over two hours, but patience was no

problem for him. That he had plenty of. What he had been through earlier in life had taught him composure, diligence and forebearance. It was that patience which gave him time to reflect on who he was, and why.

This lone assassin was an only child. His parents were forty-four years older than he and by the time he was established they were getting older and frail. They had put him through college and pharmacy school upon his return from the service. Experiences there had first tested his ability to remain calm and resolute.

After pharmacy school, rather than work in a drug store, he sought a position as a corporate representative for a major drug company.

Besides the patience, his tenacity made him a quick study and he loved to read. The job he sought demanded knowledge of many new and established drugs. His aptitude and thirst for information was recognized and his application advanced.

Securing the job he desired meant there were handsome rewards but long hours. Again, his calmness and determination pulled him through the exhausting schedule. His interest in the more exotic drugs opened doors to knowledge that would be helpful in his job and other areas later.

Waiting in that Texas brush pile allowed him time to think. He checked and rechecked the mechanism of the wire sling and the tautness of the wire. Dust and dirt could be a severe problem so he protected his weapon carefully. Doing so with movements too subtle and precise to disturb even the smallest of branches in the pile. He had become invisible but his mind stayed clear and sharp.

Concentration on his purpose did not completely block recurring thoughts of his motivation, the events of a few short years ago that lead him to this pile of brush in west Texas. Unwittingly he relived in short flashes the regrets that still ate at him. Unspoken

8

excuses of youth, ambition and lack of time did not comfort the guilt he shared with his prey.

"You were young then," his mind tried to tell him.

Like anyone of that age, he saw his parents when he could, but that had become less frequent. They lived in the same town as he and somehow that lessened the urgency to go see them. When he finally realized how badly his attentions had been diverted by his own life and new job, it was too late.

Their decline in health caught him by some surprise. The National Health Care Program rejected their requests for procedures in favor of "pain reducing" therapy as a more practical expenditure of the taxpayer's money. He had money to pay for the care the government would not provide but the doctors could not take it. Severe penalties awaited any doctor who tried to undermine the government decisions.

Lung cancer took his father two months before his mother succumbed to an infected, arthritic hip. Painful deaths in each case despite the "pain therapy" the health plan had prescribed. They were both hardly past their mid-seventies when they died.

He had talked, many times; with his state and federal representatives who assured him this was the best for the country. The government's position was that they could no longer afford to prolong life for life's sake. And then they were gone.

A vibration in the brush around him suddenly refocused his concentration. Silas moved only his eyes, straining to look to his right toward the source of the movement. The creature gently stepped from the branches and onto his arm.

The striped bark scorpion proceeded down the arm, across his shirt cuff and paused as it first touched his right wrist below the glove.

Silas' breathing ceased for the moment, but he did not move. The four-inch long being was surprised by the texture of the skin it was on, but not startled. After a momentary pause, which seemed much longer to Silas, it continued moving slowly. Onto the glove, then the weapon he held and beyond.

As the creature finally left the brush pile and scurried toward the calf carcass, Silas resisted the urge to rub his wrist where it had crossed. He did blink his dryed-out eyes several times and took a shallow breath, but other than that he remained still and calm.

As quickly as his mind had gone from it, the thoughts of his parents and how they had died return to him in a low flash of anger.

"How had this happened?" He asked himself over and over. There had been a long, drawn out national debate over the health insurance issue while he was serving in the military. He never paid it much attention; after all he had a war to fight. The issue seemed to have been resolved. What he had heard and read through the media said it was a good thing. How could it not be?

They had said everyone was to be covered and protected by this new policy. The requirement to now purchase the government's prescribed health insurance was an issue, but it had easy "get-around it" clause.

The fine, for lack of participation, could simply be attached to his annual tax return. It was considerably less than the premiums would be. $700.00 as opposed to the $5500.00 annual cost of the insurance. He considered the fine a small price to pay to help cover everybody.

His parents were fine until they reached their seventies. That's when "managed care" replaced Medicare and their world came apart.

At that point, the elderly were being allowed to die "with dignity" rather than spend money on procedures, which would only "prolong the inevitable."

He was told it was the will of the people. More like the will of the politicians, in his mind. The changes had only benefited them, the corrupt politicians.

Private insurance companies were driven out of the business by the new requirements for coverage, requirements that only a government could operate under. That meant the government had to expand their interest in health care through new agencies and administrative offices. Thousands of new government jobs were created. Appointments through politicians filled those jobs.

With the new power they controlled, their positions became even further separated from the ones they were to serve. He had always been skeptical of "public servants," but the treatment his parents received put those feelings over the top.

The brush pile moved again and again his senses went to full alert.

"*Now what?*" His mind screamed as it snapped into full reality.

No intruder this time, the cause was clearly a gust of wind that had dipped low to the surface of the plain. The brush pile rocked and settled back down just before the hair on the hide of the calf stood for a second and floated to rest.

The wind was then gone and calm had returned once more.

Silas smiled at himself despite his effort not to. As the waiting resumed his mind returned to the haunting, obsessive thoughts that would not leave him alone.

How so many politicians had reacted to his parent's plight was a major factor in his current attitude and the direction he took.

It was then that he began to study how our political leaders operated, how they manipulated their own system. He learned that very few bills were read in their entirety prior to being enacted into law. It mattered not, who was in power. The gist of the main article of proposed legislation might be known, but within the bill were many "trailers" that sponsors would prefer went through quietly and without notice.

These guys worked for themselves and each other at the expense of the people and country they had sworn to serve. Some to more egregious levels than others, but sadly, most took the path of self-preservation over public service.

Studying the goings on in the congress, he started listing members and offenses based upon the severity of the act. His aggravation grew but so did his patience and perseverance, which became resolve to dig deeper than what most citizens saw and had become repulsed with. The list soon concentrated on offenses far beyond the political.

It was the more aggressive, violent acts he learned of that spurred his interest. There was often evidence, though no legal proof, of crimes committed by elected officials against other citizens in efforts to prevent exposure or even their loss of power. The law could not reach these offenders, and more and more they molded that law to protect themselves from the people.

What he found led to and formed his direction and his plan. A regular citizen, upset by politics as usual, had become an obsessed, avenging patriot. Political differences could be ugly, but that was for the ballot box. Those variances of ideas did not deserve what he now had in mind.

Political differences were not his targets. He had uncovered the coarse underbelly of politics that most people never actually see, a harsh world of violence and death that could only be dealt with in kind. A world so devoid of conscience that it could not heal itself.

He sought to change that world because of its threat to the country he loved. Waiting in that brush pile was easy enough for him, he had plenty of patience and the waiting was no problem. It was what he had learned about certain politicians that he could not abide.

2

The senator approached from the north, as he always did. Silas could tell when his prey had noticed the downed calf. Increasing his speed to more of a canter, the soon to be victim rode past the brush pile with no notice of it at all. Pulling up the horse and dismounting in one motion, he surprised Silas.

"Still quite the horseman at his age," the stalker thought as he silently rose and aimed the device at his target.

The wire-throwing sling was patterned after a much larger unit used by the Corp of Engineers in WWII. That unit was used to string phone and telegraph lines by firing the wire at high speed to the top of the poles, where it would tie itself off by wrapping around the pole's top cross member.

Silas' model looked similar to a small crossbow and held forty feet of wire with a small lead weight on the end. With good aim, the weight would pass the target tracking slightly to the right. As the line ran out, it would drift further right causing the wire to touch the target, in this case the senator's neck. The lead weight would sharply turn 180 degrees until it again ran out of line, throwing it back around the target and completing the loop. All this took only seconds.

The lead weight had scratched the senator's cheek and knocked his hat off but that did not alter the path of the wire. Before the target could react and raise his hand to block the wire it had made a complete revolution, tightly around his neck. Silas held firm on his launcher while the wire and ironically, the senator's stiffened arm, did its work. The end came quickly, but not without a hitch.

The victim's horse had bolted, heading straight in the direction of the ranch house. This would not do at all, and Silas stared at the horse as he considered this detail he had not thought of. Alerting the ranch house too early could jeopardize the escape.

The killer remained calm and resolute. There was nothing to do other than complete his task and leave as quickly as possible.

Silas unwrapped the device wire, pulled off a glove and checked his prey for a pulse. Satisfied there was none, he wiped the possible fingerprint from the senator's neck and pulled down the top course of barbed wire from the fence. Placing it below the second course he lifted and stuck the senator's head through the triangle. He then hoisted the body over the top fence wire, in the direction of the twist, which further tightened those wires around the neck.

The killer, though he did not consider himself as such, then stuck the man's hat on a barb of the wire to further the illusion of an accident. Cleaning up was a matter of wiping the area for extra footprints and any sign of anyone else having been there. It went smoothly until he was nearly finished.

Catching sight of something moving over his right shoulder, Silas crouched low while drawing his weapon and stared in that direction. It was the senator's horse; perhaps a hundred yards out, walking slowly back to the site. He had trained the animal well and it would not leave him completely. After running far enough to get over his fright, the animal stopped and walked back to within forty feet of his master. He would stay there with him until darkness set in.

Silas let out a breath as he stood and slid the weapon back into the cut pouch on the side of his pants. He scattered the loose pieces of brush from the pile and kept one to drag behind as he turned to walk south along the fence line. Returning to the borrowed horse some four hundred yards away, he loaded his supplies and continued south to the gate. The new padlock would look out of place as it was, so the visitor

14

rubbed it with dirt and scratched the case against the post before attaching it to the gate. Then he rode on to the barn where he had commandeered the horse, unnoticed by the absentee owner.

The old pickup truck he had bought locally for this mission was a short distance from there. Changing into clothes more appropriate for the area, Silas then drove the truck into town and left it parked at a small business garage. After wiping the truck clean of fingerprints and leaving the keys in it, Silas walked the short distance back to his car, the drop car, a four door Mercury Marquis. He pulled away from the small Texas town heading southeast towards Austin. With the setting sun at his back, the assassin put forty miles between himself and the town before dark. Mission number four, complete.

The Silas persona would subside slightly as he approached home, but only slightly. Four missions completed and he could now recognize that change. The need for secrecy never changed, he remained constantly vigilant of that. The big Mercury was a Silas drop car and that kept his focus on the secrecy. The drop car was always different. For long rides he preferred the Mercury. There were others for different needs or situations. None were ostentatious. Attention was an enemy he did not seek.

There were many tags and registrations he could apply to the different vehicles, each with an identity that would serve as cover. That cover would not be permanent, but long enough. The big Mercury allowed room for his equipment and supplies. It rode comfortably and it blended in.

These vehicles were important and their need grew from another of his trusted rules. That was to never use his personal vehicle on a mission, the one that his neighbors and acquaintances might recognize him in.

Silas kept five or six drop vehicles in an abandoned warehouse across town from where he lived. One of those would carry him to the location of his mission and then home again. The transition process was quite simple and it worked.

Three blocks away, a short walking distance from that warehouse, was a luxury hotel and its high rise parking deck. He would leave his personal car there and retrieve it upon his return. The parking was free, to guests only, so that area was checked regularly. What wasn't checked was the employee parking area on the top level. That's where he would leave his personal vehicle. Seven months now, four for trial runs and the last three for missions, and there had been no problem.

His physical appearance to any onlooker would change before he entered or left the parking deck. Maybe his hair, maybe glasses or perhaps he would simply wear a different coat. But it was always enough. You could watch him walk in, but you wouldn't know him when he drove out and on to the main streets of home.

His Silas persona waned more as he turned his personal car into the driveway of his small home. This last removal had been the furthest from home. The scheduled return had only taken two days and the total duration was part of the plan. He didn't like to be away from home for more than a week. A week was an arbitrary time frame for such tasks but then; Silas operated on an arbitrary level. This man, whether as Silas or the quiet, private person his neighbors knew so little of, lived and operated alone. He always had.

His neighborhood was some forty years old and with that age came a feel, an ambiance, like something from an old New England novel. Trees lined the streets and just under their cover were the streetlights. Old-fashioned streetlights, with black iron swirls and frosted glass globes.

He had lived there for nine years and was comfortable there. His neighbors, mostly nearing retirement but a few younger married folks with small kids, saw him as a mildly eccentric, quiet but good neighbor. To them, he was still the traveling pharmaceutical representative who was often gone all week. They did not know about the missions. They were not even the least bit aware of what he did now, while away.

His home setting was perfect, or it had been until the sidewalks. To him the sidewalks still looked out of place, even now, three years since they were installed. The county had proclaimed them a necessity and declared they had been approved by a majority of the residents, although no one could find a resident who had been in favor. The homeowners paid for this "improvement" based upon their frontage and the politicians got credit for supplying jobs to the community.

Taxation without a tax and the benefits were front yards that looked undersized and driveways now too short to park cars for even a small, family gathering. It was a small thing, but his first exposure to political power and its abusive nature.

There was a twenty-year-old, or so he had been told, water oak in the front yard. He would prefer an elm but the oak was nice. It shielded all but the garage area from the afternoon sun. Under the garage, well actually the utility room behind the garage, was another of his secrets.

Several years ago, before his parents died, he became interested in a "safe room." He had read about them and even saw a movie with Jodie Foster about a fancy one. They called the one in the movie a "Panic Room," but the idea was the same, a secret room that offered security from the unknown or simply a large safe to store one's valuables away from any intruder. It would be secure, mainly, because no one would know it was there. Privacy and secrecy were concepts he held in high regard. He had started work on it just in the past year.

The interior foundation wall of the basement ended at the beginning of the garage. The garage and utility room were connected by the roofline above, but he could not tell about the foundation. Silas studied and asked around about going under the garage area. He learned that, structurally, he could not safely dig out from under a poured concrete pad such as his garage floor. The 9 x 20 utility room, on the other hand, had promise. It was a poured concrete floor, like the garage, but had more support other than the dirt. The back wall of the foundation was the full width of the basement. The outside foundation wall was only four feet deep, as was the footing for the garage, but that gave him a place to start.

Carefully removing the blocks nearest the back wall, he had begun to excavate the fill dirt under the utility room. Just a few feet wide at a time and he brought in 6 x 6 studs to shore up the pad where he had removed the dirt. It proved to be a tedious and overwhelming task, which he soon abandoned.

Digging and hauling dirt a bucket at a time had gotten old, very fast. He cleaned up the floor around the removed blocks and covered the hole in the basement wall with a side-by-side refrigerator-freezer. Not a perfect fit but it seemed to work.

The only thing he felt really good about was the foundation. It remained solid. He closely monitored the exterior walls of his utility room for any cracks from the digging and never found any.

The desire for the project was still there but he needed to come up with a more realistic plan. That would require Silas to think it through in more detail.

One day, he vowed, he would revisit this plan with a better way to do it.

3

The first removal decisions were difficult in one respect. Not that he lacked candidates, quite the contrary. There were so many likely candidates it was difficult to pick just one. Silas found that almost all fit his basic profile for removal. Some were just more audacious than others. The offense had to be verified and the intent shown to be clear. Once that was done he made plans to correct the situation. His correction method was severe. It meant the removal of that politician, permanently.

What he planned for would take money, lots of it. In a way they never imagined, his parents had provided for those means. Upon their deaths he inherited all they had in the world. Being an only child sped up the probate process. He sold his parents home and belongings of value, collected on their insurance policies and after the expenses of their services and burials he had just under a half million dollars left to him. Not knowing what to do with it, as he did not need it right now; he looked into some companies with emerging products to invest in. He found one that he liked a lot.

During this time he began to reinvest in himself as well. His physical conditioning and strength became important again. Behind his house was a stand of trees about seventy-five yards deep. That was nice, he liked the privacy and the seclusion. The new elementary school built just the other side of those trees insured it would stay that way. The trees were mature and quite tall. Mostly hardwoods, with nice strong limbs, that offered plenty of shade from summer's morning heat. The undergrowth was not too thick and he had often noticed the neighborhood dogs running their own obstacle course through the trees.

At first he would jog and jump through the path. But soon he built up to a runner's speed and cleared the obstructions with grace and ease. Add this to the regiment of exercises he would do inside his house and he quickly regained the fitness he had known before college. The trim he had left the military with.

The company he invested the money in was involved with voice recognition software. Many firms had such programs available. None had proven reliable or universal. But this company's product fit the needs of nearly every producer looking for voice software.

It would very soon eliminate the need for a keyboard or a start button. His investment went to 107 times its value overnight. The money his parents had left him, $435,875.00, had become over forty-six million. They say not to put all your eggs in one basket. This man had his own rules. He liked what he had read about the company so he invested everything in it. He spent the next year quietly reinvesting in Certificates of Deposits of varying rates and maturity dates. He kept half of the earnings in the original company. When they received the government contract for military and space utilization, his stock went ballistic.

The new millionaire bought two handguns and a carry permit for one. He would practice at the local range on weekends and even go to public firing ranges while out of town. Several new computers began to take up space in his house. He used them to study all types of weaponry, as well as the congress, through online connections.

He registered the Glock 19 in his legal name. The other, a more powerful gun, was kept as another one of his secrets for now.

Within two years of their deaths, his parents had provided him with the means to a fortune that, according to his accountant, was in excess of 125 million dollars. He remained private and confidential.

His neighbors knew nothing of the investments. His employer placed him on part time status, at his request, and he opted to stay where he lived.

The man who would become Silas bought into several businesses around his state, becoming the silent owner of a car dealership, a printing company, a computer retailer and anything else that interested him. The bottom line was that money would not be an issue, neither for him or what he wanted to do. But that was his business, his alone. What he wanted to do was the issue and deciding where to start. Deciding when would come naturally.

The first three on his list were easy choices but the hard decision was the order. It was getting that order right that mattered. Each had used their office to line the pockets of family and friends at the expense of their constituents. Re-election was a process they had perfected. Should an able adversary make it to the general election stage, they would be dealt with. A good scandal would usually do the trick. If there wasn't a real one, one could be conjured up.

These traits were sadly common and not enough to require Silas' attention. The factor that would land a candidate on the list had to incorporate harm to another individual, intentional harm, often including death. Silas found this trait disturbingly too frequent. There was one, though, who did stand out.

Most politicians, so they say, come to office with virtue and belief that they can make a difference. This one seemed to have come with a blackheart to start with. His first campaign was waged through intimidation and harsh tactics. He chose not to debate his opponent. He made statements that declared his positions to be quite clear and, in his words, "undeniable." On Election Day union members were forced, against their will in many cases, to block or slow down entrances to polling places in areas known to favor the opposition. Complaints and charges were filed but little was covered by the news media, and that not for long. Now a fourteen-term congressman from Pennsylvania, who openly brought public money to his district through influence, appeared to be unstoppable.

The corrupt influence wasn't the issue; it was his handling of the last challenger that moved this man to the top of the list.

The young lawyer running against him had been warned to back down, but did not. He pressed his bid for the congressman's job with evidence of corruption and ties to underworld figures. Getting the coverage of his evidence was hard enough. Local media outlets took their lead from the national organizations and they were "selective" in what they would discuss or make public. The young lawyer managed to get some of his documented charges into a debate, which was televised live in the district. The Congressman took this candidate so lightly that he opted to set aside his disdain for such venues.

The disclosures briefly, but deeply, embarrassed the incumbent Congressman. Coverage of the debate went mysteriously dead, during that part of the programming, but enough had gone out that the Congressman was concerned. In politics, those of his type do not confront evidence or charges to their face. They destroy the accuser.

Denials and countercharges went on for a week. The young lawyer candidate was forced to play defense against charges that lacked any corroboration, charges intended to muddy the water so that real evidence would go unnoticed.

Two weeks before the election, the young lawyer's 15-year-old daughter was found unconscious in a motel room. Drugged to the point of death, she somehow survived. Witnesses claimed she was the source of the drugs and was able to obtain them from her father whenever she wanted them.

The lawyer's home was broken into and ransacked. A warrant was issued to search the property at the request of the congressman, and during the search drugs were supposedly found.

Those who knew the young lawyer had no doubt as to what had happened, but their numbers were not enough to counter the congressman's game.

Not only was the election lost, but so was his license to practice law. That young lawyer, his reputation destroyed, shot himself after all this and his shattered family moved away.

As harsh as this case was, it won the removal decision by only a nose. Still, this would be the first job. It had to be just and deserving.

The verification trip had been a week earlier. That part was simple, but while there, the self appointed assassin scouted the area for a scheme, how to inflict death without discovery.

4

Silas made plans to gain access to his first victim's yacht. It was a 120-foot Sovereign that the congressman kept at the Presque Isle Yacht Club and Marina on Lake Erie.

The boat originally held 6 cabins. Its interior had been remodeled to make a large suite out of three cabins on the starboard side. The crew stayed on standby and the congressman was known to spend most weekends on the lake, either entertaining political constituents or just relaxing alone.

Access would take some planning. Repairs were always going on somewhere at the marina. Not all repairs were to the boats. There was an infrastructure for the marina that required attention as well.

Docked boats had access to landline telephones and this system was always changing. A maintenance truck for the phone company would likely go unnoticed.

He made arrangements and notes for what he would need and returned home. That trip took two full days and Silas had allowed another there to gather supplies.

The return drive to the lake port town near Erie, Pennsylvania took better than two more days. The route was twisted and non-direct. Having left home early on a Sunday, he was in Erie by late Tuesday afternoon. The next full day was to be spent in recon but flexibility would be allowed for if needed.

Some say luck is a matter of timing. Others will tell you it is positioning. Folks at the coffee house near the docks were talking about how the Congressman would be arriving at noon on Thursday, a day earlier than normal. He listened steadfastly to the conversations and noted the crew would be reporting to the yacht at 7:30AM Thursday morning. The slip where the boat was docked was fairly evident. There are not many 120' boats at Presque Isle. He was getting all this on Tuesday afternoon, so time was short.

He drove back into Erie and looked for a good spot to leave his drop car. He found a parking deck not far from a used car lot in town. The lot had a utility van for sale that looked like what he needed. He would keep his drop car for tonight and make the swap in the morning.

Heading back towards the marina, he stopped at Joe Roots Grill on Peninsula Drive. He wasn't a huge fan of fish, so he enjoyed a Black Diamond Steak and some onion rings while he waited for sundown.

As the evening approached, he returned to Presque Isle. The marina was considerably less active at dusk. This was good. The twilight hours are the best cover for moving about and he made note of the time. He walked down a row of boats on the opposite side of the pier from the big boat. All appeared dark and quiet. He could see the Congressman's yacht very clearly, too clearly. If there were other folks around they could also see. Fortunately, this side of the dock seemed to be buttoned down. With any luck, these boaters would not be around till Friday night. He would be gone by then.

Looking for a phone line connector box, he found one on the dock and actually near the Congressman's slip.

"Perfect," he told himself. That would put him within thirty feet of the boat without causing any attention, what so ever. Satisfied with his main plan, he now needed to find a place to sleep a few hours. He drove out US19 to I-90 and went north.

In thirty minutes he was in Westfield, New York. He took a room at the Theater Motel under an assumed name. Paying cash, he had no worries about the young man who signed him in. With his pulled down tie and briefcase he looked, for all the world, like the traveling salesman he presented himself to be.

That Wednesday morning he was up at 6:30AM and on his way back to Erie. Breakfast near the marina offered more small talk from locals about the early visit coming this week. The Congressman was a folk legend in the area. Money sent to the district blinded people as to how it had gotten there. They would give the man his privacy but were still all a buzz about the change in his schedule. After breakfast, and a quick tour by car of the marina to insure the activity level had not increased, he headed back to town. He parked in the deck and walked the three blocks to the used car lot.

At Frank's Good Used Cars he made a deal for the utility van. He paid cash and he used a Florida driver's license issued to a name he had made up last week. He flashed an Allstate Insurance card that wasn't real. The salesman was more interested in the money than any verification so the deal was quick. He drove off the lot and went directly to a hardware store and bought a short extension ladder. Then to a self-service car wash to clean up the van and apply his decals.

Back at the parking decks, he parked the van on the street and went to the car for his supplies and equipment. He mixed up his chemicals and sealed the package, tight. By the time he was ready he had two hours to kill before dusk. He parked behind the decks, off the main road, and again inventoried his equipment. At 7:00PM he headed for the marina.

The van he was driving said AT&T on the sides. He even had orange cones to put out when he parked. The signs were not a problem. He owned interest in a printing business, which made wide format screen prints for vehicles. He brought several with him and the used Ford E-250 van fit the image to a tee. The van was a $1200.00 investment in semblance and pretense, which the plan called for. With it parked near the dock, he was free to survey the area and the boat without drawing undue attention.

Silas set up the ladder at the pole with the phone box and went straight to the boat. The boat was locked and there was no one around. He looked across to the walkway he had been on the night before. All was quiet and blurred in the twilight. Locks were not an issue when you knew what to do, and he did. Once inside the yacht he put on his respirator mask, gloves and shoe covers. Then carefully looked around the yacht for the proper devise to employ his chosen weapon, Saxitotoxin with an air reactive powder propellant. The toxin was very fast acting and dissipated in minutes. It took much less to be lethal and was harder to detect than other toxins, even right after death.

A cocktail set was on the desk in the bedroom. The glasses were frosted and would be easy to glaze with the product, but that was not a specific targetable choice. He could not be sure who all might be affected and the seal from the air couldn't be assured. Inspecting the private bath gave him what he wanted. Inside the medicine cabinet were individually wrapped floss units, neatly stacked. The killer gently heated one pack and opened it. The mixture went into the package. He resealed the container as it had been and rubbed the pack to release the propellant from its sealer. It really wouldn't matter if the Congressman used the floss or not. Just opening the package would be enough. Exposure to the air would now throw the Toxin in his face. Silas placed the package back on top and carefully eased his way off the boat. Casually, he walked back to the phone box and carefully retrieved the ladder. With the orange cones back on board, he drove out of the marina and back toward Erie.

At the same self-service car wash, near the parking deck, he took the decals off the van and burned them in a trashcan. He left the ladder behind the carwash, and then drove the van to a construction site a few blocks away. After wiping it down clean for any fingerprints,

27

he left the key in it and walked away. The van was gone by morning.

The short walk to the parking deck was pleasant. Confident in what he had accomplished, now all he could do was wait. He paid the parking attendant in cash and headed for home, on a different course than the one used to get there, of course.

Rules are rules and Silas would be diligent about them.

The news of the congressman's death by stroke came over the radio while he was still enroute back home that Friday morning. Through what should have been excitement at word of his first kill, he remained calm and had no emotional response to the news. It was simply a confirmation that his first quarry had been removed.

The second and third were nearly as easy. His education in pharmaceuticals gave him hundreds of options. The delivery methods were the only variables and they took some creativity. Silas' method was undetectable. He was good.

Some months later, while on his way home from Texas after the fourth removal, a radio report on the replacement named by the Governor of Pennsylvania for his first "removal," made him realize Silas was too good.

The replacement chosen, while not proven to his standards for removal yet, had a reputation similar to the predecessor. The new representative had been named in unflattering reports relating to his predecessor. Couple this with the news from last week and Silas began to question his results. The second removal, a congressman from Virginia, had also been replaced with a suspicious subordinate. A disconcerting pattern had developed.

Silas pulled into a rest area and bought a cold drink from a machine. He sat in the car and considered what he had not before. It was all too clean. There was no message in the deaths, no reminder to do better. Silas was removing evil only to watch it be replaced by more evil. There must be a way to get his directive out without risking

28

apprehension. He would need to study on this.

The rules would require an amendment.

5

The news of Rep. Perry's replacement in Pennsylvania didn't set well with many others, either. One notable malcontent was a political writer for the Pittsburgh Post-Gazette named Daniel Seay. Seay knew the cast of characters well and Hanson was a name that rang many bells.

Most writers and reporters feared Perry. His influence was vast and could cover itself as fast as it acted. Seay had watched many colleagues suffer, and some fall, for attempting to challenge the Representatives tactics. Perry's replacement had been a staffer for him several terms ago. He became a liability through some connections with known criminals and was given a job in state government to "cool off."

Apparently the Governor thought enough time had passed and that Dewey Hanson had sufficiently cooled off. Daniel Seay smelled a rat and sat down to write about it. His editorial would be careful yet pointed. He titled it, "New Representation for the District, Advancement or Retreat." Daniel mentioned the ties to organized crime that had censured Hanson several years ago and that those ties, if true, would only perpetuate the rumors of influence on the office.

The reporter had no proof of his theories about Perry's demise. He had covered Perry for years. While the congressman was now in his 60's, he was known to still be fit. Being in shape, though, didn't exempt anyone from a stroke, so the findings were acceptable.

There were no abnormalities on the autopsy, no real cause of the stroke was evident, but nothing external was suspected. The death was quick and the congressman was not found for a couple of hours. But there he lay, on the floor of his bathroom. A towel wrapped around him and a package of dental floss in his hand. It was the end of his tenure, but unfortunately not the end of his era. Perry's legacy would live on and business would not change.

Leaks about the appointment of Hanson came into his office just before noon. Seay wrote his piece about the possible transition from one bad guy to another. It wasn't wide spread yet or reported on in the televised media. The theory was new and Daniel's editor was not yet convinced.

It was now several months since Perry's death. Two other members of Congress had also died suddenly since then. That was above the normal attrition rate but not enough to raise any eyebrows except Daniel's. To him the count was now up to three. His editor did allow Daniel's story to print locally, but only as an Op-Ed, not hard news.

Daniel was home that Friday evening, waiting for his wife to finish preparing their dinner when the news came on about the Senator Bilstock of Texas.

The story seemed clear enough, a tragic accident. The Senator had been found along a fence on his ranch. Senators were more closely guarded than other congress people, but the ranch was considered safe and the Senator always insisted he go alone. The appearances were that he had ridden up to a section of wire that was tangled and a calf had been caught up in it. While leaning from his horse to untangle the calf, he must have fallen and got caught between two courses of barbed wire. His horse had stayed with him till dark then returned to the stable and the alarm was sent out. He had been found within two hours that Thursday night, but he was gone. Texas, the report concluded, would need a new Senator.

Neat and tidy as it seemed, the hairs on the back of Daniel's neck stood out. As his wife came to get him for dinner, she found her husband sitting straight up in his chair, staring at the TV.

"Daniel, what is it? What has happened?" She saw a look on her husband's face that was completely new to her. She sat the dish she held on the table and walked over to him.

Daniel shook his head and turned to her. He realized how his actions had upset his wife.

"Honey, it's OK. I just saw a report on Senator Bilstock, that's all."

"Why would that upset you so?"

"It's nothing, really. I just think I see a pattern that may not be there."

"Don't scare me like that, Daniel. I thought something really bad had happened the way you were acting."

"It may have, Baby," Daniel spoke softly, "it very well may have."

~

For Silas, getting home was different this time. All had gone well. The removal was accomplished but a new doubt had found a home in his mind. Was it a success to remove one evil without anyone knowing the reason for the removal? The replacements appeared to be continuations of the past. Silas didn't seek credit for what he was doing. One big rule was to make no decision based on personal reasons. Another was not to leave any trace of how the act had occurred. But, without such, what would ever change? Somehow, a message needed to be sent. A clear warning against what had qualified these offenders to be removed.

The frustrated killer spent days considering his options, calling papers or television stations, leaving a calling card at the scene? He decided to work on his safe room some more to clear his mind. Three days of digging with little to show for it cleared that up. It was time to do that room and do it right, with hired, professional help.

But, the safe room couldn't be made known to his neighbors or anyone else, for that matter. He opted to say he was remodeling the basement and putting in a bath down there. That would justify the workers and he could offer them bonus money to work on the safe room in confidence.

A contractor, with a heavy Latin accent, showed him how they would shore up the wall between the garage and the utility room and finish digging out underneath. It would require a few beams and the headroom would be lowered. But, if they went down a couple of feet lower and added a step or two that would fix the headroom issue.

Silas liked the idea and gave them the go ahead. The workers were not American citizens, probably not legal. He didn't like that when he thought about it, so he didn't think about it much. He needed this done. *A hypocrite in need is a hypocrite indeed*, he thought. Their status would help in keeping his secret, so he accepted his guilt.

After a couple of weeks he had his new basement, a new safe room and an idea for his other situation. The constant student of American history and already borrowing from the revolutionary period for inspiration, he considered his work a parallel to that of the "Sons of Liberty" and what had motivated them.

There were many notable quotations credited to these brave men. He made a mental list of the best ones. He thought carefully about it and how to do it. The message must be sent. He traveled to a city some three hundred miles from home.

He bought a laptop under an assumed name at a retailer there and found a free WiFi coffee shop in town. From there, he established an E-mail account under the name "pine tree."

The message, a quote from George Washington, was sent to

both the address of the new representative in Pennsylvania, Dewey Hanson, and to the offices of the Pittsburgh Post Gazette. It read simply, *"We began a contest for liberty ill provided with the means for war, relying on our patriotism to supply the deficiency."* He signed off the instant the message was sent and closed down the computer. He ran a format C, twice. Then loaded a totally different operating system and formatted that away as well. The computer was then taken to a dumpster row, behind a grocery, broken open and thrown into separate containers.

Silas sent similar messages for the States of numbers two and three removals. Each from different cities or towns, one from a town several hundred miles north of the first one used. In each case he quoted members of the revolutionary group, Captain John Parker for the second and James Otis for the third.

For the Senator from Texas, he flew to Montana and then drove to North Dakota. From there the message was a quote from Samuel Adams in 1779. *"A general dissolution of principles and manners will more surely overthrow the liberties of America than the whole force of the common enemy."*

That E-mail went to both the new Senator's office and the Editor of the Fort Worth Star- Telegram.

The four sets of messages were several days apart but within a two-week period. Word soon spread that there may be a group claiming to be responsible for the deaths. Daniel Seay knew he had to look into this. He went to his editor to seek time and money for travel and an investigation. The editor would be easier to convince this time. Especially compared to Daniel's wife. She didn't like it when he was away.

6

"Why is it, you have to always get involved with this crap?" She stormed into the room and took one last shot as he packed his bag.

"Honey, look," Daniel didn't have a good reason, just a feeling he needed to do this.

"I've had a knot in my gut since this mess started. There is something going on and I think those messages have to do with it."

"I don't want you to go, Daniel. These people are killing folks, if you're right."

"Killing politicians, not the press, OK?" he fired back deliberately. "If I feel any danger to me, I'll back off."

"Promise?" she fabricated a whimper.

"Yeah, I promise."

And with that he smiled and gave her a hug and kiss.

"This is me, this is what I do. You know that."

She didn't respond. She did know that, but she thought he had changed. At least she had hoped he had.

"Call me every night." And with that she left the room.

Daniel had been given three weeks to come up with something. He would go in reverse order of the deaths, believing the warmest trail would be the last killing, if it really was a killing. Many experts suggested this was just some nut case trying to take credit for accidents and natural causes. Obviously, Daniel didn't think so. He flew into DFW and rented a car for the drive to Brownwood, Texas. The ranch was outside of Brownwood.

Daniel took a room at the Classic Inn near Early, Texas. The Inn was not what they call an Inn in Pennsylvania. It was more a series of cottages strung together by a common roofline. The "Ice and Concession Building" was in the middle of the parking lot. So, you soon figured out, it was best to get all the ice you might need the first trip out there. The room was clean, or it looked to be clean. He was kind of glad his wife wasn't with him; she'd probably have a fit. But it seemed okay to Daniel. The phone book listed the Senator's home and gave a number. He didn't try it. He looked up the Sheriff's office in Brownwood and called to see if he could get an appointment for in the morning. They said, "Sure, come on in, anytime." That seemed nice.

The Sheriff's name was Wilbury, Horace Wilbury and as Daniel would find out the next morning, he was quite tired of the Travelin' Wilbury jokes.

Daniel's appointment was rather open ended, so he showed up at 8:30AM. The staff had been there since 6:00, so the coffee was walking around by itself by now, and the mood in the office was not the attitude he had heard on the phone last night.

"What's your business with Sheriff Wilbury?" The clerk demanded.

"I'm here from the Pittsburgh Post Gazette and I'm looking into the death of Senator Bilstock." he stated firmly as he presented his business card and credentials.

The clerk looked at neither,

"Have a seat, I'll call you when he can see you."

With that, Daniel spun around and found the sofa against the wall. He made himself as comfortable as possible for the next hour as the Sheriff let him cool his heels.

At 9:30AM, exactly, a big, barrel chested man of about 6 foot 6 inches stomped out of his office and stuck out his hand.

"Horace Wilbury, son. What can I do for ya?"

Daniel rose and shook his hand.

"Thanks for seeing me, Sheriff. I'm investigating the death of Senator Bilstock and several other members of Congress lately, I have a few questions for you."

"He fell off his horse into the wire, son. That's what it was to it."

"Yes, Sir, I know the findings. I just have questions and wonder if..."

"Come on in, son. You're wasting your time, but come on in."

As they walked into the office Daniel noticed a huge cowboy hat hanging on the back wall. *There it is*, he said to himself and he smiled.

"Have a seat, son. What were your questions?" The Sheriff positioned himself behind his desk, which was at least 5 feet deep and 8 feet across. Even the most egotistical editor in the business didn't have a desk that big. On the side of the desk was a plaque, similar to a nameplate except it carried this inscription, *"No, I don't sing with 'em."* Daniel did not ask him what that meant.

"Are there any pictures of the scene?" Daniel asked.

"You mean the body and how they found it? Nope," he lied. "They cut him loose right quick cause his wife was with 'em and they didn't want her to see him that way. You understand?"

"Yeah, I understand. But aren't there certain procedures to follow in death cases?"

"His wife was there, son, didn't you hear me? What I saw, it was a mess. Damn near cut through his neck."

"OK, I'm sorry to press you about it. So there were no pictures. Who else found him and can I talk with them?"

"Murray, Slick and two others from the ranch crew went out after the horse came back empty. Mrs. Bilstock was right behind with

37

another ranch hand. They're all out at the ranch now. It's up to them if they talk to you or not."

"Sheriff, thank you so much. I appreciate your time, Sir." Daniel stood and turned toward the office door. He looked back over his shoulder at the still seated sheriff and asked, "Could you direct me to the ranch?"

"Take Hwy 45 South, about 10 miles, to just before the Indian Creek Road. The entrance to the ranch is on the right. The Circle B has a big gate with the brand over it. You won't miss it."

The sheriff paused. He pushed himself up from the chair with both hands and stepped around the large desk. Wilbury took three steps in Daniel's direction before ever looking up at him. Daniel turned back towards the sheriff's outstretched hand. As they shook the sheriff added, "Lunch would be the best time to go. The boys should be there then."

Daniel thanked the Sheriff again and made his leave of the office. Small town sheriffs were notorious about secrecy, *"but this guy outright lied,"* he thought. It was hot outside. This would be nearing fall back home. Texas, he thought. He shook his head and looked for his rental car.

~

The safe room was coming together. The contractors were done with their work. The basement walls were up and the heavy work was done. The plumbing was in, tub, shower and sink. The sheetrock had been finished and was ready for wallpaper or paint. Light fixtures were hung and working. There was no furniture.

He had not even thought about furniture yet, just needed to finish everything off. Paint and carpet, that sort of thing. Silas in him wasn't really thinking about the basement area. The safe room was getting his attention full time.

The door was too big for the refrigerator to hide now. A panel wall had been constructed on top of the old block finish along that wall. He removed the door his crew had installed and built a unit that looked like more wall. After finding an article on counter balancing heavy objects in Popular Mechanics and the parts at an Ace Hardware, now a simple push at the right spot would open the access to the safe room. The refrigerator rode, on a platform, with the new door. He shook his head in approval.

Having dug out through the back yard to make chases for new phone and electrical lines, the phone lines to the safe room were independent of the house phone and the electrical was on its own 200-amp breaker panel.

There were three flat screens wired to separate satellite dishes, which were hidden in shrubbery out back and near the tree line. Four computers with large back up drives, two connected to satellites and two more to cable modems lined the sidewall. There was a stack of laptops, cheap ones, but still a stack in the corner.

Shallow closets held books and clothes. Mostly disguise items for use in the jobs. He monitored news from around the country seeking fraud or worse on the part of congress people. He would use the systems there, or go to a WiFi friendly shop with a laptop to investigate the allegations. Initial investigation, anyway. If it proved serious enough, he would visit closer to the district involved for details.

He was working on a network of trust people, who knew nothing of who he was or where he was, to help with final investigations. He and he alone, would make the decisions. The network idea was risky, but he was setting it up carefully and checked out who he would use ahead of time. Some information could be kept secret for a long time, like the senator for instance.

That may have never come up, had he not stumbled over that small story. A network could help expose situations like that. They

39

would not talk about the network to anyone but him. That was the rule. If they did, he would soon enough find out about it. It wasn't a threat to their safety as much as a threat of exclusion. Those he chose wanted, very much, to be a part.

The room had provisions to keep him alive for months. He didn't know why he had that. Just seemed like a good idea and if it was ever found out he could say it was a bomb shelter. Bottom line, he didn't need to go upstairs unless he wanted to. There was one major omission to the plan. The room had no special "escape door" in the back. He'd thought of it, but not in time. He made a note.

With all this done his attentions turned. Silas had other work to do. There was a fifth candidate for removal he needed to verify some things about. He would do so away from home. It was time for a road trip.

7

Hwy 45 South in west Texas was remarkable, four lanes, neatly striped and straight as an arrow. What was remarkable about it was that it ran through a desert. There was absolutely nothing that could be seen on either side of the highway. Desolation. Daniel wondered to himself if he had taken the wrong road but he kept going.

Then, there it was. He could see the gate before the turn in the road. The Circle B. A large elevated sign that crossed over the entrance. Just like in the movies. Daniel turned in and saw a guard shack about 50 yards into the compound. He slowed but as he got close he could see it was empty. *"Not much need now,"* he thought to himself.

The road turned to dirt and the dirt turned to dust as he drove towards the house. And what a house it was. Three stories, huge front porch, four columns that rose all three stories tall and four roof top gables. The dirt became gravel for a couple hundred yards and then concrete that became a circular driveway right in front of the house.

The surrounding ground was now green, lush grass and shrubbery. He pulled up on the circle drive in front of the porch and stopped. As he got out of his car he noticed the odd square concrete pad in the middle of the grassy area. That was where you would expect a fountain or something, he thought. It was not a patio. There was no iron furniture or anything on it, just a big, flat, concrete surface.

Daniel stepped around his car and looked toward the house. He fully expected someone to come out, but that didn't happen. Lights were on in the house but that was the only sign of life. Daniel walked up the stone steps and across the gray wood porch floor. The porch had to be 12 feet deep but there were no rocking chairs. The main door was open but the screen door was closed. As he reached up to knock she appeared at the door.

"Yes?" she asked, nearly startling Daniel, "Can I help you?"

"Oh, hi. Hello, Ma'am" he started, "I'm Daniel Seay with the Pittsburgh Post Gazette. I'm here looking into the senator's death."

"That's all been takin' care of," she interrupted.

"Well, yes, Ma'am. The sheriff, Sheriff Wilbury, said I might could talk with the boys that found him."

Daniel looked around and then back at her, "are they around today?"

She hesitated a minute and then pushed the screen open. "Come in, I'll see."

She was young, maybe 30 or so, and not too shabby as they say back home. It was clear she had been working. Her jeans fit nicely but were fairly dirty, especially at the knees.

She wore a tee shirt and he tried not to stare. No boots, she wore tennis shoes instead and her hair was tied up and on top of her head.

The interior of the house was obviously being packed up. There were boxes everywhere and very little furniture to be seen. She walked to a round table in the center of the main room and picked up a base unit microphone.

"Circle one to Circle two, over."

Daniel could hear the copter's blades in the response, "Circle two, go ahead."

"Murray, there's a guy here wants to talk to you about Daddy. Can you come to the house? Over."

"Sure thing, One. Should I go by Stone Creek and pick up Slick?"

42

She looked at Daniel and he nodded his head in the affirmative, "Yeah, would you?"

"Ten-four, One. I'm on my way. See you in 15. Circle Two, out."

"So, you're the Senator's daughter? I'm very sorry for your loss." Daniel was very sincere.

"Yeah, that's fine," she stated flatly, "they'll be along in a few minutes. Can I get you a drink?"

"Thank you, yes...anything will be fine."

"Beer it is," she said and was off towards the back of the big house.

The chopper's approach was loud and Daniel stepped to the screen door and saw a dust cloud. The Bell 407 landed on the concrete pad and the motor went quiet.

As the blades slowed, three men emerged from the machine. Daniel didn't know one helicopter from the next but he knew this was a big one. It had two doors, on the side he could see, and a large window behind the rear door. There remained enough room, behind that window, for a replica of the Circle B brand to show proudly from a distance.

Two of the men walked towards the house while the third stayed with the machine. The tallest of the men came up the steps and through the door briskly. He continued without pause in Daniel's direction as Daniel reached out his hand

"Hi, I'm Daniel.........." but that was all he could get out.

The man grabbed Daniel in both hands, nearly lifting him off the floor, and pushed him against the wall.

"Just who the hell are you and what do you want?" He demanded. Before Daniel could respond the man spoke again, "These shakedowns are over, do you understand me?"

Daniel was surprised, to say the least, he looked over at the daughter who was standing with her back against a wall, a beer bottle

43

dangling from her hand and one foot against the wall. Her expression was solemn.

Daniel looked back at the man holding him to the wall and spoke as firmly as he could. "Get your hands off me, Sir. I'll be glad to explain who I am but you turn me loose, now."

After what seemed like an eternity, the man backed away and looked at Daniel with his head leaning hard to the left. He spoke in a more controlled tone this time.

"OK, talk."

Daniel straightened himself and stared directly at the man. "I am Daniel Seay. I am a reporter with the Pittsburgh Post-Gazette. I am investigating the death of the Senator and other members of Congress. That's why I'm here."

"You're a might late, friend," the man said. "There's not much left to investigate. He's dead and we're leaving, what else do you need?"

"I have reason to believe he may have been murdered."

"Murdered?" The man spun on his heels and looked at the woman who said nothing.

He stepped back toward Daniel in a threatening manner and Daniel raised his hand in front of him. The man stopped and said, "What reasons?"

"There have been messages sent to newspapers and offices in the States where four Congressmen have been killed recently." He looked around the room, at all three of them. No one moved or said a word. Daniel continued, "was there anything unusual when you found the Senator?"

"He fell off his horse and got tangled in the wire," the man stated without emotion.

"That's it? There wasn't anything odd at all?"

"No, that was it...." the man answered, but was interrupted by the other man in the room.

"Murray, tell him about the calf, man."

The room got completely quiet for over a minute. Murray glared at the other man as if he had aired a deep secret.

"Tell him about the calf," the other man said again.

Daniel knew nothing of the calf, it had not been mentioned in the story as he heard it.

"A calf was tangled and laying dead when we found him. It looked like he had reached down to release the calf and fell."

The other man pressed the issue, "That ain't all, tell him the rest."

Murray now looked resolved to be done with this, he took a deep breath, turned back to Daniel and said, "The calf was on the wrong side of the fence."

Daniel didn't understand. His look of puzzlement was enough. Murray continued,

"The herd was on the far side of that fence. If the calf had stepped into it and gotten tangled, he would have been on the other side. We don't know how that calf got on the wrong side of the fence."

Daniel's investigative side kicked into gear, "Could the scene have been staged?" he asked.

The woman put her hand over her mouth and stared at Murray. Murray stared at the floor and muttered under his breath, "Most anything could have happened. We just don't know."

Daniel let things settle before he pressed any further. He walked over to the woman and asked her, "You seem to have reason to believe it could have been an intentional act. Will you tell me why that is?"

She looked past Daniel at Murray and said, "Murray, let's tell him what we know. Its gonna come out sometime, anyway."

She reached out, pointed at Murray and looked back at Daniel.

45

"Mr. Seay, meet my brother, Murray Bilstock."

The anger made more sense now. Sheriff Wilbury had led Daniel to believe Murray was a hired hand. Daniel looked at the other man in the room, "Are you family, too?"

Murray spoke up, "Cousin. Slick is our Aunt Sue's boy. He grew up with us."

Murray looked around and asked the woman in frustration, "Don't we have any chairs left in this house?"

She gave her brother a stern look of frustration and pointed to her right. Speaking in a tone to match her expression, she said,

"they're in the kitchen," and led the way down the hall. She was followed by the three men who now had much to talk about.

8

A road trip for verification meant it was serious. It had been five weeks since the last removal but only three since the messages went out. That didn't matter. This situation had all the markings of a severely needed removal. The representative was fairly new, just into his third term. Iowa usually didn't keep them for very long. But this guy was making an impact on the drug market in a big way.

A young reporter for the Burlington Hawk Eye paper disappeared two weeks before, after a story insinuating a connection between Rep. Charles Harley and local drug ring. The story was vague but the reporter had discussed his findings about the situation with other reporters and his boss.

The findings, while not completely collaborated, were very damning indeed. The disappearance of their author was just too obvious, yet nothing legal was being done. The road trip was to get as close as he could and find out what had happened to the young reporter. He had picked up on the story through a filter on a program he used to look through national newspapers online. The filter hit on the Representative's title, mentioned in the story, and printed it out.

By the time he was packed to go to Iowa, the reporter's body was found near Sandusky in the Mississippi River. He had been shot before being dumped in the river. The purpose in Burlington was two fold. To find out if the connection was real and if it was strong enough that the authorities should be on it and handle the case. If Harley were involved, but without enough for the police to charge him, then removal would be considered.

Silas bought a cell phone at a local supermarket and used the name Israel Putnam to register it. He used it to call the newspaper's office and asked about any reporter willing to talk. Of course, they were skeptical, after what had become of their friend and colleague. Few would speak without knowing whom they were talking to.

On his second day in town, he thought of a new approach. The cell phone allowed for text messages. He texted a message to the paper's editor. *"Don't fire until you see the whites of their eyes! Then fire low!"* The real Israel Putnam had fought at Bunker Hill. That well known quotation was his. The editor knew his history and had been following the Congressional deaths story enough to put two and two together. One fact understood by those in the know was that the person communicating with authorities, about the other deaths, used quotes from a group of men in the Revolutionary War. They were known through history as the Sons of Liberty. Israel Putnam had been a member. With that, and the inquiries about Rep. Harley and the dead reporter, the editor dialed the number of the cell phone that had messaged him.

The devise is called simply a cell phone voice changer. He had several boxes of them in the safe room and had brought half a dozen units with him.

When the cell phone rang, he connected to one of the voice changers and answered, "Let justice be done though the heavens should fall."

The reference was from John Adams, another member of the revolutionary group. The voice quoting John Adams was rough, graveled and distorted by the devise. It did not sound like a voice from this world. The voice on the other end of the phone was slightly

48

trembling.

"I take it I have reached the correct party?" It said.

"You may well have, Sir. What is your business?" The voice was monotone.

"I understand you are looking into Peter Cass' death."

"That is correct. I seek the responsible party. What information do you have for me?"

"Only that Peter believed one of our Congressmen was dirty, I mean really involved with some bad folks around here."

"Do you have any proof of that charge for me?"

"No, not now but we're going through all of Peter's notes and records. There must be something in there. Can I call you back?"

"I will contact you in two days. It may be by phone but, if so, not this one. You will know it is me, be assured."

"OK, I'll work on this," the editor said. Then he realized the line was dead. The editor called his staff together and issued an order. "I want all the facts you can collect on what Peter was looking into on my desk by tomorrow afternoon. Everything." As the group dispersed he grabbed his assistant editor's arm, "We may have a ghost from the revolution trying to help us."

"What?" his assistant replied.

The editor realized how dumb that sounded, "Nothing, just get together what we can to hang the bastard that killed Peter, OK?"

"Sure thing, boss."

~

The kitchen table at the Texas ranch house was a beauty. Solid mahogany, six feet in diameter with high back captain's chairs. The lady of the house set out fresh beers for everybody and leaned against the sink. Daniel realized he did not know her name. He rose from his seat and asked, "I know Murray is your brother, but I didn't get your

49

name?"

"It's Charlene," she answered.

"Charlene, thank you." Daniel then turned to Murray and asked, "When did you know something was wrong?"

"When his horse came in after dark. They'll stay with you most of the day. But when it gets dark, hunger overrides their loyalty and they'll head for the barn."

"I see," Daniel responded. "I couldn't help but notice your helicopter. They tell me you used horses to go look for him. Wouldn't the helicopter have been quicker?"

"Sure, if we knew where we were going. We were backtracking his horse, Sir. You can't do that from the air. Especially after dark."

"Oh, I see, I'm not from around here but that makes perfect sense now that you tell me."

As he talked and listened, Daniel was making notes. He looked at Slick to ask again about the calf and started with, "Slick, is that your given name?"

"His name is Stephen." Once again, Murray had spoken for him. "We call him Slick because he can get outta trouble quicker than a snake." Murray told of how Stephen had come to live with them a dozen years ago. His Dad had died and their Aunt could not deal with Stephen on her own. He had a wild streak and stayed in trouble most of the time. Aunt Sue hoped the work atmosphere of the ranch would do Stephen good. The penchant for finding trouble followed him to Texas but it never seemed to stick to him.

His cousins took to him, renamed him and he became one of them. They were now adults.

Slick, or Stephen, twisted in his chair but said nothing. Daniel tried again to ask him, "Tell me more about the calf, if you would."

Stephen looked at Murray, as if for approval and then back at Daniel. "It was on the wrong side of the fence, like I told you."

"Did you tell Sheriff Wilbury?"

"Sure did." Stephen looked perplexed and confused.

Daniel asked him, "Did the sheriff do anything with that information?"

"I think he made a note in his book," Stephen squirmed in his seat again. "I don't know."

Daniel turned to Murray, "Does that matter as much as it sounds, I mean, something like that could be very important, couldn't it?"

Murray was unimpressed, "Don't make no difference. He's dead. He fell and he's dead."

Something was still missing from this story. Daniel could feel it. Charlene had said they should "tell him what they knew" but they were not. Not so far. He needed to bring it out.

Daniel noticed the shirt that Stephen had on. It said "Stone Creek Youth Camp" across the front. He remembered hearing that name before but he thought then it was an actual creek. That's what Murray had said over the radio, something about going over to Stone Creek to pick up Slick.

"What is Stone Creek?" Daniel asked. "I thought it had to do with water."

Everyone was quiet till Charlene finally spoke up. "It's a children's home nearby. We worked with them, real close, for years. Bunches of the kids would come here and play cowboys for a couple of weeks at a time." She went to a drawer, opened it and took out a flyer about the program. "We were real proud of that, loved those kids, everyone of them."

Daniel could see she was getting upset. "Why are you crying, can't you still do that?"

"No," she cried, "not any more, we can't." And with that Charlene left the room. Daniel stood up but Murray shook his head

51

and motioned for him to sit. Again, the table was quiet. Murray stared down at the table while Stephen, blankly, looked straight ahead.

It was Stephen that finally opened up. He got up and walked across the kitchen with his beer in hand. After clearing his throat he began to tell the story about what had happened with the kids from Stone Creek. Last year there was a complaint, from one of the boys. A twelve year old claimed he had been molested behind the bunkhouse.

"Uncle Warren paid the home to forget about it and everything seemed fine. Then this year two more complained and it got into the paper in Brownwood and almost in Fort Worth and Dallas." Stephen then explained that his Uncle, the now dead Senator, paid somebody, he didn't know who, and the story never got to the big cities.

Daniel asked who were the boys complaining about. Stephen got quiet and looked to Murray for assurance. He got none. Murray stood up and went to the refrigerator for another beer.

It stayed quiet in that kitchen till Murray finally took a big gulp from his bottle and blurted out, "Shit, go ahead and tell him. Its gonna come out anyways, hell."

Daniel didn't move or say a word. It took Stephen several moments to find his voice again. He swallowed hard and muttered softly, "Uncle Warren. Senator Warren Bilstock"

They all heard Charlene cry out in a sob and run up the stairs. She had been just outside the doorway listening. Daniel stood and tried to apologize to Murray for upsetting his sister.

"Don't worry about that." He turned and went toward the front door, "We just found out for sure this year. I'd have killed him myself if I'd caught him hurtin' one of those kids." With that he was out the door.

Daniel stayed in the kitchen with Stephen for about an hour, getting details and a few names. Stephen shared about the stranger who had mysteriously asked folks a lot of questions at the home and in town. The calls to the home and the others were not traceable. Sheriff Wilbury had tried. Nobody ever saw him and his voice seemed mechanical and very different every time he called.

One of the workers at the Stone Creek facility told the caller about the two latest complaints of molestation. She had been told not to talk to anyone but, as she explained to her boss, she felt somebody should do something. That had been about a week, maybe two, before the accident. It was obvious to Daniel now, how the senator had fit the pattern of those killed.

9

While Silas waited to call the editor again, a trip to where the body had been found was in order. The Mississippi River ran between Iowa and Illinois with no obstructions. Near Sandusky the edges of the river were still cluttered with debris from the summer's heavy rains. The reporter's body got caught on a branch from a submerged tree trunk or he might have gone all the way to the Gulf of Mexico. Two fishermen found him while walking the bank. Other than being bloated, the body was in reasonable condition for the coroner. The single gunshot wound behind the right ear would be determined as the cause of death. The bullet exited near the corner of the left eye. His wallet was still in his clothing and no other bruising was found. It appeared that Peter had been shot from behind and did not see it coming.

Most of that information was from local newspaper coverage and one call to the coroner's office. The clerk was fascinated by the voice changer and even gave the names of the men who had found the body. One of them added a few details, as to exactly where the body was, but nothing helpful about who may have shot the reporter. Walking the bank of the river, from the opposite side, he calculated that the murder happened back in Burlington, or nearby. The condition of the river here was the only place with obstructions. From what he had learned about conditions further north, the water ran free from all the way back to Rock Island. Peter's body must have gone into the river near where he lived in Burlington, and the river had carried him to Sandusky.

As he drove back toward Burlington, Silas considered who might have done the deed. The Congressman himself was unlikely though he probably had ordered it done. The killer would be from out of town, in and out, just there for the job and gone. He knew about such and how hard it would be to nail that down, hard but not impossible. The Southeast Iowa Regional Airport was in Burlington. For a job like this one, it would be a good transit point.

He parked in the public lot at the airport and walked around the terminal and noticed the airlines and frequency of flights. Peter had disappeared on a Tuesday. Flights coming in on Tuesdays were limited to two airlines and three flights each. Most flights were short hops from around the area. Hit men didn't usually live in Iowa. One carrier, Great Lakes Airlines had a regularly scheduled flight from Kansas City, Mo. that arrived at 12:50PM every Tuesday. A return flight left at 3:50PM. That was a quick turnaround, but doable.

To check it out Silas assumed yet another identity. As Special Agent Jonathan Dill, of the FBI in Chicago, he asked a booking clerk if any party had arrived and departed on those flights the day of Peter's disappearance.

One Mexican national, Pedro Jones, had done so. Pedro's address was Kansas City, Kansas. There were no other records of him using the airline. Agent Dill thanked the clerk and went toward the car rental stables.

Now, Silas became Agent Johnson of the NCIS looking for an AWOL marine of Hispanic background. The clerk at Alamo Rentals had several Hispanics renting cars in the last month. Agent Johnson was allowed to review the records and found P. Jones on the date he was searching for. Records of the rental showed the car was out for two hours and ten minutes and had used sixty-three miles.

They gave Agent Johnson a copy of the records and he thanked them and left his business card. If they saw the man again they were to call him. That was unlikely and the number, like the card, was a fake.

Back at his car, he programmed one of the cell phones to display a particular number and identification on the receiving phone's caller ID. He went into a large coffee shop with activity and talking all around, much like a busy squad room, and dialed the number for the Kansas City, Kansas police department. The sergeant who answered saw the incoming call as being from the Rapid City, S. Dakota police station.

"Shansky, homicide," he answered.

The voice, supposedly from South Dakota, claimed to be Officer Welborn; he asked if they had any information on a Pedro Jones, a Hispanic male with ID from the Kansas City area.

"Jones, huh? What did he do up there?"

"You have a file on him, then?" the voice asked.

"Hell, yeah," Sergeant Shansky replied. "He's bad people. Hangs with a rough crowd downtown, you know, drugs and prostitution. That kind of thing."

"Any convictions?" the voice asked.

"Let me look," there was brief pause, "Yeah, battery and obstruction, he served a year and half a while back. He's a wannabe bad guy looking to make his mark."

"Sergeant, I thank you," the voice said.

"Say, what do you have on him, up there?" Shansky asked. But the phone went dead.

Sergeant Shansky started to call the number back but another call came in about a robbery in progress. He went on with his job and soon forgot all about the call. Jones was a small fish anyway. Let South Dakota have him, he thought.

He had found the likely hit man. Now he needed to tie him to his target. The hit man wasn't his business, but a murderous

Congressman would be.

~

Daniel Seay left Texas assured he was on the right track. There was a killer stalking members of Congress and who knows who else? The third victim A Representative, from Louisiana, who had been rumored to be taking advantage of still suffering Katrina victims, had been five weeks after the first. Daniel called home and told his wife he was off to Shreveport. He decided to drive since the trip would take less time than airline check-ins.

The drive across I-20 offered Daniel time to reflect on the family he had met in Texas.

Murray and the third man left in the helicopter well before he and Stephen were finished talking. He did manage to get Stephen to coax Charlene down from upstairs. He apologized, to them both, for disturbing the wound that obviously hurt them all so badly.

He told them, in very certain terms, that he had no interest in further exposing the story of their father and uncle. Daniel's interests were in the murderer who was targeting men like the senator and he believed he convinced them of that.

Charlene calmed down enough to explain a bit more about the house and why they were leaving. Their Mother had no idea what the senator was doing until after his death. The grief of his loss coupled with the truth of his character was more than she could bear.

She immediately moved herself to her family's home in Dallas and would not return to the ranch. She put the ranch up for sale over the objections of her children. While grown, they still were connected to the ranch in personal way and did not wish to lose that. They pleaded the need to continue working with the children's home. To correct what had been done by their father. Mrs. Bilstock could not be reasoned with and Murray and Charlene were powerless to stop her.

None of that had anything to do with the Congressional murders, but Daniel felt bad for Murray and Charlene just the same. The ultimate losers were the children at Stone Creek.

At about halfway to Shreveport, Daniel switched his thoughts to the dead Congressman from Mansfield, Louisiana. Representative Lamar LaPointe. Politics in Louisiana was so infamous, from as far back as the Huey Long days, that many folks accepted the goings on as normal. Corruption and graft that would not stand in other states seemed commonplace down here. There was, however, a tipping point in most everything and the Congressman had found his. He had been charged with skimming money from victims of the big Hurricane, Katrina. As a member of Congress, he was able to grease the skids of the Federal Government in getting help issued for various needs. The help normally took the form of money.

The charge was, that while helping a constituent, he would have the need expedited and then as the awards came back, would keep some 40% for his offices' expenses in the venture. The victims knew they were getting hosed but it was 60% of what they were due or nothing. In the years since the tragedy, this had become a healthy business for his office and may well have continued, had it not been for one petitioner from the congressman's hometown.

Willis Dewberry was dying. He had survived several days in New Orleans after the flood but had drunk the water. His system had become so weak from fighting the various types of ills that water carried, that he could not deal with the flu bug that came last year. His lungs were nearly destroyed. A respirator was all that kept this man breathing. The cost of his needs grew, over time, to a point well beyond what the congressman was allowing him to keep. After several appeals, which were not answered, he went public through the news media. The media loves Katrina stories. The worse the better and Willis' story was bad. This embarrassed the congressman. Rep. LaPointe formally, and quite out in the public eye, apologized profusely to Mr. Dewberry, whom he described as "having been caught up in Government bureaucracy."

At the same time, others could not be allowed to believe they could go over his head, as Mr. Dewberry had done. For the locals, an example must be made. With no apparent connection to the congressman, the power on Mr. Dewberry's street was lost one evening for several hours. Ambulances called to the scene went to the wrong address. Calls for an emergency generator were misdirected and the unit arrived much too late. Rep. LaPointe was on television the next morning in full remorse for the breakdown of the system. Again, he blamed others. The message, to those it was intended, came through, loud and clear.

Some three weeks after all this, Representative Lamar LaPointe was dead, an apparent heart attack while bird hunting. His successor's office and the Shreveport Times newspaper, each received messages with quotations from the revolutionary war period several weeks later. The information out there was pretty clear. Daniel needed more than what was out there. He wanted to connect the same perpetrator to this death as the others. He would start with Mr. Dewberry's family.

10

A veteran newspaper editor was exposed to many aspects of human nature. Thomas Ames, the editor of the Burlington Hawk Eye, had seen plenty. He had even lost reporters before. Peter Cass' case was hard for him, but it wasn't his first. The interest by this unknown, mystery man intrigued him but he wasn't buying it. Ames wanted to find out what happened to Peter as bad as anyone.

This strange, hero-quoting enigma added another layer. He upped the ante and created a whole new world of possibilities for a story. He would do as the man requested, to a point. Ames increased his efforts to go through his reporter's notes and records, but not to offer them to this guy. He would get a few crumbs but only enough to reel him in. If the Congressman had any involvement in Peter's death, he and his paper would help authorities convict the man. But he would not assist some assassin in the murder of a sitting Congressman. That just wasn't going to happen. The bigger story would be the capture of the "Revolutionary Assassin." No. He didn't like that. That would be too glorious a name for this killer, if he exists. If he is real, he needs a dose of humility, a title that clearly proclaimed, to the world, his underling status.

Ames thought and recounted the quotes he and his people had received. All from well known revolutionary heroes. All of whom were members of the Sons of Liberty.

That was it; Ames thought to himself, *"This guy thinks he's a Son of Liberty. More like a wayward misguided son, if anything."* The more he thought about it the more his contempt for this guy grew. He would lure him to where the police could capture his murderous hide, and then write an expose' condemning his actions. The tag line for the story will be "*The Wayward Son.*" Ames liked that. He made himself a note.

~

Much closer than the unaware Ames would have been comfortable with, Silas sat in a local pub and listened to conversations. The pub was near the newspaper's office and he hoped to pick up on some friends or co-workers discussing Peter Cass' story or even his death.

People love to talk about their situations. If you can position yourself in the vicinity of those involved in one, it is possible to learn a great deal. He did hear a couple talking about staying late to review some notes, but they didn't say about what. These recon missions worked sometimes and then again, not so much. After three hours he left and walked past the newspaper's main building. Lights were on and the parking lot was still full. It was past normal business hours. He noted a large office on the third floor with the blinds open. From the size he figured it to be the editor's office.

"*Good,*" he thought. The editor is gathering information for him. He realized he had not found a place to sleep yet.

The walk to his drop car was several blocks in a not too great part of town. No rule was broken, he just didn't think about it. He felt in his coat pocket and it was there. The equalizer. He had many special items he could use in emergencies. Still he was relieved when he reached the car with no incident. Tomorrow would be busy. He headed toward the other side of town to look for a motel.

~

Daniel Seay pulled into Shreveport after dark. He found a decent motel and checked in. He needed to call home soon and assure his wife he was all right, she would be worried by now. He told her about the Bilstock family and she was sympathetic. They talked about her day and Daniel nearly fell asleep listening. When he told her where he was and why, she became concerned.

"You be careful down there, Danny. Those people don't fool around, do you hear me?"

"Yes, honey," Daniel smiled and pictured her face, "I hear you and I love you."

"You'd better." She continued for a few more minutes with news of her Mom and sister and then they hung up. Daniel turned on the local news and took a nap before dinner.

While he was asleep, he missed the story on channel 12 about the reporter from back east who had been poking around in Texas and was expected in their area. Rep. LaPointe's death was big news in the state. Interest from outsiders was also big news, unwelcome big news.

~

The Lincolnville Motel in Burlington, Ia. was nicer than his usual choice. Silas decided to mix it up a bit and go for a nice place. Always assumed names, always a traveling salesman, and always from somewhere different than the last time. He actually had a rotation, a schedule of names and places; made up in advance he could refer to. He concealed it in the lining of the briefcase he carried. He didn't need to be too creative. It would only be for the sake of the registration and that would soon be forgotten.

He woke early and ordered breakfast brought to the room. He wanted to have privacy while he planned his day. Pedro Jones was here, in Burlington, the day Peter Cass disappeared. He was, more than likely, the killer. The question was, who was his contact and control person. Surely the congressman would not be that close to a hit himself. There had to be at least one intermediary. The hit would have happened near the water.

Today would be a trip to the riverfront area to nose around. The spot, where the hit took place, would be near the edge between clean, upscale riverfront establishments and the older, seedier side of the river community. He looked through brochures that were in the room as he ate. The motel was on Mount Pleasant Street. He could follow that east to the river. That would be a good place to start, he told himself. He began to get dressed.

His "uniform" for investigations was not noticeable to others but it was designed for the purpose of protecting him. His underwear was the latest in Kevlar, lightweight, strong and breathable. The shirt was another layer of Kevlar that looked like a regular polo shirt.

The pants, again Kevlar, and the legs were also fire retardant. The pockets held specially designed packets of mace and other chemical deterrents he could easily reach.

The jacket held a new device he had just obtained. Lining the right sleeve were steel reinforced, fabric tubes, in a skeletal form that ran down to five glove style fingers, which remained tucked above the cuff until needed. A reservoir of hydraulic fluid was stored in his belt and was attached to the structure with a quick release valve. Small knots, in the stitching of the belt, acted as buttons to either release the connection or to activate the device. When engaged, the structure would increase the strength of that arm and hand by eight to ten times its normal ability.

He would be near deep water this day so he also carried a small re-breathing unit in his left pants pocket. His modified Glock 23 rode in its seam pocket on the right leg of his pants.

All in all, the outfit weighed only three pounds above regular clothing. The enhancements made him feel more confident of surviving awkward situations.

Silas checked out, leaving a complimentary note on the "how did we do" card for the management, and headed east on Mount Pleasant. The road dumped into US 34, a major east-west highway that cut through the northern third of Burlington. As he approached the river he could see what he was looking for. The end of commercialized, well lit social gathering places and the start of unkempt, abandoned structures just to the north. That end point for civilization seemed to be a large restaurant called Sullie's just north of Big Muddy's on North Front St. Sullie's was two stories with a huge deck that faced south but wrapped partly around the back. It had been built after the flood of '08. The main street level was elevated and the lower level was primarily storage and delivery entrances. The driveway to the lower level was not attended so he drove down to within feet of the river.

There were Railroad tracks between the restaurant and the river and everything seemed to be extremely close. He got out of the car and walked across the tracks and looked down into the river. It was big and it was dirty. Rust like reddish muddy colored water that looked thick as it swept downstream. He shook his head as he thought of someone being dropped into that brine. Everything looked old and worn along the edges of the river. He walked slowly north and found what appeared to be a rub mark. It was now aging itself, but was clearly newer than the surrounding area. Directly behind him was the underside of Sullie's deck. There was a large concrete pad, which serviced the delivery doors and stood as a foundation for the deck's pillars.

The Railroad tracks, or the ground to there, showed no remaining signs of drag marks or rubs. The weather had reconditioned most of that. Under the deck, on the edge of the concrete pad, the finish was rough. There was a slight stain embedded into that rough concrete edge. He returned to the car for a test kit. He sprayed the stain with luminol solution and the telltale blue glow appeared. It was blood.

Still kneeling over the bloodstain he looked, quite deliberately, around the area. It was damp and dark from the heavy shade of the deck. Light from the sun touched only the very back third of the concrete pad.

He glanced at his watch. It was only 10:30AM. Pedro could not have gotten here before 1:30PM on that Tuesday. By 1:30 there would be no daylight under here at all. He stood and slowly turned in every direction, staring intently the whole time.

"This wasn't it." He told himself. *"It's too dark and foreboding."* Even the eagerest reporter would not meet someone in a place like this, especially alone. He stepped to his right and tilted his head to look straight up. He was directly under the corner of the deck, that most remote corner of the restaurant's deck. With his left hand raised to his chin he looked back again toward the river. The rub marks did not lie. Pedro was here, but Peter was not. Not alive anyway.

Pedro was not from Burlington.

"Why would Peter meet someone he did not know, especially in a place like this?" He looked back to the deck above him.

"He didn't," he said almost out loud, *"Pedro wasn't the killer. He was the catcher and the dump man."* Silas picked up his test kit and walked back to the car. He had been down here for over twenty minutes and had not seen a soul. He could hear activity above on the deck, yet no one appeared to know he was beneath them.

Silas drove up to the main road; went past the restaurant and stopped. He parked on the side of the main road and got out of his car. He walked back toward the restaurant building looking for an egress point, somewhere that a man might climb down to the lower level. There, next to the building, lay a rope. Not an old worn rope, but fairly new. He had not noticed it from below. It was tied off to a large rock and extended down most of the side of the building. That was it. That was how Pedro got to the lower level that day. He simply parked right on the road and let himself down the steep incline with the rope. Pedro most likely used that same rope to pull himself up after his job was done.

Silas walked across the street to a bench along the road and sat. He stayed there for another thirty minutes just watching and studying. His car was not noticed or bothered. No one even drove by. The road on that side of the building was not often used. The only access street north of where he stood was High Street and it was not a busy connector.

The scene was becoming more and more clear. Peter came here to meet someone, someone he knew. They met on the deck. Somehow the person Peter met here shot him, with no one the wiser. That person then dropped Peter over the side, still unnoticed, to the waiting Pedro who dragged and then dumped the body in the river.

Pedro would have had to be there no more than 30 or 40 minutes and it was back to the airport. Still that was quite a lot to go unnoticed by anyone. But stranger things have happened. He would wait around for lunch to further check this new theory. Perhaps a burger on that deck would help.

11

Morning at the Hawk Eye paper started before dawn. They hit the street in the afternoons, one of the few that still did, so the final touches of the final edition were being polished.

Along with that was Ames' decree that all relevant notes and scribblings of Peter Cass be gone through. Peter's desk had been left much as it was the day he disappeared. They found multitudes of small notebooks in almost every drawer of the desk. Reporter's size notebooks, 3.5" by 5.5", but none with the date he went missing. Obviously he had that one with him. If all the contact and where he was to meet them information was in that one missing notebook, it would be hard to place what had happened.

Earl Johnstone was a feature writer and friend of Peter's. He had spent several hours at Peter's desk going through everything when he suddenly stopped. He jumped out of the chair and nearly ran into Thomas Ames' office.

"Chief," Johnstone shouted, "I think I've found something. It was right under our nose."

"Found what?" The boss demanded.

"A scribble in Peter's hand, in the margin of his desk calendar. It's in his shorthand but I've seen enough of it I know what it says."

"Show me," the editor said as he led the way back to Peter's desk.

There, on the left side margin, was the cryptic message. A note he left for himself but was now key evidence. It said, *"Sul/dk – 115p – THarp."*

"What does it mean?" Ames seemed perplexed.

"Sul/dk is Sullie's Deck and 115p is the time 1:15PM. THarp is who he was meeting." The young reporter looked at his boss. Color had drained from the editor's face.

"Boss, do you know who 'THarp' could be?"

"Yeah, I think I do," said Ames. "Good work, kid." He looked straight at his young reporter and put a hand on his shoulder.

"Look, you found this, its yours. But before I tell you anything about what's in my mind you should know, if I'm right, we're both in danger."

"Sure, boss." Johnstone's curiosity was on overload.

"It could be Terry Harper."

"Where have I heard that name?" Johnstone asked.

"He's a personal aide to Charles Harley. US Congressman, Charles Harley."

"Oh, shit!" Now Johnstone's color faded.

"Yeah, you can say that again. Keep this under your hat till I say different, understand?"

"Yes, Sir." With that his boss went back to his own office and Earl Johnstone walked slowly back to his desk. He had a copy of Peter's story, the one that caused all the trouble. Johnstone needed to read it again.

~

Daniel Seay had slept late. He had not realized just how tired he was. His adrenalin had kept him in high gear since he left home. His mission started out to prove his theory about a serial killer. A theory not shared by many others at the time. It was a strange effect for a

68

person to have. But finding proof, that a serial killer was loose, released pent up tensions and allowed him to relax. It had been his first restful sleep since leaving home. He was now in Shreveport, Louisiana, the home of Lamar LaPointe. LaPointe, a congressman from the area, had been the third victim several months ago.

If Daniel could find ties to this death that mimicked the Texas Senator's death, he may not even worry about the second victim. Two out of three would be plenty of juice for a story, a national story. By the time he was dressed it was nearly lunch. Daniel drove into town, towards the LaPointe main headquarters and office complex, to see if anyone was still around. One room on the first floor was lit. Daniel parked and went up to the door. Before he could knock the door opened. Deja vu he thought, remembering the Texas ranch house. Again, it was a female and again, she had an attitude.

"What is it, we're closed or didn't you hear?" She was quite rude for a southern girl.

"Sorry, I don't mean to be a bother," he pleaded. "I'm Daniel Seay with the Pittsburgh Post-Gazette. I'm here doing some research for a story about the congressman's death. I was hoping I could talk with you a minute."

"What kind of story?" she asked. Others had been here before Daniel. Having heard the rumors about the corruption. They all wanted to win prizes for their character assassinations. She would have no more of it.

"Lamar was a good man. He helped lots of folks. That's all I'm gonna say." And with that she shut the door. Firmly.

He thought about knocking again but why further aggravate her? Daniel drove a few blocks and found a friendly looking diner. It was lunchtime anyway. Maybe he could strike up a conversation and learn something.

~

Sullie's, along the Iowa banks of the Mississippi, was a busy place at lunch. The interior dining room filled quickly and the crowd expanded to the deck. He walked in at 1PM; about the time he figured Peter would have met his killer. The hostess asked the standard, "how many" and then where would he like to sit? He told her he had some work to do and would prefer to be alone, if possible. She mentioned the backside of the deck but cautioned him, "You may need to remind us you're there. We don't have many customers who wish to sit there in the daytime." He assured her that would not be a problem and as they walked across the deck he pointed to a table in the far corner.

"That one will do, nicely."

"Yes, sir." And then she took his drink order and left.

He sat in the corner with his back to the rail. It was isolated for sure. He could not see any other customers and there were no windows from the main dining room looking this way.

"*Odd*," he thought. Looking over the rail he could see the train tracks. They appeared to be much closer than they actually were. He could see a great deal down the southern side of the tracks but the northern route turned fairly sharp to the right about a hundred yards out. The view was definitely to the south.

He was checking out the floor around him when she reappeared with his Diet Coke. She stood silent for a moment, watching him in wonder.

"Is everything all right, Sir?" she asked.

Almost jumping, he sat upright and smiled. He had let her walk up on him undetected.

"Yeah, just dropped a pen. I think it went through the crack."

"I'd be glad to get you another one, sir," she suggested.

"No thanks, no. I've got plenty," he shook his head and waved the suggestion off. "I think I'll have that burger plate, no onions, please."

"Yes, sir." She made a note and was gone again. He smiled at himself once more about letting her sneak up like that. Silas would not approve.

He could find no sign of blood on the deck itself. He had brought in a small spray bottle of luminol and tested a couple a spots, but nothing. He continued to study the area and did find a rub on the railing. Could have been a belt buckle, maybe not. Just before his food came, he decided to wash his hands.

Walking back through the main dining room he noticed a face he recognized. It was Thomas Ames, the editor of the paper, looking very true to his likeness in the research notes. He delayed his trip to the bathroom and stood near the bar. He could hear the editor talking with the hostess, and then they walked out onto the deck. He followed carefully, staying out of their sight.

Stepping to the far side railing, he watched as the hostess pointed out his table. She looked around, as if for him, but didn't seem concerned. The editor thanked her and shook her hand. They reentered the main building and Ames left through the main doors. Watching the activity from the deck, he noticed as the editor got back into his car and drove away. Then he waited for the hostess to come back out on the deck, so he to go around her to the bathroom.

On his way back to the table, he made a point to run into her.

"Oh, there you are," she stated.

He did his best to seem surprised, "Did I miss my burger, or what?"

"No, no," she smiled. "I just had another guest asking about the area you were sitting in. Your exact table, actually."

"Really?" He asked with deep interest in the situation. "What was so special about that?"

"A local reporter, name Peter Cass, ate here the day he disappeared. That's been some time back now, I don't remember the date."

"Disappeared?" He asked. "I'm a fan of mysteries. Was he here alone?"

"No, Mr. Harper had made the reservation and had asked for that table. They needed to talk in private, he said."

"Did they leave together?" He couldn't catch himself. The question just came out.

"You know, I hadn't thought about it, but no. I don't think they did. Mr. Harper said something about Mr. Cass not feeling well and that he left early. I missed it, didn't see him leave but it was Mr. Harper's check so there was no problem."

"Sounds like a good mystery story to me." he quipped. He noticed his burger being delivered to his empty table. The server was looking around for him. He waved and went back to the table. While eating he considered this new revelation. He had been right again. This is where it happened and the editor knew it. But the noise level wasn't high enough to cover a gunshot.

"*Even with a silencer someone could notice,*" he thought to himself.

He finished his burger and while wiping his face, it happened.

The earth rumbled and shook. Then the whistle blasted. The piercing sound that announced the arrival of the freight train. It was heading north and it was coming fast. The noise and air movement stirred by the speeding train made it hard to hear your own thoughts.

He stood up and stared at the train over the railing.

"*That was it!*" His mind screamed. "*The noise drowned out everything.*"

72

Walking along the rail he noticed the crowd's attention was entirely to the south, where the train was coming from. His table sat in the most northern corner of the deck. He sought out the hostess and checked his watch. It was 1:46PM.

The train and its noise lasted 4 minutes and some change. When it had passed and he found the hostess he asked if that was a regular event.

"Yes, Sir." She smiled. "That's what we call the 1:45 around here. Everyday, it's almost like clockwork. It was actually a bit late today."

Back at his table he recalled the information the coroner's clerk had offered. The bullet passed through Peter's head at an angle that would be toward the river. It may not have gone too far having cleared all that obstruction.

He paid his check and walked back to his car. Driving back under the deck area, he took his metal detector from under the seat. After about twenty minutes he gave up. No bullet. Back to the car, he retrieved a file folder from the trunk. Inside the vehicle he looked through his notes on this case. He had a list of the Congressman's assistants and known associates. There he was, listed as an aide de camp, Terrence Harper. So, Harper was the shooter and Pedro was brought in to do his job, dump the body and go away. He was anxious to hear from the editor, but that would be tomorrow. Now it was off to see what he could learn about Mr. Harper.

He drove south along Front Street and turned right on Market. After one block he turned back south again on S. Main. He remembered S. Main was the street the newspaper office was on. He followed the road down to the area he had been in last night. With all the buildings around, he had not noticed how close he was to the river the day before. In the daylight, the city looked old to him. It was neat and clean, just old.

Driving around he got a feel for the types of businesses that were in this area. It was light commercial, mainly shops and coffee houses. The bar he had visited last night was among them. He got gas at a corner station and asked the clerk where the industrial park was.

"Get on Mt. Pleasant and go west," he advised. "Its an area we call West Burlington."

He remembered Mt. Pleasant Road. He headed north and then west to check out that area.

As he drove toward the west side of town, he reconsidered his thoughts on looking into Terrence Harper, for right now anyway. The editor of the paper has demonstrated that he knows about the restaurant and he must know who Peter had met there. Having been to the restaurant meant the editor was looking into it himself. It would be quite possible that his investigation might cross paths with the editor's. That could cause the people in the congressman's camp to be aware someone was on to them. He could not control what the editor did but he could be patient himself, he had the time and he could wait.

The plan was to call the editor in the morning. That will work just fine. He decided to look around the industrial area without asking direct questions about Harper.

The industrial area of a town is always where the rough and tumble types could be found. Someone might mention Harper without a question. He figured a guy who could handle a shooting would have associates of similar character. It was several hours till dinnertime.

He would look the area over and then find a spot to have dinner; and listen a bit.

12

Thomas Ames was more nervous than ever. He returned to his office to think what he should do. It was clear people from the Congressman's office were involved in Peter's death. If not Harper directly, someone he knew. This was not good. He was aware of Harper's reputation. He was a persuader. He managed to get people who weren't inclined to cooperate at first, to do so, rather abruptly. Ames wanted no trouble with Harper. He would let the police handle that. Neither did he plan to allow this "Wayward Son" to take revenge, warranted or not. He picked up his private line and called a Lt. Draper of the Burlington Police. He had worked with Draper many times and felt he could rely on his counsel in this mess, both ends of it.

Not sure if his office building was being watched, he asked Draper to meet him at a coffee shop a block west of the building. Ames went out a back door, wearing a dark jacket and a hat, and walked to the coffee house to wait for Draper. From his booth, he kept an eye on the front window and all seemed OK. Draper came in, wearing civilian clothes, and sat with his friend in the booth.

The editor shared his stories with the officer. Draper responded that they were already suspicious of Harper and he appreciated the confirmation. On the tale of the assassin, looking for the Congressman's guilt, Draper was fascinated. He had heard stories about this guy and now he could be real and in his town. Ames told him about the call he was expecting tomorrow. They decided to set this guy up and let Draper bring him in for questioning. If he was real, it would be a big deal for the town and Draper's department. As for Terrence Harper, that was an on going case and would continue to be.

~

Daniel Seay had lived in South Georgia, not far from the Florida border, as a young boy. It could get hot in Georgia, he remembered it well, but this was ridiculous. The Louisiana heat and humidity was far worse than Texas.

His luck wasn't nearly as hot. He had struck out at the Congressman's old office and the residence was closed up.

It didn't appear that the grass had been cut in several weeks but heck; hot as it was the stuff may grow faster down here. Without any other plan at the moment he looked up the offices of the Shreveport Times Newspaper. When in doubt, find kindred people and ask what they know.

He drove back onto I-20 toward midtown looking for the Spring Street exit. He saw a sign or two mentioning the street but not an exit. Before he knew it he was crossing the Red River so he got off I-20 at Traffic Street and turned around.

Once across the river again, he saw the exit this time. As if luck was now with him, the exit dumped right onto Lake Street where the Newspaper was located.

The parking lot area for "visitors" was full but he found a spot not too far from the doors and went in to introduce himself. Sherrie, at the reception desk, took his card and called for Editor Matt Turlock.

Daniel had a seat and checked out the headlines mounted on the walls. Framed and lit from above, they told of the events the Times reporters had covered over the years. From the Mars probe, of last month, all the way back to the Kennedy assassination, the headlines were there. On the wall, about a third down from the Mars headline, was their lead on the Congressman. "LaPointe Dead," it read in bold type.

Daniel stood to look at it closer when he heard the man's voice from behind him.

"Daniel? Mr. Seay, I'm Matt Turlock. Welcome to Shreveport and how can I assist you?"

Daniel turned and reached out to return Turlock's handshake.

"Hello and thanks Mr. Turlock. Pleasure to meet you, Sir."

"Call me Matt, please." Turlock looked to be a good ten years older than Daniel's 39. But he was trim and fit looking and certainly seemed friendly enough.

"Matt, I'm here investigating the Congressional deaths that have happened in the last few months. I believe I see a pattern leading to a possible single perpetrator. I believe Representative LaPointe was one of the victims."

"Really?" Turlock turned his body and pointed with his arm to an open door just down the hall. "Come, please, tell me more. I think I heard something about this theory just recently. Didn't you say you were from Pittsburgh?"

"Yes, the Post-Gazette."

"That's right. So you're the guy with the idea about all this, huh?" Turlock's office was very nice. Probably twice the size of his boss' office back home and the décor showed a woman's touch.

"Nice office," Daniel commented.

"Thanks, my wife is an interior designer. She did all this on a napkin at a restaurant. Came together pretty neat, I suppose."

"Very well." Daniel smiled. Changing the subject he continued. "So, you heard about my theory? My boss mentioned something about a story on it in a phone call, but I haven't seen it."

"Channel 3 carried the story here, last night in fact, your timing is excellent. They say you're nosing around in the affairs of others."

"Nosing around?"

"Harsh, huh? Folks down here can be that way. The money flow that LaPointe had kept going, has dried up since he died. Or whatever." The last part was just thrown in for contempt.

"He wasn't a very 'loved' man," the editor continued, " but that money sure was. This new guy in the job doesn't have the flow back up to speed yet. The folks are impatient. They see you as an impediment."

"Must have been quite a flow! I was thinking small stuff. How many people were using LaPointe to get funds?" Daniel asked.

"Eight, maybe nine thousand."

"You are kidding me."

"No, old Lamar was squeezing over ten million a year for himself out of it all."

Daniel was amazed. He thought about the man LaPointe had made an example of, Willis Dewberry.

"How are the Dewberry's doing? I wanted to talk with them."

"They all packed up and left Louisiana. I tried to get one of them to talk about it, no one would. They all left within a month of Mr. Willis' death."

"So, LaPointe still had pull from the grave, huh?" asked the visitor.

"Oh, yeah. That kind of power runs deep. So, what can I do to help you?"

Without the Dewberrys and with no cooperation from the Lapointe people, Daniel had to think about that for a minute.

"Before the Congressman died, was there any report of a stranger asking questions, like I am now?"

"Not that I am aware of, but I tell you what; I'll check with Phil Stone down at the police department. If anybody reported anything like that, Phil would know about it."

Matt Turlock walked around and then sat at his desk.

"Have you had dinner? I'll call Phil, right now, and see if he'll meet us for dinner. Show you some good Louisiana cooking, how bout it?"

"That's mighty nice of you." Daniel answered. "Thanks. I believe I'd enjoy that."

Matt Turlock did reach Phil Stone and he agreed to meet them at Cub's.

"Phil wants a steak. This place is so great, you'll love it." Matt smirked.

"Can I ask an odd question about LaPointe?" Daniel injected.

"Sure, if I know the answer."

"When he had that heart attack, he wasn't flossing his teeth at the time, was he?"

Matt's expression changed back to serious.

"That is odd, Daniel. He was at a friend's hunting cabin. He wasn't flossing but he did have his tooth brush in his hand and lather in his mouth when they found him."

"I don't suppose there was any foreign residue, anywhere?"

"None found around or in his system for that matter. What's the connection?"

"Our guy was flossing. Dropped dead with floss in his hand. Nothing found with him, either," the visitor proclaimed.

"Damn, guy. You could be on to something here. Think it's the tooth fairy?" Matt was smiling again. Daniel laughed with him and they headed out to go meet with the officer.

13

After several hours of touring the area west of the mall, Silas found a dive on N. Agency. If it had a crowd, they would likely be a rough bunch. The parking lot was gravel. It wound its way around to the back of the building. A spot that could be trouble in the dark, but there stood a light pole with what appeared to be a huge halogen bulb. He walked in and looked around.

Since it was early, there was not much happening. He sat at the bar and sipped a diet coke while pretending to look through a day old copy of the Hawk Eye. As dusk set in the bar began to fill and conversations filled the room. Silas moved to the other end of the bar and ordered a cup of coffee. He heard about drug deals and a prostitute who got beat up last night, nothing about Mr. Harper. The coffee made him hungry so he went to the rest room and washed up, the best he could.

The rest room was an exhibit of human depravity. Dope deals were happening right in front of everybody. A man was snorting cocaine off the top of a urinal. He could see four boots in one stall as he went for the door.

His hunger had been tempered a bit, but he knew he still needed to eat. This place was bad yet it was where he would hear about bad people if the food didn't kill him. He looked into the kitchen and was mildly surprised.

Despite the goings on everywhere else the kitchen was neat and clean. There actually was an inspection certificate hanging just outside the door showing a 96% on the latest check. Silas smiled to himself and shook his head at the same time. Grabbing a menu off the bar he looked for a table.

The waitress, a pleasant enough though large woman in a short dress with a "Z Z Top" tee shirt over it, pointed to a small table near the window. It was further away from the main group than he wanted but it was available. He ordered the steak and fries. After taking an hour to eat he had still heard no mention of Mr. Harper.

"Rough place but maybe the wrong place," he thought to himself. He paid his check for dinner and sat back at the bar. He nursed a beer for another thirty minutes still to no avail. He hoped the moving around had made him less conspicuous but no one really seemed to care.

At 8:15PM he gave up. Time to find a motel and get some rest. He tried to go to the restroom again; more to throw off anyone possibly watching him, but it was standing room only in there. Once outside he took a deep breath and could tell right away that big, parking lot light was not working. The only light in the lot was from inside the bar or across the street and it was faint at best. He walked around the corner toward his car. A large van had parked next to his driver's side.

As he walked across the lot he thought he caught a glimpse of a shadow in a car mirror. He hit the power lock button for the vehicle through his pants to leave his hand free. As he stepped to the car door he heard a man's voice.

"Give me the money."

"I don't have any money, friend," he replied calmly.
He then felt something in his ribs from behind,

"I said give it up, man." The voice was agitated now.

"OK," he said as he touched the top button on his belt. The five fingertips dropped down to where his digits could slip inside them.

"Calm down. I'll get it for you." As he touched the second button and the fluid rushed into the skeletal structure around his arm. The fingertips slid back up enough to be firm in his grip.

The attacker was getting impatient.

"I said now." And he pushed the object further into Silas' side.

"OK, I said." He responded while he bent the arm at the elbow and brought his hand up to his waist.

In the blink of an eye, Silas spun to his right with tremendous force. The arm struck the assailant and knocked him into the van. He immediately stepped into the attacker, grabbing him under the chin with the hand.

Silas felt the object his attacker held hit him in the stomach area with great force. He stiffened his back and raised his arm. The attacker was lifted off the ground by his neck. The object, now clearly a knife, dropped to the ground. He held the man in check and slowly tilted his own face up to look at him. Rage filled him. He increased the power of his grip and the man's legs began to twitch.

Silas held him there for another few seconds and then stepped back and dropped him in one motion. The attacker was not conscious. Silas leaned over to check for a pulse. It was still there, slightly.

He dragged the man to the front of the van placing him out of sight. Squatting back down, he picked up the knife. It was a hunting knife with at least an 8" blade. He could feel his rage building again as he stared at it. Standing and throwing in one motion, he launched the knife onto the bar's roof.

With the arm still activated he drew the Glock from its pocket. Holding the weapon behind his back Silas walked to the rear of the car and looked around carefully. No one else was in sight. For the first time he could sense the tender spot above his stomach. Feeling the area he could tell the Kevlar had done its job. There was no puncture.

He turned, re-holstered the gun and got in his car. Backing out slowly he continued to search for any possible witness. He exited the parking lot and headed up Agency Drive to South Gear Street. A block away from the bar he finally pushed the buttons to relax the arm. The fluid returned to the belt and the fingertips dropped off his hand and slid gently back under the jacket cuff.

Going north, on South Gear Street, he saw a motel just north of the Westland Mall. Silas stopped the car and took a deep breath before he drove up to the office and checked in.

~

Ames and Draper decided on how they would lure the assassin into their trap. Ames would tell him they had found notes about a thug named Dobbs, who hung out at the pub around the corner. Dobbs had no connection with the Congressman, but was an independent drug dealer. Ames would tell the assassin that in those notes was a threat from Dobbs against Peter.

He would say witnesses had spotted Dobbs following Peter out of the pub that night and they suspect he killed him and threw the body in the river in that area. The lure would be the offer of copies, of both the notes and the threat, to be left for him in a specific place.

After a bit of fine-tuning Ames finally said, "That should work."

"Of course it'll work. I do this all the time."

~

Cub's in Shreveport was indeed a very nice place. They knew Matt Turlock by name and told him Capt. Stone was already there. Phil Stone wasn't just a police officer. He was Captain of the Homicide and Major Crimes Division.

83

Daniel felt underdressed for the first time he could remember. The restaurant was highly ornate with tablecloths and chandeliers. The serving staff wore uniforms based upon their activity. The maître d' wore a black tux. The waiters, and they were all males, wore gray and the expediters were dressed in red. The busboys wore dark blue jackets. The service at every level was very military and choreographed. It was quite impressive to Daniel.

Capt. Stone stood as they approached the table and reached out toward Daniel to shake his hand.

"Good to meet you," the Capt. stated. "I've ordered a beer. What are you guys having?"

"Same for me," Matt declared. He grabbed a chair and looked at Daniel.

"Sure, I'll have a beer," Daniel said as he sat down.

As the dinner progressed Daniel could tell the men were close friends and had worked together for many years. Matt told Stone the details of Daniel's theory. The Captain's eyebrows rose a bit. He was intrigued by the idea but had no evidence the death was anything except natural causes.

"That's the same as in our case in Pennsylvania," Daniel interjected. "Until the notes arrived the only thing that seemed odd was the number and frequency of the Congressmen dying."

Stone knew about the notes and had not taken them too seriously.

"You give credence to those messages?" he asked.

"That's what I'm trying to determine. My gut says yes." Daniel then told what he had found out in Texas. He told them of the apparent motive for wanting the Senator dead and the "odd" voice on the phone calls before he died.

The mention of the mechanical voice caused Stone to lean forward.

"One kid I interviewed said something that didn't make any sense till now." The captain remembered.

Stone went on to tell about the investigative canvas of the Congressman's Headquarters and that one young man who worked there told him of a phone call about a week before LaPointe's death. The caller had asked the kid questions about Mr. Dewberry and the circumstances around him dying like he did.

"He said the voice was like Darth Vader's," Stone added.

"Did anyone else mention that?" Daniel's eyes became as wide as his dinner plate as he pressed for more information.

"Not that I'm aware of, but I'll check with my officers."

Stone's normally confident look became puzzled. He cupped his chin with his hand and leaned back in obvious deep thought.

"That's kind of a weird thing to write in a report." He finally stated. "I don't even know if I did, now that I think about it. It never seemed important. Not till you said what you just did."

Matt glanced over at Daniel but neither said a word.

"Just a coincidence," Stone uttered as he shook his head and looked up firmly; his confidence restored. "That's all, a coincidence."

The rest of the evening was good food and conversation. Some included facts and theories of the case. The veteran police officer was not impressed with the floss and toothpaste connection that Daniel offered either.

"Men that age die everyday and most early in the morning," he said flatly. "Those activities are normal and I don't think it's anything but a coincidence."

"Coincidences were starting to pile up," Daniel thought in silence.

But it was not a coincidence. No one would ever know for sure, but Daniel was dead-on with the manner of the murder. Silas had managed to gain access to the cabin, through the crawl space,

85

undetected by the guards. He came up through a scurry hole in the closet floor. Once in the bathroom he saw only rolled floss so the concoction was applied to the congressman's toothbrush. The rubbing action of brushing released the deadly fumes. It was over quickly.

Daniel still believed the two were relevant but did not press the issue with his expert. Nothing else tied this death to the others, just the strange voice. But that voice thing could be enough. Daniel already felt his trip was justified.

~

In the motel room, in West Burlington, Iowa, the man paced back and forth. Silas had stripped down to his shorts and would stop every so often to look at the bruise developing on his abdomen, just below his ribs. He was livid, but not just with what had happened. He had allowed himself to be in a very dangerous position. It wasn't the injury that concerned him.

It was the possibility of being discovered. Besides that, he had nearly killed his attacker. He didn't have time for explanations of things like that. He walked and talked to himself till he fell onto the bed in exhaustion.

On the side chair lay the arm unit. It had performed to perfection but he had not taken time to consider that yet. He had obtained it like he did his other toys, through the Internet. Not a simple Google search. One of his computer systems is programed to search special websites for items submitted to the military.

The arm had made it to the prototype stage but was rejected for unspecified reasons. The website listed two prototypes, with manuals and spare parts for $75,000.00 each. He ordered both, using an account set up for one of his dummy companies. He had them delivered to one of his empty warehouses in town. The day of the expected delivery, he hired a young man to sweep up the place and sign for anything that came in.

Silas understood the mechanics of the unit but as for the operation through nerve impulses, he determined to just accept what the manual said. It appeared to work exactly as stated it would. Once up and running, the unit acted as an extension of his own arm and reacted as if it were. This was a keeper. As was the special Glock handgun.

The Glock 23 was already known as a very concealable weapon. This one was slimmer and lighter overall. The carbon fiber reinforced materials used for the barrel and slide cut the width down to ¾". Other measurements remained the same but the total weight, with standard, loaded magazine had dropped to 24 oz. There was only this one and he had been lucky to get it. The only problem would be if any repair parts were ever needed. There were not any. Continued use caused the barrel to overheat, so it was rejected. He didn't plan to fire it that often. The concealability factor was his issue. One magazine of fifteen rounds did not cause the heating issue. For him, it was ideal.

14

The morning found everyone at the Burlington Hawk Eye once again busy. Thomas Ames had his script at arm's reach, the details of what he and Draper had decided to tell the assassin to set the trap. Ames was working steadily on his story for this afternoon's release. The capture of the "Wayward Son" would be picked up nationally, he was sure.

Draper was already preparing the area for the trap. Officers were in place high above the site and would stay there, out of sight till notified. They did not know exactly when he would call. So they decided rather than have Draper sit there all day, Ames would let Draper know as soon as he could.

When the phone rang at 9:05AM Ames did not expect it to be him. The voice made him realize he was wrong.

"These are the times that try men's souls," the distorted voice announced.

Gathering himself, Ames tried to be cool. "You're up early."

The voice was not amused.

"What do you have for me?" it asked.

Ames looked at his script. "We got lucky, really lucky. I think we know who did it."

"I'm listening," the voice said.

Ames relayed the story about the nonexistent Dobbs. He went into detail about the threat and the notes and the copies he had for the man.

In his motel room, the man leaned back and thought to himself, "*so this is how it will be?*" What he spoke into the phone was quite different.

"So how do I get these copies?"

"I can leave them for you down near the boat ramp about four blocks from here." Ames worked at remaining calm. It appeared as though the killer was going for his story.

The voice was quiet for several minutes. The risk of being traced was not a problem. He had routed the call through several phones so that would prove fruitless.

"I will meet with you, personally. No one else and I don't care for your spot," he declared.

"Me?" Ames asked. "You want to meet with me?"

"If you have no interest, that's fine," the voice said.

"No, wait. I can do that. Where do you want to meet?"

"There's an abandoned building behind the Westland Mall area. On the right side of Layne Drive off West Huston Street," he read from the map in his lap.

"Layne Drive? I'm not familiar with that." Ames stalled.

"Get a map or forget it," the voice was firm.

"Okay, I'll find it. What time? An hour or what?"

"Four O'clock this afternoon," he said.

"Four? Why so long? Can we do it earlier?"

"Find a map and a watch, I don't care. Be there or not."

"Okay, I'll be there."

The phone went dead. Ames called Draper to tell him what had happened. Draper was not pleased, at all. Now the meeting was on his terms. They had no control.

"I'll send a unit to the area, now, to keep watch," Draper told his friend. "We'll be right there when this goes down."

Ames wasn't happy with the conditions either. He had wanted the deal done when his story hit the street this afternoon. Now it would be nearly simultaneous.

"Risky business," he said out loud.

~

A quick check of inventory in the trunk of his car and Silas was off to the Layne Drive building he had noticed yesterday. His motel was less than a mile from the warehouse. Trip time there was three minutes. He placed three .00002 LUX, wireless lipstick cameras in areas to check the doors. They could see in the dark. One mini 4.4GHz wireless remote control camera was set near a crack in the wall. It could move around the floor less noticeable than a cockroach and keep an eye on the outside area.

He set up a cardboard box with a jacket over it then placed a baseball cap on a wire just over the coat. In the dark of the warehouse it was deceiving. Three wireless speakers were placed around the interior space and set to pick up the two cell phones he had wired together. The speakers were set on a delay of less than ½ a second from each other. The effect would be an echo added to the disguised voice. When he called in it would appear that he was in the building.

The cameras would allow him to see who and what was there. Adjusting his receiver unit to all the frequencies he would be using, he set the range to maximum. That should cover 20 miles even in bad terrain. He was inside the warehouse for less than fifteen minutes and gone 5 minutes before the patrol cars arrived in the area. They set up on two ends of Gear Street and monitored access to the warehouse. Within the hour, unmarked, stakeout vehicles replaced them. Those would wait there all day.

Back at the motel, Silas went deeper into his trunk supplies. He dug out a UPS uniform and a telephone company repairman's outfit. At 11:00AM he checked out of the motel room and headed toward town. He would find a position near the Hawk Eye Building, to watch and wait.

~

Daniel Seay awoke and returned to the office of the Shreveport Times to thank his host from last evening. He had thought about it after dinner and still wanted to ask around town a bit himself. He asked if that would offend Captain Stone?

"Hell, no. He's not that kind of guy." Turlock assured him. "If you learn something we missed, we'd both be tickled to hear about it." They shook hands and Daniel was on his way.

He rode to the Dewberry neighborhood. The house was still empty and there was no "For Sale" sign to be seen. He parked in the driveway and walked toward the back of the house. A woman's voice challenged him.

"What are doing there, Mister?" she asked.

He explained who he was and why he was there. He added for her, "Did your house lose power when Mr. Dewberry's did?"

"Yep," she replied. "Everybody around here did. It was dark for blocks."

"When did it come back on?" Daniel asked.

"You know, it was the day Willis died." She paused a second. "Never thought about that before. We were all caught up with him passing and didn't notice."

Daniel was making a note in his book when her attitude shifted.

"Don't go judging us harsh for that now." She warned. "When you live down around here, you soon learn there's a difference. There's what you can do something about and what you can't. It's best, the quicker you learn that difference."

"I'm not judging anyone." Daniel assured her. "I'm looking into another matter that all this might have caused."

"Ok, now I know who you are. I saw a story about you on TV the other night."

"I don't know, I didn't see it. I thank you for your time today, though." Daniel tried to get her to leave so he could look around. He finally just asked her permission.

"Do you think anyone would mind if I look in the back?"

"Can't think of why they would," she told him. "Help yourself." And she was on her way.

Daniel found nothing out of order in the yard and decided to try to find which blocks were with power and which were without. He drove several streets over and asked a man working in his yard. He too, had lost power.

Daniel went a couple more blocks and finally nailed down the end of the disruption. He drove around looking for a transformer or something that could have been fooled with. Quite by accident, he found a pole with a series of newer cleat marks. Someone had been climbing that pole, from what he could see, much more recent than any other pole in the area.

He didn't know electrical work, but this pole seemed to have some heavy lines coming in and going out towards Dewberry's street. Daniel made his notes and continued to look around.

~

Thomas Ames hung up his phone. He was concerned about the arrangements he had made and the talk with Lt. Draper had not helped. Still his reporter's sense pulled on him to get busy and finish his story. The timing sucked. His final edition would hit the street at 4:05PM. He would not be able to stop it after 3:45.

They teach you not to let your story get ahead of your facts; but if he waited on this he would lose a full day to TV and other papers. It was his call to make. He made his decision quickly. Opportunities like this don't happen often. He would go ahead with his scoop, his exclusive and possibly his ticket to New York and a larger publication.

The headline would be attention grabbing. "**Hawk Eye Editor Foils Wayward Son Assassin**." Two lines for the headline, he thought. Inspired again, he dove into writing his story. His deadline for submission was just over two hours away.

Draper went to the warehouse on Layne St. in an unmarked car. In contact with his spotters, he checked to see if anyone else was monitoring the building. Opening the main door, he looked inside. It appeared to be empty.

The large space was visible though not completely. The box, jacket and cap were placed where they would not be noticeable until the afternoon sun came through a high window on that side of the building.

Draper could not see them. He did not want to disturb anything so he backed out and pulled the door to. He didn't like the set up, not at all. The Lieutenant feared for the safety of his friend, the newspaperman.

He made a decision he would not tell Ames until the last minute. He would exchange places with his friend. Draper would confront this potential killer posing as the editor.

~

A fire escape had allowed Silas access to the roof of the building next door to the Hawk Eye. There was a good thirty feet of separation. The Hawk Eye building was five stories tall with a flat roof.

He was a full story above that but a transition from one roof to the other didn't appeal to him. It was too far to jump, and too exposed to try a wired slide across. He could see three sides of the newspaper building from his perch. There were no obvious access points or fire escapes.

To get in, Silas would need to walk in the front door.

His inspection did lead to a big discovery. Phone lines to both buildings came from across the street. He couldn't believe his luck. The main drop lines came to the higher building and were tied off. Lines for the Hawk Eye building then dropped from the taller structure to theirs. He had full access to the phones in the newspaper's offices.

He checked his equipment in the car's trunk and did not have a phone test handset with him. A quick trip to the local Radio Shack and he was in business.

The phone lines were tied off on the roof just beneath a knee wall that surrounded the rooftop. He sat with the wire cluster and cut through the heavy tape that combined them. Several main strands branched off toward the Hawk Eye building. His tester unit had clips that could bite into the wire and make contact. This allowed him to listen in and identify where those lines connected to the phones.

It took over an hour to isolate the pairs of wires he sought, but find them he did. Checking the time, it was 1:25PM, too early to start his plan.

He wrapped the total wiring harness in a black plastic bag to mimic the tape he had removed. Once satisfied it wouldn't draw any attention, he cleared the area, brushed it to remove any sign of his having been there. He stretched a very thin line of thread from the front edge of the building to the side. Anyone bothering his work would break that line without knowing.

Silas looked around one more time and climbed back down to the street. He walked around the Hawk Eye building, at ground level, just to make sure there wasn't something on that far side he needed to know about. The proximity of the next building over made a transition more possible from that side, but it was still risky, too risky. He decided to stick with the current plan. Checking his watch again, he walked around the corner to the coffee shop he had visited a couple of nights ago. It was time for a sandwich.

~

The editor reread his work for the third time. After all, he was the editor. It had all the aspects of a Pulitzer nomination. What was really perfect about it was the inference cast upon Representative Charles Harley. Without any direct, libelous statements from his paper, the story clearly showed that the assassin was satisfied with the Congressman's guilt or at least his culpability in Peter Cass' death. Ames didn't care for Harley to start with and the connection of Terry Harper to Peter's disappearance was too much to ignore.

Ames sent the headline and the story files to his pre-press department. The old type setting days were long gone. Today's electronic world had font design, type setting and pagination done on computers. Spell checking was still a function of human beings, but that could be done much quicker than the old days. The whole process, from submission to plates being set on the presses, normally took 4 hours. This story would be on the street in three.

Ames called Draper on his private cellphone; he wanted an update on his progress at the warehouse location. He was taken aback in hearing that the police were doing little else than watching the area.

"Aren't you setting a trap, or something?" he asked the Lieutenant.

"Let me handle this, will you?" his friend responded. "Patience, Ok? We don't want to spook him, do we?"

The editor rubbed his forehead. "Alright. This is what you get paid for."

"Thanks, Pal. I appreciate your confidence." Draper muttered sarcastically.

"Come on, you know I have faith in what you do. I just thought there would be some elaborate trap." Ames said apologetically.

"Sometimes you let your prey set his own trap."

Draper told Ames where he wanted to meet him, in the Westland Mall parking lot, at 3:30PM. They agreed and Draper hung up the phone. The editor leaned back in his chair with his phone still in his hand. The newspaper business could get rough at times but this meeting had the potential to go way beyond the norm. He had to admit he was concerned. One life had already been lost over this mess. Now he was in the middle of the blender ready to stir it up even more.

Ames reminded himself of something he had read many years earlier, *"Courage was not the absence of fear. But rather the ability to recognize it and work through it."*

Well, he felt the fear part just fine. Maybe the courage would kick in soon.

~

Daniel Seay was ready to go home for a few days. His trip to Louisiana wasn't as fulfilling as the Texas venture, but he had discovered enough to make the connection he needed. The second Congressman to die had been in Virginia. Daniel had hoped to have conclusive facts without going there. He knew that wasn't the case. A trip to Virginia would be necessary after all, but he would go home first. Besides, he missed his wife.

He could have turned the rental car in and flown out of Shreveport. Daniel needed to think and he could think more clearly while driving. He opted to drive to Memphis and fly from there. He called the airline and made his reservation. The drive would take 5, maybe 6 hours. The flight would take two more. Add to that the time difference and he'd be too late for dinner at home, but not too late for a little fooling around.

He left Louisiana to catch I-30 in Arkansas. He thought about Charlene back in Texas. He wondered what she, her brother and cousin would do. He thought about the Darth Vader voice Captain Stone had told him about. The people at Stone Creek Children's Home didn't use that term, but the description was the same.

He was on the right track. He just had to decide how to write about it. The approach would need to be just right. The drive toward Memphis went by fast with all he had on his mind. He had not even stopped to eat but was already within an hour of the airport.

He had no idea about Iowa or what had happened there while he drove that afternoon.

15

At 2:15PM, Silas was back on the rooftop next to the Hawk Eye building. Everything looked as he had left it. Even the monofilament line he had left across the corner where the phone wires were. Sitting back down, he took the wires leading to the newspaper's office and stripped small sections of insulation from several of them. He then tapped the exposed wires with the blade of his knife, crossing them out with each other. The effect at the newspaper was a very static noise on the phone line. He connected his test unit to the receptionist line and listened in as he continued to short out different phones.

Within ten minutes, the receptionist had been ordered to call the phone company for a repairman. She was told they would have someone there before 6PM. He figured that meant 5 or 5:30 at the earliest. That would be enough time. Silas continued to short out various phones for ten more minutes, and then he left the rooftop. He needed to change clothes.

He put on the UPS uniform first. The AT&T outfit was intentionally looser and fit over the other nicely. His lightweight "tool box" was actually made of cardboard and contained nothing. It could be refolded, inside out, to look like a package. He watched the parking lot entrance, from the building's basement until he saw the editor leave in his car. The same car he had used to visit Sullie's. It was 3:05PM as the car pulled out and turned to go west.

At 3:15PM an AT&T repairman approached the receptionist desk on the third floor. He explained he had had a cancellation and came on over to see about the trouble. He was waved in and given access to wherever he needed to go. He checked a couple of desk phones in the main area, looking over the papers laying about as he did and then went into the editor's office. Taking apart the phone in there, he went back to the receptionist to inform her he had found the problem. He would need to rewire several parts of the editor's phone and asked if that would bother him. She explained that the editor would be away for a while and that he could go ahead and work in there. He set his "tool box" on the desk and set about looking like a repairman.

He took his monitor and receiver from his inside pocket and set them up. While checking the papers on the desk, he watched the scene play out from across town. All was quiet inside the warehouse but activity outside was picking up.

Quite by accident, he bumped the keyboard on the desk. The screensaver on the editor's computer monitor went off and exposed the story he had been working on. He hit "print" and saw several options. One was "office." Looking around, he saw a small printer across the room. He punched "OK" and heard the unit come to life. It produced several pages, which he folded and carefully put inside the UPS uniform under his current outfit.

~

Thomas Ames drove to the southeast corner of the parking lot at the Mall. Draper was waiting for him in a brown Crown Victoria. Draper got in Ames' car with him and did not waste any time.

"I'm going in. Not you," he said defiantly.

"What?" Ames was confused, "What do you mean?"

"I mean you're not trained for this shit, I am. Give me your coat."

"Whoa, I can do this," Ames argued.

"Maybe, but I can't let you. The coat, now."

Ames could tell his friend wasn't kidding or in a mood to discuss things. He took off his coat and gave it to the Lieutenant. Draper got back in his Crown Vic and drove toward the warehouse. He sat in the car till 3:58PM, then got out and headed for the door.

~

Silas went through every drawer in the desk and every cabinet and shelf in the room. Then he noticed the folded piece of paper under the keyboard. It was a torn off piece of desk calendar. His eye caught the note in the margin. "sul/dk – 115p – tharp." The "tharp" part was the giveaway to him. Perhaps because he was looking for anything about Terrence Harper but, then the sul/dk made sense to him. He had been there, Sullies' Deck. The 115p had to be the time they met. He had guessed 1:30.

"*Close*," he told himself. He knew it had to be Peter's. It didn't match anything in the editor's office.

He walked out into the main area, pretending to check the other phones again. He found Peter's desk by the torn page missing from the desk calendar. He lingered there, fooling with the phone while trying to see if any other information was evident. It really wasn't needed at this point. The editor had the note about the appointment. The editor had been to Sullie's. The editor knew who had killed his reporter. His verification of this case was sufficient. Normally he would return home, make his plan and be back in a week to finish the removal. But this editor was a wildcard and that story on his computer could be a problem. He went back into the editor's office.

It was show time. Almost 4:00PM.

He turned on his monitor and set it for the main door. Using the phone on this desk, he dialed the cell phone he had left in the warehouse. As he watched from the office across town, the door opened and a figure entered the dark warehouse. Through the speakers, the distortion unit and the two cell phones he spoke to the man coming through the door.

"Is life so dear or peace so sweet as to be purchased at the price of chains?" Silas spoke quoting Patrick Henry.

Draper was stunned by the voice and the quotation. "Where are you?" he challenged.

"Do you have what you promised?" the voice came back.

"Yeah, I've got it." Draper reached out his hand with a folder.

"Come to your right, five steps." the voice commanded.

Draper did as he was told while stating, "Why don't you come out and face me? Where are you?"

Silas could see through his monitor that this was not the editor. With what he already knew, that made sense. He manipulated one of the cameras for a better look.

"Who would I be facing? You are not who I was to meet," the voice asked.

Draper's eyes had adjusted some and he could see the silhouette in the corner. He moved toward the object.

"Don't move, you're under arrest," the officer ordered.

The voice waited for Draper to discover the ruse. As the policeman looked at the coat and the box, he turned and shouted in anger, "Where the hell are you?"

The voice stayed calm.

"Whoever you are, Sir, when you see Thomas Ames would you tell him I have what I needed from him. From under the keyboard."

Draper threw the box and the coat across the floor. The cap remained hanging. The officer never saw the cameras but he found the speakers. He stormed out of the warehouse and waved off his troops. Ames was there. He walked up to his friend and said sullenly, "He's not here. He tricked us."

Ames was in shock, "No, what do you mean, he's not here?"

"Tom, he said to tell you he had what he needed from you."

The editor didn't say a word but his face asked the question.

Draper looked him straight in the eye, "something about 'from under a keyboard'."

"Oh, no." The editor fell back against the car. "He's in my office."

The two men jumped into the Crown Victoria and with siren and lights at full, raced back toward town.

~

"That should do it," the repairman told the receptionist as he headed out the door toward the elevators. She thanked him while she answered her phone. As the repairman turned the corner in the hallway, she heard something over the line that made her lose color in her face. She screamed for Earl Johnstone, who was in the back of the room.

"That was Tom on the phone," she stammered, "he said the killer was in his office."

Johnstone grabbed the receptionist by the shoulders,

"The phone guy. Where is the phone guy?"

"He, he just left," she managed to answer.

Johnstone ran into the hallway. He looked both directions and to the elevators. Nothing. He hit the down button on the elevators and waited.

Silas had walked down one flight of stairs and found a rest room. There he pulled off the AT&T outfit and refolded the toolbox to look like a package. Now in uniform as a UPS driver, he placed his discarded clothes in the box and checked his hair. He went to the elevator and pushed down.

Johnstone had already cleared the elevator and was outside running around to the back. Ames and Draper pulled up outside the building. Ames had talked with the receptionist again. She told him about the phone man.

As Ames ran toward the elevator, the door opened and a UPS man stepped out. The deliveryman could see someone running to catch the elevator so he stepped back and held the door for him.

"Thanks man," Ames said to him. "Say, you didn't see a phone repair guy, did you?"

"Yeah, I think I did. Up on three," the UPS man responded.

The elevator door closed and the UPS man went out the front door and across the street.

Draper and Johnstone met at the back of the building. They knew each other and gave equal looks of frustration.

"How did he get out that fast?" Johnstone asked.

"He was just here a minute ago."

Ames got off the elevator on the third floor and turned directly to his offices. Through the glass wall panels he could see his receptionist still looking around with her hands up to her mouth. Staffers were looking out the windows and checking their papers.

He meant to ask if everyone was all right but his mind changed gears and the first words he uttered were,

"Can we stop the final edition?"

The receptionist looked at him as if he speaking in a foreign tongue. The question did not even register.

Several other staff members gathered around their leader and he asked again,

"The final edition, can we stop it?"

One of the staffers checked his watch. He shook his head and told the boss,

"It's been on the street for 15 minutes."

One block over and two north of the Hawk Eye Building the UPS man walked toward the prepaid lot he had parked the drop car in. He could hear the sirens of several patrol cars as they approached the newspaper's offices. There, on the street, sat a metal box that distributed newspapers. The logo all over the box declared it to be The Burlington Hawk Eye. Silas glanced down as he passed and the headline stopped him. He stepped back to look closer. It was the story he had printed out. He did not carry any money on jobs so he could not purchase a copy from the box.

At the car, he got in and changed his shirt. He looked in the glove box and found two quarters. Driving back to the newspaper box location, he stopped and bought a copy. He would study it later. Right now he needed to leave Burlington. As he crossed over South Main St. he noticed an AT&T van pulling up to the newspaper building.

"That guy's life is about to become interesting," he thought to himself.

The phones in the Hawk Eye office began to ring off the wall. Many were asking about the police presence but most were trying to get verification of the front-page story. Local TV was on the air at 5:00PM with the tale of the lost opportunity. National TV news had picked it up and the story was on the air by 6:30 and 7:00PM. Ames went into his office to construct his retraction story. It really wouldn't matter. The damage was done.

16

At 6:15PM local time in Memphis, Daniel's cell phone rang. It was his wife.

"Hey, honey, what's up? I've got a surprise for you," he answered.

"Daniel, have you got the news on? There's a story about a guy killing congressmen. It sounds like your story."

"What?" Daniel walked through the terminal looking for a TV screen. "Where is this from?"

"Iowa," she said. "Burlington, Iowa. They thought they had caught him but he got away."

He had found a TV and it was telling the story. "Honey, I'll call you right back."

He watched and listened intently to the tale of embarrassment on the part of the local paper and police department in Burlington. There was little detail about the killer, whom the national news was calling "The Son," only suspicions that he was there to kill a congressman.

Daniel wasn't shocked that someone else was on the case, but the fact that it was now national news caught him by surprise. Daniel went to the ticket counter to change his destination. From Memphis, the closest he could fly would be Peoria and then catch a connector flight to Burlington. It was only about 100 miles from Peoria to Burlington so he asked for a car to be ready for him when he landed. He called home to tell his wife what he was doing. The call had to be hurried; his flight would leave in 20 minutes.

~

After driving south for a couple of hours the freshly labeled "Son" stopped for dinner and to change out of the rest of the UPS outfit. He read the newspaper while he ate. The national report was on the TV in the diner. His anonymity was being challenged but here was one good thing. Though he held affection for the Silas name, he liked the new name he had been given, the national network version, much more than the editor's. It suited him and his perception of himself.

"The Son" would continue south for several more hours before turning in the direction of home. There was much to think about. He had confirmed this guy's qualifications for removal, but really by accident. Without the "by chance" sighting of the editor at the restaurant and the opportunity to get into that man's office, he would be left with speculation. He never would have taken the editor up on his meeting, not on those terms. Knowing the editor was lying to him was again, because of luck. The whole verification had been by providence.

So, now where was he? The congressman needed to be dealt with, there was no doubt. But the circumstances for the return trip were now very awkward and dangerous. Congress would be back in session in three weeks and the target would then be in DC. That made it complicated, but still doable.

He would go home and patiently consider a plan. If it had to be Washington, DC, so be it. He wouldn't make that decision right now.

~

Thomas Ames spent the night in his office. His wife came down to help. She brought Chinese take out.

They both had been around the newspaper business their entire adult lives. They were aware of what this mistake would mean.

They talked as they cleaned out and packed Ames' personal items. She wasn't judgmental toward him, not at all. She understood the reasons he had taken the chance he did. It just didn't work out. It should have, but it didn't.

The morning would bring visitors from the paper's home office. They would tell him he had to go. He was close enough to retirement that they could get by even if he did not catch on elsewhere. Ames was sad about one thing more than the rest. He would have liked to help catch Peter Cass' killer. Now that would be up to someone else. He and his wife packed and talked about the good times.

Now and then they would stop for a hug. By morning, they had his things ready to go.

~

Daniel arrived in Burlington after midnight. He found a motel room, called home to let her know he was there, and looked up the address of the Burlington Hawk Eye. Sleep came quickly despite the excitement of the day.

~

Congressman Charles Harley made three phone calls that evening after watching the news. He wanted to know just what the Burlington newspaper people had and how they got it. He wanted an update on Terry Harper. He wanted a meeting with his key staff at 8:00AM in the morning.

Those contacted would work through the night to get the information they were expected to have for that meeting. As Harley finished his last phone call there was a knock at his door.

"Yeah, come in," he bellowed. The door opened and a young man came in and walked to the sofa where Harley was sitting.

"I have a copy of that paper you wanted."

"Good." The Congressman reached out and grabbed the folded newspaper.

"Anything else tonight, Sir?" the courier asked.

"Naw, that's it. I've got some reading to do and then some sleep to get ready for a big day tomorrow. Be here at 7:15 sharp, in the morning, to pick me up, got it?"

"Yes, Sir. Got it."

~

Daniel arrived at the Hawk Eye offices around 7:25AM. He asked to speak with the editor but was told he was in a meeting and could not be disturbed. After 30 minutes of waiting, Earl Johnstone came over to the area where Daniel was sitting.

"Hi, I'm Earl Johnstone. Mr. Ames is going to be tied up for a while, I'm afraid. Can I help you with something?"

Daniel identified himself and explained why he was there.

"So, you're tracking this killer too, huh?" Johnstone asked.

"Actually, I was trying to prove he exists."

"Well, something exists, I can assure you of that. He was right here yesterday afternoon disguised as a phone repairman."

Daniel went into his detective mode, "do you remember anything about what he looked like?"

Johnstone didn't know how far he should go. This was a reporter from another paper looking into their story. "About my height, a white guy. Maybe 200 lbs."

"Facial hair or tattoos?" the visitor pressed.

"Look, my boss is in there getting his career ended right now, over this. I'm not so sure I should even let you stay here, much less share information with you."

Daniel didn't understand until Johnstone explained how they had gone to press before the story was real. A calculated risk that went bad.

"At least nobody got killed." Johnstone stated. "Hopefully, we ran him off. He knows we were on to him."

"He'll be back," Daniel warned, "his MO is to do surveillance first, then come back for the hit."

"You sound like you know a good deal about this guy."
Daniel shared what he had learned, to a point. Enough to let Johnstone feel they were being equal in this.

After about another 30 minutes of small talk, the two men exchanged business cards and handshakes. Daniel thought about going to the restaurant mentioned in the story, but realized he had as much as he would get already. He left the offices of the Burlington Hawk Eye with the information he wanted and the name of a new friend in his pocket.

The meeting in the editor's office was still going on as he left.

~

The meeting in Representative Harley's office didn't go too well. No one had any idea who the guy was that had, supposedly, come to Burlington to check on the reporter's death.

Terry Harper was not informed of the meeting, but the report on him was nothing out of the ordinary. Pedro Jones had been back in Kansas since that day and there was nothing different about his activities.

There just wasn't anything except the paper's story about some assassin asking embarrassing questions.

Harley shook his head, as if to say, "all is OK" and excused everyone with one exception.

"I can't take any chances with this shit. I don't need to be tied to Harper or Jones in this. Clean this up."

The exception asked for clarification, "Both of them?"

"Yeah, and be quick."

17

It was after 4PM when the enigmatic assassin pulled into the driveway at his home. It could have been later, much later. For the first time there had been a snag with the parking deck. Some other "employee" had parked in such a way that blocked him in. As he stood there trying to come up with how he would handle the situation, a young man came walking up the slope from a lower level. Ducking behind another vehicle, he watched as the offending parker moved his car.

Total delay time, 20 minutes, it could have been much worse.

There was plenty of daylight as he drove into the neighborhood and his house stuck out from the rest, which was unusual.

Something was different about the yard. He noticed it right away. The grass had not been cut.

For four years, he has had a deal with the neighbor kid who he had known since he bought the house. The kid, now about 18 he figured, would keep the grass and yard looking good and watch over the house while he was away on business.

He paid the kid well, took him stuff for Christmas and his birthday; basically they had a good working relationship. Something was wrong but he was sure there would be a good explanation.

Inside the garage, he parked and went to the door to his kitchen. There near the entrance was a note; the explanation he knew would be somewhere.

"Sorry about the grass. I got injured and can't do it for a couple of weeks... Ben."

"*Injured*," he thought. That didn't sound good. He put down his bags and instinctively started walking next door.

He liked Ben. Ben was a good kid. He really had not thought about how much he liked and respected the young man till this note about his being injured. He knocked on the back door and the boy's mother answered.

"Hey," she seemed shy. They had met before, but only briefly. "Ben's really upset he's let you down about the grass," she continued.

"That's not a problem," he assured her. "How is Ben? What happened?"

"He's in the living room," she pointed the way. "I'll let him tell you."

As he stepped into the room he was taken aback. There his young employee sat on the sofa. He had a huge black eye, one arm in a sling and a cast on his right leg.

"What happened to you?" he asked.

"Oh, hey there." Ben was surprised by the visit. "Nothing, I just ran into some trouble."

Ben's mother stepped up and nearly scolding him said,

"You tell him the truth, tell him what happened. All of it or I will."

Ben fidgeted in his seat a bit and spoke slowly.

"I saw a kid getting shook down for his lunch money earlier this week. I stepped in and stopped it. There were just two of them at that time."

"At that time?" the older man asked. "What does that mean?"

"They jumped me after school. There were more of them then."

"How many more?" he asked, anger building in his voice.

Ben's mother spoke for him.

"About six at least. Ben got what you can see, plus two cracked ribs, a tooth is gone and more bruises than I care to count."

"Who are these guys?" he asked Ben.

"A bad group. A gang I guess. They just push people around and scare everybody all the time. The school administration seems to be afraid of them too."

He put his hand on Ben's head and gave it a gentle rub. "You rest up. Before long we will go see about these guys, Ok?"

"I really appreciate that, but no. It would just make it worse."

"All the more reason to stop it completely. Don't worry right now. I'm gonna be home for a week or more. If you need something, let me know."

He put an arm around the mother's shoulders and restated that he would be home for a while.

"I'll check on him later, Ok?"

"Sure," she said. "Thank you."

As he walked back home he tried to calm himself. What they had done to that kid was vicious. No need for that in society, no need at all.

He would see about this gang. There were things he could do. Things they never considered.

Unpacking the tools and "toys" he had in his personal car, he noticed a lipstick camera he had not used. He took it with him to the basement and the safe room.

The room was a mess. No one had been in there, yet there was paper on the floor and lights flashing on computer systems. He tried to calmly figure out what was going on.

His systems that monitored the Internet for equipment had been on overload. The printer was out of paper. There were printouts of all manner of gadgets lying everywhere on his floor. He gathered them up, best he could and looked at a couple.

A spring loaded vault pole that could propel a man 60 feet into the air.

"If his arms can take the torque." He thought to himself.

There was armored baseball cap with three 22-caliber barrels mounted into the cap's bill. It weighed in at over 6 lbs.

"A six pound hat. No thanks." He sat the other papers aside and went to the systems that were connected to his unknown assistants. The network of those who were to evaluate and recommend elected offenders for removal. In the week he had been gone, they had sent files on over twenty-two candidates.

He went to one of his storage cabinets to get a couple more cameras. He still had seven here. He was sure there were more at one of the warehouses. He pulled open a drawer and took out three laser switches. Checking one against one of the cameras, he convinced himself they would work.

He wired the lasers to the cameras and set them to transmit their video to three recording devices he had on the worktable. Outside, it was now dark.

He set two of the cameras to monitor Ben's front and side yard area. The third was positioned to watch the rear patio door. Any movement across the lasers would start the cameras recording for 25 seconds.

Neither Ben nor his mother was aware of what he was doing, but the cameras were still on his property and they were not "peeping" so there were no laws being violated. He wanted to keep a check, for security purposes. He didn't believe that people, who would do what they had to Ben, were done yet. Ben's beating was a message to anyone else considering interfering. When his use as a message was over, they would eliminate him. Preventing any further intrusion into their business and emphasizing the message. He did not plan to sit by while that played out.

Satisfied with the hook ups, he returned to his basement to finish cleaning up. He sat in a swivel chair and looked around. It wasn't even a full week old and it was too small. The idea was sound. The space he had for it was not adequate. He decided to have some dinner and get some sleep. He was tired and upset about Ben. Maybe tomorrow this would all look better.

~

Daniel Seay was back in Pittsburgh a day later than he planned. He slept in a bit longer than usual, mainly trying to think how to approach his boss. He had been scooped, but by a source that knew less than he did. He could add to the national impact of the story, if he did it right. His editor may wish to toss the entire idea after what happened in Burlington.

Daniel had breakfast with his wife and organized his notes. He was back to the thought that the Virginia hit could be assumed to be part of this. The messages sent there were obviously by the same guy. A trip there and more money spent would likely turn up more of the same. He entered the offices of the Post-Gazette at 10:00AM.

"Well, about time you got back," his editor greeted him. "Got the bad guy in your pocket?"

Daniel knew that wasn't a good start to the conversation.

"All but his name and address, boss. I'm working on those."

"Really?" came the response. "How so? Tom Ames was a good newspaperman. He got taken down in this. And for what?"

"You know Ames?" Daniel was excited. "I need to talk to him."

"I know of him," the boss said flatly. "Met him at a convention or two. We're not first name basis or like that, but I know he was a respected newsman. One with a heck of a lot more experience than you."

"Why the 'was', he didn't get hurt?"

"He got canned." The Post-Gazette editor stood up and stared Daniel down. "Is that what you want to drag me to with this?"

Now Daniel understood his boss' reaction. Everything he did reflected on him. If this went sour, like it did in Iowa, it would be his head on the table, not Daniel's.

"Sir, I won't make a mistake like they did. Neither would you."

The editor didn't reply. He sat down and held out his hand for Daniel's notes. After several minutes going through them he looked back at Daniel.

"Name and address, huh?" he smirked. "You need a bit more than that. Any more leads?"

"From what I've learned about this guy. I expect him to lay low for a week or two. Then he'll resurface to do the job."

"The job?"

"Yeah, he looks at these killings as a job that needs doing. Its not personal with him, its just what he does."

"Makes him more dangerous, Danny." The boss handed him the notes back. "Stay on it but keep me close. I don't want any surprises."

"Thanks, Chief. Do I write about what I know so far?"

"Wait a while on that. My gut tells me that would only draw attention to you, not him."

The boss was right. All he had was evidence that backed speculation, solid speculation but no real facts. What happened in Iowa had exposed and put pressure on the Congressman currently at the center of this mess. How he would react was not known. "Yeah, I see your point." The reporter paused a second. "I'll wait."

" You bet you will. Now leave me alone, will ya? I've got a paper to get out."

Daniel went to his desk. Sitting down, he glanced back at the editor's door and smiled.

Daniel was pleased. All in all, that went well.

~

Most of the morning had been spent organizing the safe room. He looked over a few more gadget printouts but his mind wasn't into it. He refilled the paper on the printers and reset the systems that had gone down. Every few minutes he would check the monitors on Ben's home. He could not understand why his concern continued to grow. He was not prone to overreaction, yet his instincts were amplified.

At 10:30AM he went upstairs. It was time for a break from this. The grass would be dry enough to cut but he didn't own a lawnmower. He walked next door to see about borrowing Ben's. Ben's mother was in her kitchen mopping the floor. She was glad to see him.

Ben's mom was a few years older than her neighbor. He wasn't sure just how many, but she was still young and quite attractive. He didn't know the whole story, but he knew she was a widow. Her army husband had been killed in action around ten years ago. That was a subject he tried to stay away from. He knew she worked in an office somewhere, but wasn't sure just what she did. Obviously, she was staying home with her son right now.

Ben had always been athletic. He met Ben in the yard while Ben was throwing a baseball against the side of his house. That was eight years ago. He had spent many hours playing catch with Ben since that day. Listening to stories of what all Ben's dad had taught him to do, hunting; fishing and even a small amount of mountain climbing. They never talked about his dad's death. Ben would have, he was proud of his soldier father, but his friend and neighbor would always shy away from that conversation.

He asked her how Ben was doing and if he could see him.

"He's still sleeping this morning." She smiled. "First time he's slept good since the attack." She reached out and squeezed his arm slightly. "Your coming to see him last night calmed him down. He was really glad you're home."

He could have easily lost his composure at that point, but he stiffened his jaw and looked her in the eyes. "Do you think I could borrow the lawnmower?"

"Of course, it's in the garage. Let me get the key."

The garage was immaculate. The mower sat in the back corner looking nearly new. Assorted other yard tools hung from assigned spots along the sidewall. All clean as a whistle. Gas cans and oil dispensers were stored in the safety cabinet. He was quite impressed but not surprised. Ben often talked about how his dad had kept things just so.

"This is one together kid," he said to himself.

"Cutting grass isn't so hard," he thought. *"But how did Ben keep the edges so neat?"*

He set himself a pattern and tried to keep it straight. On the fifth round he noticed the dark sedan with the three men inside... again. This was their third time to go by and they slowed in front of Ben's house. He kept his pace but looked to see if he could get a license number. "AT 22..." but then they were gone. He wasn't even positive about the "22". Could have been "ZZ." What bothered him the most was that these were not kids. They weren't even young men. The driver and front seat passenger were Hispanic. The man in the back looked heavy. Overweight with hanging jowls and thick black hair. His guess was Italian. In the next ten minutes it took to finish the front yard they did not come around again. He took the mower to the back and tied off

117

the "dead-man" lever and parked it where it would not roll away. The sound would appear he was cutting in the back. There was a tall hedgerow between his yard and neighbor opposite Ben's house.

He positioned himself in those bushes and waited.

They came by again within five minutes. Not as slow this time, but still staring holes in Ben's house as they cruised past. The license was still a mystery. He paid more attention to the men than the tag. It was definitely "A 22" and then "G" or maybe a "C." The guy in the back of the car was, for sure, Italian.

He turned the mower off and went into his house. He sat near a front window and watched the street for another 30 minutes. The dark sedan did not return. In the safe room, he set up a scan on one of his computers to identify the dark sedan. Nothing came up right away so he let it run and went back upstairs. He made himself a sandwich, PB&J and then went back to finish the yard.

It took him an hour to clean the mower to what he hoped would be Ben's standards. Placing it back in their garage, he took the key back to the kitchen door. He checked the lock and the deadbolt before knocking for her attention. It seemed ok.

He would not say anything about the sedan right now. No need to add to her concern. He had the house monitored and had picked the spot for yet another camera, to watch the street.

18

Daniel was in the office earlier on his second day back in Pittsburgh. He was still reviewing his own notes and thinking about Virginia. He could not decide about that case. It was likely there would be nothing to add, but you never knew. He was filing the business card for Earl Johnstone, of the Burlington Hawk Eye, when his phone rang. It was Earl.

"Hey, man," the new friend started. "Glad I caught you in."

"Good to hear from you, Earl." Daniel thought about telling him of the coincidence with the business card, but let it go. "What's going on up there?" he asked.

"Well, could be something big." Earl said. "Not sure yet." He took a breath and continued. " I told you some of what we knew, but I didn't name names. One of the characters that Peter Cass had uncovered was a guy named Terry Harper. Harper worked as a aid for Congressman Harley."

"Ok, I'm with you, so far." Daniel leaned back in his chair to listen.

"We believe Peter was going to meet with Harper the day he disappeared."

"Can you prove that?" Daniel injected.

"Well, I'm sure, myself. But I don't know if we have proof in the legal sense."

"OK."

"Well, Harper turned up dead late yesterday."

Both men were quiet until Daniel finally spoke.

"Somebody didn't want him to talk."

"Yeah, that's what I think, too." Earl coughed and then his voice got lower. "Look, our new boss is green and he doesn't want to touch any of this. He won't even let me contact the main paper in Des Moines. I figured since you were already looking into it, you might like to know what happened."

"So, this guy, Terry Harper, worked for Harley and was linked to Peter Cass' disappearance?"

"That's right."

"And he's dead within two days of the assassin fiasco and the story about the congressman is renewed?"

"You got it."

"Any other bodies lying around?"

"Not that I'm aware of."

Daniel thought before his next question. "Is your paper going to report on this Harper guy's death?"

"Yeah," Earl responded, "That's why I'm calling you. There will be no mention of his connection to Harley in our story."

"Even though he worked for the man?"

"None. And no mention of a possible connection with Peter either." Earl's voice was agitated. "Its like he was some ordinary Joe. Its not right, this story needs to advance."

"Ok, Earl. Thanks. Let me see what I can figure out to do." Daniel paused and then decided to be upfront with his new friend.

"My boss wants me to keep a lid on this here till I get more. I don't know if this will qualify with him but I have another idea if he doesn't go for it."

"Do what you can, man. Peter was a good friend. I don't like the way this is being washed and watered down."

"I'll be in touch, Earl. Thanks again and be careful. These are not nice people."

"I heard that." And the call ended.

Daniel rocked in his desk chair and thought. He looked at the boss' door and thought of his other idea. The boss wouldn't go for it. It was too soon after he had told him to stay calm for a while. Daniel turned his Rolodex to the other new contact he had made. Picking up the phone he dialed Louisiana.

~

Ben improved with each day. His spirits were better. Noticeably better to his mother, since his neighbor had gotten home. He planned to return to school on Monday. The neighbor asked if he could drive him and pick him up? That neighbor had continued to monitor the cameras he had installed. There had been nothing new in the last couple of days. The sedan had not returned. His computer scan had found a car matching the description with a Tag # A22G48. It was registered to an Esteban Juarez of a local address. Mr. Juarez was listed as 44 years old. Why would he be interested in a high school kid? The report showed Juarez worked for Argus Importers, again with a local address.

"*Argus?*" He thought out loud. That name wanted to ring a bell with him. How and where had he heard that before? It wouldn't come to him, not right now anyway.

~

Matt Turlock was having a great morning. Shreveport was quiet, the weather was cooler than normal for this time of year and he had plans to get in nine holes at Northwood Hills Golf Club right after lunch. Nothing could spoil this day.

His phone rang and the caller ID said Pittsburgh Post-Gazette.

"Hello Daniel, what are you up to now?" he laughed.

"Morning Matt. Can I ask a favor?"

"Absolutely maybe. What are you into now?"

Daniel explained what had happened in Burlington and the lack of coverage there. He explained why his boss didn't want smoke on their turf right now.

"Your boss is a smart man," Matt told Daniel.

Daniel made his best pitch,

"This guy Harper is tied to the congressman. The man I'm after knows this and is going to kill Congressman Harley, and soon. If that happens, those responsible for a fellow reporter's death may never be exposed."

"Why did I answer this phone?"

"Because you have a nose for news, Matt." Daniel tried to butter him up a bit.

"Doesn't the Times have a ghost reporter? Most of us do."

Matt was quiet for a minute.

"Orville P. Norwood is still on staff. We haven't used him in some time."

"Let Orville write the story." Daniel pleaded. "We just need to get the word out about this Harper fellow and his connection to Harley. With the mess from last week in Burlington, the national media will pick this up and so will the authorities. It could save Harley's life and maybe get him put away."

"Phil has called me twice about your investigation. That Vader voice thing really has him fired up. He wants a piece of your bad guy."

"Because of LaPointe?" Daniel asked.

"He doesn't give a crap about LaPointe personally, but Phil's a good cop. He doesn't like anybody getting killed in his territory and walking away."

"Can you help with this, then?" Daniel asked one more time.

"Damn. Fax me the details and we'll get it out today."

"Matt. I owe you another one."

"Yeah, Thank Orville."

Matt rehashed the story of Congressman LaPointe, inferring that the death might not have been natural causes and that there were similarities to other congressional deaths. He wrote that they had information that a death in Iowa may be connected as well. He named the reporter who had been shot in Burlington and his ties to the man recently killed. Then the hook was set, the fact that Harper worked for the Congressman in Iowa. National TV news did pick up the story. The tale of "The Son" once again filled the airwaves with speculation. But it also pointed fingers at Congressman Harley in Iowa.

Daniel saw the story while having dinner with his wife. She was upset that his story was getting away from him. "Oh, Daniel. Your story is on again and you won't get any credit this time either."

"Honey, that's Ok." He was pleased with the Shreveport Times' work. "Orville is a good man. I've met him."

~

He saw the television news' account and use of his new nickname while looking through papers from his trip to Iowa.

"*So, they took Harper out.*" That didn't change anything, far as he was concerned. If they arrested Harley that could screw things up, but until then he would proceed with his plan.

Sorting the papers he had collected in Iowa he got to the ones from the airport. The car rental guy had made copies of Pedro's rental form. He looked at it and then laid it down on his desk. That's when it jumped up at him. The sign-in line for Pedro included what company he represented. Pedro had put down Argus Imports.

19

This was an example of times he wished he had someone else to talk to. It would be easy to overreact to this. The Argus connection, what the hell was it? This was too weird. Calmly, he set up two computers to search for information about Argus Imports. Within ten minutes, the printers were humming and spitting out paper.

The company did operate an import business. Most of the initial information found references to lines of merchandise offered by them. Household items, junk décor stuff, baskets and small tables. Things you walk past in those tiny mall stores. Location information began to pour from the computers. They were everywhere, or almost. The entire east coast was covered with over seventy-five locations, again mostly shopping malls. They had three major distribution hubs, Miami, Cincinnati, and here.

"*Here*?" He'd never heard of them before. Checking the local address showed the hub to be two blocks from one of his empty warehouses. That didn't make sense either. He had picked his locations based on lack of activity. That area of town was nearly deserted.

He made a mental note to go by and check it out later. Googling the local mall, he looked for anything with the name Argus. Nothing. The stores were named something else.

The systems began to recycle the same info in different ways so he reset the parameters of the search. He asked for names of principals of the company. That exposed Miami as the US

Headquarters of Argus and the name Saul DeMarcos appeared. No title was given to this corporate leader but his name was quite prominent. More names began to print, as the program's requirements for connections to Argus were lessened from obvious to anything.

The location of Pennsylvania caught his eye as several names from that area printed out. Fifth on the list was Dewey Hanson. That name struck a cord with him. He tried to concentrate on the name and where he knew it. Jumping up from the chair he went to a file cabinet where he kept copies of his correspondence to the areas of the first removals.

"Pennsylvania, of course. That's where that name came from," he thought out loud as he pulled the file on Representative Perry, his first removal. He remembered Hanson was Perry's replacement. There it was, his copy of the message sent to the offices of Representative Dewey Hanson.

"Hanson is involved with Argus?" he thought. *"But was Perry before him?"*

Quickly he set up a new search for two of the computer systems. They ran Perry's name for a connection to Argus, but none came back. If he was a part, he kept himself insulated well.

On the desk was the stack of paper he had picked up from the floor when he got home. The lists of candidates his "network" had recommended for removal, twenty-two names from all over the country. He ran those names for a link to Argus.

While the program ran he refilled his records and tried not to obsess about why these guys were interested in Ben. That still made no sense. The printer began to spit out paper again. Of the twenty-two names he requested information on nine had links to Argus. Ok, Argus was into more than black lacquer tables, but what?

The computers were asked to find where their merchandise came from. It was imported, but from where? The point of origin for

125

the imports was listed as Colombia. Embarking from Cartagena, Colombia to Miami. Many of the items had been manufactured elsewhere. Peru, China, Greece and Indonesia as well as Colombia were listed as producing countries. The headquarters for the exporting company was in Bogotá. That spelled one thing. Somehow there were drugs involved.

The logo caught his eye. It was a round, gold plaque embossed with a smiling face, an emblem from ancient Greek mythology. A Sun God perhaps. What that had to do with merchandising was beyond him. He took an instant dislike to that face in the emblem.

To him, the smile was a smirk. He took it as the symbol of an arrogant jokester having dropped a line no one would understand except him. The smirking face angered him. It represented the pain inflicted upon Ben. He did not yet know how Ben's actions deserved the attention from these thugs with the smug logo, but he fully intended to find out.

He decided to check more names for details. Esteban Juarez was first. An immigrant in this country for only four years, he had a fairly substantial criminal record. His sheet showed three charges of small time breaking and entering, a list of assault charges and one drunk and disorderly. No drugs charges of any kind. His occupation was "driver" for Argus Imports and the home address was a flophouse across town.

Saul DeMarcos was different story. No rap sheet at all. Clean as a whistle, but then again he was only twenty-two years old. That's young to be a baron of business, even a lowly import business like Argus. He lived by himself in a penthouse on Miami's South Beach and ran the operation from that address. The report on DeMarcos listed an uncle, still in Colombia and still in prison, Santonio Lendono. Lendono had been a member of the Cali Cartel.

Both the Cali and Medellin Cartels had been broken up in the 1990's. The Colombian government killed many of the leaders and the rest were captured and imprisoned. Cocaine continued to flow from Colombia, even to this day. Authorities in this country and in Colombia do not know the source of the drugs. If they do, they don't acknowledge it. Lendono could be running the operation through his nephew and other family members, but there were no clear ties.

Circumstantial evidence may not be good enough for a courtroom, but it was just fine in his safe room. This was beginning to make sense, all except the Ben part. He still had one more name to run. Good old Pedro, the catch man, from Kansas City. The very first computer hit was a news story from the local Kansas City paper, The Star. It was dated two days ago.

"Local Thug Found Dead of Overdose," the headline proclaimed.

"Well, now. Harper and Jones both dead after that story in Burlington." He stood up and paced the room. "These guys play rough." He became more worried for Ben. The beating was a message, but to whom? He needed to talk to Ben without alarming him or his mother. He could feel Silas rising.

~

In Pittsburgh, all Daniel could do was wait. The story from Shreveport had done its job well. The national news was back with coverage of the American Revolutionary Assassin known as the "The Son." Surely this would back him off for a while, maybe even indefinitely. Daniel decided to use his time looking into Dewey Hanson. He didn't care for Hanson's appointment and it appeared that few did. Hanson and the Governor could use some exposure and Daniel set out to see what he could find.

A background search on Hanson came up with the same stuff that had caused Perry to distance himself from Hanson a couple years ago. Hanson was into influence pedaling and loan sharking, through accomplices of course. A check on one of those accomplices led to the connection of Hanson to several members of a group called Argus. In fact, Hanson was on payroll with Argus for ten months. Daniel went to his boss to see if the editor knew anything about this Argus group.

"Did you try the internet?" the boss asked.

"That's where I found this, I've just never heard of them, have you?"

"My wife buys crap, all the time, from this mall shop called 'Sundown Corner.' She likes the wall hangings and ordered this wicker chair I hate, last year. The shipping paperwork said it was made in Greece, like I'm gonna believe that. But the papers also said, 'imported by Argus Imports of Miami'." He smiled at Daniel. "They import shit."

"You remembered that? Just now?" Daniel was surprised at the editor's retention.

Without looking up, his boss replied, "That's why I'm here and you're out there."

Daniel began looking into Argus Imports. Why would a man like Dewey Hanson be on payroll with an import company? He found the local Pittsburgh address of the Argus warehouse and headed out to see what he could find.

20

In the office of District Attorney George Vincent, a senior attorney hollered across the room to an aid.

"Is Doris coming in today?"

The assistant answered him, "She'll be in later, Boss. She's still staying with her kid this morning."

"George knows about this?"

"I assume so," came the reply.

It was Monday and Doris had been out since Tuesday afternoon of last week. They had a big case and they needed Doris back, her and her expertise. They finally had something on the group and they needed to act quickly. Her kid getting beat up wasn't her fault but it sure messed up the case schedule.

Doris Shaw had worked with the district attorney for the last eight years. She wasn't a lawyer but she was more than a legal assistant. Doris had been going through volumes of evidence against a group of men thought to be smuggling drugs into their city. Her findings and testimony would be crucial and they needed to go over it before the indictment was issued.

Doris was still at home that morning. She was helping her son, Ben, get ready for his return to school. The new walking cast on his leg was lighter and made getting around easier. He could also get in and out of a car and ride without needing to lie on the back seat.

Ben was ready and waiting for his neighbor who would drive him to school. His Mom finished his lunch and checked his backpack. The knock at the door would be him. Ben hugged his Mom and stood with his crutches. Ben opened the door and greeted his friend and neighbor.

"You ready to go?" the friend asked.

"Yes Sir, Let's do it." Ben smiled. He was ready to get back to school.

"Are you comfortable?" The driver asked Ben.

"Yeah, this is good. It's good to get out."

The drive was quiet till the man asked Ben if he had ever heard of Argus?

"Argus?" Ben thought. "No sir, I don't think so. Why?"

"I'm just looking into something and wondered if that name meant anything to you."

"Does it have anything to do with the guys that beat me up?" Ben asked.

"That would be a stretch right now, I'm looking into several things, don't get ahead of me."

"That's what Mom says all the time."

~

Back at her home, Doris was gathering her brief case and checking her hair preparing to leave for her office. She didn't hear any commotion outside.

In the safe room next door, the warning lights and a bell went off. The monitors had picked up motion at the Shaw's house. He wasn't there to hear or see.

~

As they drove up to the school, the car was parked near the front door and his neighbor walked around to help Ben from the car. A group of rough looking youths stood to one side and stared.

"That's some of them over there," Ben whispered.

"Who's the leader?" His friend asked him.

"See the one with the gray jacket and the blue hat?"

"Oh, yeah."

"That's Cesar. He's the top dog."

The man just nodded and grabbed Ben's backpack.

"I can get that." Ben asserted and he grabbed the bag and smiled. "Thanks."

"You got it, big guy. Have a good day."

The neighbor stood and watched as Ben entered the school. The group around Cesar looked at Ben hard, but did not move. Once Ben was inside the building, the man looked toward the group and Silas emerged within him. He moved at a firm pace towards the group. They seemed startled by this. He continued, deliberately in their direction until they broke away from each other and left the area. Silas stopped but made Cesar the focus of his attention.

Returning to his car, Silas drove to a spot almost a block away, to watch. Several of the group went into the school, but three did not. Cesar was one of those three. They got into a car and drove south.

He followed them out of their viewing distance, and watched as they drove into an old building in the deserted warehouse district of downtown. The large door closed behind them.

He parked two blocks west and walked to the building, approaching it from the side. He could hear voices inside but could not tell how many. He had worn his Kevlar but did not have his other toys. This was not the address for the Argus warehouse. That would be several blocks away.

He went back to his car but had no supplies with him today. No cameras or microphones. He had been so busy with the research all weekend; he had forgot to restock the car. Not all was wasted. He now knew the leader of the school thugs, by name and face, and he knew where they hung out.

"*Patience,*" he reminded himself. He drove back to his home to think about what he might need, and to restock the car.

He parked the car and went into the house through the garage. He got himself a cold soft drink from the refrigerator and walked toward the den. He noticed the red light. He had wired a red bulb on his microwave to act as an upper level notification that he was needed in the safe room. Something had been picked up on the monitors.

He did not go downstairs right away. He knew what it had to be.

Quickly grabbing a full sized Glock from a drawer near the backdoor, he ran to his neighbor's patio.

The door was open, kicked in. The lock and dead bolt had not held as he had hoped. The bolts had torn the door jam from the door. The side rail of the door was broken just under the doorknob.

It had been a violent entrance. He called for Doris. No answer. He stepped inside and immediately saw blood on the floor. Not much, but there was blood. A short look around made it clear that they had taken her. There was nothing to be done here.

Back in the safe room he queued the recordings. They had picked up three men, the same as from the car the other day. It was Esteban kicking in the door. All three went in with near military precision. He watched his clock for the time. They were in the house for five minutes.

Doris was alive as they pulled her from the home, he could tell that. The blood wasn't hers. One of the men had cut his hand on the broken glass from the door. The police would have DNA. He couldn't show them his recordings but he could call the cops. They needed to get started, and so did he.

He loaded his car as he waited for the police. They were there in 7 minutes. He identified himself and explained he had taken Ben to school and was reporting back to Mrs. Shaw. But she didn't answer at the front door. When he went around back he found the damage and had walked inside a few steps.

They took his information. He told them about the car he had observed cruising the neighborhood and gave them the tag number. With what he was sure they knew already, that should point them in the right direction to getting Doris back quickly. The recordings would have to remain his secret.

He checked the time. It was 10:30AM. Kidnap victims were either killed right away or held for about 72 hours and then disposed of. He would allow about 24 hours for the police to do their job. If Doris wasn't found by then, he would go after her himself.

The police realized that Ben could be in danger. They asked the neighbor if he would go back to the school, with an escort, to notify Ben and bring him back here. He didn't look forward to telling his young friend about his mother, but he would rather do it than somebody else.

It finally hit him as he drove back to the school. It wasn't Ben who was the target. It was Doris, but why her? He drove up to the front doors and went inside to the principal's office. They called for Ben. The police escort, two cars, stayed a half block back.

Ben was beyond upset, but he held his anger till they were in the car. As they pulled away from the school, Ben slammed his hand on the dashboard. Clearly, he blamed his friend.

"I told you not to interfere. What did you do?"

"I haven't done anything, not yet." He tried to assure the young man with his tone. "Listen to me. We'll get her back, but we have to stay calm."

"What caused this? You must have done something," Ben repeated.

"Son, I haven't done anything yet. But I can and I will if you'll let me."

Ben calmed down some and listened to the man.

"These are bad people, but they don't even know I exist at this point. This isn't about anything I did. It may well be more about what you did."

"Me? What did I do?" Ben cried.

"When you helped that kid, you may have kicked this off. I don't know that for sure but it's the only connection."

"The guys that beat me up took Mom?"

"No. But the people they work for may have. What do you know about them? Who are they?"

"Nothing. Mom might know." The kid looked scared even more. "Mom doesn't talk to me about work but sometimes it's about bad people. I've figured that much out."

"Where does your Mom work, Ben?"

"At the District Attorney's office."

"Holy Shit." The man shook his head as to say *no*. "Damn it, Damn it!"

Back at Ben's house, the police were still there. So was Doris' boss. Ben got a hug from the Legal officer and then introduced him to his friend.

"Can you tell me anything about what Doris was working on?" the man asked.

"I understand your concern, Sir. But no, I can't. It's an ongoing case that's in big trouble without Doris." He turned to catch up with a police officer, and then turned back.

"Nice to meet you. Doris has mentioned you many times. I know you're a good neighbor to her and Ben. I'll let you know as much as I can, Ok?"

"Thank you, sir," the man answered. "I'd appreciate that."

Police were on the scene for several more hours. During that time, it was determined that Ben could not stay in his house alone. The
134

neighbor had a guest room and offered it to Ben. That was acceptable to the authorities there.

He wanted to get out to look, but he had a responsibility to Ben first. Besides that, where would they take her? The warehouse was too easy. That would be the first place the police would look. The District Attorney knew about Argus, the man could tell. They knew more about the group than he did right now. He ordered a pizza and he and Ben tried to stay focused. He thought about sharing more about what he knew with the kid, but not now.

During dinner, he thought about the building the kids had gone to. He made an excuse of needing more milk for the morning and went out. At the building, he was disappointed. It was dark. He parked and walked up and all around it to listen. Nothing. He found a loose window and pried it open. Inside, he found a couch and a TV with a video game hooked up. There were remnants of drugs on the floor but little else. She wasn't here. This was a gang hangout and that was about it.

21

When he got home Ben was standing in the den with a box in his hand. It wasn't a large box. Slightly worn blue cloth lined the outside with a red and white stripe running across the corner. It shouldn't have been left out. He liked to get it out from the drawer now and then to sit with it. To him it was more than a box with things in it. It was memories of people who had given their all for him. If he had just thought to put it away the kid would not have found it.

"What are these?" the kid asked. "Are these yours?"

"Yeah, they're mine," he answered.

"But, what's with you anyway? You never even wanted to let me talk about Dad. He has medals too, but not like these. You are a real hero from what I see in this box."

"I'm no hero, Ben. Your Dad was a hero." The man walked across the room before turning back to Ben and declaring, "I just got saved by some heroes."

They talked for a while. Ben understood the box and the medals in it. He knew they were special and represented brave acts by his friend and neighbor. As they talked, his friend acknowledged the importance of the awards, but tried to deflect his merit to others. He never really told Ben the entire, real story.

The box held three Purple Hearts, an Army Commendation Medal, a Silver Star and the Distinguished Service Cross. He maintained it was more about those who had saved him and to some degree it certainly was. But the whole story was this:

He joined the Army at age 18, just barely older than Ben was now. The country was still upset over the big attacks in New York and Washington DC. Patriotism ran high and his was no exception. He wanted to fight back and help search for those responsible, primarily Saddam. For basic training they sent him to Georgia's Fort Benning. Advanced Infantry Training was in Georgia and then Fort Jackson, South Carolina. After his training he was sent to Afghanistan.

His disappointment in location was made up for by the action he saw. The first of two six-month tours found him with the 10th Mountain Division as perimeter support and on desert patrol behind two Marine companies. After a short break, he was now a corporal and assigned as a reserve support for a Ranger Battalion. He sucked up knowledge like a sponge from these veteran fighters. Impressing the commanding officer so that, after that second tour, he was offered Ranger School back at Ft. Bragg. Within two years, at the ripe old age of not quite 20, he was a fully trained Army Ranger and back in the Afghan war region.

Now an E-5, Sergeant, he led a squad of ten fellow Rangers within the company that went into the mountains on that last mission. They set up a command post, in the round, on top of a mountain and spent a day lining the post with sandbags, four high. Internally there were dugouts and tunnels for, what they thought would be, safe movement within. The post was approximately eighty-five feet in diameter at its widest point. From that vantage point they were to keep an eye on two mountain passes for insurgent movement.

The initial attack came during the second day they were there. Insurgents hit them from all sides at once. The enemy had been alerted to their presence and had not used either of the passes. Rather, they came over and through the rough mountainous terrain and set up completely surrounding the Ranger Company.

The mortars did the most damage. It was a tough shot to land one within the small circle of their compound, but the enemy managed to do so way too often. Almost every other shell was an airburst. The damage done by those damned things was inhuman. Rifle fire peppered and bounced around the compound constantly. Men died almost every minute. They fought hard, throwing heavy fire back at the enemy, but they were outnumbered by at least five to one.

Two days of continuous fighting left his company in ruins. The barrage of fire slowed somewhat that second afternoon. The enemy was apparently out of mortar shells and had only small arms at that point. Rifle rounds still poured into the circle. He could hear the trucks going down the mountainside. The enemy had sent for more mortar shells but that would take them days. Little did they know the casualties they had already inflicted. Of the 96 men in the Ranger Company, only he survived. He did not intend for them to know that.

It got quiet that first night after the mortars went silent. The insurgents did not like to fight and die at night. He was alone with his dead comrades. He set up about forty bodies along the sandbag line and placed weapons in their arms. Half a sand bag over each barrel would keep the recoil from causing the weapons to jump around too much. Clips were reloaded and weapons cleared and cleaned. He reset the flag at the center of the circle and laid grenades where he could get to them in different areas. He found two radios and set them to play on different settings. You couldn't make out the language but there were voices in the air. It sounded like men talking. He did anything to portray numbers that didn't really exist.

The lone survivor spent the next day going back and forth across the circle, dodging bullets and firing from the different positions, giving the impression that he was not alone. After day one of that, he feared his ruse would not hold for long. The shots were from separate areas but with too much time between them.

138

He spent the next night tying wire to the weapons' triggers and stringing them to the center of the compound. He tied the wires to a board he had torn from a munitions box. The dead Colonel's periscope binoculars still worked. From this new position, he could watch and fire in all directions. He also set up three mortars of his own at a steep firing slope. If needed, the rounds would fall only feet outside the compound. Should the enemy attempt to breach his post from the flattest side of the mountain, those rounds would hopefully drive them back. The entire night was spent in preparation. Sleep wasn't even considered. He had to stay alive.

That next day was still small arms fire from both sides. He stayed down in one of the trenches, below the line of fire until a weapon needed reloading. His wiring allowed him to seem as many, some firing at the same time. That was a long day. He had food but no time to eat. The water had been shot up so he didn't want to use what was left just yet. That night he ate a small bit as he reloaded magazines and cleaned several M-16's. Though he still did not sleep, the night seemed short. The smells of his dead comrades and all the gunpowder began to get thicker than the air.

He spent another day firing, running back and forth to refresh clips and trying to just stay alive. It rained that day and that helped cut down the smell but it made moving around more difficult. On the third night it became calm again. He tried to remain alert. He sat with his back against a mud wall and fed rounds into magazines. He splashed some of the remaining water on his face but sleep caught up with him. Just how long he slept would not be known.

He didn't know what time it was. He didn't hear them come in. The black-gloved hand woke him as it covered his mouth. His eyes opened with a start to see a man in total black, only the eyes were exposed, holding his finger up to his mouth.

"Hush," the man in black whispered to the Ranger.

It was a member of Seal Team Bravo-six. His unit and team Bravo-nine had dropped from 42,000 feet in total silence. Using the coordinates the Ranger Commander had filed with HQ the day before the attack, they fell like rocks toward the compound. They had dropped to just above 900 feet before deploying the mini-chutes. All but two landed inside the sandbags. The others were only a few feet outside and quickly found their way into the compound. Twelve other men now backed the lone, surviving Ranger.

The Seals had brought ordinance, plenty of it. They had flamethrowers that could cut a path down the mountainside. They brought grenade launchers and bazookas that could move a tank. Rolling claymores that could blow up the area of a city block. These guys came to fight.

Looking around the compound as day broke, the Seals could tell what had been going on. The dead soldiers with weapons, the wires pulled to the center of the camp. They looked at the young Ranger with deep respect. Realizing what he had been through they swore to get him out. When the fighting started they made a mess of the insurgents that first morning. Pouring firepower, death and destruction on them in relentless fashion. Then, quite suddenly, it was time to go. The Seals could hear the enemy trucks, with the additional mortar shells, climbing the mountain.

The fight to the pickup zone was as bad as the war on the mountaintop. The Seals fought like nothing he had ever seen and he with them. They fought as one. They were a unit with the strength and firepower of a brigade. The Seals did not know they were coming for only one man that night, but it really would not have mattered to them. They'd have come anyway. Of the twelve that dropped in that night, seven made it out with him.

It took them four days to get down the mountain. It was on the third day the Seals realized how badly the Ranger was hurt. There were wounds to both his arms and his right leg, and a cracked rib from his Lieutenant diving on him. The officer gave his life to protect him from a grenade. Shrapnel from the explosion left him with a serious head wound, to the right side, behind his ear. The Seals took time from the descent down the mountain to patch the young man's wounds. Against his protests, they carried him the rest of the way to the landing zone.

They stayed with him at the field hospital till he was airlifted out to Germany. The Seals were impressed with this young Ranger. He had the heart of a warrior they told him. They made him an honorary Bravo Team member. The military gave him medals and ribbons.

After six months at Ramstein hospital and some physical rehabilitation he was sent home. No more war for him. His several requests to take Special Forces training were denied because of his injuries. The wounds to his arms and leg had been superficial and healed well. Physically he was in good shape. The doctors were concerned about the head wound and what it had caused. His psychological profile had changed dramatically. That disqualified him from further service. At 21, he was a hero and in his own mind, a reject. He went home to his proud parents.

He lived at home through college and worked out every day. He continued to shoot and keep his skills sharp. His Ranger training would stay with him. Then he entered pharmacy school. That would take another two years. About midway through that, he bought his own house. That was just over eight years ago.

Ben got some of the story as they talked, but some of the significant details were left out. His friend finally let Ben talk about his Dad. They sat and talked for three hours until Ben's exhaustion overrode his anxiety about his Mother's safety. His host and neighbor remained awake for another hour. He put together in his mind how Ben's interaction with the gang had triggered the kidnapping. The gang members would have beaten anyone who interfered with the same viciousness. They didn't know who Ben was, but their overseers found out after the fact. Concerned that the beating might have an effect on Doris' influence with the DA, they had to find out what she knew. That's why she was taken. Once they had what they needed from her, Doris would be killed. He had to move soon, if the police couldn't find her.

22

News of the DA assistant's kidnapping made it to Pittsburgh and Daniel Seay read about it in his own paper. It didn't mean anything to him at the time. He was searching for information on Argus and that didn't connect to it, so he moved on. His research was turning out much the same as the assassin's. They just didn't know they were working on the same lead. Daniel started to ask if he could go to Miami and dig around there but he knew he didn't have enough to justify that expense. He talked with both Earl in Burlington and Matt in Shreveport. Earl had heard of Argus, he thought they had a warehouse in Des Moines, but nothing in Burlington. Not even a mall store. Matt had not heard of them in his area but would have his people look into it. Matt had been getting a bunch of attention since the Assassin story, but it was not bad. His buddy, Phil Stone was put off mildly by it, but he was fine.

~

Charles Harley read about the kidnapping in his Congressional office Des Moines. He knew full well, what the connection was, but that was in another region and not his responsibility. Exposure anywhere could be a great hazard to the entire group. But all he could do was wait and hope it would blow over. It was the same with Pennsylvania's new Congressman, Dewey Hanson. He wanted to talk to somebody about it, but was afraid to try, believing he was being monitored. He was.

~

It was nearly 9AM when Ben woke him with a strange question. "What's with the red light flashing on the microwave?" he asked. "I've never seen anything like it."

"Stay here," he commanded as he jumped to his feet. He ran through the kitchen and grabbed the Glock. In his hurry he left the drawer open.

The back door to the Shaw's home was pushed back open again. He dropped below the windowsill level and looked inside. There was movement headed toward the stairs. He slowly eased his way into the house and to the staircase. Waiting quietly alongside the wall just around the corner, he heard the steps coming back down. When the first foot hit the foyer floor he reached around and grabbed the intruder. It was the DA.

"I suppose you have a permit for that?" he asked the neighbor.

"Yeah, I kind of had it handy after yesterday."

"I can understand that."

"Ok, what are you doing here?" he asked the DA.

"Doris had a briefcase with her at home. It didn't have much in it, we don't allow sensitive materials out of the office, but I wanted to see if it was still here."

"And?"

"Can't find it. They may have taken it with her."

Not wanting to let on what all he knew, he asked the official if the police had done anything with the tag number he had given them.

"It came back to a local thug, but they couldn't tie him to this."

That didn't make any sense. He just did not want to tell him. Juarez was employed by Argus. They had to know that, the tag was in his name. He turned away from the DA and there stood Ben.

"What is going on?" he demanded of the men in his home.

"Ben," the DA asked, "do you know anything about your Mom's briefcase?"

144

"She kept it in her room, why?"

The neighbor walked back toward the rear door to return home. He had all he could get from this and knew he needed to prepare and act, soon. He could hear Ben and the DA talking as he left.

Inside his kitchen he saw the drawer he had left open. A spare magazine was now lying on the counter. There would be more questions from Ben. He just didn't have time for them now. He couldn't stock his car from the safe room, not with Ben around. He would need to go to a storage warehouse for his supplies. He dressed, in his casual Kevlar. Ben and the DA heard him drive out of his driveway.

At his warehouse he picked out a few items. The arm he had used in Iowa was in the safe room, as was his special sized Glock. He had the full size gun with him, no problem. The spare arm unit was untested but it would have to do. He took several mini explosive charges and a smoke bomb the size of a quarter. There was what looked like a little league, batting helmet that he had just ordered last month. It was made of two layers of Kevlar coated in resin, lightweight but effective, weighing less than a pound but offering full protection down to his collar on both sides. He really liked Kevlar. This was the first molded piece he had owned.

He picked out a vehicle for this trip. The Chevy truck would do. It was a ¾ ton pickup that had been armored around the cab, glass included. He could drop wheel protection shields with the push of a button and it had a spring-loaded bumper that could deliver a wallop. He put local tags on the truck and rechecked himself. It was time to go, time for Silas to find Doris.

He drove around the gang's hideout three times before he parked. There were lights on and music came through the walls. He found the window that was still loose and climbed inside. The three gang members present were engrossed in their video game.

Simultaneous taps, behind the ear with billy clubs, took the two on either side out quickly. Cesar, sitting in the middle, jumped to his feet and spun around. The gun in his face froze him where he stood.

"Where is Esteban?" the man asked the punk.

"Who?" Cesar pretended.

"You have one more chance, son. That's it."

"Wait, wait, I don't know where he stays, man," he pleaded.

The man racked the slide on his weapon and repositioned it at Cesar's forehead. "Then you're no good to me."

"No! No! I'll tell you. Just don't kill me."

Esteban and his two sidekicks usually hid in a basement bunker they had below an abandoned store. It was five blocks south of where he was now.

He put Cesar to sleep with a tap similar to what his friends had received. He then tied them firmly and hung them upside down from a rafter behind the couch. He turned the TV to a game show and turned the volume up.

The storefront was boarded up, probably from looting after it had closed some years ago. He found access to the basement through a vent window on the side. The basement was not lit at all. Daylight did not find its way down the hall to the steel door. He had to use a small flashlight taped to the Glock.

Listening at the door, he could hear voices. He counted three. So far, that's what he expected. Looking at the hinges and the lock showed they were substantial. He wrapped a small explosive cord charge around each hinge and one around the door's deadbolt lock. All three were tied to one detonator which would set them off simultaneously.

Stepping back, he activated the arm unit and checked his protective clothing. The glove fingertips came down perfectly. The batting helmet fit and he pulled the chinstrap tight. With the Glock in his power hand, he pushed a button on the remote detonator with the other.

He wasn't supposed to look at the explosions, but somehow could not stop himself. As if in slow motion, smoke swirled around the hinges and the lock for a microsecond before the charges fired. The door jumped off its frame and fell two feet into the room.

Following the door into the room, Silas stayed low and scanned the room with his eyes. As the man to his left drew a weapon, he fired two shots and both hit their target. Another of Esteban's associates jumped off a couch to the right and raised his weapon.

Silas could feel the round strike his helmet. The hydraulic arm snapped in that direction and two more shots were let loose. That man also fell in a heap.

Behind his desk, Esteban stood and reached for a large Colt. A 40 caliber round from the Glock tore through the back edge of the desk and into Esteban's right knee. He fell to that side.

The assassin was on top of Esteban in a second and grabbed his shirt collar and tie with his normal hand. He pulled the hoodlum toward his face, glared directly into his eyes and spoke.

"Listen to me carefully, I'm not going to ask you twice." The voice was calm, clear and brimming with resolve. "You will answer my question," he proclaimed, "or you will become a quadriplegic with no testicles. Right here, right now."

He pulled the man closer and placed the Glock on the inside of the man's left elbow.

"Do you understand me?" The voice was now louder.

"Yes, yes, what do you want?" Esteban was in near panic and extreme pain.

"Where is Doris Shaw?" was the question.

Esteban hesitated and then defiantly looked away from his tormentor.

The Glock fired into his elbow.

His screams echoed through the building as Esteban tried to flail about, but he felt the barrel of the gun move to his left knee.

"No! No more, por favor. El' cabana," Esteban spit blood from his mouth. He had bit his tongue clenching from the pain. "I'll tell you, I will tell you."

Esteban told the man about a cabin ten miles outside of town. That's where they were holding Doris.

"You're coming with me," the man told him. He wrapped Esteban with duct tape, mouth, arms, legs and all, and dragged him to some stairs. That didn't look too promising.

Even with the arm's added strength, Esteban had to be at least 260 lbs, so he opted to leave the thug in another room of the basement. He hid the wounded gangster behind some cabinets, making sure he could not cry out or move. Pulling the door closed, he then headed out of the building and to his truck.

The road out of town became farm and forest land at about the 6 mile mark. It was two lanes with a bit of a crown along the centerline. You felt like you were leaning as you drove. As the ten miles approached on the odometer he slowed down. There was a clearing ahead on the left.

A small, unmarked drive went back into the woods. He could see the cabin.

There were no vehicles in sight. Continuing down the road another hundred yards or so he saw a small access from the road into the woods. He turned in and off roaded his way back and behind the cabin. Turning the truck toward the road he parked near some heavy brush and cut several pieces of the shrubbery to obscure its visibility from the cabin.

He approached the small building from an angle, listening carefully as he stepped. There was no sound coming from the cabin. At
148

the corner, he slid around to a window and looked inside. It appeared to have two rooms.

He saw no one inside. The window in the smaller back room was not locked. He opened the lower pane and eased into the room. Taking a pair of boot covers out of a pocket and putting them over his shoes, he cleaned the area where he had stepped in and began to look around. There was no one in either room.

The cabin had little furniture. The larger room consisted of a small kitchen, a fireplace and a large table with three non-matching chairs. The smaller room obviously intended as a bedroom held no bed. There was a four-drawer chest against one wall and another wooden chair on the other. No rugs anywhere and the place was dusty. The air was damp from humidity and it smelled of mold.

Then he saw the closet in the smaller room. A chill ran down his back as he walked toward it. He pulled the door open and was nearly sickened by what he found. It was Doris or he believed it was.

Her eyes were swollen shut and her face bruised heavily. Blood ran from two cuts along her scalp and from her left ear. Two fingers on her left hand were clearly broken.

He checked for a pulse. It was there, barely. Silas pulled her from the closet and checked for other broken bones. None were apparent but he couldn't be sure.

As he picked her up he could hear vehicles approaching the cabin. He could not be sure how many, but it sounded like more than two.

Quickly he lowered her out the window and climbed down behind her. The window sash jammed for a second but with a bit of coaxing, it closed. As gently as possible he gathered her over his shoulder, then crossed the back area to some bushes and laid her down.

She was still unconscious. He crouched quite still beside her, hidden by the bushes, as the men came running around to the rear of the cabin.

They looked hard but did not venture into the woods. There were four that came to the back area but he could hear still more in the cabin. After the men returned around to the front, he picked her up again and moved through the woods to his truck.

The door creaked, but ever so slightly as he placed her on the passenger seat and tightened the safety belt and shoulder strap around her.

Closing the truck doors, either of them, would create too much noise. Once he fired the engine they would hear that as well. Silas tied a short piece of rope through the passenger door handle and tossed it across Doris' body. He eased the driver's door open and got into position with the key in the ignition. He waited and listened.

Carefully, he looked and studied the path back toward the main road. It would need to be as smooth and gentle as the situation would allow. Doris couldn't take much more.

Within five minutes, he could hear the sounds of several of them coming his way. He let them get as far from the cabin as he could and then pulled the rope while starting the engine. Gunfire rang out from the direction of the cabin as he aimed the truck back to the road. A few rounds struck the vehicle but did no damage.

It was a rough and bouncing ride but he found the road and turned right to go back to town. That would take them past the cabin, but he had little choice.

Flooring the older model pickup, it roared and sped down the road directly into the first severe test of its protective systems.

Two of the vehicles from the cabin tried to block the roadway, forming a "V" across the road. Men lined the highway on both sides, maybe six or more.

Silas touched a lever on the left side of the steering wheel. Armored panels moved into position blocking the wheel wells. As they roared past the first of the men gunfire poured at them.

The truck was hit many times but the armor plating held firm. Several rounds struck the side window and windshield to no avail. The added weight of the armor slowed acceleration but not dramatically.

Stepping on a pedal near the brake, he activated the pneumatic shocks that held the front bumper. They would extend out two and half feet within a tenth of a second. He aimed the truck directly at the cars blocking his way. Sensors fired the shocks forward the second before impact.

The two cars were lifted and thrown to the side. The car on the right side spun and landed on three of the men who had been shooting. The pick-up rocked side-to- side but stayed fairly stable.

He pulled the lever retracting the wheel panels and the bumper keeping the truck running at full speed till they came to the edge of the town. As he slowed, he thought he heard Doris moan slightly.

Turning hard onto the main street of town they sped to the hospital. Pulling up under the Emergency entrance, he stopped hard and jumped out. As he ran to passenger side and pulled open the door, he screamed out, "I need help here."

Two orderlies came running with a gurney. As they gently loaded Doris, he noticed a car driving by slowly. There were four men in the car.

"Get the police here, now," he yelled into the hospital. "This is Doris Shaw."

23

He pulled the truck to the lower part of the hospital's driveway and waited till the police were in sight. He then drove calmly to his warehouse, changed vehicles and continued on home. The police were already there as he drove up. When the call went out that Doris was at the hospital, they sent a unit to protect Ben. Parking in his own driveway, he ran over to the Shaw house. Ben Shaw stood inside the doorway. Police were everywhere.

Ben looked at his friend and asked if it was true, that his Mom was alive.

"It's true, Ben. She's in rough shape but she's alive."

Ben gave him a hard look. "We really need to talk, you know?"

"Yeah, I know." The man glanced at the police officers and continued, "Let them do their job and get out of here first."

"Did you find her?" Ben whispered.

"Yes, now can we talk later?"

"I want to go see her." Ben's eyes were swelling with tears.

"No you don't. Not right now," the man said. "Let the doctors clean her up some first."

"I want to be there." Ben was adamant.

The man took a deep breath and walked over to one of the officers. "He wants to go to the hospital. Can you escort us over there?"

"Sure thing, Sir. Do you want to ride over with us?"

"Naw, I'll drive if that's Ok."

The ride to the hospital was anything but quiet.

"How did you know where Mom was?"

"I told you, there are things I can do. I'll explain it to you more later. I can't have you knowing too much right now. If you did, I would have to ask you to lie." He looked right at Ben and squinted his eyes.

"I don't understand all this." Ben shook his head.

"Be patient and work with me and you will. Right now we need to be concerned about your Mother. This thing isn't over yet."

"She's hurt that bad?"

"Well, yes. But it's more than that. These are bad people and they may try again."

They turned into the hospital parking lot and the man looked at the boy and asked again, "Can we finish this conversation later? Not here and not now? Later. Will you trust me?"

Ben was still and quiet for a minute. "I do trust you."

As they walked into the hospital an orderly pointed to the man with the boy and told an officer, "That's him. That's the guy that brought her here."

The officer told the DA, who had arrived a short time earlier, and they walked up to the man.

"You brought Doris here?" the DA asked with surprise in his voice.

"I did," he responded.

"What... how... where did you find her? How did you know where to look?"

"Ben had pointed out one of the boys who beat him up when I dropped him at school. I took a chance and found the punk. I asked what he knew about Doris."

"A high school kid?"

"He was hanging out there, I don't think he's actually in school."

153

"So," the DA continued. "This high school kid told you where to find her?"

"He told me about a cabin he had heard things about. I decided to go look for myself and she was there."

He left out the details between those two events. The only question the officer followed with was about the pickup truck. He stalled for a minute and then said there had been a pickup parked at the emergency entrance when he pulled up. He told them he had parked behind the truck. The attendants must have gotten confused and thought the truck was his. For the moment, the DA and the cop bought it.

"Well, I'm thankful you found her," the DA concluded. "Thanks for what you did."

"She's a neighbor and a friend; you don't have to thank me." He smiled.

They stayed at the hospital for several hours. Ben saw his Mother but she had not regained consciousness. They sat in the hall; they went downstairs and got coffee. They walked the halls and then sat some more. All the while he was watching and waiting for the other shoe to drop. How long till the cops found the bodies in the store? When would they find Cesar and his troopers? He waited but nothing ever happened. He finally told Ben he needed to check on a couple of things to do with business and left the hospital.

Driving in the opposite direction and then doubling back, he went by the gang hideout. Cesar and his friends were gone. So were the sofa, the TV and any sign that anyone had been there in a long time. He rode to the abandoned store and there were no police in sight. He drove around the block twice and then parked. A door was open on the side of the building. He went in and cautiously looked around. He went down the stairs.

He could smell bleach. There was no blood on the floor at the bottom of the stairs. In the room where he had left Esteban there was nothing. Esteban was gone. He crept down the hall slowly, to the room that had the steel door. The room was open. There was no door, anywhere. Again, there was no blood, no bodies. The only proof that he wasn't losing his mind was the telltale burn marks on the doorframe where the hinges had been.

He halfway ran to his car and drove out the road toward the cabin. As he approached the area he saw red lights flashing. Lots of red lights but no blue ones. As he drove past the area there was no sign of the cars that had been wrecked hours earlier. No bodies along the road or any of that. The cabin had burned down, completely. It was still smoking around the edges but there was nothing left. That's why the fire department was here. A few of the trees were scorched and the brush was gone. But there were no signs that he had been there earlier.

"These guys are thorough," he thought to himself, "And they are not done with this."

That's why the police had accepted his story. There was no evidence to conflict with what he had told the DA. The Argus Group didn't want any evidence. He said to himself again, "*these are bad people.*" He drove back by his home to make sure all was ok there. It was quiet. Inside, everything appeared to be as he had left it. He checked next door as well. There was yellow tape up across the rear door, but that's all that seemed new.

He returned to the hospital. Ben was now in his Mother's room with her. She was still out but the Doctor's report was fairly good. She had a concussion, a bad one. Her ribs on the right side were broken and had collapsed her lung. Her left arm was broken, as was her left leg above the knee. Her left hand was wrapped completely. He knew those fingers were broken when he found her. The good news was that she would make it. It would take months, many of those in the hospital, but she would recover.

Doctors determined that Doris should be moved to the Trauma Center Hospital, a satellite of the main Hamilton Medical Center. They specialized in intensive care and potential long-term cases. Doris qualified under both categories. The move was made quietly and Doris tolerated it well. They set her up in a large second floor room with a rollaway for Ben and three soft chairs for guests. Monitors and tubes were everywhere.

He found them at the new building and was directed to the room. To him, Doris looked like she was sleeping. He walked up to the bed in silence and looked at Ben.

Ben was awake but not talking. He sat and stared at his mom. As his neighbor came in, he looked at him for a second, and then turned back to his mother. He still planned to have that talk, as his friend had promised, just not now. The three of them spent the night in that hospital room. It was another long night.

24

The morning paper brought news that the assistant to the DA had been found alive. The story mentioned her pending case against Argus and its delay. It was a big story, even for the small local paper, and it was quickly picked up by the national news.

Another story caught Silas' eye. A home in the east side of town had been shot up over night. Over fifty bullets were fired into the abandoned house just after dark. The address looked familiar to him. He looked at it for a while and then realized what it was. He had used local tags on the truck yesterday. That was the address he used to register those tags. The Argus people had traced the truck's tags to that address. How long till they figured out where he really lived?

He spoke with the police officer on duty outside Doris' room. Ben was still asleep in a chair and he didn't want to disturb him.

"Tell Ben I'll be back in a bit," he asked of the officer.

He rode through his neighborhood to check again. All appeared to be fine. He had brought the paper with him. He turned to the "Homes for Sale" section and found several that interested him. One was in the process of being built on the side of the mountain just outside of town. The builder had run out of funds and was looking for an interested party with money and ideas. He had both. It took twenty minutes to get there.

What he found was a nearly completed foundation set into the mountain. It appeared to have more than one level of basement area. The framing that was in place, had been exposed to the weather for too long. It would need to be redone, in total. The wood was a loss but the concrete outline of the house was intact. Basically, the footprint was some 3500 square feet per floor and could go as high as he wanted.

The basements were very intriguing to him. The possibilities were endless. He called the builder, who was out of the big city some hundred miles south, and set up a meeting in town for later that day. He looked back at the area as he prepared to leave. A smile came across his face. This mountainside would be his new home, one day.

Activity at the hospital had picked up considerably. News trucks everywhere, as were reporters and cameramen. He thought about trying to sneak in somehow but wasn't familiar with the hospital enough to do that. Putting his head down, he walked forward at an even pace. That got him to the elevators and the floor where Doris' room was. On the floor the questions started. A microphone was shoved into his face along with a rude question.

"Who are you, Sir? Do you know the victim?"

"I'm just a friend." He pushed his way past the man.

Not ready to give up, the reporter jumped back in front of him, "Are you the man who found her?"

"Nope, wrong guy," he replied tersely. "That's another neighbor, a real big guy. And he hates reporters."

He found the DA standing in the hallway outside the room. Looking past the man he could see Ben in his Mother's room. There were several other people around him. One, a woman in a serious business suit and a briefcase at her side, was doing the talking. He tapped the DA on the shoulder and asked, "What's going on?"

The DA turned to him, stuck his hand out for a greeting and replied to his question.

"It's people from the State Social Services department," he started. "They are going to make Ben a Ward of the State."

The man was puzzled. "Why, Ben is 18, isn't that age of consent?"

"Not in this case. It really doesn't have to do with his age as much as other factors."

"What others factors?" the man asked.

"What you see in front of you," the DA began to explain. "Ben is in no shape or condition to care for himself right now. Plus, the court has determined that his life could be in danger." He looked at the man he was addressing to see if it appeared he was understood. It did, so he continued, "Doris will also be a Ward until we resolve this and she can care for herself. My department will be her Guardian. We have resources to keep her guarded 24/7."

"Will Ben need a Guardian?"

"Yeah, the court will meet tomorrow morning and appoint a foster parent to do that."

The man said nothing. He stared at Ben in silence. The DA could tell he was in deep thought.

"Say," the DA interjected, "I came back to see you yesterday afternoon. Ben said you had to deal with some business."

"Yes, I did. Is everything Ok?"

"I was just going to tell you, I think we found that cabin. It was where you described but it was fully engulfed in flames when we got there. We had to call out the fire department to keep half the woods from going up with it. It's not going to be much good to us for evidence now."

After a minute of quiet, the man asked sheepishly, "I noticed you didn't accuse me of starting the fire. Thanks for that."

"Well, if I thought you could have, I would." The DA smiled. "That fire couldn't have been going for more than 30 to 45 minutes when we got there. I knew where you had been for the last several hours." Shrugging his shoulders, the DA patted the man on the arm, smiled and walked toward the elevators.

The man waited till the State officials were done and had left. Walking up to Ben, he put an arm around the young man and asked, "How's she doing this afternoon?"

"About the same." Ben stated. "I have to go to court in the morning."

"Yeah, I hear. I'll go with you if you like."

"Thanks," Ben muttered.

~

The next morning Daniel had not noticed the report on the TV news. If his wife saw it, it did not register with her. Argus wouldn't at this point. Daniel hadn't really discussed that part of the mystery with her. It wasn't till he was in the office and going over the wire reports that it jumped out at him. **"North Georgia Assistant DA Kidnapped, Found Alive."**

The first line explained about the case the assistant was working on against Argus.

Daniel grabbed his map, *"Where is Dalton, Georgia?"* he asked himself while looking it up.

Finding it, just below Chattanooga, Tennessee, he went to the boss' office, wire report in hand.

"Did you hear this about Argus?" he asked.

"Yep, saw it on TV last night." He was way ahead of Daniel.

"Do you think I need to get down there and see what's going on?"

The editor looked up at him and shook his head, no.

"Not yet," he replied. "It's just a local issue right now. May not have anything to do with your story or anything else."

Daniel was disappointed. He told the boss he was right and headed out the door. As he got to the doorway, the editor hollered out at him. "Mr. Seay."

He never referred to him that way. Daniel froze where he stood.

"Don't forget I'm a reporter, too," the boss continued. "Keep a bag packed at home. This could break any minute in our direction. When it does, I want you down there. Got it?"

"Yeah, Chief. I got it."

25

Back at his house that morning, he stared into the mirror considering what he would do later that day. Silas and The Son were looking back at him. They reminded him of the need for secrecy but he realized that things were changing. He walked to his closet, picked out a suit to wear to court and looked back at the mirror. They were still there but now standing to the side.

He went next door and into Ben's room to find the same for him. It wasn't hard. Everything was organized and orderly. They were pretty much staying at the hospital right now, but that didn't change the facts. They could never live back here again, either of them. The police were guarding the residences for now, but that wouldn't last.

The meeting with the builder from Atlanta had gone well the day before. He was motivated to work and get his people busy. Things were slow and they needed the work. He had brought the original floor plans, but the man had other ideas. They drew out what the customer wanted on a couple of napkins and the builder said he could have it rendered professionally. He gave the builder a nice retainer check and asked if they could get started tearing down the old framing right away. Contracts could be drawn up when the new floor plan was approved.

"We'll be up here in the morning," the builder replied.

"Great. I'm busy in the morning, but I'll be by the site later in the day."

"See you there, Sir."

"Oh, and one more thing. Please be flexible in this build. I may want a few special things added. I will pay for it, but they may come late in the plan and I want everything kept between you and me. Understand?"

"Sure, I think so." The builder seemed confused a little. "No telling anyone else, right?"

"That's exactly right."

"Long as it's legal, it's your business." The builder made his rule apparent.

They agreed and shook hands. The new home and the new safe room would be much different than the little house.

He went to the hospital and waited for Ben to get changed. Doris was still unconscious but the doctors were still being positive about her progress. He stood and stared out the window. The news people were still thick as thieves. "How long will that last?" he thought to himself.

The DA stuck his head in, "You guys ready to go?"

"Yeah. Ben is getting changed, right now."

"I'll be in court with you guys. I've got three people plus the police who will stay here with Doris."

"Thanks," he told the DA. He was beginning to like the man.

Ben came out from the restroom and was ready to go. He leaned down and kissed his Mother. The three men walked down to the elevator and took it to the basement service-parking garage. The hospital had made that available to them due to the circumstances.

In two cars and with four others in escort, they made their way to the courthouse. The parking there was all at street level. They had to push their way into the building. The courtroom was on the fourth floor.

News people were lining the walls. Cameras stuck out into the walkway and microphones were at the ready. They stood in the hall until their case was called and then entered the courtroom. Ben and the DA went down front and sat at a table. The DA was acting as Ben's counsel. The man sat near the very back.

As the proceedings got underway, the judge read all the legal documents filed by the State Social Services people. The DA stood at one point and made a statement in Ben's behalf. There was nothing contradictory to the State's position, just asserting Ben's rights.

As the judge declared that Ben was indeed to be a Ward of the State, he began to assign a foster parent when the man at the rear of the courtroom stood.

"Your Honor, May I address the Court?" he asked.

"Who seeks to address this Court?" the judge demanded.

"I do, your Honor," he said louder this time.

"And what is your name, Sir. And your business in this case?"

"Your Honor, my name is Jonathan Crane. I apply to be Ben Shaw's guardian."

"Step forward," said the judge. "Have you filed the proper papers in this matter?"

At that point, the DA stood and asked to be heard.

"Your Honor, I can vouch for this man. Our office can have the paperwork filed with the Court by this afternoon."

As he walked past the bench where Ben and the DA were, Jonathan could see Ben smiling.

The judge noticed it as well.

"I don't suppose I need to ask if you have any objections to this, Mr. Shaw?"

"No, Sir," Ben replied.

Looking him over, the judge spoke again. "If the District Attorney's Office speaks for you, I'll not stand in the way. You will be sworn in after the papers are signed." The judge raised his gavel, paused and started again.

"It is so ordered, that at such time that the paperwork is filed and accepted, Mr. Jonathan Crane shall be considered the legal guardian of Mr. Benjamin Shaw. This appointment shall last until such time that this court considers it no longer necessary. Court is dismissed." The gavel hit the bench.

That was it.

The afternoon paper ran this headline, "Hero Neighbor Named Guardian." If Argus was still confused as to who he was, that should clear it up for them. "It was on now," as they used to say in the Rangers. Plus, he had managed to eliminate, either directly or indirectly, all the local Argus actors that he knew about by name. The town was full of new ones and he didn't know who they were. He was at a disadvantage.

Returning to the hospital, Jon told Ben they would need to live elsewhere. Ben seemed to understand and asked how he could help.

"I'm going to need some time to look around for a place," he told the youth. "You stay with your Mom as much as you can."

"Ok, but is that all I can do?"

"For right now, yeah. We'll talk more. There's a lot for you to learn."

He already knew where they would move until the new house was ready. He just needed time to pack and move the safe room contents to the warehouse. He decided that warehouse would make suitable living quarters for the next few months, suitable and secret.

He was already a week behind schedule on the Iowa removal. That was Ok, since he had planned to cool things for a while anyway. But he had planned to use the time coming up with his manner and weapon for the job. That's what he was behind on, and it looked like it would get worse before it got better.

This new situation was important and above all, unavoidable. He hadn't been completely aware of it before all this took place, but these people were important to him. Something was missing from his life before. He would have to learn how to fit these new feelings in without interfering with his work.

There were actually fewer media types at the hospital this afternoon.

"Good," he thought. *"Maybe they're getting tired of this."*

Ben didn't seem to notice. He was anxious to get back and check on his Mother. Still unaware, but alive, her machines beeping and blinking, Doris' appearance was less chalky and more human. Her color was better.

26

From Miami, Saul DeMarcos was on the phone to an Atlanta number. He was not happy.

"You telling me, I still have a leak problem?" he demanded of the man on the other end.

"We took care of the clean ups but we can't get to the guy responsible, not just yet."

"Nobody messes with this family and," DeMarcos realized he was on an open phone line and caught himself. "I need that leak fixed. I need the flow restored, you understand me?"

"Yeah."

"How many are on the project?" the Miami boss asked.

"I sent eight up there yesterday. Lost three so I'm down to five."

"Five counting you or plus you?"

"Counting me, boss."

"So, there's only four up there right now, huh?"

"No, I'm here too. My cell is out of Atlanta, I'm up here too."

"Fix this mess," DeMarcos yelled into the phone and hung up. He was in dire straits. The pipeline went through Dalton. They were concerned about sending any more product through there till the heat was off. Their old carpet plant on the south end of town was the distribution hub for the east coast. Black Lacquer tables were processed and directed for shipment depending on the logo and its color. Gold logo was a real table made of plaster and painted black.

The ones with a greenish gold logo were more valuable. They would be melted down at the proper receiving warehouses. The tables were X-rayed several times on their way, looking for false pocket or other voids where drugs could be stored. There were no voids for the X-ray machines to find. These tables were made of drugs. Not solid cocaine but enough worked into the plaster that it could be reheated and filtered out. Strained from the plaster, with the right equipment.

It had worked for them for several years, but some blonde in North Georgia got a hold of one and broke it open. The dogs she had with her went nuts. They couldn't smell the drugs through all the lacquer, but they could when it was busted. Saul knew she was making a case but they didn't know how strong it would be. When her kid got worked over for messing with a small time shake down, they thought maybe he was empowered by his Mom's case. Feeling his oats. So they decided to find out what she knew and what she planned to do with it.

That was going OK, until some independent rodeo clown stepped in and screwed everything up. They needed to get him out of the way, her as well. He needed to get back to business and soon. DeMarcos' family in Colombia was getting impatient with him.

Soon the five men in Dalton would have Crane's name. It would be easy after that.

~

The man the media called "The Son" spent the next two nights moving computers and other items from his safe room to the warehouse. He got the computer systems back on line as quickly as he could. He couldn't handle the cabinets himself but he did get them emptied and pulled out into the regular space of the basement. By that Monday he had almost everything out of the secret room.

He had not "talked" with Ben yet about who he was and what he did. He kept rehearsing in his head how to tell someone you killed people. None of the attempts worked for him.

He really didn't know how he would handle it.

Life and death were bigger issues at the moment. There were men in town. How many, he didn't know. But they would be looking for him and Ben to kill them. They would also like to finish the job on Doris when they could get to her. His problem, he didn't have any idea where they were hiding. The Argus warehouse was not listed. He figured they had to be nearby. There weren't any mall stores in Dalton that sold the stuff they handled. So, he figured he would find the closest one and follow a truck back to the nest.

Monday night he headed to Chattanooga. He found a store, carrying Argus merchandise, in a mall on the south side of town near I-24. The rear of the mall had the receiving doors marked so that was simple enough. All he had to do was wait for the delivery truck.

The next day he had parked in a grocery store lot across the street and sat in a stand of trees just to the back of the mall. Vision was clear from there and at about 3PM his wait was rewarded. The truck was marked Argus Imports. Convenient enough. It was unloaded and sent back on its way in less than twenty minutes. He walked to his car and got on I-24 East till it merged with I-75 South. He had not yet caught up with the truck, but knew it had to be going this direction. About four miles down I-75 he saw it. The damn thing was going over 80 as it pedaled toward Dalton. No wonder it was hard to catch.

The truck went past the main Dalton exits and finally got off on the last exit considered to be the Dalton area. It was heavily industrial with plants and warehouses everywhere. The Argus vehicle made several turns and ended up at an old carpet plant's loading dock. Worn out painted signs on the building said Miracle Carpets. They had not been cared for in years. He parked to the side and cut his lights.

169

The dock doors opened and two men were at the door as the truck backed in. The driver got out and went inside with the others. Crane considered his option for tonight. He didn't have the arm with him but he did have his Kevlar jacket. This was not the night to confront them, just to find out what he was up against.

The side of the building was solid block, no doors or windows. The front, opposite the loading dock, was dark and the offices there looked empty. He could see light under one of the doors, but only one. That must lead to the warehouse area, where they were. Back to dock end of the building, he eased himself onto the dock itself. There were no security cameras that he could see. Leaning into one of the metal roll up doors he heard voices inside. He really needed to know how many he would be dealing with and voices through a metal door didn't cut it. He looked high and low around the dock. There was a vent fan mounted about twelve feet high at the other end of the dock. The fan was running. No ladder or anything to climb on anywhere, but he did find a rope. He tied a 6" metal bracket that he found to the end of the rope forming a "T." Tossing the bracket gently, it landed on the lower ledge of the fan's framework. It made a slight banging noise.

Leaving the rope hanging, he jumped down off the dock and hid in the shadows along the side. The dock door opened and one man came out. He looked around, saw nothing and went back inside. He said something in Spanish as he closed the door. Crane climbed back onto the dock and pulled himself up, hand over hand by the rope, till he could see through the revolving fan blades.

They were at a table playing cards. There were five in all. He hung on and waited to be sure there wasn't another one or two walking around. It became clear that the five he could see were it. Leaning as far as he could, Crane scanned the entire visible area of the warehouse. It was piled with boxes marked Argus. Some had a gold logo stamp and others the logo looked more green than gold. Off to the side he could
170

see what looked like cars. They were banged up. One was on its top. Those must be the cars from the cabin. There was no doubt. These were the guys he was looking for.

Lowering himself quietly he considered what to do about the rope. Should he just leave it hanging or would they notice and realize he had been there? The fan was blowing out, exhausting air from inside the warehouse. He found a long stick and a piece of rag. Tying the rag to the end of the stick, he first dripped the rag end into the trucks gas tank. He had a lighter in his car. Lighting the rag, he held it up with the stick to a spot about a foot under the fan's frame. The rope caught and burned. Not with bright flames but more a slight glowing cinder. It burned up to the frame and the lower section fell to the dock floor. Little sound was made. The little smoke or smell created was blown out away from the men inside. In two minutes the rope was gone.

He placed a magnetic tracking device under the front wheel well of the truck and a mini microphone just inside the door. He did not slam the door but pushed it as tight as it would go. Satisfied with what he had accomplished, it was time to leave.

He thought about just calling the authorities. That would involve explanations about the wrecked cars. Who knew what they did with the bodies and where they might show up? Nope, he would have to handle this a bit further. The group he was dealing with was large and powerful. But at what point would they cut their losses and get out of Dalton? If he knew who was making the decisions he could better estimate that answer.

~

It was a nice evening in Pittsburgh. Daniel and his wife, Lori, were out for a movie. It was some new superhero flick playing at the Cinema 16. The theater was located in the mall near their home.

It was late when the show let out and all the stores and shops were closed. Bars and heavy screens across the storefronts kept passersby out, but they could see in just fine. Daniel noticed a shop with small tables and lamps. Wall hangings and plastic flowers. The kind of shop the boss said his wife liked to shop in.

He stopped Lori for a moment and pointed out the shop.

"Would you buy anything in there?" he asked her.

"Maybe. Depends on what I'm shopping for, or perhaps just my mood." She smiled.

Daniel was half listening and half concentrating on looking. One of the tables was on its side and he could see the underneath. There was a logo stamped on the bottom. It was not quite upside down, but almost. The logo was a round face with a smirk, all in bright gold. It looked like a Sun God medallion or something he had seen in a Sinbad movie. Under it read "Argus."

"So this is the kind of stuff that got Dewey Hanson in trouble?" he thought out loud.

"What?" Lori asked.

"Nothing, Baby." Daniel took her arm and they walked on their way. "Just thinking."

He finished his thoughts quietly this time, *"Makes no sense. Must be more to it."*

27

In almost a week, the builder had made great progress. He and his customer had agreed on the basic floor plan and the contracts were signed. There would be three floors to the main house and a two-story garage to the side and slightly behind. The basement was a big change. There were already two foundation levels but his customer wanted yet another. The concrete was set into solid rock so the structure would be fine. It was just the excavation that would be costly. Down another 15 feet in every direction, plus another cut out area, 80 wide by 22 feet deep. It looked like an underground garage for maybe six cars, but how would you get them there? It was the customer's money and he seemed sure of what he wanted so the builder had brought in mining excavators to dig and haul the rock away. They could remove their debris through the first level basement so it would not hold up the framing on the main house. They could work at the same time.

Half a mile from the house he was having built, Jonathan Crane had found an old, abandoned service station. It was built into the mountainside with the front half of the station exposed from the rock. This had been done because the highway ran very close to the mountain. It was the only way to have a building there. Time and progress had claimed the highway and the station. The new Interstate had diverted most of the traffic away years ago and the highway was now only an access to a small subdivision.

He purchased the station and the part of the mountain it was protruding from. His plan was to leave the building as it was, obviously closed. Through the service bay was the back wall, which connected to the mountain. That's where he planned to have the mountain dug out. Other than its small size, his only error with the planning of his first safe room was an emergency exit. It didn't have one. This would be costly, but worth it. That back wall would be replaced with a secret door, which looked like the original wall. Behind it would be a tunnel. A tunnel that turned left in a slow curve and then straightened out. That tunnel would continue and connect to the new third level of his basement. Work on this project would begin next week. It would be done mostly at night.

The builder knew Crane's name but had been asked to secure all permits and paperwork in the name of Crane's company, J. Tremain & Sons. The tunneling company was working for the Liberty Tree Service Company. He would also need to find a way to move from the current house, or houses, to the warehouse without being seen. He would have to share some information about himself with the DA and perhaps even the Police Chief. They could help. But he needed to talk with Ben first.

Near the end of the first week staying at the hospital, they developed a standing agreement with the police. Dinnertime meant some form of subterfuge to help Jon and Ben get away to eat. Tonight they were taken out in the back of a squad car from the hospital basement. Ben felt like chicken so they went to the Market Street Shops. Jon started mumbling about needing to explain a few things and Ben finally interrupted him.

Ben had had a lot of time to think lately. Sitting with his Mother in that hospital room. Ben had three men in his life that he looked up to and respected, his dad, his mom's boss and his neighbor. His dad was gone. Mom's boss was nice but was busy and they didn't talk much. His neighbor stayed away a lot but did spend time with him when he could. They played catch and talked about the world. Politics and history, what was right and what was wrong.

As Ben had grown older the discussions became more involved. Jon revealed his deep love for his country. His understanding of what it had been founded on and his concerns for the direction some were taking it. New ideas and attitudes can make change and that's not a bad thing. In fact, that's the America he believed in. But some in power were now effecting change based upon what Jon saw as immoral concepts. These people would hide behind words like "greed" and "bias," or worse, to gain and maintain their control over others.

Lives were destroyed and some others taken in the name of their desire for power. When that power was obtained they would act with complete disregard for the rights of others. Acting out their personal selfish wants with lavish extravagance and, in the worse cases, the depths of human depravities. What these people would do had no limits and no shame. They would one day have to be confronted before the entire country slipped over into the abyss.

Ben thought about those discussions and what he had learned about his friend's ideals. He knew Jon's convictions were deep.

He thought about the medals in the blue box, the gun in the kitchen and Jon's reaction to the red light on the microwave. He thought about the books he found in Jon's den and his abilities. The way above average abilities that Jon had just demonstrated so recently.

Then in the hospital room, there were the news magazines with the stories about the strange revolutionary character that had claimed he killed the congressman. The stories called him "The Son," as in Sons of Liberty. There was even a thing on TV about it.

Ben had thought about these things a lot while he sat with his mother. Two and two became five but he wasn't really sure. As he had added everything together there was but one possible answer. He hadn't been sure, not till now. Now, Jon sat there with him, stumbling and mumbling over how to tell him something.

With all they had been through this past week, all he had done for him and his Mother, his friend was suddenly having trouble telling him something. All the addition came together for him. All his thinking now centered on one thing. He couldn't let his friend continue to trip over himself. He interrupted him.

"You have a bunch of Revolutionary War books in your den."

Ben watched his friend closely for the reaction. It wasn't one of confusion by the subject, but more of caution. Wanting to be sure to answer correctly.

"Yeah," Jon responded in his surprise. "I've been a fan of that period since I was a kid."

"I kind of figured as much," Ben continued. He took a bite of his meal and looked Jon right in the eye. "I'm not stupid, you know. Those jerks deserved what they got. I read about them and what they did."

Jon laid down his fork and leaned forward to whisper, "You read about who?"

"Those congressmen that you believe broke the law. The ones that got taken out."

"Be careful what you say." Jon paused and then asked, "Ben, exactly what is it you think you know?"

"I know you're the man who saved my mother in two hours when the whole police force couldn't do it in a day." Ben took another bite of chicken. "I know you can 'do things,' as you put it. I know who you are."

Jon leaned back in his chair this time. He rubbed his brow and the bridge of his nose. His appetite had left him for the moment.

Ben took a swallow of iced tea. He sat as straight as an arrow and spoke again. "I know who you are, Jon. It has to be you."

Jon Crane raised his head and stared across the table. The young man with him didn't look frightened or the least bit concerned. He looked quite calm.

"I'm proud you are my friend, Jon," Ben told him. "You don't have to be concerned about your secrets, not with me." And he took another bite of his meal, and he smiled.

"There's still much for you to learn, my friend," Jon stated.

"I know. I'm a quick study," Ben smiled. "Just tell me what you need from me."

The rest of the meal was much quieter. Jon had worried about this talk and how Ben would take it. He "took it," by taking it over. This, like so much else lately, would take some getting used to on Jon's part.

Back at the hospital, Ben played his role as if nothing had happened. His new persona as a secret keeper didn't show at all. He was calm and relaxed. They talked as they always did and welcomed visitors that they knew.

Just before 9:00PM another milestone past.

Doris came to for a few minutes that night. This was a good day. The doctors told Ben they would need to put her back into a coma for a while yet. To let her brain rest, but that this was a very good sign. He got to hug her and make her aware she was safe and with him. Jon stood in the corner and beamed. Doris smiled the least little smile, and the drugs took effect.

Ben stayed with her and Jon went to the warehouse, by way of several stops and changes, to continue setting up the secure part of their new quarters.

Organizing his supplies and resetting the computers, he would stop every so often to check the tracking device he had left on the Argus truck. All was quiet. There had been no movement and there was no noise from the cab. There had been five guys in the warehouse. Could they be waiting for reinforcements? Most likely, yes.

He looked through a drawer he had just refilled. Three cameras left, but only one with enough range to do any good. He checked the unit and it was working. One slight moment was allowed for self-deprecation over not having taken a camera out there the first time.

Things were happening so fast he was making amateur mistakes. *"Learn and get better"* he told himself. Enough time had been wasted on reflection. He needed to take another trip down to the old carpet plant and find a good spot for this baby.

In the lower level of this warehouse he had three vehicles. One was a Jeep Cherokee. Not new, in fact it was several years old and had a few dents. But it could run and run fast. The lightweight frame and chassis held a 427 Chevy V-8. No armor on this one, just speed and agility. He took it in case he needed to get out of there in a hurry.

28

The plant was dark and the Argus truck was parked where it had been. Parking a block over, he checked for other cars as he walked toward the building.

"Where did the men leave their cars?" He wondered. None were parked nearby that he could see. The only visible access to the plant was through the dock doors and they were raised above ground level.

He found a tree just off the corner of the building and climbed to about 10 feet off the ground. One limb needed to be trimmed and no one would notice it missing. He spiked the camera's mounting bracket into the tree and set the range for maximum. The mount could swing 15 degrees in either direction so he checked for clearance. The camera was set into position and the battery power turned on. He checked the swing and the focus with his remote before placing a cover over the unit. The cover looked like tree bark and left only the lens exposed. It would be hard to discern even in daylight. Climbing down he heard a door open; it was the dock door of the carpet plant.

With his back up against the tree trunk, he stood still and listened. A vehicle drove into the area. He heard voices and the dock door being rolled down. The vehicle approached and stopped. Jon slid down into a sitting position so he could turn to look. Two men got into a new car, a black Cadillac sedan. He could not make out anything about them. The car drove away toward the freeway onramp going right past his Jeep. He looked around for a few seconds more and then ran, half bent over, to his Jeep. He wanted to follow that Cadillac and see what the men were up to.

There were three men in the Cadillac, the driver and two other men who had been inside the warehouse. The driver was Juan Castrono. He worked for Argus out of Atlanta. His normal duties were that of distribution. Moving the product after its recovery from the mold it arrived in.

The other man had been sent in by the higher ups, either in Miami or perhaps Colombia. Juan did not know and it didn't matter really. What mattered was the product had been stagnant for too long. The man flew into the Atlanta Airport and wanted to see what inventory was left, first thing. They counted the boxes with the greenish gold logos and then he wanted to see what the holdup was. Where was this woman? Where was her kid and whoever had interfered with Esteban and his men? Why was this taking so long to resolve?

They did not notice the green Jeep following them. It would stay a couple of blocks back and then, when it became obvious the Cadillac was headed for the hospital, he slid over one block and ran parallel to them. The black sedan drove past the hospital, turned around and came back. They stopped in front for a few minutes and Jon thought he could see a flash from within the car. They were taking pictures.

Jon guessed that their next destination might be his old neighborhood. He drove in that direction three blocks and pulled into a driveway along the side. When the Cadillac went past, he waited a couple of minutes and then took a short cut he knew. He killed his lights and parked along the main drag outside his subdivision and waited again. The black Caddy turned in and proceeded to the first left in the neighborhood. Jon got out of his Jeep and started to walk that direction. The Cadillac suddenly came back out and turned toward the freeway. He remembered the police were still guarding the houses. That probably prevented the guys in the sedan from getting their pictures. He got back to the Jeep and headed after them. Did they go straight to the freeway or did they know about his warehouse? The Caddy was not in sight, so he had to make a choice. He guessed they could not know about his hideout and were heading back south to the carpet plant.

Roaring down I-75 at over 85 miles an hour it was hard to tell what was what. Then he passed the car he was seeking. Went right by them. The exit for the carpet plant was next on the right so he sped up even more and got off there. Waiting at the top of the exit, he was surprised when the Caddy kept going south and did not get off. He put the Jeep in reverse and got back on the freeway. Where were they going now?

Two hours and half a tank of gas later, both the Cadillac and the Jeep pulled into Atlanta's International Airport. The lines of traffic were thick as they approached the drop off zone for departing flights. Jon pulled into a spot next to the curb, got out on the driver's side of the Jeep and waved, as if he saw someone. He kept his eyes on the Black Cadillac.

It pulled to the curb, maybe 100 feet ahead of Jon. The two men in the back got out and went to the trunk. As he waited for his associate to get his bag, the other man looked up and around. Jon could not believe his eyes. The man was very familiar to Jon. He was on his quarry list. In fact, he was the next one on that list. He stood in a line of traffic at the Atlanta, Georgia airport and stared at the man he had just spent nearly a week investigating several hundred miles to the north. Representative Charles Harley of Iowa.

He didn't really need any further confirmation on Harley. He had made up his mind already, but if he had needed any help in deciding, this would be it. Harley was suspected of being involved with drugs, but no one knew through what organization. Now, Jon did.

This upped the ante considerably. Jon knew that Harley played rough. The reporter in Iowa, Terrence Harper and Pedro Jones could attest to that, if they were alive. Harley's involvement could only mean they were getting impatient and preparing to move. The pictures of the hospital made more sense now. He had to get busy with his own plan, before these guys could hit. He pulled the Jeep out from the curb and slowly drove past the Cadillac. He did not look, but the Cadillac's driver stared at him. Jon needed to get back to his warehouse, but first, he needed gas.

~

Earl Johnstone of the Burlington Hawk Eye called Daniel around 11:30 that morning. He had young reporters in Des Moines keeping watch on Representative Harley. They reported that he had boarded a flight to Atlanta with no further destination listed. What would he be doing in Atlanta? Neither Earl nor Daniel could figure that out, but the proximity of Dalton to Atlanta did cross Daniel's mind. He made a note of it.

29

The first thing Jon did at the warehouse was to check on the camera and see how it was working. He ran the tape back a couple of hours and something odd caught his eye.

He backed it up and ran it again, then again. The same thing happened. It looked as if a car was driving out from the side of the building. Not through a door, but through the solid block wall. He backed the tape up again and ran it slow. Sure enough, the car emerges from the solid concrete block.

He knew it had to be a hologram, but it was a good one. He had walked right past that area, within feet of the wall and didn't notice. Next time there he would study the area more closely. The whole idea of the thing, the hologram, gave him the thought of an application he could use in the future.

The current situation was getting more and more serious. Problem was, only he knew it. He needed to bring the police in on this. But then, how would he retain control of how to handle it? Was there any way he could control an attack on the hospital by himself? How would they do it? How many men would they use? He needed to think like a criminal, he could do that.

The first thing that came to his mind was Doris' location. They would need to move her and do so quietly. No one could know except the trusted and cleared doctors and staff who were working with her. They could then use the old location as a trap. Allow the assault to happen and catch them at it.

The second thought was what if they went the old fashioned way, messy? Maybe a rocket propelled grenade, an RPG, through the window where Doris' room was. Using fewer men would be harder to stop.

The thought of that made him shutter. He would need spotters on the roof watching everything in the area. Other buildings, cars and trucks coming in and out, even pedestrian traffic could be suspect.

Or would they try to kidnap a doctor or nurse and gain access by pretending to be them? What about the timing? Jon assumed that the presence of someone like Harley meant that Argus' situation was crucial.

But, why? Unless that carpet plant was special.

"Yes, of course," Jon told himself. *"That's it."* The hologram door, no markings other than the truck and a Congressman from another state coming to check on it. The plant was a major distribution site. The local address listed for Argus was that empty storefront in town. The plant was the real "business location."

He had been traveling the country eliminating congressmen with ties to this drug ring, three of the four anyway, and all the time their hub was right where he lived. He'd laugh if it weren't for the danger his friends were in. This had to be stopped here and now. That damned smiling, joker-faced logo of Argus. It and those behind it would pay for what they had done to Ben and Doris.

Finally it came to him, the best way to deal with this bunch and protect Doris at the same time. He put a call into the DA and told him he was suspicious the gang would try an assault on the hospital.

"Let us handle that." The DA said.

"Look, I really need you to trust me on this." Jon begged. "I know more about these people than I've told you, but I will tell you. Just cooperate with me now, please?"

"Crane, you and I need to have a talk." The DA did not sound cooperative. "I'm aware that you are into things you haven't let on about. I don't even want to imagine what all that could be right this minute. My employee and her son are in extreme danger, we agree on that, right?"

"We do," Jon answered.

"I have enough trust to let you have guardianship of Doris' son, right?"

"You must have."

"And I don't really know where that comes from, just a feeling I have about it."

"I appreciate that," Jon interjected.

"The rescue deal, I don't know how you did that, but I know there was much more to it than you let on, right?"

"I can't say just yet."

"You need to level with me, consequences be damned. If I don't have a basis to trust you we can't work together, got it?" The DA's voice was getting higher and louder.

"Can you meet me at the house?" Jon asked.

"What house?"

"Doris' house."

"Twenty minutes?"

"Yeah, that'll work." And the phone conversation was over.

Jon would get there a bit quicker than twenty minutes. He would watch the house from a yard across the street. If the DA came alone, he could be trusted to some point. The conversation would determine how far. If he came with police backup, the conversation would be really short.

~

185

Daniel Seay couldn't concentrate on much else. Why was Harley in Atlanta? What is Argus? Are those two things connected? He had many questions but no answers. He remembered Dewey Hanson had been connected with Argus when he got into trouble some years ago. Was Argus the entire reason for that? Are Hanson and Harley connected, other than by their job status? More questions.

He went back to the last one, are Hanson and Harley connected? The other common denominator in that was Argus. Could there be a connection between Harley and Argus?

He got on the phone and called Earl Johnstone back.

"Hey, do you have time or maybe some fresh information on this angle?" he asked the Iowa reporter.

"What angle are you talking about?"

"Sorry, I was wondering if your boy Harley had any ties to a group called Argus? Argus Imports."

"I've heard of that, but not in direct connection to Harley."

"Can you look into it for me?"

"I can't do much here, the new boss lectures us every day about what happened. But I know a guy in Des Moines who can. In fact, he's closer to the situation there than I would be here."

"Great, may not be anything, I know that. But it could be a big deal. A very big deal."

Daniel thanked his friend and thought about LaPointe in Louisiana. Was he into Argus?

He hung up with Iowa and called the Shreveport paper. The conversation was pretty much the same. Matt Turlock said he'd look into that, but threw in, "Aren't you getting tired of that horse, yet?"

"Not really, I've felt all along these murders were connected. This Argus thing could be the thread."

"Yeah, maybe. I'll check it for you, like I said and I'll ask Phil if he has anything on Argus."

186

"Thanks, man. I owe you another one."

"Yep, you're falling way behind in that department, pal." Turlock laughed.

Daniel tried to smile. He knew he was pushing his luck with these new friends, but he also knew there was something big in all this. He was sure of it. He just needed to be careful and not fall into a trap like the editor in Iowa had.

30

From his vantage point he watched as the DA drove up. Not only was he alone, he told the officers who were on the scene to back off to the end of the street.

"Keep an eye on the area from there for a while." He told them he needed to look around a bit. "Oh, and let Crane in when he gets here."

Jon drove around the block and was waved through. He pulled into his own driveway and the DA walked up to greet him, hand extended. Their handshake was in silence and Jon stretched his arm toward the door of his home. The two men walked inside and Jon went to his bar in the den.

"Drink?" he offered.

"I'd love one, but I can't. Still on duty."

"Ok, I think I'll pass as well," Jon put the bottle down, reached into the mini-frig and grabbed two colas. The DA took one of those and walked across the room. "You know you won't be able to live here after this."

"Yeah, I've already considered that. Gonna need your help in some respects," Jon replied. "There is something about that you should know first."

"And that is?" The DA was curious.

"I have means. Considerably more than I let on."

"Good for you." The reply was very flippant.

"Seriously, I have money. I've been fortunate in some investments with the money my folks left me."

"Just what do you call, fortunate?"

"Last time I looked it was over $155 million. Interest changes that everyday."

The DA was quiet this time. He did shake his head several times before saying, "I suppose I can cancel that benefit I was going to throw for you." He smiled and sat down. Looking straight at the man, the DA asked, "Alright, let's quit foolin' around. What is it you can or will tell me?"

"Where do you want me to start?"

"How about the rescue, that's what's bugging me the most. How did you do that?"

"I didn't lie to you." Jon paused for a minute. "Everything I said was completely true. I just left out a couple of steps. I thought for sure you would find those steps, but when you didn't say anything I went back. They had been cleaned up."

The DA leaned forward in his chair, "You said you were going to explain, this is just more mystery."

"I left Cesar in his warehouse playroom, him and two of the kids who worked with him. Cesar told me where to find Esteban. They were alive when I left them."

"Who's Esteban?"

"The guy I filmed casing out Doris's house and then breaking into it."

"Wait a minute, you filmed the break-in?"

"Yeah, I set up cameras to watch the house. Esteban drove by several times before the kidnapping and I took the license tag and had it traced," Jon explained.

"You had it traced?"

"I have connections," Jon stated.

The DA stood and walked to the other side of the room. "So where did you find this, Esteban?"

"He was in the basement of the old building downtown. The one that Argus uses as its mailing address in Dalton."

"And he told you where Doris was?"

"He did, after a little persuasion. Esteban only understands rough, so I had to use his language."

"Was she alone at the cabin?"

"Yeah, when I got there. They had stuck her in a closet, the bastards."

"What did you do with Esteban?"

"I left him in that basement. He had two holes in him and his two buddies were dead."

"You killed people?"

"Self defense," Jon shot back. His expression became even more serious than before. "I don't hurt innocents," he finished.

"Ok, I'm forgetting that part for right now and don't tell me about anybody else you may have killed, alright?"

"Sure, fine," Jon agreed and glaced at the man sideways.

The DA was taken aback by the response, but continued. "So, you believe more of this Esteban's friends came behind you and cleaned up your messes?"

"I do. They didn't want you guys to know, worse than I did. This Argus is a mean bunch."

"How do you know that?" the DA questioned.

Jon went into his story, leaving out the killings, of how he had been tracking certain government officials who had done very bad things. He told how after the fact, it turns out several of these guys were connected to Argus. That Argus was into drugs but he didn't know exactly how, just yet.

As the story continued, the DA lost more and more color from his face. Finally, he walked right up into Jon's face and asked straight out, "You're the guy they call "The Son?"

"I can't answer that. You made me promise I wouldn't say anything more about that."

The DA spun and half staggered to the chair in the corner. He sat and looked back at Jon.

"I don't believe this."

"You going to arrest me?" Jon asked.

The DA was quiet. He slowly stood up and took a step toward Jon. "Arrest you? Hell, I don't know. I don't know if I'm going to arrest you or buy you dinner." He laughed. "I'm supposed to be one way on this type thing, but I know about those guys, the ones you...."

"Removed." Jon lifted his eyebrows and suggested a term.

"Whatever! I read about them, I have friends who worked in areas near them. They'd like to give you a medal."

"I have medals," Jon quipped.

"You know what?" the DA said. He turned away slightly. "I'll take that drink now."

The discussion continued with details of how Jon had tracked and filmed Esteban and learned of his employment with Argus. He was asked where he did all this tracking from.

He explained about his safe room. The DA seemed puzzled by that.

"It's empty now, I've been moving stuff all week. But I'll show you the room."

They went downstairs and Jon opened the section of wall. The DA was amazed.

"What all did you have in here?" he asked.

"Computers mostly. Monitors for cameras, storage for my gizmos and records."

"Can I see the tapes of the kidnapping?" the DA asked.

"I'll have to take you to my temporary place. It's in town."

The District Attorney suddenly thought of someone else who would be affected by this.

"What about Ben, what does he know?"

"Well, less than you, right now. I tried to talk with him last night but he got the jump on me. He knows who I am but I haven't filled him in on the details yet."

"Ben knows who you are and he's okay with it?"

"I believe so. He's a pretty smart kid and cool as a cucumber. He seems fine about it."

The talk turned to the current problem, the danger that Doris and Ben were still in.

The DA wanted to make a point very clear. "What you did for Doris is something I'll never forget. I believe you saved her life."

"She's a fine lady and has a fine son," Jon added.

"She's extra special to me, if you haven't noticed."

"Yeah," Jon answered. "I've noticed. I sure hope she'll recover for both your sakes."

"Thank you, thank you for that as well as the other. Now, what is it you think is going to happen?"

Jon explained about the carpet plant and the surveillance he had on it. He told him about the Congressman he followed all over Dalton and back to the airport. He expected a move on Argus' part and soon. "We must have their product bottled up and I don't even know exactly what it is."

"Do we move Doris and Ben, what do you think?"

"I considered that," Jon went on. "Where do we move them? We need to get prepared and stop their attack. Remember, they don't know about me except that I'm the neighbor.

They know I got Doris out, so they will be after me. But they don't know what all I can do."

"Don't say it like that, ok?" George looked at Jon sternly. "I'm trying to pretend I don't know what you've done already."

With that, Jon offered to take his friend to the warehouse and show him the surveillance, all of it. He looked at the DA and added one more thing.

"I kinda lied about the pick-up truck. It was mine. I just couldn't explain it right then."

"I know," the DA assured him. "We have cameras, too."

George Vincent turned his glass up and drained it. He then sat the glass down on the counter and looked back at Jon. "I couldn't figure out what you were up to and decided to play along. Like I said, you saved Doris." The DA paused for a moment and then continued. "That scored a bunch of points with me."

31

George Vincent had been the District Attorney for Whitfield County and Dalton, Georgia for 9 years. He had seen a lot in those years, heard a bunch as well, but this situation beat everything. A nationally sought, serial killer was taking him to his hideout. And he was going voluntarily. Why was this guy here now, he wondered? All the times those bad guys got off on some silly technicality just to go and hurt more people. Several times they actually killed after getting released. Where was this guy then, huh?

Their car turned into a parking deck for a hotel and went to the top floor. Jon jumped out and told him to "follow me." They ran down the stairs at the back of the structure and it was a short walk to the first warehouse building. Half way down the backside Jon grabbed a handle on what appeared to be a double window. The "window" swung open on hidden hinges enough for the men to enter the building. At the far end of this otherwise empty space sat a green Jeep Cherokee. Jon opened the driver's door of the Jeep. The DA climbed into the passenger's seat and they were off again. Several blocks over, Jon turned right and then back to the left. He hit a button on his dash and a side of the building they were next to opened up. They drove over the low curb and inside. The building closed behind them. Interesting, George thought. Dim lights came on inside the structure and George could see ramps at the far end, one going down and one going up. They went down.

At the bottom of the ramp the lights were brighter. They were below ground level and no one could see. There were several other vehicles parked down there. One was the pick-up they had talked about earlier. George got out of the Jeep and walked over to the pick-up truck.

"*My God,*" he thought as he rubbed his hand over the many dents and scratches from the bullets fired at Doris and this man he was with. George could feel both knees weaken as his thoughts invisioned the hail of gunfire this truck had been through. He looked at the huge, front bumper. It too, was dented and had blue paint on one side and gray on the other. The pick-up told him what the conditions had been that morning. It had been rough. His near stupor was broken by Jon's call.

"Come on, man. This way."

Jon was already at the elevator, holding the sliding door. George hustled over and the two went up. One, two, three levels to an area that was well lit though the windows were all blacked out. George could hardly believe what he was looking at. A row of computers just like he had said, with printers and monitors flashing. There were other monitors and flat screen TVs set up across from the computers. Jon went to those first. He hit a knob that looked like a joystick on a video game, then turned to the DA and signaled him to come see. The monitor showed an industrial building. It had a loading dock on one side and a flat, concrete block wall on the other.

Jon pointed at the screen and simply said,

"Watch."

George didn't know what he was watching for until the car drove out from the solid concrete wall.

"What the hell?" He asked Jon. "What did I just see?"

"Money can do many things, my friend," Jon retorted. "You just saw a small example of what it can do."

195

He then explained to George what the building was and about the hologram. He reiterated his belief that the key to the mystery was in that building.

"I need to get in there," he told George.

Another car drove up to the wall and stopped. Then, they both saw it. A man opened a personnel door just beyond the garage door. It too, was covered by a holographic allusion. He looked at the car and waved them through the other opening, then retreated back into the building.

"Aw, that's it." Jon smiled. "That's my way in."

~

The small clinic was about 5 miles outside of Ringgold, Georgia. Esteban had been there for several days. He wasn't sure how many. The pain was still intense. The doctor had taken his right leg just above the knee and the left arm didn't look good. He had lost a lot of blood. When the men from Atlanta found him he was nearly dead. Two of them took him to this clinic and left. He had not heard from anyone since.

The commotion in the other room woke him. The two men came in and turned on a light. He recognized the first man. It was Armando Diaz. He was the head of the Atlanta distribution network. Armando leaned over Esteban and asked if he knew who had done this. Esteban told him "No." He had never seen that man before.

"Are you sure?" Armando pushed. "The paper said he was a neighbor.

"No, no. Mr. Wayne is an old man."

"What about the other neighbor?"

"We cased that street for two months. He's hardly ever around. Crane, I think that's his name."

"What else do you know about him?"

"Nothing. He sells drugs on the road. Drugstore drugs. That's all."

"Ok, then," Armando finished and turned to walk away.

"Is that it?" Esteban tried to sit up.

Armando looked at the man who had come in with him and nodded. "No, Esteban. Saul has one other message for you."

Armando went into the other room. The doctor was being held by two of Armando's men. They heard a shot. Armando looked at the doctor.

"I think he died. Bury him, quietly and do not speak of it."

~

George Vincent was back in his office the next day. He had the Police Chief coming in to see him in one hour. George wanted to know where Esteban was and who else was in town. The recordings that Jon had shown him were clear. Argus, or at least Esteban, was the guilty party. Doris' investigation of Argus put any speculation of "why," to rest. One huge problem remained. He couldn't use the recordings.

His phone rang, not the cell but his desk phone. He grabbed the receiver and gave it his usual. "This is Vincent. Speak to me."

The voice was distorted. It was the first time he had heard it. But he knew what it was.

"Washington and Essex," was all that the voice said. It was a code Jon had asked him to use. The reference was the street corner in Boston that had been the site of the Liberty Tree. There were many before the war was won, but that was the first. The response to that would indicate if George could talk or not. The positive response was to be "Boston is clear." If it wasn't a good time, the negative would be, "Taxes are rough on everybody."

He responded in the affirmative.

The voice remained distorted. "There is much traffic at the carpet plant."

"Men coming in?" George asked.

"Vans, large vans from all over according to the tags."

"Are they bringing in men?"

"No, quite the opposite. They are taking something out."

"How can you tell?" the DA wanted to know.

"The vans sit higher as they go in, then much lower, on the wheels, when they come out. They are loading something inside and not using the regular loading dock."

"Any ideas?"

"That's why I have to get in there and soon. Set some decoy in the area for me, can you? Have the police block some streets near there and act like they are looking for somebody."

"Alright, give me about an hour. Be careful, will ya?"

"Always."

32

Jon dressed in his uniform without the arm, grabbed a duffle bag and several items he would need. The special Glock was in its pocket on his leg. A dark wig and moustache with the backward baseball cap would serve as his disguise. He went to the basement to pick a vehicle. The lavender '69 Dodge Charger would likely fit into the area unnoticed. The foam dice hanging from the rearview mirror was a classic touch. He threw the duffle bag onto the rear seat and fired the 440-magnum engine. He left the downtown area going east, rather than toward the expressway. He would connect with the bypass highway and then go south to the industrial park. It would take longer, but that was fine. George needed some time to get his cops set up. Besides, he wanted to approach the area from a different direction than the expressway.

As the Charger neared the industrial area, he pulled to the side of the road and took out his remote monitor. The screen showed the carpet plant. There was not any activity at the moment but that would soon change. Sirens filled the air with noise and blue lights were visible from the expressway and two other surface streets.

"George had come through," he thought.

A small gray car suddenly roared past him. It was headed for the carpet plant. Jon sat where he was and watched his monitor. The small car slid into the lot of the building and stopped outside the hologram. Within seconds a hand extended from the visual illusion and the small car went inside. Two minutes after that, three white vans emerged and then the small car came out. Two of the vans came past Jon, the other vehicles went out toward I-75. Jon cranked the Charger and drove into the carpet plant's lot.

He parked a block away and grabbed his bag. Alongside the block wall he admired the holograms. Close inspection of the larger one clearly showed a repeat of a mark that was further down the same wall. They had taken a picture and used that for the cover. He could reach through the opaque visual and feel a wooden door beneath. Stepping back, he could see marks on the pavement that showed the location for the drivers. They were not heavy or overt, but enough once you knew what they were.

Feeling his way down the wall, he quickly found the personnel door. The handle was there as was the lock. He reached into his bag and got his kit. It would be like working a lock in the dark, but he'd done that before. The lock clicked slightly and the knob turned.

He gently propped the door with his foot and put his kit back in the bag. Opening the door barely enough to see, he looked around. There was nothing right around the two doors. Most of the boxes and the table were up at the front end of the building. The bad news in that was, there was no cover once he went inside. Fortunately there were no windows and the interior was dark. He slipped inside and closed the door, realizing that the small crack from the door could let in light. He stood perfectly still and continued to watch for any movement.

"*Had they all left?*" he wondered.

He found a small rock near his foot. He picked it up and launched it high and to the front of the space. It landed near the table and the sound echoed through the building. No reaction.

"*They are all gone. Beautiful!*"

Jon moved quickly. He noticed that the stacks of boxes he had viewed through the fan had changed. The ones on this side were less in number. The others appeared to be about the same. So, it was those

200

boxes they were moving out. Both stacks seemed to be the same size and model number. The marking were exact. Then he looked again.

"The logo was different." Those had a solid gold logo and these were greenish gold! He remembered he had noticed that the other night. They were moving the ones with the greenish gold logos.

He shook one of the boxes. It was light, maybe 10 pounds, if that. The boxes were glued shut. If he opened one it would not be resealable. He reached back into his bag and took out a small hand drill. He put a ¼" core boring bit into the chuck and drilled a small hole into the box. The first hole hit nothing. He withdrew and tried another spot. That time the bit hit something inside. He pushed the drill bit into the unseen item as far as it would go.

He pulled the drill out and the hollow center of the bit was full of white powder. He put the bit, powder and all into a plastic bag and packed up. Stacking the box where it had been he quickly started toward the rear doors. He heard the motor of the overhead door start up. Light poured in from the garage door area. He crouched down and looked around. Up on the dock level was another door, behind the boxes with the gold logos. He jumped up on the platform and pushed the door open. It was clear out on the dock. He slipped out and worked his way to the end of the building. The men returning were all on the other side and did not notice him. He walked the block to his Charger and drove back to his main warehouse compound. The police were still in the area, but the men must have figured out it was not about them.

Jon called George again, to let him know he was away from there and that he had some powder for them to analyze. Going back through his warehouse and reversing the steps to his personal car, Jon showed up at the DA's office as Jon Crane and asked to see Mr. Vincent.

In the privacy of George's office, he handed him the bag and told him.

"I have a field test kit. I checked a small amount from the outside of the drill bit. It's plaster cut with cocaine."

He told George about the different logos and that the men were likely back and continuing their work. He estimated that half the boxes he had seen the other night, the ones with the greenish logo, were gone already. Jon told George he had more news. While at his warehouse, he had focused the camera on the vans and the tag numbers. Two were from Kansas and he gave the DA those tags. One other had an Alabama tag and he gave him that one as well. The last one was from Pennsylvania.

Jon figured the Alabama van probably had made it to its destination by now. But the Kansas vans and the one headed for Pennsylvania might still be on the road. If they put out an APB, an All Points Bulletin for the east of the Mississippi, they might find them before they got to their home base. George agreed and grabbed his phone. The Police Chief could make that happen.

George put on a pair of rubber gloves and reached into the plastic bag. He took the drill bit and shook the powder off it and from within the core. He handed the bit back to Jon.

"This would mean too many questions right now. All I need is to verify what it is, not how I got it. We'll worry about that detail later."

"How about the carpet plant?" Jon asked.

"Chicken and egg situation, Jon. I can't go busting in there without valid reason. If we catch one of the vans we can try to trace it back to the plant. As we stand now, I don't have enough for a warrant, unless you want to explain how you got that sample, and I don't have an exigent circumstance to act on either."

"What kind of exigent circumstance would you need?" Jon asked.

"A scream from inside, maybe a gun shot, something like that."

"Give me forty five minutes and have your troops in the area."

"Hey, what are you up to, now?" the DA demanded.

"Just an exigent circumstance." Jon smiled at him. "Oh, beef up security at the hospital, too. They may be trying something there."

Jon had almost left the DA's office when he stopped, reached into a pocket and pulled out the small remote monitor. He went back to George's desk and handed him the devise.

"Keep an eye on this, will ya? And I'll want that back when we're done."

The monitor showed real time images of the carpet plant. When George looked back up, Jon was gone.

33

Activity within the carpet plant was high. Armando Diaz was now there issuing orders. The vans from all over were coming and going. They normally used large trailers to move the product. But without knowing the extent of the DA's evidence, they couldn't risk the normal procedures right now. The big guy from up north had reviewed the situation and told Saul they needed to get the stuff out of there. At the rate they were moving, it would take another full day. Perhaps they could reestablish this location later. Right now it was possibly too hot. A chance they couldn't take.

Armando was walking the floor, supervising the movement of boxes into stacks for the different locations. That would speed up the loading. He noticed a small amount of white dust on the floor.

"What the hell is this?" He bent down and picked up what would stick to his fingertip. The sniff test was not conclusive to him. He called for a chemical kit and dipped his finger into a solution of cobalt thiocyanate. The solution turned blue. Armando turned red.

"Who spilled some product? How did it get out of the box?" he screamed.

No one knew.

Armando grabbed box after box and looked at it. Then he walked over to one of the first stacks to be set up. He pulled a box from the bottom. There were two small holes in the box. Tearing the box open he saw the hole in the leg of the table.

Armando screamed again, "Someone has been in here." He pulled his cell phone and hit a rapid dial button.

"Yeah, it's not good here. Send me as many as we can spare. Fifteen? That'll have to do. I need them here now."

A van came in through the hologram door. It carried a Louisiana tag. "Get him loaded and out of here." Armando was clearly concerned.

~

Jon was in and out of his warehouse quick. He had his Kevlar and his batting helmet. He had both Glocks and a couple of new items he had not tested yet. He took the Jeep this time. He would have preferred the pick up and its armaments, but it could be recognized.

He saw three marked and two unmarked police units in the area as he turned on South Dixie Road toward the carpet plant.

He parked in the same spot a block away. It had been lucky to this point. Walking around the building, he held a weapon in each hand. From the backside, opposite the loading docks, he climbed the slight, tree filled incline along the side. He secured his balance behind a wide pine tree and took aim at the exposed projector lens, the lens that supplied the hologram in front of the garage door. His aim was true and the lens exploded. The wooden door was now exposed and he aimed over the personnel door. As he started to squeeze the trigger, the door opened. A man with a gun of his own came out, frantically looking around. Jon popped the lens over that door and the man dropped to the ground and fired in his direction. Several rounds chewed into the tree he was behind and into the ground around him. Jon reached around the tree and fired off five shots at the door. The man retreated inside and the steel door closed. It was time to move.

Jon stepped laterally behind one tree and then another. When he was beyond the garage door, where he could see the dock area, he settled in again. The garage door started to lift. He fired three shots into the pavement at the door and it closed again. In his peripheral vision he caught movement on the dock. He emptied the first magazine in that direction and reloaded in one motion. It had been only two minutes since his first shot at the lens, but it seemed like an hour. Jon could hear the sirens. They were coming from all directions.

He put three holes in the garage door and two more rounds in the direction of the dock.

Sliding down the bank, he hit the pavement and ran for all he was worth. Once he got to the block wall he walked toward the garage door, paused and then crossed in front of it.

He continued around the corner and crossed into the lot behind the carpet plant.

The police were now lined up across the dockside of the plant and moving down the side where the other doors were now exposed. Jon lay prone, behind a stack of landscape timbers.

He was waiting for his opportunity to get to his Jeep when the carpet plant erupted.

The explosion went up and out. Parts of the exterior walls withstood the blast but the roof was falling back down everywhere. Blocks and pieces of wood flew into the timber pile he was behind. Corrugated metal fell on him, but he was not hurt. He worked his way to the Jeep and from there could see the front where the dock had been. Police were staggering around and some were lying motionless. Other units were still coming into the area. He wanted to see what was left of the insides but knew he had to go. He guided the Jeep out of the area using the same back roads he had earlier.

Three blocks away, he dialed the DA from his cell. He didn't have a voice unit with him.

When George answered he didn't say a word at first. Then the DA started the conversation.

"Jesus, Joseph and Mary, guy! What did you do?"

"I'm not sure what happened inside. That wasn't me."

"Then they had the building wired up. These boys don't like to leave evidence."

"Does the camera still work?" Jon asked.

"Yeah, I've got a view of the scene."

"How are the officers?"

"So far, two are banged up pretty good but they are moving. Three others have bumps and bruises and aren't hearing too well at the moment. It looks like the explosion mainly went skyward. We were lucky."

"Thank goodness. I swear, I didn't see that coming."

Jon went to his warehouse to clean up and wait for the report on what was found. The report would take longer than his patience allowed. He had other responsibilities.

He went to the hospital to check on Ben and Doris. Ben was all excited. The news was all about the big explosion. "You were in on that, weren't you?" he asked.

"Not here." Jon was not amused. He looked around the hallways and outside the windows. "Where's all the police?"

"A bunch left right after word of the explosion," Ben told him. "About an hour ago."

"I don't like this." Jon was concerned. "Come with me." He walked out to the hallway and found a doctor.

"Is there another room we can move Mrs. Shaw to?"

The doctor seemed surprised by the request. "I could find something."

"Then do it. A different floor and the other side of the building if you can. Make sure her son is with her."

The doctor went to see what he could do. Ben stepped in front of Jon and asked, "What's wrong? What's happening now?"

"I'm afraid they might make a move on the hospital. There are some big shots that want to limit what is known about all this."

Jon walked to the elevators, "I'll be right back. I just need to go to my car. If they move you before I get back, meet me here in 15 minutes."

~

At that same moment, three cars were on I-75 passing the Highway 20, Rome, Georgia exit and coming north. They would be approaching Dalton in 30 minutes. The lead car had last heard from Armando just before he blew the building. His instructions to them were simple. Eliminate the witness in the hospital.

They were on their way to do that.

34

The first reports of the explosion did not mention Argus but it obviously was about Dalton, Georgia so that caught Daniel's eye. Cable news stations were all over it. They had broadcasts of local helicopter footage and local reports. When the local reports began to speculate on the Argus Import Company, Daniel reached for his phone. Before he could pick it up, it rang.

"You got that bag packed?" his boss asked.

"Yes, Sir," he responded. "I was just about to call you. I'm heading for Georgia."

"You haven't heard about the other yet, have you?" the editor asked.

"No, what other?"

"State police stopped a van along I-75 in northern Kentucky. They had a tip it might be carrying drugs."

"And?" Daniel inquired impatiently.

"Fifteen boxed, black lacquer tables. Cocaine mixed in with the plaster. The logo says Argus on everyone of them."

"Hot damn, I knew it...err.... I mean that's great, boss. Thanks!"

"Hot damn, works for me. The GPS on the truck says it had left Dalton, Georgia yesterday. Now, go get the story."

~

Jon had his full size Glock in the car and five magazines. The smaller one was in his pants pocket. He had three mags for it. He had

also brought the untested items he didn't need at the carpet plant. He had an extra Kevlar jacket. He brought it for Ben to wear if things got tough. His instincts were off the chart. He could feel something bad building up like it was coming his way. Jon stopped and looked at the building. He would need to find a way to defend this building against whatever was thrown at them.

Hamilton Trauma Center was a satellite of the main Dalton Hospital. It handled extreme and long-term cases and was much smaller than the main medical facility. Doris had been brought here from the emergency room of the medical center. Dalton, Georgia was not a major population center, 33,000 residents, give or take. The primary hospital housed 285 beds. This trauma center had 120 beds in 85 rooms. The three floors faced the main road and general parking was in the front. Jon noticed the main doors were in the center of the building and side access was at both ends. A large fence screened off the rear with entrances through sliding gates. Offices, treatment rooms, coffee shops and a general purpose waiting area occupied the first floor of the building. Patient rooms were on the second and third floors. From the numbers of vehicles in the parking lot, Jon assumed the occupancy was low. In fact, due to the high profile nature of Doris' case, any patient that could stay or be moved to the main hospital had been.

Adding up all the factors for his plan, Jon was still uncomfortable with his available manpower. He called George again and asked why the security at the hospital was so low. George didn't know why the Police Chief had done that. "He must have overreacted when the building went up."

"We need support here, George. I've got a real bad feeling."

"Ok, I'll try to turn some of them around. How many are there with you now?"

"Looks like three, plus the regular security guards. There's four of them."

"Are they armed?"

"Sort of," Jon complained. "Small 38 revolvers."

"The police units should have back up weapons in them. I'll talk with an officer on site and get those guards some firepower. How about you?" George was concerned.

Jon paused and then replied, "I'm good. Just get some more guys up here, OK?"

On his way back into the hospital he could see an officer on his phone. He called to a security guard and they headed to the police unit parked in front of the hospital.

On his way in, he thought about the other patients and doctors. How could he protect everybody from an unknown force of unknown strength? He asked the desk clerk to get him the Hospital Administrator. After a short talk they set off on separate duties. The Administrator began moving everyone he could to the back of the building on all floors. The low patient count would make that doable.

Jon went to find Ben and Doris. They were on the third floor near the right end. Ben apologized for not meeting him as they had planned. He had gotten tied up making sure his Mom was all right.

"That's no problem. Here, I want you to wear this." He gave Ben the jacket and explained what it was.

"Cool," Ben commented.

"Yeah, well I hope you don't have to find out how cool it is."

He made mental note of the new room they were in and pulled the door to. He then went to the elevators and disabled them. He found the side steel doors that connected to the stairwells and placed metal bars in the door handles. That would make them more difficult to open from the outside. Jon asked one officer and two guards to station themselves at the side doors. The remaining police officer worked with Jon. They blocked the revolving front entrance doors with file cabinets and desks. He placed a couple of surprises inside those doors before blocking them. If there was no danger, he would look rather foolish. Right now, he didn't care about that.

From the second floor window, over the main entrance, Jon and Officer Gil Gartner watched and waited. Jon looked at the officer's weapon. He realized that ballistics would identify who shot who when all was said and done.

He asked the officer, "What is that? A Smith and Wesson?"

"Yeah, it's a 4506. We're talking about getting a few Glocks next year if the budget is OK'd."

"I like mine," Jon told him and held it out. "Want to try one? It's a 23."

"Sure, I'd like that," Gil said as they exchanged handguns. "Actually, I hope we don't have to use 'em."

"Same here, but I don't care for the odds on that."

The two men stood and watched the road from both directions. The officer checked, by radio, with the other officers at the doors. They were ready.

Within ten minutes Jon and Gartner looked at each other as the three sedans drove up.

Reaching to his shoulder, the cop pressed a button on his radio and said, "They're here."

Five men per vehicle got out and walked toward the building. They spread out as they approached. Four of them moved directly toward the front doors.

Jon opened one of the smaller window sections and hollered out. "Get on the ground, you're surrounded."

That didn't work. He didn't think it would.

The fifteen men pulled their weapons and began firing at the hospital. Jon fired and hit three almost at the same time. The Smith

212

and Wesson kicked more than his Glock, but its knockdown power was good.

The officer looked across at him in amazement, but then turned and fired at the attackers himself. The remaining twelve spread out and advanced toward the building. The four in the middle continued on to the front doors. Jon had rigged a surprise there. Two of the untested items were remote controlled smoke bombs. He had injected some concentrated chloral hydrate solution into one of them and a dose of nitrous oxide in another. As he heard the men breaking through the glass doors he pushed his igniter button and the smoke went off. The four were overcome almost instantly. They would sleep for several hours. The count was down to eight.

Gil Gartner ran downstairs to the left side of the first floor. His other officer and one guard were exchanging fire with three of the men. One of the security guards had bugged out when the shooting started. The intruders backed off for a moment and headed to the rear of the facility where the fences would turn them around. If they made it through, the rear doors were sealed shut anyway.

Jon went to the right side doors to check on them. The cop was down, wounded in the arm, but the guards were still firing.

"One of 'em got past us." A guard said. "He went up those stairs." One of the Argus men outside stood for a second to take aim at the guard as he spoke. Jon fired twice and that threat was gone.

Then Gil showed up and Jon turned to run up the stairs. He could hear a commotion on three. That's where Doris and Ben were. He burst into the hall and dove behind the nurse's station. The assailant fired twice and missed. Jon could see him going door to door. He had a picture in one hand and a 9mm in the other. Jon looked down the hall and could tell it was only a matter of time till he got to Doris' room. He stood and fired. The Smith and Wesson was empty after two rounds. He laid it down on the counter and reached into his pants pocket. With his special version Glock in hand, he tried to move forward. The man shot in his direction again. Jon remembered his Kevlar and stepped out away from the counter. He yelled at the man and walked towards him, firing as he went. The man fired again. Two 9mm slugs hit the Kevlar jacket Jon was wearing and went no further. His knees buckled, but only for a second.

Then Jon saw movement behind the man. Doris's door opened and Ben stepped out into the hall. He yelled, "Hey, Asshole!"

The man turned toward Ben and fired. The impact of the shot knocked Ben down.

In the time that took, Jon had moved to within three feet of the assailant. He fired once and struck him behind the left ear.

Rushing on to Ben to check on him, he found the young man on his face. Jon rolled him over and the 9mm slug fell out of the Kevlar webbing of the jacket Ben was wearing. Ben started to groan and move his arms. He would have a good bruise on the right side of his chest. Ben gasped for air. His breath had been knocked out of him. But that was about it. Score two for the Kevlar jackets today.

The shooting had stopped and it got quiet for a second. Then Jon could hear the sounds of sirens. He was beginning to like that sound. The attackers had either been killed, put to sleep or were standing with their hands up when the reinforcement got there.

Gil and his guys cuffed the survivors. All fifteen were accounted for. Six were still alive. There were no casualties in the hospital other than the one officer who was hit in the arm. He would be fine. Not bad for a rag tag group left to fend for themselves against a near army.

Jon walked by the nurse's station and picked up the borrowed weapon. He and Ben went down the stairs and found Gil.

"I'll take that back, now." Jon told him with a grin.

"Man, where did you learn to shoot like that?" The officer asked.

"It was all you, my friend." Jon winked as he stuck his Glock back into his belt. The smaller one was already put away.

"Me, hell," Gil retorted. "That was the finest shooting I've ever seen."

"Like I said, it was all you, OK?" Jon looked him right in the eye. "I don't need the publicity, please."

Gil Gartner looked back at the man. He smiled and shook his head in the affirmative.

35

Daniel Seay got into Atlanta a couple of hours ahead of the crowd. The shoot out at the hospital added to the industrial plant explosion had put Dalton on the national stage. Media types from New York and L.A were on their way to Georgia and Daniel was only hours ahead of them. He got a rental car and a map. He opted to go around Atlanta and connect with I-75 North on the west side of town. He would get to Dalton as the others arrived at the airport in Atlanta.

It was twenty-four hours after the excitement and ripples were being felt in many places. News was being made all around the eastern side of the Mississippi River. Raids were conducted on any store or kiosk selling Argus goods. Two other vans had been stopped in transit and the drugs uncovered. It would be a matter of days until authorities figured out the greenish logo significance and then track the locations where those boxes went. Argus was busted.

Federal agents went to the offices of Saul DeMarcos in South Beach but found the rooms empty. At about the same time, a small private jet lifted off from Miami International heading south. Saul had been called home.

Representative Charles Harley was in Washington with the other members of Congress. His insulation from the Argus Import scandal was solid. There were rumors in isolated areas but nothing that could be used. It was the same with Dewey Hanson. His one time connection to the group now appeared to be dissolved. Harley held a meeting in Des Moines before leaving for Washington D.C. In attendance were those who had been his local operatives in the Argus

Organization. Harley explained that things would be different. But he emphasized he would not allow it to be over. He demanded time to reorganize what was left of Argus. He asked his people to reach out to other areas and find who was still out there. "Tell them to hang on." The Congressman stated. "The customers are still there. We'll find a way to service them."

~

Daniel started his process in Dalton at the offices of the Daily Citizen Newspaper. The Publisher and Editor, William Gaines welcomed his visitor from "up north" with opened arms. "Welcome south, brother," he quipped. "What, do I need to guess, brings you here?"

"Thanks, Mr. Gaines. I've been following this story for some time. Perhaps not the way you would expect, but with what continues to be a growing lead."

"Now, that's a mouthful. Can you be a little more specific?"

"I'm tracking the serial killer that's been labeled as "The Son.""

"The guy who kills Congressmen? What does that have to do with this?" Gaines asked.

"Like I said, I'm following the story where it takes me." Daniel squirmed a bit in his chair then continued. "This shoot out at the hospital, the hero was a local Police officer?"

"Yep, Gil Garnter. He's a good young man. Known him quite a while."

"I see here," Daniel was holding a copy of Citizen, "that Jonathan Crane was also there. Is that right?"

"He was there. Do you know Jonathan?"

"No, sir. But isn't he the same guy who rescued Doris Shaw from the kidnappers?"

"Well, his position is 'he found her.' We pushed him really hard about it and he maintains he's no hero. 'Right place at the right time,' is what he says."

"And he was involved in the shoot out at the hospital?" Daniel asked.

"According to Gil, Jonathan was there visiting Doris and offered to lend a hand when the shit hit the fan." The editor didn't care to be questioned like this and it started to show.

"Do you think he would talk to me?" Daniel tried to soften his tone.

"Can't say. He's a pretty private guy." The editor thought for a minute. "He grew up here but never made any news till just recently."

"Do you know where I could find him?" Daniel asked.

"He spends a lot of time at the hospital with Doris and her son, Ben." He went on to explain the Trauma Center from the main hospital for him. Daniel thanked him and offered a business card. "If we can ever help you," he said.

"Yeah, thanks for that," the editor replied.

~

Jon Crane was spending the day going through papers in the new warehouse residence. George, the DA, was planning a way to help them move their other belongings. It needed to be done without anyone knowing where they moved. It would take a few days to get that organized, with all the hubbub over the shooting. Guards continued to watch the old neighborhood and the hospital where Doris lay asleep. Ben had held up well through the questioning by the police and FBI. Jon was proud of him. Jon's other new friend, Gil Gartner, reluctantly took the credit for the hospital standoff. George was suspicious of it, but Jon explained that Gil was doing so as a favor to him. The DA understood and in fact, that saved a bunch of explaining on his part as well.

Jon was trying to concentrate on the printouts of special items offered for sale, the ones that his computer programs had found. There wasn't much that interested him. He wondered how the progress was going on the house. He would need to tell Ben about that at some point.

He had called for a wrecker from Gainesville, Georgia to come get his pick-up truck. It needed some repairs to the armor and front bumper. This wrecker was covered. It was more a flatbed with a canvas top. The pick-up could travel without being noticed. The guys in Gainesville had built the truck for him and they would know what to do with it.

As Jon thought about calling his builder and riding out there, the phone rang. It was Ben.

"Hey, there some guy here who wants to talk to you."

"Oh, really?" Jon asked. "What's his story?"

"Well, he says he's following the trail of the Congressional killer." Ben's voice was calm and even.

"Cop?"

"A reporter from Pittsburgh. Says he'd be happy to buy dinner."

Jon took a deep breath and told Ben, "let me talk to him."

Ben handed the phone to the visitor.

"Hello, Mr. Crane?"

"This is Jonathan Crane. How can I help you?"

"Like the young man said, I've been working on a story about the guy they call "The Son." That story seems to be connected to this Argus mess in several ways. I wondered if I could share that with you and maybe you can help me?"

Jon was quiet for a few seconds. Then he offered this, "Can you find the Depot Restaurant? It's on Depot Street off North Hamilton."

"I'll find it, sure." Daniel sounded thankful.

"Alright, 7:30PM. I'll call and put the reservations in my name."

"Thanks, see you there."

Jon asked one more thing. "Put Ben back on, will ya?"

Ben took the phone, "Yeah, Jon?"

"Call me the minute this guy leaves."

"Sure thing." Ben responded and hung up.

Daniel thanked Ben for his help and offered best wishes for his Mom. He left the room and Ben watched from the door till he was on the elevator. Immediately, he redialed Jon.

"What kind of car is he driving?" Jon demanded.

"I don't know, but I can go to the window and watch for him."

"Do that, please." Jon continued. "What is he wearing and what general description can you give me?"

Ben thought about his answer. "He's about 6 feet maybe 190 lbs. Dark hair, clean shaven. He's wearing tan pants and a light blue pullover type shirt. Dark blue jacket and a briefcase."

"Great job, Ben. Have you seen the car, yet?"

"Yeah, he's in a light gray Ford, four door. Like a Taurus, I think."

"Good," Jon was pleased with Ben's details. "This is a white guy, right?"

"Yep," Ben confirmed.

"Ok, I'll see you later tonight, after dinner. Can you deal with it yourself tonight?"

"George is bringing in Chinese, I just need to let him know you won't be here."

Jon needed to clear his head and get ready for tonight. A trip to the new house would do it. He didn't even call the builder.

"Time for a surprise drop in," he told himself.

~

Daniel drove around and asked for directions to the Depot. He wanted to find it now so he wouldn't have any trouble later. After that he rode out Walnut to the expressway area. All the motels were there.

He found a room and good thing he did. Traffic from Atlanta was starting to pour into Dalton as dozens of rental cars and numbers of satellite trucks turned off the expressway, seeking a spot to camp. The media zoo was in town.

36

The house was looking great. Workers were all over the place, some framing the new layout and others in the basement area, removing rock from the new third sub-level.

His builder was a bit surprised but not offended.

"Hey, Sir." He shouted across the first floor. "Good to see you."

"It's looking great. Any problems?"

"No, Sir. Everything is on schedule. Even the excavating."

Jon looked toward the back left corner of the floor.

"Remember I said I would have changes?"

"I sure do, what's on your mind?" The builder grabbed his notebook.

Jon walked him to the corner and spread his arms out wide.

"I'd like a big closet in this area on each floor."

"Each floor?" the builder specified.

"Yes, that includes the basements."

The builder paused, then continued writing and asked, "what size closets?"

Jon tried to step off some distances. "How about 8' X 10'?"

"Sure, we can do that. What else?"

"I want some stairs in there or some way to get from one floor to the other fast."

"Both directions?" the builder asked.

"Mainly down," Jon told him.

"We could do a series of chutes or maybe a fire pole?"

"Interesting." Jon answered. "I like the way you think. Can you get me some examples of your ideas?"

"Yeah, when do you want to come see them, tomorrow?" the builder asked him.

"How about the end of the week?"

The builder was fine with that. They walked around a bit more and Jon asked what the time schedule looked like for completion.

"Four to six months, depending on the weather till we get dried in."

"Ok, that's sounds good." Jon thanked the builder and got back in his car.

"This guy was good," he thought as he backed away from the site. *"I'll need to give him a nice bonus when this is done."*

Jon then drove down the old road. The road that lead toward his gas station project. It was still daylight so there was no progress being made. They only worked at night to keep from drawing attention. The crew chief estimated that they would be far enough into the mountain in about two and half weeks that they could start working 24 hours a day without causing too much notice. That would mean 14 feet per day and at that rate the tunnel would take about six and a half months. That should work out.

He pulled into the station and walked inside. It was dusty and still had junk lying everywhere. Tire displays were mounted to the sidewall and a sales counter, with broken glass front, sat as if untouched for years. A sign in the corner read as it had the day it was taken down, "Regular - $1.42 and 9 tenths." He didn't plan to bring this station back to life. But he did have a use for it, as it was.

The plywood covering the hole in the back wall was awkward to handle, but he moved one piece out of his way. Stepping into the "tunnel," he imagined what would be. The escape route he had not planned for in the old safe room. It wasn't much to see yet. It only went back about 12 feet. But that was still on schedule. At $4500 per yard it would be a $4 million dollar tunnel.

"*A good investment*," he told himself.

~

George Vincent had spent the whole day at the site of the plant explosion. The interior of the space was blasted away and what was left was burned. They collected body parts of eight or nine men in and around the blast site. There were chassis of two vans and three smaller vehicles still inside and they found the tags from the vans. One was Tennessee and the other from North Carolina. It was weird to look at. The chassis, with engines and drive trains, sat on four steel wheels. There was nothing else. They couldn't figure what became of the steering columns or other major components. It was as if they had evaporated.

His experts told him the C4 explosives had been shaped and adhered to the interior walls at about three feet from the floor. Some warehouses put a rubber bumper rail along walls where they plan to use forklift trucks. The C4 could have been molded to look like a bumper rail. Whatever shape they had used, it was intentional.

It directed the force of the blast to the interior of the building. That force traveled from four sides to the middle where it met and then expanded upward and back out with tremendous power. Everything within the building was consumed, other than those chassis, and the particles cast with the debris cloud.

Placement of the charges had been well thought out to accomplish the cleansing that occurred. A lot of trouble to go to, but these guys spared no expense. Not even in human life. The blast was intended to destroy all evidence of what had been in that building. It almost did.

They found enough white powder residue to test for cocaine. The best samples were actually stuck in the tree bark of the pines along the bank. The huge dust cloud created in the explosion had carried some of the plaster and cocaine mix upward. While most was consumed in the flash of fire, enough of the dust was thrown clear and blown into the trees. The samples tested positive, there was no doubt about the cocaine. But the boxes and the black lacquer tables Jon had talked about were gone.

Enough of what Jon had told him had been confirmed. George did not doubt the extent of the operation that had been here. He could use the obvious evidence. The dust in the trees, but that was about it. The gunfire that alerted the police to the area was a mystery. How that building became suspect would never come up. George knew but couldn't say.

His personal quandary was now at a turning point. This guy was useful. In this case alone, it would be impossible to estimate how many lives would be saved. He knew what other things the man had done. Murder could not and should not be condoned. But when George allowed himself to really think about it, he agreed with each "removal."

He couldn't erase what Jon had done for Doris from his mind. What he was doing for Ben. Some of what this man did may be misguided, but there was a need for someone willing to do what he does. If George were to ever turn him in, it had to be now. From this point on he would be considered an accomplice.

George walked to a spot about a block from the destroyed building and turned to study it. The extent to which the Argus people were willing to go would have put them out of reach of the legal system. They knew our legal system's rules and the limitations to justice caused by them. Because of Jon's actions they were out of business. It hadn't taken years and millions of dollars. It didn't cost hundreds of lives in the delays justice would demand. It was just a few days.

George Vincent never said so, even to himself. But he had made his decision.

~

Ben had started walking the halls of the hospital. The cast on his right leg was tolerable and he didn't need the sling for his arm anymore. Exercise was what he lacked. He still stayed close to Doris' room, so he could keep an eye on it. But he knew he needed to walk.

School occupied much of his time these days. He was so far behind he wondered if catching up were even possible. The principal and his teachers were being very supportive. Sending work and even tests to the hospital so Ben could try to stay with his class. Graduation would be next June and no one wanted him to miss that.

He thought a lot about his friend, his guardian and his secret. When feelings of doubt would slip into his mind, the overwhelming respect he had for this man took over. He knew some of what his friend had done was considered wrong. In pure terms, Ben saw them as wrong. Yet another term he had learned, that of mitigating circumstances, would suppress even those scruples. He understood Jon Crane to be a good man. Good men were not perfect. But in the balance of things, you would prefer them to be on your side.

Ben returned to the room from his latest walk and dove right into the books. He had to get the studies done before his other good friend, George Vincent, showed up with dinner.

~

Rep. Charles Harley had a message waiting for him when he returned to his office in the Rayburn Office Building. It was from Saul DeMarcos. The message had been hand carried from Miami and given to a guard at the front desk. After being X-rayed and sanitized it finally got to the congressman's office about a week later. The message was simple and straightforward. *"Received your consul. Much at Stake. Reacting Now."*

Harley's face was flush by both the note and the fact that DeMarcos had sent it directly to him. He walked over to the fireplace in his office and pulled a lighter from his pocket.

The congressman lit the paper and held it by a corner, watching as it was consumed. He threw the last, burning piece into the fireplace and rubbed his hands together.

He asked himself again, *"Why would he do that?"*

37

The Dalton Depot was an actual former train depot. It sat literally on the train tracks that still ran through Dalton. The building is full of history. A mark on the floor that still exists just to the right of the main doors indicated the center of Dalton in 1847. The Dalton Depot played major roles in the Civil War. In hot pursuit of the stolen train engine, The General, Confederate troops ran their engine, the Texas, in reverse. They found a young telegrapher walking his way back towards Atlanta. The telegraph lines had been cut and he sought the location. The stolen train had passed the young man, Edward Henderson, before the Texas found him near Calhoun, Georgia. The Texas picked him up then slowed at Dalton's Depot to let Henderson off. He tried to telegraph Chattanooga to alert forces about the stolen train. Most of his message made it through before the Union highjackers stopped the General long enough to cut the lines again. The rest is history.

The Depot was also the demarcation spot for thousands of troops who would fight in the Battle of Chickamauga.

The interior of the dining room greets guests with a large lobby and huge grain scales reminiscent of the days when produce was shipped through there. Large wooden booths line the sidewalls and the center of the dining room; booths that offered privacy to each set of guests. The open rafter ceiling now housed several ceiling fans. One section of booths sat along the outside wall overlooking the tracks. A good conversation would have to take a break when the freight train came through, and that could be depended on.

Jon arrived early, as he usually did for most things. He sat about a block down on Depot Street and watched the parking lot. At 7:20PM a car, a gray Ford like what Ben had described, pulled into the restaurant's parking area. The man got out and leaned back into the car. He had picked up his notebook. He walked to the front doors and went inside. Jon started his car and moved to the lot himself.

They had seated Daniel, as Jon had requested, in a booth by a window trackside. The hostess walked Jon toward the booth. As they approached, Jon recognized the man he was meeting, touched the hostess' arm and waved her off. "I see him," he told her quietly.

Jon stepped alongside Daniel Seay and reached out his hand.

"Mr. Seay?" He offered.

Daniel stood, causing Jon to back up, and returned the handshake.

"Yes. Call me Dan, please. I take it you're Jonathan Crane?"

"I am. Nice to meet you."

They both sat and Jon asked the man, "Have you ordered a drink?"

"No, I just got here myself. Let me see if I can get the waitress' attention."

"She'll be along in a minute," Jon assured him.

They halfway stared at each other. Not impolitely but still staring. Daniel was sizing this guy up. Could he be the killer? He seemed fit enough. Not really big, but fit. Looked like he ran a lot.

Jon looked down at the table and wondered what this man knew or thought he knew.

"I've been traveling a good bit lately," Daniel started just as the 7:40 from Atlanta to Chattanooga came roaring through. Daniel all but jumped out of his seat and then watched out the window. Completely mesmerized by the train, so close and so loud.

When he looked back at Jon, he was smiling. Jon was recalling Iowa in his mind.

"Got ya, didn't it?" Jon laughed.

"Well, yeah. That was unexpected."

"There'll be another one before we're through. Oh, here she is to take our drink order."

With the drink orders on the way to the bar, Jon restarted the conversation. "So, you were saying you've traveled a lot?"

"Yes, I have. I'm from Pittsburgh and I write political editorials for the Post Gazette. When Rep. Perry was found dead on his boat, I didn't feel too much regret for him. Most Pennsylvanians didn't. But it didn't feel right to me. The way he died."

"So, you're a doctor, too?" Jon fiddled with his glass but didn't look up while asking.

"No, no. I couldn't tell why. It just seemed odd, that's all. Then the others began to pile up."

"Others?" Jon asked.

"Wright in Virginia, LaPointe in Louisiana, all in about 5 or 6 weeks. It just didn't set right."

Jon smiled at the reporter. "Set right?" he repeated. "You don't talk like a Yankee."

"Born in Valdosta and raised in Moultrie till I was 12," Daniel asserted.

"But now you're from?"

"Pittsburgh. Yeah, lived up there 23 years. Met my wife there."

"Well, good. So these men you were telling me about, the ones from Virginia and Louisiana. These men were politicians?" Jon redirected the conversation.

"Right, I thought you knew. Yeah, both were also congressmen."

"That is interesting."

"Then a senator gets his neck caught in some wire and I start thinking there's a connection here somewhere."

"Ok, now there's a senator in this story?" Jon inserted. "I'm having trouble keeping up."

"Oh, yeah. I'm sorry. About the time they announced our replacement for Perry in Pennsylvania; a senator in Texas, well, let's just say he gets dead."

"So, you found a connection in all this?"

"Not just from that. But then somebody started sending messages to the newspapers and the dead congressmen's offices."

"No kidding?" Jon leaned in with feigned interest. "A terrorist group?"

"Well, we don't know. Can't rule it out, I suppose, but it looks more like domestic stuff to me."

"You must have an interesting reason for that idea."

"All these guys were dirty," Daniel explained.

"Dirty?" Jon's expression became more questioning as he cocked his head to one side.

"Mob connections, getting people killed, involved with drugs. One was even a child molester."

"Now I'm really wondering why you wanted to talk to me?" Jon seemed indignant.

"Yeah, it's not like that. I don't think you're in with them or anything." Daniel started to stumble around. "It's the drugs. They seem to connect several of these guys through one company."

The drinks had arrived so it was time to order dinner. Jon took a gulp of his beer and offered, "The filets are great. If you like steak."

Daniel agreed and they ordered.

"So that I can enjoy my meal," Jon started back. "Would you mind explaining how I am connected to your theory? And the drug part especially"

Daniel realized he'd been coming on strong. "I don't mean to offend you, Mr. Crane. Can I call you Jon or Jonathan?"

"Jon will be fine. But please...continue."

"You're kind of a hero around here lately," the reporter tried to tread lightly.

"What?" Jon sat up and tried to look perplexed.

"You're in the papers as the man who saved your neighbor from kidnappers. Then you make national news again at the hospital shootout."

"Being there and being a hero are quite different things, my friend." Jon was dismissive.

"But both deals involved Argus," the reporter insisted.

"Ok, if you say so. What's Argus?"

"They were a big drug cartel working out of Miami. They appear to be out of business at the moment."

"I'm still lost, man. Can you put a bow around this so I can see what you're trying to say?" Jon twisted in his seat and leaned forward over the table.

"It looked like you were going after Argus. I just wanted to ask you about it."

"No. I don't know Argus from Arby's. How does that connect with your dead politicians?"

"Three of the four who died and then had messages sent to their offices, were connected to Argus." Daniel spelled out what he knew.

Jon realized he could make this work in his favor if he played it right. He took a breath and looked up at Daniel.

"I'm not flattered, but I can see how you came to your questions." Jon was firm and sounded offended. "My involvement is coincidental, period. My neighbor's kid got beat up and one thing led to another. That's all."

Daniel tried to apologize for the implications.

"Maybe I got caught up in my own story. I've been talking to so many people about this in the last weeks. I've been to Texas, a real sad story there. Not so much for the senator but his family. They knew about him. He wasn't into the drug thing, but he hurt little kids. It was really bad." Daniel took a swallow of his drink and continued.

"Then to Louisiana. The guy there, LaPointe, was a piece of work." The reporter's eyes were darting about as he recalled what he had learned. "The bastard let some poor guy die to make a point... nice, huh?"

Jon looked concerned but did not change his expression.

"Then I get called to Iowa." Daniel looked directly at Jon who tried not to react, but he knew he had. He took a swallow of his beer, in a delay to allow his mind to settle, and then asked calmly,

"Iowa? You hadn't mentioned Iowa, before."

"I think the next one to die is from Iowa." Daniel confided.

"Next one? He's still alive, then?" Jon was being coy.

"Yeah, but I know the guy was there. I just missed him."

"The guy?" Jon asked, looking right at him, "So you have a suspect." Leaning back in the booth, he finished, "Who is it?"

"I don't know." Daniel got quieter and took a swig from his drink glass. "The press calls him 'The Son.' Surely you've read about it? They say he almost got caught in Iowa."

"I don't pay much attention to the news," Jon said bluntly.

"It was a very big deal." Daniel continued. "Made the national news. An editor lost his job over it."

"Like I said," Jon was calm and firm, "I don't watch the news that much, except cable sometimes."

"Well, anyway, the man I believe is the next victim. He was in Atlanta last week."

Jon squirmed again. He thought to himself, *"How could this reporter know about that?"*

He gathered his composure and asked, "You followed this man down here?"

"Oh, no. But we had folks watching him. He came down here, all right. Charles Harley, himself."

"Interesting." Jon replied and finished his beer. He waved for the server to bring him another. "How about yours? Could you use another Sam Adams?"

"Yeah, thanks." Daniel watched the man across the table. He was cool. He was calculating. But he did seem vulnerable in one area of the discussion.

The servers were arriving with their dinners. Jon placed his napkin in his lap and looked back at Daniel. "Let's enjoy our meal, OK? I hope you can find this guy, I really do. I just don't see how I can help you."

"It was just some questions I had. Thought it best to just come right down here and ask you in person."

"You certainly did that." Jon smiled.

"Jon, I appreciate your taking time to talk with me. It has helped, it really has."

They ate and talked about other things for an hour. Local fishing, a little trash talk about college football, some discussion of family, mostly just guy stuff. The train interrupted them once more during dinner.

When they had finished and walked to the door the two men shook hands. "Thanks again, Jon. I appreciate your time and I'm glad I met you."

"You're a little hard to get to know," Jon laughed. "But I'm pleased to meet you. Good Luck with all this and thanks for dinner."

"My pleasure, Jon. Thank you for coming."

Jon went to his car and Daniel went to his.

Inside the gray Ford, Daniel made one note in his book. Jon Crane's reaction to the mention of Iowa had not gone unnoticed.

38

Washington D.C. was busy this session. Summer was over and the congress was out to pass everything they could, spending wise, while the public's mind was still on vacation.

Dewey Hanson had received a letter from Ft. Oglethorpe, Georgia. The letter said little to Hanson other than asking if he would forward an enclosed note to Rep. Charles Harley of Iowa.

Hanson had one of his aids walk the sealed note to Harley's office. The entire letter had been through the screening process, so Hanson saw no harm. The aid left the note with Darlene, Harley's receptionist. Darlene, believing the Congressman might not be in the office till after she left for the day, put the note on Harley's desk.

Charles Harley got to his congressional office after 6:00PM that evening. He made a couple of phone calls back to his district to check on activity there. While on the phone, he noticed the note. It was in the same hand as the first note, the one he had burned.

This was not the way they communicated. DeMarcos knew that. Why was he doing this?

It wasn't Harley's fault that things went haywire. Was that young jerk trying to implicate him with the Argus Group?

He unfolded the message. Similar to the last one, it was printed and direct in its remarks.

"Plan Failed, Trucks Found, Your Trip Failed."

Harley was livid. He crumbled the note in his hand and pounded his fist on the desk. Who was doing this? This wasn't DeMarcos. He would never dare to threaten him like this.

Harley unwrapped the note and set fire to it. His trashcan was empty, so he dropped the flaming paper in there. He called for head of staff.

"Who left this note on my desk?" he demanded. The man didn't have any idea. "Well find out, damn it. I want to know who's doing this."

~

Jon Crane got to the hospital after visiting hours. George had gone home but remnants of the meal he brought lingered.

"Want some Kung Pao Beef?" Ben asked his friend.

Jon waved his hand in front of his face and declined.

"Thanks," he teased. "But I could smell it all the way up in the elevator. Did ya'll have a good evening?"

"Absolutely. The doctors say Mom's condition is much better. They are going to wake her up tomorrow." The young man was beaming.

Jon shook his fist and then grabbed the kid in a hug. "Oh, man. That's great. It's been a long couple of weeks. We all needed some good news."

"How was your evening?" Ben asked.

"Fine. He thinks he knows more than he does." Jon tried to sound convincing.

"I got a great steak out of the deal." He laughed and hugged the kid again. Then Ben looked at him with a serious expression.

"We had a bunch of reporters try to get in here tonight. George turned them away."

"Good for him. It's going to be that way for a few days I'm afraid."

"They were looking for you." Ben looked concerned.

Jon grunted and shook his head, " We just need to be patient and concentrate on your Mom. Ok?"

"I hear ya." Ben turned his attention to his mother and they both got quiet.

They stood around Doris' bedside for a few minutes and then Jon stated very matter of fact, "I'm getting out of here so you can get some sleep. Big, big day tomorrow!"

Jon walked and took the stairs down to the first floor. He left through the far side doors of the hospital, just in case. No one was there. He drove back to his warehouse residence with his mind spinning. He couldn't get what that reporter had said out of his mind.

~

In Atlanta, Georgia Juan Castrono patiently waited for word of what to do. His boss, Armando, was gone. All normal connections to the leadership were severed. He had only three men left in his camp and enough money to pay them two more weeks. Juan was the thinker. Armando was the heavy. That's why Armando was in charge. But now it appeared that no one was in charge. Things were coming undone.

They had two loaded cargo ships still at sea. The Cheri' and the Austin Matel were already taking the slow route to New Orleans. Each was loaded with black lacquer tables from Columbia, half with the gold logos and half with the markings of the more valuable load. The Feds would be looking for the tables so their usefulness was gone. Or so Juan thought.

The message came in through an alternate but acceptable channel. It was from the "Bird."

Juan had met the Bird only one time. He had been instructed to pick him up at the airport and drive him to Dalton to look around. The man never spoke to him directly. He and Armando had done all the talking. The plan they had devised that day ended poorly. Now here were instructions of yet a new plan, much more involved and incredibly expensive.

The Bird ordered the ships to return to Cartagena, Colombia to be unloaded. New greenish gold logo boxes were to be sent to the port, empty. The regular plaster tables from the Cheri' were to be repackaged in the new boxes. The cocaine tables from both ships were to be returned to Bogotá for a new configuration. The Austin Matel would be reloaded with all regular plaster tables. But half would be in boxes the Feds thought they were looking for. The port for arrival in the U.S. would now be Jacksonville, Florida.

The cost of this would be substantial. But it would keep the U.S. Government busy and frustrate them at the same time. There was no mention of a new location for the product's distribution or what new shape it would be in. That would come later.

Juan was relieved to have some communication from somewhere. These instructions were major responsibilities and he knew it. Failure would not be tolerated. Using procedures already in place, he contacted the ships and gave them their new destination.

~

Representative Charles Harley of Iowa would miss two important votes that day. In his mind, it couldn't be helped. Another of those damned messages had arrived. This one from Tennessee and sent directly to his office. The message shook him to his core. "Peter says to tell you, Terrence and Pedro are fine. They could not stay long. They were expected in another location." The references to these three people could only come from someone who knew. No one was supposed to know. Harley fought the urge to panic. He'd been in tough situations before. Right now he was attempting to reconfigure the entire drug enterprise. He didn't need this distraction.

He picked up a direct line phone to his office in Des Moines. The office manager answered on the second ring. "Yes Sir?"

"Put Henry on the phone, now."

"Yes, Sir."

There was a pause for a minute, maybe less and people could be heard scurrying around.

Then the response he was waiting for. "This is Henry."

"Get together everything, and I mean everything, you can on that situation in Burlington last month. I want information on who knows what, got it?"

"Yes, Sir."

We'll meet for coffee at the usual place at 10:30AM tomorrow. Is that clear?"

"10:30 tomorrow, got it."

The line went dead on Henry. He knew the usual spot was a diner just outside of Winchester, Virginia. It was quiet and had only light traffic on weekdays. The Congressman would drive over in about an hour and a half. Henry would fly to Baltimore and then rent a car. They had met there many times. They could speak in private without worry of being overheard.

Henry started putting out calls for information. He couldn't show up there empty handed.

That would not be wise.

39

Daniel's morning started off early. He had talked with his boss for an update on his progress. Earl Johnstone had called from Iowa and left his number. He would return Earl's call after this appointment. The Police Chief of Dalton had told Daniel he needed to talk with the DA for any information on the cases, either of them. They were treating the kidnapping and the building explosion as separate issues.

George Vincent was in his office at the appointed time and asked the reporter to come in.

"They tell me you've been following this case around the country."

"Well, sort of," Daniel answered. "I feel like its pulling more than me following sometimes. Things seemed to come to a head here."

"Oh, really? So our little town is the center of this nation-wide crime spree, huh?"

"If I thought that might be your fault, I'd apologize. But its not and your general statement is more accurate than you might like to think."

"Look," the DA responded, "I may be a little defensive right now. And there could well be more for us to learn about what was going on out at that old carpet plant. If you have anything that can enlighten me, I'd love to hear it."

"Sir, I had dinner with Jonathan Crane last night. Do you know him?"

George was taken back but didn't show it. "I know Mr. Crane. He's the neighbor of my employee who got hurt."

"He's also the man who rescued her, isn't he?"

"What did you say your name was, again?" George asked deliberately.

"Daniel Seay, Sir."

"Daniel, Jonathan Crane did a brave thing. He tells us he just found her. He's sticking to that and we have nothing to the contrary. That's all I can tell you because that's all I know." George gave the man a look that said the interview was over.

Daniel didn't pick up on it. "Did you question Crane about the shoot-out at the hospital?"

"Our police department did. And they were quite satisfied and thankful for his help in that situation." George stood this time, "I appreciate your interest but I don't understand where you are going with this."

Daniel stood also and extended his hand in gratitude. "Like I said Sir, it's not so much going anywhere as being pulled. I thank you for your time. Nice to meet you."

George walked him to the door and Daniel nodded as he went out. Walking back to his desk George thought, "it isn't going to be easy keeping a lid on this. What have I gotten myself into?"

Daniel's thoughts were more in line with his awareness of political answers and knowledge of human behavior. The man he just left was either naive or protecting a friend. He didn't look too naïve to Daniel. There wasn't much he could do except gather more information. He needed to find a quiet phone so he could call Earl back.

~

The doctors gave Doris a stimulant to counteract the induced coma at 6:00AM. By 9:00AM it was starting to show signs of working. Her fingers on her right hand moved.

It was very slight, but Ben could see it. The nurse agreed with him.

Jon arrived around 9:25AM and was asking Ben questions about the progress so far when they both heard a very soft voice, "Ben?" it asked.

"Mom, Mom, yeah, its me. I'm right here." Ben grabbed her good hand and held on. Jon stepped back out of the way as the nurse worked with one machine and a doctor came running into the room. Jon stretched his neck to see what he could. Doris' eyes were flickering.

"Easy now," the doctor stated to her sternly. "Just breathe easy and relax."

The flickering eyes began to stay open longer and Ben said she squeezed his hand. He smiled through the tears running down his face and softly repeated, "Mom," over and over.

After a couple of minutes her eyes appeared to focus and she turned her head toward her son. The doctor let him hug her gently and then asked him to step back so they could check her further. Jon was standing four feet behind the bed, his left arm across his chest supporting his right elbow. His right hand was cupped over his mouth. Ben grabbed his friend and hugged him, muttering "thank you, thank you" to the man that had saved her from the evil.

Jon could see someone, through the corner of his eye, at the door. It was George Vincent.

Jon turned to the door. "George," he called to him. "You're right on time, man. She's awake."

~

Henry Dowd sat in the parking lot of the Triangle Diner. He had been there since 9:45AM, but better early than late. The Congressman's car pulled into the lot at 10:20AM. Both men got out and walked toward the door of the diner without any wave or acknowledgement of each other. The lady behind the counter pointed to a booth near the end of the building. Dowd and his boss went and sat down.

"What did you find out?" Harley started with. The waitress was there and they ordered coffee.

Dowd let the server leave the area before he answered. "You were being watched for one thing." He told the congressman.

"By whom?"

"The paper in Des Moines hired some smuck, private investigator to watch your movements."

"What did they expect to get from doing that?" Harley asked.

"Well, they know about the trip to Atlanta, I can tell you that."

The congressman's face flushed red. "I told DeMarcos I shouldn't do that. He insisted I look the situation over and tell them what to do. Damn."

"The private dick is now off the case." Henry Dowd puffed out his chest and continued. "I suggested he find another avenue for employment."

"Who at the paper, did he work for?" Harley asked.

"He didn't know. It was just the paper. They were doing it for another paper. At least that's what we think."

The coffee arrived. Harley looked out the window and fumed. He didn't want the server to see his expression. Henry Dowd added his sugar and cream and asked the boss, "Sweet and Low?"

"Why do you think there's another paper involved?" Harley demanded.

"This guy from Pittsburgh has been all over Burlington asking questions. They say he'd been to other murder sites, you know, Texas and Louisiana." Henry told him.

"Is this about the story the Burlington paper ran?"

"Yeah, that's the one. The Pittsburgh guy thinks you're on the list. Next maybe."

"Who's doing the killings?" the congressman asked.

"Nobody knows. That's the thing, he's in the wind."

Charles Harley sat quietly and drank his coffee. He thought and considered what to do about this. Then he looked up at Dowd and said. "I've been getting these dumb messages. They are supposed to be from Saul but I know they aren't. Could this reporter guy be sending them?"

"I don't know about that, boss."

"Ok. You know what we're doing with the two shipments, right?" Harley changed the subject.

"The coke?" Henry blurted out.

"Yeah, don't say that in public. You know what's going on there, right?"

"Yes, sir."

"Alright, I don't have time to screw with this reporter right now. I want you to put someone on his ass and keep up with his goings on. Make sure the hubs are manned and ready for the new product when it ships, we are way behind."

"Ok, boss. You want me to just get this reporter clown out of the way?" Henry had handled such as that before.

"No, we don't know what all he's into. That might bring attention to us we don't need. Just keep an eye on him till I'm ready to talk to him."

"You're going to talk to him?" Henry Dowd seemed surprised.

"Just do what I said. And make sure those guys at the hubs are ready. I haven't heard what the new shape will be yet." Harley leaned in toward Henry's ear, "But it won't be lacquered tables, I can tell you that."

With that, Congressman Charles Harley put two dollars on the table and left. Henry knew to wait and let his boss drive away before he got up. It was what they did.

~

Daniel had called Earl Johnstone back and the news wasn't good. Johnstone reported that his contact in Des Moines said the investigator had quit.

"Wouldn't discuss it with them, he just quit." Earl told him. Somebody got to him, was the obvious conclusion. But, there wasn't much you could do if the man would not talk.

"How are you doing in Georgia?" Johnstone had asked Daniel.

Daniel was cryptic but had told his friend he had some verification to his theory. He didn't want to over sell just yet. Truth was, it was about time to head for home and let things settle for a while. The man Daniel suspected was busy with other things right now. He felt "the Son" would act slowly and deliberately anyhow. The Harley hit was still on, he was sure of it. It was simply in a delay.

What had happened in Dalton, Georgia would only add to the time delay.

40

Other than a severe headache the first couple of days she was awake, Doris' recovery was very pleasing to the doctors. The leg and arm had been set, as had the fingers. They would heal in time. Her ribs had been reset and the lung re-inflated while she was out. Her comatose state had been a benefit to her in the early stages of the healing. The pain would have been nearly intolerable for a conscious patient.

Her concussion showed no signs of permanent damage. The blow had been dangerously close to causing a fracture, but her skull was intact. The doctors said the headaches were a good sign and would diminish over the next few days. She was kept sedated most of the time, awake but not too alert, in effort to help with the pain.

The doctors suggested that Ben could be away some now. It was no longer necessary for him to be there every minute. School was still out of the question for security reasons. But he could leave with his guardian. Doctors reworked the cast on his leg again and made it more comfortable for him to move around. Leaving the hospital took a good bit of convincing but Jon managed to gain his interest. He told Ben there were several things he wanted to show him. Ben didn't know what they were, but he knew what it meant.

Jon let Ben out of the car near the first warehouse. The stairs from the parking deck and the walk would be too much for him right now. Within five minutes Jon was back, on foot, but only for a few minutes. He directed Ben to a side panel on the warehouse that he opened with the push of a button. The button was under a window ledge near the panel.

In the center of the floor sat a 2007 Ford 500 sedan. Jon had picked this one because it sat higher than a regular car and had wide door panels. That would make it easier for Ben to get in and out of. It was a new car in the stable. Jon had driven to North Atlanta to find it, just for this purpose.

As Jon drove the car toward the corner of the building he took a remote switch from his shirt pocket. There had not been time to have one wired into the Ford yet. Ben looked at Jon with concern as they picked up speed in the direction of a solid wall. Jon touched the remote and a large panel slid open. The Ford was suddenly in an alley alongside the warehouse. When the remote was activated again, the panel closed. Jon slowed at the intersection with the main street and then turned right. Ben's education was just beginning.

Several blocks later, they were approaching the main warehouse. Jon laid the first remote down and picked up another one from the seat. At forty-five miles per hour he hit that switch and veered the car to the left. The side of the warehouse opened and they were inside the building in an instant. Their speed decreased only slightly as they went down the ramp to the basement area. Jon parked close to the elevator and got out. Ben sat where he was and looked around at the vehicles.

"Are these all yours?" he asked

"Yep. One is out for repairs, but it should be back next week," Jon replied.

The elevator ride to the third level was quiet. When Ben stepped out and saw the equipment there he stopped and looked at Jon.

"How can you afford all this?"

"Ben, you need to sit down and let me tell you a few things."

He sat Ben in an Executive desk chair in front of the main computer screens. Reaching into a drawer Jon took out a passbook from a bank.

"This one is for you," he told the boy.

With a very puzzled look, Ben flipped open the passbook and his mouth fell open.

"This can't be for real," he said.

"It's real enough. If you're going to work with me I need you to have access to resources you might require."

"But, this says there's five million dollars in this account."

"There will be times I need you to get me a few things. I don't want money to be an obstacle."

"I don't understand." Ben started.

"There's a signature card you need to sign and I'll get that turned in for you."

"What is all this, Jon?"

Jon paused, almost as in disgust. He turned and walked to the end of the aisle he had created with the computers and the flat screen TVs. He rubbed his mouth and walked back to Ben, with much quicker steps this time.

"You know what I do," he said. He took a deep breath. What he wanted to say next was extremely important to him and he wanted it to be just right. He decided to make it simple.

"Do you have any idea, why I do it?" He asked the young man.

Ben stared at him. His mind raced looking for an answer. The men Jon had killed were bad. They had all done very bad things. Some would say they deserved to be killed. But that didn't justify it, not really. He decided to remain quiet and wait for Jon to finish.

Jon pointed to a row of books on a temporary shelf. "You've seen my books, you told me you noticed them," he started.

Ben looked toward the shelves. They were all there. He had looked at them at the house but had not noticed that they were here. The sense of just how important they were to Jon began to take over in Ben's mind.

"Have you read any of them?" Jon asked.

"I looked through several of them at the house," he answered.

"I want you to read as many as you can." Jon walked to the shelf and continued. "There was a reason this country was started, and rules for how it was to be run. The ideal that men could govern themselves was basic. There was sacrifice involved in serving as a representative back then. Today the sacrifice is demanded of the people rather than the servants of the people. Our representation has changed. It's been taken over by professional politicians. Those who spend their time staying in power instead of working for the people."

He grabbed another chair and sat down beside Ben.

"Nearly all of them are what I would call criminals. They have violated their oaths of office and taken advantage of their positions."

Jon paused to gather his thoughts. He didn't want to say this wrong.

"Those congressmen are responsible to the people and the people should deal with them."

Looking directly at Ben, he squeezed the arm of his chair firmly and let out a breath before continuing.

"It's up to the people to remove them, not me or any other individual."

Jon seemed to relax somewhat having gotten that out. His gaze then went to the floor and his voice became softer.

"But there are the exceptions. Those who go beyond the pale and do things that prevent the people from having the truth about them, or prevent them from acting on it."

Jon's head tilted up toward Ben and the young man could see the anger in his mentor's eyes as he spoke again.

"Some even destroy others who attempt to expose them. By destroy, I mean even having them killed."

With that Jon stood again and stepped back toward his books. He reached out, touching several volumes at once and continued.

"That sort of thing sets a very bad example. It can't be allowed to work for them. That's the message I'm trying to get to these elected officials. If the people they represent want to send them back by legitimate vote that's their business. But there's a line they should not cross just to insure that happens. They don't get to hurt or kill others to curtail the truth."

Ben finally spoke. "Are you sure they did what you think they did?"

"I spend more time, money and effort verifying the accusation than I do exercising the removal." Jon was very assertive. "If I have any doubt, any at all; I leave it to the people."

He sat back down and pulled his chair right up to Ben's. He looked directly into Ben's eyes.

"If there is no doubt, I act. These criminals spend the peoples' money to maintain their power. I spend my own to remove them."

Jon pushed his chair away from Ben's and leaned back into it. He stared at his young friend and asked, "Still proud to know me?"

The young man, who had known this friend for years without really knowing everything, suddenly knew and understood. It was this man and his thinking processes that saved his Mother's life. Someone who could not act, as Jon was capable of, would not have saved Doris.

Ben answered the question in a firm voice, "Yes, Sir. I sure am."

"Good," Jon shook his head affirmatively. "This business with Argus has taught me there's more out there to be dealt with. Not just the evil politicians. I will need help. I will need your help."

Jon stood and smiled at his protege. There was no ceremonial handshake, only the shared look of complete agreement. With a brief nod, Jon turned and left.

Ben looked back at the books, and smiled. He knew about Jon before today, now he understood.

The next several days, when not visiting his Mom, Ben spent time reading and checking out the computer systems. Ben was a techno geek. He had immediate ideas on how to improve the data streams and filters to get what Jon needed from his systems.

He looked through the gadgets that printed out and was fascinated by some of them. Jon showed him the toys he already had.

Ben commented that there was so much more available that should be in their arsenal.

"You've got a bank account. Use it," Jon said firmly and then he explained the delivery methods that he used.

"In a few weeks we'll go check out the new house," he told Ben.

"New house?" the boy asked.

"Yeah, its not ready for you to see it yet. It won't be ready to move in to for months, but we'll go see it when it gets to a certain point."

Jon realized he was supposed to meet with the builder about the slide system. The method he would use to get to the subbasement in a hurry. He left Ben to his work and excused himself.

41

The DeMarcos family had their black lacquered, cocaine tables melted down and the product extracted. It took them a while to come up with the new shape for smuggling.

One of Saul's cousins was in the auto parts business. He imported shocks and brakes from Japan, China and Taiwan. They were concerned that the same basic idea, molding the cocaine into shapes, would be discovered too quickly. They came up with the idea of small touch up paint spray cans. The cans were made of heavy aluminum and packaged under pressure. Rather than paint, a liquid solution of the product could be placed in the cans and marked by certain colors. The main idea of a central distribution facility remained in the plan. Most imported products are handled in that manner. The legitimate cans would still go to the shops that sold spray paint and the special colors would be directed to the hubs. There, the product would again be reconstituted and sent to dealers on the east coast.

The issue would be gaining control of the main receiving and distribution warehouse. For the east coast, that the DeMarcos family controlled, that facility was in Richmond, Virginia. This was not far from the port at Norfolk where the goods came in. The warehouse handled many other items besides the cans of spray paint. The family was not in position to take over the entire operation, that's not what they do. So they set up a dummy corporation claiming to sell touch up paints and bondo products. They offered a price slightly higher than its value to the company receiving the paint and its distribution rights.

Harley, AKA the Bird, didn't like the Richmond location because it was too close to Washington, DC.

They went down the road to Charlotte, North Carolina and found an empty warehouse there. The Patch and Paint Company was born. They took over the distribution of existing brands of touch up materials and co-opted the brand names for use on the cans of cocaine solution. The cans would be intermingled before loading on the ships and sorted out in Charlotte. Quite similar to the Argus tables but still completely different.

The first several shipments were completely legitimate. Regular products were shipped as usual, establishing the business and rerouting the goods to retail stores east of the Mississippi. The coming product vans made test runs during this time. Carrying regular paints, again, to establish their presence as a normal part of the business. Juan had his units staffed and ready. His Atlanta area location moved from the south side of town to northern Atlanta suburb of Doraville. The Birmingham plant moved similarly as did all the locations for receiving the cocaine.

Through the proper channels, Juan Castrono notified Charles Harley that they were ready. Harley contacted the DeMarcos family and a date was set to begin moving the product.

That date would be five and a half weeks after the Dalton explosion.

~

Writing regular opinion pieces and covering local political haggling was a boring change from being on the road and chasing a killer. Daniel went back to being a reporter though, while he waited for something to break in the other case. There was more than one time he felt like he was being watched, but couldn't confirm it. That seemed silly anyway. Reporters were the ones who did the watching.

Lori Seay was glad to have her husband home for a while. Chores had stacked up and she had a list waiting for him. They went out to dinner and the movies again. Life went back to normal for several weeks.

~

The builder was making great progress on the house. Weather was good and he was motivated. The first floor was completely framed out and they were working on the second. The third level basement was dug out and the blasting was under way for the recessed garage area down there.

Jon had called this time so the man was expecting him. He had the prototype of the elevator on site. It was a cross between an elevator and dumbwaiter, a three-foot round cylinder that rode on a pole through its middle. The unit had a floor and a control panel. The single rider could select whatever level he wished to go to, up or down. That was a plus. It was quiet and would only take up a portion of the space Jon had set aside on each floor. Jon was pleased with the idea. The only thing was, he would need two, one for Ben.

They walked to the area set aside for Ben's room, that Ben didn't know about yet, and asked the builder could he fit one into the closet there as well. He might need to move a wall or two a few feet, but basically the answer was yes. Cost for each unit was reasonable, around $40,000 each, plus installation. Jon shook his builder's hand and thanked him for his effort and what he had found. They would be perfect. He wrote the man a check for his additional expenses on this new feature and received a copy of the change order marked paid.

The service station work had made the curve and was now well into the tunneling toward the house. Work was progressing 24 hours a day and they were averaging 13 feet per day. Slightly behind expectations but enough that could be made up as they got the bugs worked out. As he walked into the station area, his cell phone rang. It was Ben at the warehouse.

A strange message had come through one of the computers.

"Sorry to bother you with this but it looked like it might be important." Ben started.

It was from a member of Jon's unknown assistants group. Normally they only monitor the Congressional representatives but this note was different.

"He's concerned about some new company moving into the Springfield area of Illinois," Ben continued. "He says they had bought an empty 40,000 square foot distribution center building off I-55 and paid above going prices in the area. They moved in very quickly and set up shop within a week. Trucks coming and going daily."

From what the person relayed in the message the new company sold patching materials and spray paint for cars.

"He doesn't like the looks of the people who hang around the building." Ben told Jon. "That's a weird thing to say."

Jon told Ben he would be there in a few minutes.

"Its probably nothing, but could be worth looking into further," he told his young helper.

Jon got into his car and headed to his warehouse hideout. His inspection of the tunnel could wait.

~

The "assistant" from Illinois was taking a chance. He figured it was 60/40 but still worth it. A 56-year-old man who had lost a daughter to drugs, he had been an "assistant" for about five months. His daughter had died three years ago, that ordeal refocused his life.

He had appealed to his congressman when he found the plant in Peoria a couple of years ago. Nothing was done. He felt sure that

Congressman was dirty. He heard about "the missions," as they called it, through a web chat room and sent a message offering to help.

After three tries he was answered and accepted as an assistant. While working in the Internet technology department of a major company for years, he had developed skills in tracing Internet messages. He had traced an auto response to his first offer to help. The IP address came back as from somewhere in north Georgia. He remembered that fact.

The congressman he thought was involved in the drugs turned out not to be. He had no real evidence to offer in that regard. But, the coincidence of the Dalton, Georgia explosion and the plant in Peoria shutting down at practically the same time, was too much to ignore. He had watched the activity in Peoria for years. Taking pictures and several tag numbers of vehicles frequenting the plant. The trucks in Springfield were different, they didn't say "Argus" on the sides, but three of the tags were the same. He smelled relocation of the drug operation and local police were not interested. He didn't know whom else to contact.

Remembering the Dalton IP hit and guessing the guy he was helping had something to do with the Dalton bust, he took a risk. If the man now known as "the Son" had been involved in the Dalton drug bust he needed to know about this possible resurgence. If it wasn't him, well, then it wasn't him.

He would never turn him in or cause him harm. He wanted to help with what the man was doing, for his daughter and himself.

42

Jon arrived at the warehouse and looked over the message. It was as Ben had relayed it. Not much more and none less.

"I'll need to talk with this guy to evaluate his information. Sending messages back and forth takes time, even with the internet," Jon lamented.

"I can set you up with a blind chat room," Ben offered.

Jon had no idea what that meant. He didn't ask he just looked at Ben inquisitively.

"Here, let me show you." Ben sat down and started acquiring the protocols for the chat room. "Ok, now all you need to do is send him one message, asking him to use this code to enter the chat at the time you want."

"Then what?" Jon was getting interested.

"Then you two talk back and forth in real time. He doesn't see you and you won't see him."

"Huh?" Jon's response wasn't as dense as he sounded. "Make it happen," he told Ben.

Ben typed out the message in Jon's regular site, asking the assistant to sign in at around 5:00PM EST.

"Now, we wait till just before 5PM and then we watch the chat room," Ben told Jon.

While they waited for the appointed hour, Ben showed Jon a couple of items he had found in web searches of gadgets.

"Do you have night vision goggles?" he asked.

"Not really, I hear they can be dangerous if a light comes on, even outside."

"These adjust. Seriously, the lenses adjust like your pupils and just as fast. The Army didn't take them because of the weight. I can fix that," Ben boasted.

"How would you fix the weight?" Jon asked.

"Simple. I'll remount the lenses on lighter frames. That's what the inventors are going to do. We can get three pairs, as they are now, for $50,000."

"Ok, do it." Jon liked being a CEO.

"Oh, and you need a black out suit."

"I don't wear costumes. I have my Kevlar clothes."

"Think of the Seals," Ben challenged him. "It's not a costume and it has a new liquid armor system. They call it STF, for Shear Thickening Fluid."

"I have Kevlar. I'm used to that." Jon was insistent.

"Jon, this stuff soaks into Kevlar. It molds to it and bends and flexes like skin. When it gets hit the liquid stiffens and stops the projectile."

Jon wasn't sure about the suits. But he knew he needed to give Ben the benefit of the doubt at least once on decisions like this. "Go for it, you can get my sizes from the other stuff."

"I'm not ready to suggest this right now, but I'm looking at some neat rope, too."

Jon gave a look of disgust.

"Really," Ben continued. "They are repelling ropes re-enforced with your favorite stuff."

"Kevlar ropes?" Jon laughed. "What do I need with that?"

"Let me check them out and then I'll tell you. They could be very useful."

They spent the next couple of hours checking their inventory and reordering what was getting low. Delivery addresses and accounts used were dispersed as usual. Ben turned a monitor on at 4:50PM and punched in their protocol and codes. This put Jon in a "queue" outside the chat room but where he could watch for the other party. At 4:58PM that other party signed on.

"334512 here as asked," he typed.

Jon verified that number as the assistant he was expecting, then asked for further verification.

"Last three words of your last transmission on regular site," Jon entered.

There was a delay while the other end looked up what he had sent. Finally the screen displayed, "still can help."

Jon shook his head. "That's right," he told Ben.

Ben tapped Jon's shoulder. "Tell him," he said.

Jon acknowledged and the talk began. Jon asked why the man had sent him the info?

The response was, he hoped that Jon could do something. "I was hoping you were in on the Dalton, Georgia bust of Argus." he typed.

Jon looked at Ben. "That's the first mention of Argus he's made, isn't it?"

"Yeah, he didn't say anything about Argus in the first message," Ben confirmed.

"What makes you think I care about Argus?" Jon typed.

"I was just hoping you did. If not, then I took a shot and lost," was the answer.

"Maybe I do care," Jon returned. "What street address in Springfield is this new building?"

"Thank God," the next message said. "This bunch just can't stay in business."

Jon did not respond to that one.

The Illinois assistant sent the physical address of the new plant. Jon responded and asked the man to stay back and keep his ears open.

"I'll be in touch," was the last thing Jon typed to him.

Jon and Ben looked at each other.

"They're back!" Ben stated.

"They never left," Jon corrected him.

~

The DA had spent considerable time with Doris since she regained consciousness. The headaches were much better. The doctors had cut back on her medication levels to allow her more awareness. Conversations were much better. George didn't interfere with Ben's time. Ben never missed mealtime to help his Mother with her meals. Jon made sure of that. Ben also spent more time away. That gave George more opportunity to be with her. They would talk small talk about the office and her friends there. George bragged on Ben and how he had stood by her through the worst days. He told her bits and pieces of Jon's involvement in her rescue. She wasn't aware of any of that and George figured Jon wouldn't have much to say about it.

They talked a little about the drug case she had been working on. Her case was really over with. The discovery of the carpet plant and its destruction had sealed that. George gently explained that situation to her and tried to figure out what had happened to her briefcase. What was in it, if anything? Her memory was not solid in some short-term areas. She knew the briefcase had important papers in it, but wasn't sure if they were still there when she was taken. She really didn't remember much about her abduction, and George didn't push that. He preferred she didn't remember that.

What had motivated the Argus people to go as far as they did was still a bit of a mystery. George took Jon's theory into account. Jon still felt that Ben's interference with the shakedown of that kid, and his getting beat up for it, had set things in motion. The fact remained; they knew Doris was working on a case against them. How did they know that? Nothing was public at that point.

The current case against Argus in Whitfield County and Dalton was down to paperwork. The local players were gone or dead. The operation was closed. There wasn't much to do except clean up the mess and close the books on it. Records of the evidence they had found would be kept and shared with other jurisdictions. Argus had been there, but the effects of the explosion had all but erased any sign of their presence.

He told her he would have to miss their afternoon visit today. Jon had called this morning asking a favor. He wanted to know if George had any contacts in Illinois, particularly the Springfield area? He hadn't given him any details over the phone. They planned to meet later that afternoon to discuss it. Ben would come in early to be with her. Doris smiled and closed her eyes. She took several naps each day. It was time for one now.

43

Representative Charles Harley was generally pleased with the progress of the Patch and Paint Company. There were rumblings about the Springfield hub making too many waves with their move, but nothing had come of it. All seemed set and ready for the start date.

Each hub had made trial runs to Charlotte and brought back regular spray paint. Those cans were recycled back into the inventory for normal distribution to retailers.

The reports Harley had received about the Pittsburgh meddler were of no value. He was apparently home and doing what a political reporter does. Harley still felt that Daniel Seay was somehow involved in what had happened to Argus. The idea that he knew about the congressman's trip to Georgia was unsettling. Harley asked Henry Dowd to find a house or vacant building in the Charlotte area. He would need a place to question Seay when the time came. Somewhere they would be alone. One more false move on Seay's part and they would pick him up. Better he disappeared than have another Dalton experience. He'd rather deal with heat from the FBI than that from Bogotá.

~

Jon had asked Ben to handle several research projects. A major one was to look into Congressman Harley's staff and associates, all of them. He felt he would need to know the players and have some familiarity with what they looked like. The list was vast, but Ben was thorough.

One undefined "associate" was a man named Henry Dowd. Ben found several pictures of this guy and they were included in the file. He was one of three undefined members of Harley's entourage. From the pictures Ben had found, Jon considered Dowd to be a high ranking something or other. Worthy of remembrance for sure.

The meeting with George Vincent was good. George did know a public defender in the Springfield circuit and had confirmed he was still there. George told him a friend might be calling and that he'd appreciate any help he could offer him. Jon was impressed and grateful. He shared the information about the possible new drug receiving facility in Springfield. The connection to the old Argus plant in Peoria got George's blood boiling.

"I knew they'd come back in some form." He told Jon.

Jon Crane gave George the address of the building in Springfield and asked George to have his friend look into it as deep as he could. Names on the purchase agreement, principles of the Paint Company and anything else he could find. Peoria had not been a facility like Dalton. Peoria had been a meltdown plant that distributed the cocaine to the street vendors. Springfield was more than likely the reincarnation of that. Jon had no idea where the new "Dalton" style plant was. He intended to find out.

Jon was planning a trip to Springfield. He would leave in two days and planned to be gone a week. Jon planned his trips to the minute. Every detail was considered. Travel time, vehicle needed, supplies he would or might need. He decided to take the Mercury Marquis. It never brought any undue attention but was an excellent road car and could carry what he needed, much of it concealed.

A major consideration for his absence would be Ben's mobility. He really wanted Ben to be available at the warehouse for certain hours. Could Ben drive with that cast on his right leg? They took the Ford 500 out and Ben drove around a shopping center parking lot. The cast was a little heavy but did not interfere with his ability to handle the pedals. Jon had installed the switch for the warehouse entrance. It was on the steering wheel. He had installed a "close switch" on the rear bumper that would activate as the car cleared the doors.

Ben wouldn't have to worry about that as he aimed for the ramp once inside. He cautioned Ben to be aware of who was around as he came and left through the secret panel doors.

"If there's any doubt, go around the block a few times first." Jon counseled him.

The plan in Springfield was simple. Identify a truck making runs to the new main plant and follow it home. It had worked before. He also planned to install a couple of observation cameras to watch the Illinois plant. He would connect them to cell phones he could dial from the warehouse. The normal transmission distance for the cameras was about 35 to 40 miles. The connections to the cell phones would extend that range over the phone lines. He could now monitor the cameras from anywhere he needed to be.

Jon and Ben packed the Mercury with what he would need. Several cameras, a bunch of cell phones, his regular Kevlar gear, the small Glock with three magazines and those new night vision goggles Ben had ordered. He was still working on the new frames but Jon liked the way the lenses worked. Several other emergency goodies were packed, as were his files and test kits.

Jon told Ben that he and George had agreed on how to handle the furniture and other items from their old houses. Jon had arranged for movers to pack everything and load it on their trucks. The loads would be taken to the police impound storage building. There, the boxes would be crated into larger containers and those containers shipped, a few at a time to the warehouse. Only the items they needed would come to the temporary home. Most would stay at the impound building until the new house was ready. There would be a room for Doris in the new house if she wanted it, Jon assured Ben.

"We'll leave that up to her and George," Jon said.

Jon left Dalton at 5:00AM that morning. The road trip took 10 hours. He pulled into a motel near the industrial park and checked in as a traveling salesman from Florida. The tags on the Mercury verified that. He called into the warehouse to let Ben know he was there. He asked about Doris and how the driving was going. Ben was positive on both counts. Ben had not heard any follow up from George on the principals of the Paint Company.

"I'll talk to you later this evening." Jon told him and decided to take a nap. He would start his surveillance tonight. Should a truck leave for the new main plant right away, he'd need to be ready to follow it. He pulled his notes and rewrote the three tag numbers his assistant had mentioned on his arm. Setting the alarm for 8:30PM, he pulled the drapes and lay down.

~

Activity at the building in Springfield was low. The men there kept trailers parked at the loading docks. They used the floor level rollup door entrance for the vans. Vans were the proven transport for the product. State line inspections were easier, the vehicles were less costly to operate and they could carry enough product to be economical.

The men were expecting one more test van and then the first load of the new spray paint.

Special machines would open the cans. The liquid would then be spun and then poured through screens before the final step, evaporation. The purified product would then be placed in tubes for the "mules" to carry and sell to the street dealers. It was like opening night at the theater. Excitement and expectations were high.

Jon pulled into the industrial park at 8:50PM. He found the building in question and looked for the best spot to set up. It was a sprawling building with the dock doors at one end and the rollup door some 100 feet away. Based on what he had learned from these guys in Georgia, he guessed they would use vans. That meant the small door, the drive-in door. Parking the Mercury around the corner and in the dark, he walked to a position across from the rollup doors. The area was well lit but he found a spot behind a dumpster that was in the shadows. The first van drove into the driveway within twenty minutes of Jon's arrival. It turned quickly as the rollup door opened and the van was inside in a hurry. Jon caught a look at the license tag. He couldn't repeat the whole number if he had to. But he saw enough to know it was not one of the ones he had written on his arm. He got out a digital camera and focused it on the side of the building. There would be no flash. His meter told him the shutter speed and the light in the area would be enough.

The temperature fell about 15 degrees in the next two hours. It neared being downright uncomfortable. Jon slowly breathed in and hunkered down. At least the cooler temperature cut down the smell from the dumpster. It was almost 11:15PM when he first heard, then saw, the other truck. Again, it was a van and again it was moving fast as it entered the area. The rollup door opened as before. This time Jon pointed the camera at the door and began pulling the trigger on the shutter. When the door closed he turned his camera over and reviewed the shots on the 3"LED. One shot caught the truck right at the door and the tag was clear. He knew without checking but he looked at his arm anyway. There it was, Illinois tag 6687 AG 4 on his arm and the truck in the picture.

He packed up and tried to stay in the shadows on his way back to the Mercury. He drove around the backside of the building to an intercept point, a spot where the van would have to pass on its way out. It took them 30 minutes to unload. The van roared around the corner and sped toward the Interstate.

He cranked the Mercury and eased out behind it, keeping his lights out till they got to a main road. They headed south on I-55 toward St. Louis. As he got used to the van's profile in the dark, Jon dropped back further, staying out of sight. The trip would take I-64 east from St. Louis toward Lexington, Kentucky. They both stopped for gas somewhere in Indiana and Jon grabbed a few snacks and a couple of soft drinks. He bought bottles with screw tops so he could reuse them for another purpose later. He didn't have time to risk going into a restroom. These guys were in a hurry.

Jon called his motel back in Springfield around 6:00AM and checked out by phone. He had not left anything in the room so it was not an issue.

Daylight changed the game. On long stretches he would actually pass the van and lead for a while. Then dropping back in heavier traffic to as much as a mile behind them. He assumed there were two drivers but he never really saw either. The blackout glass on the van was completely opaque. The next stop for gas was near Knoxville, Tennessee. Jon would not use the same station as the van but one just down the road or across the exit. It was 1:20PM when they drove through Knoxville and turned onto I-40 towards Asheville, North Carolina. Mountains, mountains and more mountains.

"At least they broke up the monotony," he thought. Some 4 1/2 hours and another gas stop later, they pulled into Charlotte, North Carolina. It was rush hour and the traffic was as you would expect. He stayed back behind a semi and peeked out every minute or two. He just didn't need to lose them or get caught now. When the van finally got
268

off the freeway and headed into the industrial park, Jon knew he was about to see the new main warehouse. The new Dalton.

Slowing down from the pace they had maintained, the van made several turns and stopped at one point, apparently calling in before proceeding to the side door. The van pulled into the building and disappeared. He had them. Driving around in the parking lot, Jon made a note of the address and the building number. He needed some sleep. Badly. The next order of business was a nice room. He would investigate this building tomorrow.

He checked in with Ben as he almost swallowed his burger whole. Hunger as it turns out, is not a good candidate for multitasking. During the call he learned that Doris was getting stronger with each day. As tired as he was, he managed a smile at the news. He asked Ben to let George know where he was and see if he knew anyone in that area.

"Oh," Ben interjected before they hung up. "The black outfits came in today. The coated Kevlar is terrific."

"That's nice," Jon answered and hung up. Sleep came quickly. He felt good. He had them. They thought they had slipped away to start their deadly drug trafficking all over. But he was on them again. He didn't just feel good. He felt great.

44

Jon slept for 14 hours. When he did wake up he had to think about where he was. As Silas he didn't get disoriented too easily, but Jon was close. He cleaned up and actually ate breakfast. The room was nice so he kept it for another night. He wasn't sure how long the surveillance would take.

He needed to learn how he could gain access to the building and more importantly, how to hurt them. He would wait for the cover of darkness to set up cameras and count the vans coming and going. Today he just wanted to get a good look at the surrounding area where the building was located.

He changed the plates on the Mercury to Virginia tags and drove into the industrial park.

Dressed as he normally did, he kept the digital camera around his neck. He looked at several of the buildings as if he was shopping for a site to move his operation. Cars and trucks passed him but no one was concerned about his presence. Pretending to be looking at other buildings, he was able to get great shots of the target from all angles. He tried to get pictures of the men around the building but none came out on foot. The vehicles always had blackout glass. It was illegal but that was a matter of degrees. Seldom was anyone stopped just for that.

After lunch Jon left the Mercury at the motel. He had changed clothes and rented another car to revisit the industrial park. He picked out the locations for the cameras he would set up that night. At around

4:15PM he decided to turn in the rental and gas up the Mercury. After that he planned on a good nap before his night's work. Everything was going well so far.

At the gas station off I-77, Jon looked up from pumping gas into the Mercury Marquis. The face at the next pump over was familiar to him but he had trouble placing it. He was a middle-aged man in a suit, a crumpled suit. The car looked like a rental, in fact, there was an Avis sticker on the rear glass. Jon left his nozzle in the car and went to his notebook. Flipping through his trip notes, there he was.

He had pictures of the man, several pictures of him. It was Henry Dowd. Henry Dowd of Iowa.

"What the hell was he doing in North Carolina?"

Jon finished pumping his gas and pulled away from the station. He waited for Henry to pull out and followed him. He really needed to know what old Henry was up to.

He followed him to an older part of town. It was a rundown section of town. Consisting of many vacant buildings, mostly old houses and converted houses. Some had been used as a business.

Henry Dowd stopped at one and went to the door. He took keys from his pocket and opened the lock. Jon made a note of the address. The buildings on either side of this house were also vacant. Dowd wasn't in there for very long, but he relocked the door and put something behind a post on the porch. Then he got back in his car.

Jon continued to follow the man back to the airport where he turned in the rental car and took a shuttle to the Delta Airlines gates. Jon parked in the lot and called directly to George's office. He gave him the address of the house and asked him to find out what he could about any recent transaction. He then drove back to his motel for that nap.

George woke him with a return call an hour later. Real Estate transactions could be found within minutes once posted to the

Internet. The house in Charlotte had been leased to a Virgo Stern of New York. The leasing agent was Todd Manley of the Jackson Realty Company in Charlotte. Jon thanked him and made notes. He would check all this out tomorrow. Right now his priority was to get back to sleep.

~

Ben had spent more time organizing and going through the different messages Jon's computer programs would spit out. He did find some time for reading. He had started John Ferling's <u>A Leap in the Dark </u>but got sidetracked by another book in the same shelf. A Frenchman, Alexis De Tocqueville, spent some time here between the Revolutionary and Civil wars. He then wrote his thoughts about the new form of government the Unites States had chosen.

He predicted that while it was interesting, our Representative Republic would last only until those who vote realized they could vote themselves largess. His timetable for that was just over 200 years.

The attitude De Tocqueville described created the atmosphere in which Jon's removal candidates flourished. Society became concerned with what government could do for them as individuals rather than what it was established to do. Politicians came along who gladly offered to expand the government's welfare programs in exchange for more power. That in itself does not constitute the evil Jon sought to remove. But the power such conduct offered tempted some to go to any length to retain and build that power.

The more Ben read, the more he understood. Killing was not something individuals should take upon themselves to dispense. Yet what was the answer when evil used its power to protect and empower itself? He knew the answer. If there was an acceptable one, it was well beyond him. Jon's reasoning for what he did could be argued. But not by the ones whose lives he saved with his actions. Ben decided he would not make such decisions himself. What he would do was help with fact gathering. He would trust Jon's judgment after that point. Should the time ever come that he felt he could no longer do that, he would re-evaluate his position.

It was time to go to the hospital. He checked the monitors and the printers. Everything was in order. The elevator to the basement squealed slightly. He made a note to tell Jon about it. The Ford 500 came to life as he turned the key. He aimed for the ramp and once on the street level pointed his chariot at the corner. The switch on the steering wheel opened the panel to the street. He slowed as he approached the main road and looked both ways. Turning right and punching the gas at the same time he was off. He thought about the leg cast. It was due to come off next week. His arm was a little slower healing. Ben would be pleased when both were memories.

~

The clouds were light today, Henry Dowd thought as he rode the Delta flight back to Iowa. He was pleased with his find in Charlotte. He had almost missed his flight because he forgot to leave a key and copy of the lease for the boss. Lucky he remembered while gassing up the rental car for its return. When the time came it would be a nice place to ask someone a few questions. A nice place where no one else could hear what it might take to get answers. There was no furniture at all in the house, but that could be fixed. He had called the power company to have the lights turned on. He'd call the water department when he got back to Des Moines. He wanted to tell the boss about it anyway, before he had too much done to it. Congress in session made it hard to get hold of Harley at times. He would leave a message for him tonight.

"*Look at that cloud,*" he thought. "*It looks like a tractor. Ha!*" Henry leaned back and smiled. He had done good today.

~

The alarm went off at 8:30PM. Jon dressed quickly and headed to the industrial park. He grabbed a burger and a shake on the way. It was quiet there this night. He parked the Mercury around the corner and stayed in the shadows as much as he could. There was no hologram projector here. Not yet anyway.

He placed his first camera where it could watch the roll up door. Another further back for a wider shot of the area. He wanted to get inside. The far corner of the building was away from the lights. He crept to that corner and took out his listening devise. It looked like a stethoscope, but was stronger. It wasn't strong enough to hear through concrete blocks. He slid himself carefully to the roll up door. Being aluminum, it would transmit sound much better.

The device picked up several men walking around and talking. Some of the conversations were in Spanish, some in English. Regardless, there were too many voices in there. He looked for a fan or anything he could see through. No luck. This building used roof top air conditioners and he could not see a wall fan.

He brought an 8mm video scope but needed a crack or hole to slide it through. He felt around the block walls and found a broken spot on the far wall that was in the dark. Mortar was gone between two blocks almost clean through to the inside. He took his knife and gently worked the joint. When a pinhole finally allowed light from inside to show, he stopped with the knife, took a ballpoint pen and stuck it into the space. As the pen broke through Jon pulled it out and gathered his stuff. He hurried across the lot and hid among the trees. He could not be sure that they hadn't seen or heard his boring.

Jon waited for about twenty minutes. No one came out and the small light from the hole did not change. He unpacked his video scope and hooked it to a 3" monitor. He looked at his beige pants and blue shirt and thought about the black outfits Ben ordered for him. He understood the need for such apparel much better now.

Creeping back to the wall, Jon inserted the 8mm tube into the hole. He adjusted the frame and the focus. There were six men in the warehouse that he could see. They had settled down. Sitting in chairs watching a TV that looked like it was connected to cable. As he watched them another man walked into the frame. That made seven. He was glad he hadn't tried to sneak in.

Jon unscrewed the monitor and attached a camera. He took several pictures in Hi Def mode that could be blown up with his equipment back home. Other than the men watching cable, there were stacks of bundles. The bundles were of spray paint cans. Small cans of spray-paint in four colors. He snapped shots of the different stacks. Withdrawing the video scope, he went back to his vantage point across the lot.

Jon stayed in the area for three more hours. No vans came in. It was quiet. He finally packed up and went back to the motel. He would be going home now, but needed to see the real estate company in the morning. That house bugged him. He would stay to see what he could find or figure out.

45

The offices of Jackson Realty opened at 9:00AM, or so the sign said. It was 9:25AM and no one was around. Jon tried not to be impatient, but he had other things to get done today besides this. And, this may be nothing. He organized the folder he would take in with him once again. Fake papers about a fake client looking for a "fixer upper" in town.

He had one of the pictures from his files in there as well. At 9:40AM a car drove up and a young man unlocked the office. Jon gave him two minutes and then went to the door. The young man's name badge said "Todd."

"Hi, Todd," Jon smiled. "I represent an artist looking for a quiet place to work. I noticed a house over on Greenway that appeared to have vacant houses on either side. Can I look at the property?"

"You've got to be kidding me." Todd responded. "We couldn't beg anyone to look at any of those houses for months and now in two days there are two of you wanting the same one."

"I'm sorry," Jon pretended with his most sincere look. "Two of us?"

"Yes, Sir. Some guy from New York just leased that property yesterday."

"Not Virgo?" Jon said very coyly.

"Why, yes. His name was something like that. Come in and I'll double check." The young man led Jon into his office and desk area. He pulled a folder and looked up at Jon.

"Yeah, Virgo Stern from New York City."

Jon opened his folder, as if to it make a note in it. The picture slipped out onto Todd's desk.

"That's him, you know Mr. Stern?" Todd asked.

Jon smiled at the young man. "Yeah. We're in competition sometimes. Looks like this round goes to Virgo."

The young real estate agent seemed confused.

"We both work for this artist. Whoever finds what the guy wants first gets paid. No big deal."

"So, Mr. Stern will be pleased that he beat you to it, huh?"

"You know, I'd really rather he didn't know. Professional pride, you understand?" And with that Jon handed the young man a fifty-dollar bill.

"Why of course." Todd responded happily. "He won't hear it from me."

"Thanks, I'll try you again next time." Jon walked out of the office now knowing he needed to find out what was happening or going to happen at the house.

He drove to the neighborhood and rode around the block twice looking for activity. There was none. Jon parked a half a block down from the house itself and walked up to the front door. He remembered Dowd bending down as he was leaving yesterday. Jon felt around and behind the railing post and there it was, a key.

Checking over his shoulders for anyone watching, Jon unlocked the door and stepped in. The house was small. Three rooms up front if you count the foyer area, then a living room and a dining room on either side of that.

The kitchen was behind the dining room and there were two small bedrooms to the left of it. The one bath was in a hall that joined the living room to the bedrooms. The living room was the largest, 12' by 14' maybe. The dining room was 9' by 8'. He couldn't imagine what size table would fit in there. The bedrooms were hardly big enough for a double bed and it would have to be stuck in the corner. Each had two windows for cross ventilation.

This place was built before anyone thought about air conditioning. In that same hall as the bathroom was an odd door, maybe 18" wide. It opened to a set of very steep stairs headed up to an attic. He guessed the width of the staircase to be two feet. One could hardly carry anything up or down those stairs. Watching his steps carefully, Jon went to the top to check it out.

The attic mimicked only a part of the floor space of the house. A rear-facing dormer allowed an adult to stand but it was necessary to stoop as you walked around to the front to the matching dormer's space.

"Not too usable," Jon thought, as he turned sideways to climb down the steps. *"What could they intend to do here?"* It was way too small for meetings and there was no parking. This was truly odd.

The kitchen had a door to the side so with that, there were two doors into the house. He walked around the outside. The foundation wall was stones stacked about four feet high. There was a crawlspace door in the back. Underneath the house there was no insulation. He figured you could hear everything and probably see some through the cracks in the floor. This house had to be seventy or eighty years old. He took a few pictures, just in case. Jon still had no idea what a house like this could be used for. He made a page of notes about it to be safe.

"You never can tell these days," he reminded himself.

As Jon moved to the front door to leave several overhead lights came on. Startling as that was, the man he could see standing on the porch was more so. Jon could tell he was in uniform, a power company uniform. Jon opened the door.

"Mr. Stern?" the man asked.

"Yeah, how are you doing?" Jon answered him.

"Didn't think you'd be here, Sir. We're just turning the power on as you requested."

"Sure, I had to come back and check on something. You go ahead."

"I'll need to check all the switches and lights before I leave," the man told him.

"Of course." Jon thought about the situation. "You know where I was going to leave the key for you, right?"

The power company man looked at his paperwork. "Says here, behind the post on the front porch."

Jon handed the man the key. "That's right. Just put it back when you're done, Ok?"

"Yes, Sir. Do you want to sign this work order?" he asked.

"Uh, you're going to be here a while, right. I have to leave. I wouldn't want to sign before you were done. Just handle it like we had set up. Like I wasn't going to be here."

"Sure thing," the power man said and Jon slipped away.

He drove directly to I-85 and headed for Atlanta. He didn't care much for going through Atlanta but that was the best route from here. The time was 11:15AM. He could be home by 6 or 7PM if traffic wasn't bad.

~

Daniel had been home for weeks. There had been no further activity by the assassin, or at least none that made news anywhere. The Argus story had wound down and lost interest. Everything seemed to be happening in Washington. Daniel asked the editor about a trip there to get some fresh news for his reports.

"You're wanting to dig into Harley some more, right? He's there now, I know what you're thinking," the boss told him.

"So are over 400 other representatives and the Senate. That's where the news is right now, boss."

"Alright, keep your nose clean and stay in touch daily."

Daniel grabbed his gear and headed home to once again pack. Lori was not pleased but she planned to go see her Mom in New Castle for a few days, so she didn't throw much of a fit.

He made his reservations and settled on leaving the next day. He did hope to find something more on Charles Harley. "The guy was just too slick." The thought made him remember the folks he'd met in Texas. He finished packing and took Lori out for dinner.

46

Progress at the house was coming along. They had had some rain but not much of it. The contractor told Jon he would be "dried in" in another week. He learned that meant the roof would be in place and the outside sheathing and windows would be in.

The house appeared as if it were emerging from the mountain and creating its own outcrop ledge while doing so. The ledge level was only a slight incline above the main road. The driveway to the ledge came in from the side and the house had a three-car garage built into the end. There would be parking directly in front of the house for guests and company. The ledge next to the house was large enough for up to seven vehicles in that area.

The lighting around that area would be subtle yet striking.

The elevators were roughed-in. Another building term he learned about. The round chutes within which the platforms would ride stood but were visible only from the ledge. The home's wood framing was so intricate that it obscured the chutes from on-lookers.

Jon's chute went the entire height of the house. He had it extended to his study, which would be on the third level of the house. Ben's started from his second floor bedroom closet and went to the third level sub-basement. Which, by the way, was working out terrificly.

The dugout garage came in at 11 feet high. That should be fine for what he planned to keep there. Sighting it from the road, Jon was pretty sure the level was right for the tunnel, which was coming that way, day by day. It would soon be time to discuss with Doris about her plans, if she cared to live here with her son, or somewhere else. George never said anything, but Jon could tell his feelings for Doris were strong. So he didn't set aside any possibilities there either.

Jon planned to bring Ben out to the house as soon as the interior walls were all up. That should be very soon. Ben's room would be across from his on the second floor. He would have a workshop in the second level sub-basement and access to all computers throughout the house. Ben's Ford 500 would park in the main house's garage but he planned a surprise for him with another vehicle in the sub-basement parking. Budget wise, both the house and the tunnel were on or near budget. His accounts continued to grow, even with the heavy spending of late.

Jon was pleased with Ben's skills, both in organization and picking out special items from the web sites. Those black outfits were coming along. Ben had several ideas for modifications, particularly spots to carry the Glock and other gadgets. The Kevlar rope had possibilities but those possibilities required some acrobatic skills. Jon wasn't too sure he had them.

He also thought about the distractions the new Argus plant had caused. Jon had already sent three messages to Congressman Harley attempting to throw him off his game. Harley was tough and seasoned. He would need some anxiety in his life to make him more approachable, for Jon's purposes anyway. Those cryptic notes were now old news. He would need to start them up again. Get this creep's attention and make him sweat.

The cameras in Charlotte and the pictures of the men in the warehouse there were coming up dry so far. He felt that would change. But he also knew he didn't need to waste too much time. He would construct a new message for Harley. One intended to really shake him. If he got on it, he could have it to him by the end of this week.

~

The Best Western at Georgetown was Daniel's usual base in Washington, DC. He checked in and called Lori to let her know he was there. It was still a couple of hours before dinner so he headed over to Capitol Hill to see who might be out and about.

Daniel's beat was Pennsylvania. He had 19 Representatives and two Senators to keep up with for his paper. Charles Harley wasn't his responsibility, in that Harley was an Iowa Representative, but he had become Daniel's obsession. The killer was after Harley and Daniel knew it. If he could stop that from happening, and document it, it would be a major story. In fact, it could be a huge national headline besides preventing a murder.

There were several areas around Capitol Hill where reporters could bump into congressmen. Daniel's favorites were the Capitol Building and grounds, Union Station, The Capital Grille and Charlie Palmer's restaurants. This evening, those areas were nearly vacant. Giving up for the time being, he walked back toward his motel. Daniel wasn't aware that it was he who had been noticed. One of Henry Dowd's men was already on the phone to Iowa letting Dowd know of Daniel's presence.

Coincidences can be strange things. Several had worked in Daniel and Jon's favor already. This one would go in quite the opposite direction. Jon's continuing of his campaign to "shake up" Charles Harley was about to have a consequence he never thought of. The last message Jon sent was aimed at both redirecting the congressman's attention and throwing him off his normal routine. It came to Harley from his Chief of Staff who received the e-mail. That e-mail showed it had been sent from the White House, a trick Ben had showed Jon how to do.

The message was simple, *"You're not forgotten, I'm coming for you."* Direct and to the point as were the others. Time had lapsed since the last one so Jon wanted to be sure Harley got the message.

At almost the same time that Henry Dowd was being informed of Daniel Seay's presence in Washington, Harley was calling Dowd about the latest message. Harley was angry.

"That's it," Harley screamed into the phone. When he learned that Daniel was in Washington it set him off even further. "Come get this bastard. He's involved in this, if he's not the one doing it."

"Boss, I'll be there in the morning. We'll take him to the house, Ok?" Dowd told him.

"Keep him there. It'll take me a day or two but I'll figure a way to break away from here. I really want to talk to that smart ass. People don't do me like this." Harley was livid.

That next morning, after having breakfast in the motel dining room, Daniel walked toward his rental car in the back lot. As he stepped into the row for his car, a van pulled up and the side door opened. Two men jumped out and grabbed Daniel.

He struggled and managed to kick one of them in the jaw. The thug wobbled for a second but stepped right back into the van. As the other man held Daniel down he put a hood over the reporter's head. The hood had a rag with chloroform inside it.

Daniel twisted and tried to kick but the fumes were overwhelming. The reporter was soon unconscious and on his way to North Carolina. Eight and a half hours later, they had Daniel tied to a chair in a small house. When he woke he had no idea where he was.

The editor in Pittsburgh was not pleased when Daniel didn't check in at noon. He was worried when he hadn't checked in by 5:00PM. He tried Daniel's cell phone but there was no answer. The phone had been dropped in the parking lot when Daniel was abducted. Having been run over several times, it was no longer working.

284

Daniel's boss called the local DC police. They asked around town, talked with other reporters who knew Daniel well, and checked at his motel. No one had seen him all day.

The editor called Lori; she had not heard from him either. He tried to reassure her that everything was all right, but it wasn't. They both knew it.

The word went out, a reporter was missing in Washington, DC. Although the police were not yet ready to declare him missing, it was on the national wire and cable news within hours. Some locations didn't pick up the story till the next morning.

The news media went all out. They wanted to protect and find one of their own.

Doug Dahlgren

47

Jon left the new house that afternoon and went by the hospital. It was dinnertime and he expected to find Ben there. He didn't see the Ford 500 in the lot but maybe Ben was running late.

The hospital building was looking better. Most of the repairs to the facility had been completed. New glass and doors along the front and both ends of the building were in. The bullet marks in the concrete and brick had been smoothed over or rubbed out the best they could. The building hardly showed the trauma it had been through just a few short weeks earlier.

Jon walked off the elevator and turned toward Doris' room. He knocked on the slightly open door and pushed it open. He found George was there, not Ben. George was sitting on the side of the bed. His hands cradled Doris' good hand as they looked at each other.

Jon realized he had interrupted a heavy conversation.

"Oh, sorry," Jon stopped at the door and didn't go in. "I thought Ben would be here. Didn't mean to barge in like that." He told them.

George turned his head and smiled. "That's fine. I had asked Ben if I could handle a few of the meals for a while. He said I could."

Doris was also now looking at Jon. She looked like she felt good. Her color was much better and she raised her arm with the bandaged fingers to wave. "Come in. Good to see you," she smiled and told him.

Jon felt a bit awkward. "Ben should have told me about this and I wouldn't have walked in on them," he said to himself.

It was the first outward display of affection Jon had noticed between them, intentional anyway. He knew something was there all along but they had always been very careful about it. It appeared the days of total discretion were over.

George offered what the conversation had been about. They had talked about Doris' progress. George mentioned that she would be well enough to leave the hospital in a couple of weeks. He had explained to her about her house. She understood she would not be able to go back there.

George also told her about Jon's guardianship of her son. She was pleased with that. She thanked Jon for being so thoughtful. George told Jon that they had been discussing the options of where Doris should go after leaving the hospital. George insisted that he fix a room for her at his place. He could have round the clock care come in for as long as she needed it and security would be easy to provide. Doris knew that Ben was staying with Jon. She thanked him again for that and expressed her relief that she didn't need to worry about Ben's welfare while she was recovering. Jon smiled and just nodded his head in the affirmative.

The room suddenly got awkwardly quiet. Like when no one is sure what to say next. Jon winked at them as if he understood.

Then he asked them both, "Well is that it? Any other news?"

George smiled and took Doris' hand again. He looked right at Jon and answered him.

"That's it for the minute. But I hope things might get more detailed in the near future."

Doris was smiling. Jon could tell there would be more news, but later. Not everything all at the same time.

Doris' dinner was being delivered so Jon said he would get out of the way. He shook George's hand and patted the bed as he turned to leave.

"I'd better go see what that boy of yours wants for dinner." He laughed and pulled the door closed behind him.

The news wasn't surprising to him. It would make his new house and room layout planning easier now that he knew for sure what they were thinking about. Jon wondered if Ben had any idea about his Mom and George. Ben never talked about it and it sure wasn't his place to tell him. Jon headed to his car and called Ben to see what he wanted to do about dinner. Ben asked for fried chicken. That wouldn't have been Jon's first choice, but he agreed and said he'd pick some up on the way.

They looked at Ben's projects after dinner. He had the night vision goggles mounted on the new frames. They were much more comfortable than the rigid old frames. Ben had molded sections of the Kevlar rope around the frames to further protect the wearer from any projectiles. The black suits were ready. Ben demonstrated the STF; shear thickening fluid that was soaked into the Kevlar of the fabric. The flexibility of the fabric was better and softer than his other coverings. When something struck the fibers, they stiffened and stopped anything at any speed. Gunshots, blows, knife attacks even explosions would not penetrate the covering.

The hood was a bit hot to Jon, but not too bad. It allowed breathing through the nose and mouth and only exposed the area for the goggles. He didn't care for the idea of a tight, black suit but Ben kept reminding him of the Navy Seals and their getup. Jon asked about the hydraulic arm.

"Oh, yeah," Ben smiled. "That worked out great." He had dyed the tubes and connectors black. The structure would now be worn on the outside of the new uniform.

"What about the finger tips?" Jon asked him.

"I rewired the system. The glove tips stay on your fingers all the time. They won't interfere with anything you do with that hand.

When you activate the arm, they read your impulses and tell the arm what to do, just like before." There was a black glove for his left hand. It felt like leather but was more natural in flexibility and grip. Jon liked it.

Ben had devised a new holster for the special Glock. It strapped the weapon to his right leg at the exact same height the old pocket had kept it. Only now it would be on the outside. Again, everything would be external to the suit. That was a big difference. But the suit was for tactical operations only. It wasn't intended for walking around looking like a comic book character. Ben had contracted with a clothing manufacturer for a break away outfit of beige pants and a blue shirt. They were sized to allow Jon to wear over the black suit. The pants still had the breakthrough seam so he could get to the weapon without removing the cover outfit. When Jon needed to disappear in the dark he could tear off the outer layer in seconds. It could also be reapplied in just about two minutes.

The Kevlar laced rope was still being worked on and studied. It took a special tool to cut it. Normal blades, saws or even a gunshot couldn't cut through it. Ben had tested it to over 2500 lbs of lift strength. It could hold more, but he wasn't sure how much more. He felt it would be handy for Jon to have in any circumstance. Ben had dyed a forty-foot section of the rope black to match everything else and hooked it to a mounting bracket for the belt. Jon could either take it or leave it, depending on the situation. Ben was still trying different applications for the rope material but none were perfected yet. For now, it was just an unbreakable rope.

Other improvements incorporated into the black suit were the wireless ear bud for the cell phone and a microphone embedded into the fabric of the hood. It was near his mouth but Jon couldn't feel it. Small, battery powered high intensity lights were mounted on either side of the hood. They were less than a ¼ inch protrusion on the sides yet offered light to wherever he looked. So if the goggles weren't needed for cover he could touch the switch on his belt and see what he was doing. A pouch on the back of the belt carried his spare magazines and smoke bombs half the size of a golf ball. The smoke bombs could be lethal if needed. The pouch had room for other items Jon might decide to carry as well.

All in all, the suit would take some getting used to but had great potential. Ben had worked really hard on it and Jon was appreciative.

The next morning Ben called to Jon as he was preparing to leave the warehouse.

"Hey," he hollered. "Isn't this the reporter fellow that came here to see you?"

Jon walked up to the TV monitor Ben was watching. The news report was about Daniel Seay's disappearance in Washington, DC.

Jon froze for a moment. His mind seized on the news and added to it what he had stumbled on during his last trip. He then grabbed a phone and called George Vincent in his office.

"George, who do you know at the Dalton Airport I could get to fly me to North Carolina, quickly?"

"One of our County Commissioners has a flight training school and charter service there. What's going on?" George demanded.

"I just need to get to Charlotte and fast." Jon was talking and thinking at the same time. "Oh, I can carry my equipment in a private plane, right?" he asked the DA.

"That's between you and the pilot. When did you want to leave?" George asked him.

"In one hour." Jon said firmly.

"I'll call Gordon and see what he can do. If there's a hang up, I'll call you back. Other wise be at the Dalton airport in one hour."

"Thanks, George." Jon hung up and looked at Ben. "I need the stuff you were showing me last night packed up to go, quickly."

"What's going on?" Ben asked.

"It's that reporter. I know where he is," Jon told him.

"You know where he is in Washington, DC?" Ben was confused.

"He's not in Washington, DC. It makes perfect sense now," Jon answered. Then he dialed the phone again, this time to call the Charlotte airport. He wanted to arrange for a rental car to be waiting for him. As he held on for reservations, he looked at Ben again.

"Get that bag ready, will ya? I need to move and fast."

48

As Jon drove into the Dalton Airport he could see a man standing by his plane with a sign. He rolled closer to the plane and finally could see the sign said "J. Crane." He pulled up next to the plane and asked through the window. "I'm Jon Crane, where should I leave my car?"

The man pointed to building about a hundred feet away but said, "Leave your bags here and put it in that building."

Jon dropped his duffle and drove to the building. He left his keys in the car and ran back to the plane. "Hi, sorry to be in such a hurry." He reached out his hand to the pilot and said again, "I'm Jon. I appreciate you doing this."

"It's what I'm here for. My name is Harvey, you can call me Harv," he said.

"What kind of plane is this?" Jon asked him.

"It's a Cessna 182T Skylane. She'll do 135 kts. That's about 155 miles per hour."

"How long till we're in Charlotte?" the passenger asked.

"Hour and a half, give or take clearance to land. Shouldn't be a problem though."

"Great." Jon responded. "Whatever this costs, I hope George told you I'm good for it."

"That's been worked out between him and my boss. You ready to go?"

Jon nodded and they threw his bag in the back and loaded up. The plane rolled to the end of the short runway and turned around. Harv revved the engine to a high-pitched roar and the Cessna lurched forward. They were airborne in a matter of seconds and Harv banked the plane to the east. It was 11:15AM. Jon thought about Daniel Seay. Was he still alive? The trouble Harley's people had gone to with the house told him he was. They wanted to spend time with the reporter before they killed him. But kill him they surely would.

At 12:40PM Harv had received clearance to land in Charlotte, North Carolina. They taxied to a private hanger and Jon could see a blue Lincoln Town Car sitting there. It was his rental. A bit fancier than he cared for but it would do.

Jon jumped out of the Cessna and grabbed his bag. The attendant there verified the car was for him and loaded his bag into the trunk. Jon went around the plane and thanked Harv again. He then climbed into the Lincoln and headed to town. As he left the airport grounds he could hear the Cessna rumbling down the runway again. It was back in the air on its return to Dalton.

He went through his memories of the house as he drove. He brought the pictures he had made when he was here before. They were in the file. Midday traffic wasn't too bad. It took twenty minutes to get to the neighborhood. Turning into the street it struck him how desolate the area was. It was 1:25PM and there was not a soul to be seen on the street. The house was about half way down the block and on his right. The Lincoln cruised by slowly. He could see two vehicles there. A van with Maryland plates sat in the driveway. A small sedan with local tags was parked on the street. Jon sighed with relief that the vehicles were there. They confirmed that Daniel was there and that he was still alive. Had they killed him already, they would be gone. Jon drove two blocks down before he turned to go around the block. He finally parked on the adjacent street behind the house.

The building there appeared to be vacant as well. A small fence separated the two structures and he could clearly see the backside of the house. He approached the house from the left rear and at an angle. There were no shrubs, only the foundation wall of stones and then the house.

He listened at each window and finally heard voices in the room on the right. They spoke Spanish and it did not sound like they were addressing a captive. Jon stepped back enough to look up to the attic window. It was open. Not much but it was open. The chimney ran up between the first floor windows and along the side of the attic window.

He went back to the Lincoln and put on his rubber soled shoes and a pair of gloves. On the side opposite the room the men were in, he scaled the chimney slowly and quietly. At the level of the attic window he still needed to cross the backside of the chimney. The reach was difficult but he gripped the far edge with his fingertips and found a foothold in the mortar. Using all the strength he could muster, he transferred his weight and slid across the back of the brick surface. There was only two feet between the chimney and the window. Jon grabbed the top of the window frame and eased himself into the corner created by the chimney and rear of the house.

Jon leaned toward the window and peeked inside the attic. There was a man sitting in a chair. He was tied to the chair and had a hood over his head. Jon could feel the heat coming out the slightly open window. It was hot in that attic. The ventilation provided by the open window was barely enough to keep the man alive. It had to be nearly unbearable in there. Jon started to raise the window further when he heard a door open. It was the door at the bottom of the stairs. Two men came up into the attic. They untied the man from the chair and one dragged him down the stairs. The other carried the chair and the rope. Jon needed to reverse his course and get back to the other side of the chimney so he could climb down. His strength was not as good in his left arm but he made it.

Once across he got to the ground and under the window on the right. He could hear the men were talking again. It was more than two this time. He could hear at least five different voices now. That changed the odds, and not in his favor. A cell phone rang and the man who answered did so in broken English. He answered several questions with "yes" and then repeated "three hours". He finally finished the call with "Yes, we will be here."

Jon went back to the left side of the house and crept to the front. There was another car there now. Parked on the street, right in front of the house. Something was up. He wanted to get Daniel out of there but that in its self would take some planning. Plus, the extra guys and the phone call about "three hours." Jon slipped back to his car and moved around the block to a spot where he could watch the front of the house. He moved every twenty minutes without ever driving past the house directly. He checked his watch. It was 3:35PM. The original "three hours" would be over at 5:30PM. It would be dark two hours after that.

"Does Daniel have that long?" he thought.

He got out the pictures he had taken of the interior. The room they held Daniel in now was the back bedroom. Access to that room was either through the house or one of two windows, the side unit or the rear window. These were not good options for what he needed to do.

"Did that room have a closet?" He asked himself. The picture said it did. Maybe that was what he needed. Maybe there was a scurry hole in the ceiling of that closet. Jon considered that as an answer but decided to look for another option as well. Getting into the attic was an issue and the chances of there being a useable access hole in the closet were 50/50 at best.

He remembered the crawl space. It was four feet high and went under the entire house.

He got the pictures he had taken under the crawl space. The plumbing pipes ran together before heading toward the front. The water pipes also came together in nearly the same place. It was under the bath. They had emergency cut off values and a plumbing clean out accessible under the bathroom. There had to be a hole in the floor there. That's where he would look.

At 5:45PM a late model sedan pulled into the drive behind the van. Two men got out and walked toward the house. It was Henry Dowd and Charles Harley. Jon cranked the Lincoln and rode around behind the house again. He used the same path to the rear of the house and got as close to the bedroom window as he could.

He could hear Harley's voice and he wasn't pleased.

"You guys have him unconscious. I can't talk to an unconscious man. Get that hood off him, Christ." Harley grabbed the hood and held it to his own face. "Damn, this thing still smells of chloroform!"

He looked at Dowd and demanded, "How long till he wakes up?"

Daniel was groggy, but not out as he pretended. The smell did persist in the bag but it wasn't enough to keep him unconscious. He was aware enough to know he needed to stall. He didn't know the men who were tormenting him. He didn't recognize Harley at that point either. All he could do was concentrate on stalling. The more he could stall the longer he could stay alive.

"Sorry boss, I didn't know these morons would keep the hood on him." Dowd excused.

"How long till he wakes up?" Harley repeated himself, but louder this time.

"An hour, maybe two. Can't be sure." Dowd was nervous about his answer.

"Damn it." Harley started. "I came all this way. I will get answers out of that slug. He's been dogging me for months and now I have to wait for this." He stepped into the other room but could still be heard. "Somebody go get me something to eat while I wait."

"Yes, Sir," Dowd responded.

In a few minutes Jon could hear one of the cars leave. He slipped to the front to try to see who had left but the car was already gone.

Jon went back to the Lincoln and unpacked his bag. It was time to put the uniform on. Silas had a job to do and Ben's work would soon get a field test.

49

The officers in Washington, DC had little to go on. There was simply no sign of Daniel anywhere. Legally they weren't supposed to be looking for him yet. Not enough time had elapsed to declare him missing. The press corps in Washington was a tight knit group. They demanded and expected action. The police did their best but it was as if their fellow reporter had floated away. Lori Seay had arrived that night, flown in by the Post Gazette. They put her up at the same motel as Daniel's room. The cable stations and the local news had interviewed her already. She kept to herself the belief she held in her heart, that the congressional killer had taken Daniel. As scared as she was, she knew Daniel would not want her to say anything about that. Not until it was proven. It had been two days.

"*Surely they will find him soon,*" she told herself.

~

The sun went down at 7:25PM in Charlotte and it was dark within ten minutes. Jon/Silas crept back to the access door in the foundation and pulled it open slowly. He could see the light from above coming through the cracks in the floor. It was almost enough light to navigate by, but not quite. Jon pulled his goggles up and tried them. They adjusted to his eyes instantly and while everything was greenish, he could see shapes and tell distances well. As he went under the bedroom he could hear activity up there. Harley was half yelling at Daniel. Demanding to know what Daniel had on him. What did he know and how long had he known it? Jon could hear Daniel moan and then there were the sounds of slaps.

"I don't know what you're talking about." The reporter insisted. He wouldn't allow his eyes to focus, still pretending to be out of it.

"You've been following me and sending me messages, you little creep. What are you up to?" Then the voice got even louder. "Tell me what you know, damn it."

Harley hit him again.

Jon hurried quietly to the area under the bath. He looked to the sub-floor and there it was. Right between the water cut offs and the drain clean out. A cut out section in the floor above him, it was about two by three feet. He pushed the boards up gently and brought them down into the crawlspace.

It opened into the bathroom closet. He had done this before to gain access into an older building.

There were shelves next. Each in two sections that came up and twisted to where they fit down through the hole. Had this been a lived-in home that closet would be full of towels and bottles of shampoo. What he was doing would have been nearly impossible.

Slowly and quietly he took down four sets of shelves. That cleared a path where he could stand within the closet.

Jon cracked the closet door. The light was off in the bathroom and the door to the hallway was closed. He stepped out into the bathroom and closed the closet door. He opened the bathroom door enough to look out. The small hallway was there and the door to the attic was across from him. The bedroom was to his left.

There was more yelling in the bedroom. Daniel maintained his ignorance to what Harley was asking him. Then he heard Harley say he needed to take a leak. Jon stepped back into the closet and pulled the door to. He could hear Harley come in and take care of his business, then leave.

He went to the front of the house this time. He was giving orders for some of the men to go get some plastic bags and a shovel. He was tired of screwing around with this guy.

"Time to wrap this up and get out of here." He said.

Jon wasn't sure how many left, but there wasn't time to wait any longer. He stepped into the hallway and looked to his right. There were sounds coming from the living room area but he could not see anyone. He looked to his left. There was one man in the bedroom with Daniel. The hood was off now and Jon could see it was indeed Daniel Seay. The man in the room was facing Daniel, standing over him while twisting a silencer onto a handgun. It was really none too soon.

Jon touched a button on his belt and the arm powered up. He stepped quietly into the room and grabbed the man from behind by his neck. A sharp twist with his wrist and there was an audible pop as the man's neck broke. The body gave a quick jerk and went limp as the gun dropped. Jon caught it with his other hand and laid the body on the floor.

Daniel was looking at the man in black with fear in his eyes. Jon got down in his face and softly quoted Thomas Jefferson, "One man with courage is a majority."

Daniel's eyes enlarged to the size of saucers and he uttered, "Crane?"

Jon raised his finger in front of his face in the universal "hush" signal. Jon was standing directly in front of Daniel with his back to the doorway. Reaching across the tied up man to undo the ropes he saw Daniel's face become excited.

"Look out," Daniel tried to warn his helper. Shots were fired and Jon could feel the impact against his back. The fabric did its job well. The bullets stung, but very little. Two more shots struck as Jon pulled his Glock from the holster. As he turned to fire back, the man shot again. The round grazed past Jon's back and struck Daniel in the upper chest. Jon's arm with the Glock pointed at the threat. In an instant he fired three shots that dropped the man in the hallway.

There was something happening in the living room.

He saw Charles Harley step into the door and yell,

"Get me the hell out of here."

The front door slammed open against the wall and the sound of feet leaving the house echoed through the hallway.

Jon moved Daniel from the chair. The reporter was not conscious. He checked Daniel for a heartbeat and it was there. The danger was far from over.

Jon rose up and stepped into the hall. He could hear a car start up and pull away. Then another shot came at him, this time from the kitchen on his left. The bullet struck him in the arm but again the STF fabric allowed no penetration. Jon pointed the Glock to the kitchen and fired off three more rounds. Two found their target and the man fell.

Jon quickly searched the house but found no one else there. He checked the wound to Daniel's chest. It was high on the right side but looked like it missed anything vital. The reporter was bleeding heavily. Jon grabbed a roll of tissue from the bath and pushed it against the wound to stop the bleeding. He wrapped the tissue in place with Daniel's belt and put the man over his shoulder. With the reporter over his right shoulder and the Glock in his left hand, Jon Crane went out the front door and around the back. He went through the back yard and the other building's yard to his car. He lay Daniel in the back seat and drove around to the front of the house where he had been captive.

Jon ran back inside with his camera and took pictures of the three men who were still in there then went back to the car to find a hospital.

Realizing he needed to change out of his "uniform" he found a house with an empty carport. Everything in and around it was dark. He parked under that carport long enough to change his clothes and check on Daniel's condition once again. He was still unconscious but the bleeding seemed to be less than before. His pulse was still strong and his breathing was not labored.

Jon put the duffle bag in the trunk and it was on to the emergency room. As he drove the thought came to him that he needed to make a phone call. This situation had developed in a way he had not considered and he needed help.

Jon called back home to George and told him he had Daniel and might need some interference to get out of Charlotte.

"It's a mess right now," He told his friend. "I've got him but he's been shot. I can't just leave him. I have to get him to a hospital."

George was surprised but not that much. He could have asked many questions at that point but his instincts told him this was not the time. Besides, he remembered, he probably didn't want to know the answers anyway. He told Jon he knew a couple of people in the DA's office there and would make a few calls.

"Stay put till somebody gets there who knows me, got it?" George told Jon. "It may be a police officer or somebody from the prosecutor's office, I don't know which yet."

"Alright, I understand, thank you." Jon responded. "I keep getting into messes lately, George. It's not supposed to be this way." He took a deep breath, and then added, " I have rules, or I did have."

Jon pulled the Lincoln into the Carolinas Medical Center Emergency ramp and called for help. They unloaded Daniel and Jon told them who their patient was. They rolled the missing reporter into a trauma room and Jon sat in a chair outside the ER. He waved off questions from the staff and the security guards. The police would be there soon. He would wait until somebody claimed they knew George Vincent before he said a word.

After they had cleaned Daniel up, he awoke. He asked if the man who had brought him in was still there. An orderly came to Jon and told him Daniel wanted to see him.

"Have they called his wife?" Jon asked.

"Yes, they let him talk to her a minute," the orderly told him. "Now he wants to see you."

Jon walked into the small area and looked at the reporter. Daniel shook his head as he managed a small smile.

"I can't believe you came for me," he told Jon.

Jon tilted his head sarcastically and looked back at Daniel.

"Me either," he replied. Then he paused for a moment. Jon Crane tapped the gurney Daniel was lying on with his fist and continued, "I really need to stop getting to know people."

Daniel nodded in appreciation to the man who had saved his life and Jon went back out to his chair in the hallway, and he waited.

Shortly after 11:00PM two officers in uniform and a lady in a raincoat stormed down the aisle toward Jon.

"Are you Crane?" the woman asked.

"I am," Jon answered. He lifted his head and looked directly into her eyes.

"I bring greetings from Mr. George Vincent," she continued. "You need to come with us."

50

Lori Seay was on her way to North Carolina. The news of Daniel's escape was out but details of the ordeal were still few. Whatever he had told his wife she was keeping to herself. Daniel was thinking clearer now. He wasn't sure who had grabbed him. He thought he recalled Charles Harley being there but that was a blur. He needed to talk to Jon again before he said anything. If Harley was there, where was he now? Lori could be in danger. He told the doctors he wanted to see Jonathan Crane. They told him that Crane had left with the police.

"Can you get word to him, please?" Daniel asked them. "He and I need to talk."

~

Representative Charles Harley sat in the private plane in Greensboro. He had flown there earlier in the day and Dowd had picked him up. The drive back had taken two hours but now they just sat in the plane. The pilot was waiting for his orders. Where did Harley want to go? The pilot would need to file a flight plan but that was a formality. Harley was clearly a shaken man.

"Who was that in the house?" he wondered. *"How did anyone even know about that house?"*

He was mumbling out loud and downing shots of bourbon to try to calm his nerves.

"Could I go back to Washington or do I need to go elsewhere and try to establish an alibi for the time?" He thought, and he considered going home. That wouldn't work.

"Myrtle Beach!" He almost shouted. "That's it, let's go to Myrtle Beach."

Harley owned a place there and had enough friends to say he was taking in some shows on the strip. The pilot filed his plan and they were in the air in twenty minutes. Harley's story would be that he had flown to Greensboro earlier in the day and driven down to the beach. Sometime later, he realized he had left his wallet on the plane so the pilot flew on to Myrtle Beach to bring the Congressman his wallet. With friends verifying his presence there all afternoon, the story would hold. This solution or the booze, or a combination of the two, had calmed his nerves. He turned his attention to the man who set this plan up.

"Get Henry Dowd in here," he demanded.

~

Lt. Marsha Hurst, of the Charlotte Police Department, began with questions right away. Most, at first, were about George and how he knew him. That was the extent of the subject in the car, but when they got to the station the questions got much more serious.

"Where did this happen?" she asked the mysterious man her friend had asked her to help.

He liked what he saw even though she was being a bit official right now. The Lieutenant looked to be in her mid-thirties, maybe a little older. She might even be older than he but that didn't matter. He liked her hair. It was blonde with a touch of red and her eyes flashed as she spoke. Try as she did to remain business like, she was attractive to him. Jon tried to see if her left hand was empty or carrying a rock. The way she held the arm of the chair made it hard to see.

"I asked you where did this happen? " she repeated herself.

Jon gave them the address and told them they would find bodies there. He went through how he had gotten into the house and the shootout. He didn't mention the Congressman.

That would remain his business, for now anyway. Lt. Hurst called for three units to respond to the location. The scene was three hours old already and had not been reported. All the commotion and gunfire and no one called it in.

Jon was dancing around the question of how he knew the reporter was there, when the lead unit from the scene called in to the Lieutenant.

"There's nothing here," the officer stated. "We can smell bleach really strong but it's clean."

Jon could hear the report over the radio. He shook his head and thought to himself, "*Just like at home.*"

The radio cracked and the officer on scene continued. "The closet in the bathroom is like he described. The floor is out and the shelves are missing. We found the closet door closed so it went unnoticed." They realized the site had been cleaned up.

The Lieutenant looked at Jon. "Who the hell are we dealing with?" she asked him.

"It's Argus. The drug cartel," Jon told her matter of fact. "They are still active."

Jon explained how he had "found" his neighbor after Argus kidnapped her.

"You're that guy?" One of the officers asked.

Jon took a deep breath and continued his story and how he had been accidentally dragged into the mess. He said he saw a man he recognized as an Argus member while on a business trip there in Charlotte. He followed the man and that lead to the house.

The female officer leaned back in her chair with a look of total disbelief. She took several moments considering her next question. In leaning back she put her hands in front of the chair's arms. Jon saw no ring, on either hand. Before she could ask her question the phone rang. It was the hospital with Daniel's request to talk further with the man who had saved him. She hung up and looked at Jon.

"We need to take you back to the hospital but we're not finished with this just yet." Her tone was stern.

Jon nodded and smiled. He didn't mind her not being through with him yet, not at all. They all got up and headed back to the hospital.

Daniel was sitting upright and in a private room. He looked pretty good for what he'd been through.

"You wanted to see me?" Jon said flatly as they walked in.

"Yeah," Daniel replied. He looked at the officers and the doctors and asked them to step outside for a while. They did so.

"Lori is on her way, she'll be here within the hour they tell me."

"Your wife's name is Lori, then?" Jon said. "You told me about her but I don't recall you mentioning her name."

"Yes, I'm sorry. Her name is Lori. The point is, she knew what I was doing. She knows about you and who I thought you were."

"Thought?" Jon injected.

"Well, yeah. It's pretty clear now, don't you think?"

Jon nodded and waved his hand for Daniel to continue.

"Lori thought you had taken me. She didn't tell anyone, but that's what she thought."

"You straightened that out?" Jon asked.

"Yeah, absolutely. My problem is this. Was Harley there? Is he in on this? I can remember thinking I heard his voice but I'm not sure." Daniel was concerned.

"He was there." Jon told him. "But he got away."

"Got away? So he's out there somewhere? Does he know we're on to him?"

"I guess we'll see how he acts the next few days." Jon leaned in and spoke softer. "I haven't told anyone else about him, OK? It would be very difficult to prove his involvement, but I know he was there."

"What are you going to do?" Daniel asked. "My wife and I could still be in danger if he suspects we know."

"Then don't mention him to anyone." Jon got closer and quieter as he continued, "I will take care of Harley, and soon. I promise."

Daniel looked at Jon. He knew exactly what the man meant. It went against everything Daniel stood for, until now. Now, with his wife in possible danger, it made perfect sense.

"Can I ask how you knew where I was?" Daniel pleaded.

"That's complicated. I'll tell you that Argus is still going. I tracked them here and, by chance, ran into one of Harley's henchmen at a gas station. He led me to the house. It didn't make any sense that day. But when I heard you were missing, it all came together."

"You're kidding, right?" Daniel could not believe the circumstances.

"That's it, man. I wouldn't lie about something that weird," Jon grinned.

Daniel's face got serious again. "Your secrets are my secrets, friend," he said.

Daniel Seay reached out to Jon with his right hand. They shook on it. Jon smiled and turned to go.

"Lori says 'thank-you'." Daniel shouted after him.

Jon got to the door and looked back, "Tell her she's very welcome." And he left the room.

Lt. Hurst was waiting for him in the hall. Her outstretched arm suggested they return to the car.

"Ok," Jon thought to himself. *"The reporter is on board. Now what do I do?"*

As they walked to the car a limo pulled into the covered entrance at the front doors. A very pretty brunette jumped out and was led into the hospital by two escorts.

"Lori." Jon told himself. *"Nice to see you."*

Lori Seay never noticed him. She had other, more important things on her mind.

~

From a condo twenty-four stories over the Atlantic Ocean, Charles Harley anxiously monitored the news. There was coverage of the reporter's escape but no mention of his rescuer and no mention of the Congressman. He calculated that Argus had been compromised again but so far he wasn't. Harley wasn't sure where the screw up had occurred but he knew Dowd would not fail him again. Henry, with the help of a few others, had left the plane on the approach to the Myrtle Beach area. The pilot was instructed to swing out wide over the ocean and Dowd left the Congressman's employ at about 2200 feet. A body would wash ashore between Jacksonville and St. Augustine several weeks later. No identification would be made.

Harley would need a new right hand man. With the drug business going quiet again he thought of Juan Castrono in Atlanta. Harley liked Juan. It would be a waste for him to just be sitting around doing nothing. He didn't care for his name, too much. "Maybe I can call him John," Harley thought. He told one of the men with him to call Juan and arrange for them to meet in Washington in three days.

~

Daniel and Lori's reunion was a happy one. She tried to be upset with him but when she realized it wasn't what she thought, she just rejoiced that he was alive. Daniel explained, in confidence, that he had been wrong about Jonathan Crane. "Well, not wrong about what he did. But wrong about him."

Lori didn't completely understand. That wasn't important now. They were back together.

Daniel asked about when they could return to Pittsburgh.

"The doctor told me you could go home in a couple of days," she responded. "Oh, Mr. White says to tell you 'Hi'."

Daniel looked worried, "Do I still have a job when I get back?" he said half joking.

"I think so," Lori told him. "I believe he's expecting a big story on all this."

"I know he is," Daniel said and he hugged his wife the best he could with his injury.

51

Back at the station, Lt. Hurst tried several times to get a better answer from this mystery man. Each and every instance and event, he claimed to be an innocent bystander, a simple passer-by caught up in the occurrence and finding himself needing to help.

"I've got a gunshot victim to settle charges on." She stated. "Who's the shooter?"

Jon sat back and answered her, "Assailants unknown. I told you, I shot the guy that hurt Seay, but they took him away. It's not the first time they've done that."

"And you're permitted to carry that gun across state lines?" she asked.

"Yes, I am. My former job required me to carry controlled substances around the country. My permit is national. You can check with George."

"I already did," she snapped. She then stood up and walked around the room a bit.

"You know you sound like a character from a movie," the Lieutenant challenged.

Jon didn't care for that analogy. He wrinkled his brow and squinted at her, "How so?"

"You know," she stumbled, "That guy in the movie who's everywhere all the time."

"No. I don't believe I do," he countered.

"Gump. That's it! Forrest Gump. You're like Forrest Gump."

Jon smirked at her, "Are we through here?"

"I guess so. There's nothing else you want to say?" she asked.

Jon did a double take at that statement. A great set up line and she didn't even realize it. He looked at her and asked, "Yeah, what are you doing for dinner?"

Marsha Hurst stared at him hard. "Do you know what time it is?"

Jon looked out a window. It was pitch dark. The wall clock read 4:15AM.

"Well, breakfast then." He had lost track of time.

She tried to hide her laugh by looking down. She cocked her head towards the man.

"Breakfast?" she countered.

"Sure, where do you suggest we go?" he smiled.

"Whoa, I didn't say I would..." she started but got cut off.

"You didn't say 'no' either. Come on, we both need to eat. I go back to Dalton in the morning." He closed one eye and tilted his head, "I am free to go, right?"

"You like pancakes?" she offered.

"Love 'em. When can I pick you up?"

Marsha Hurst took a shallow breath and looked him right in the eyes.

"Shifts over at 7:00AM. I sign out at 7:20." She smiled for the first time.

"See you at 7:21." Jon headed out of the building, on his own this time.

Jon hated holding out on her. He had pictures of the three men he had killed at the house. But he wanted a chance to compare those photos with the ones from that new warehouse building. Right now, those pictures were his.

"If," he thought suddenly, *"They haven't gone through my car."* His rental Lincoln was in the impound lot but it had not been disturbed. He called the desk and the officer released it to him. Everything was there, just as he had left it. Jon drove away to find a room. He might catch a nap but mainly he needed a place to clean up for his "date."

He grabbed his cell phone and put a call into George Vincent.

"Thanks, man. You have some strong pull."

"Lucky you weren't in Savannah. They hate me over there." He laughed and then demanded, "Do you know what time it is?"

Jon had awakened his friend at 4:45AM. He tried to apologize,

"Sorry, that's twice I've been asked that in the last hour. I need to tell you something."

"It better be good," the DA mumbled.

"Look, I have some pictures I didn't tell them about. I have my reasons and I'll make it clear to you when I see you. I just wanted you to know, Ok?"

"Jon, you make this job more fun every second, you know? Withholding evidence now, are we?"

"You make it sound like a bad thing, George. I'll get 'em to you. I just need to check a couple things out myself first. Thanks again, Oh....I have a date this morning."

"A date?" The DA was curious. Then he thought about it a minute and continued, "Not Marsha?"

"Why not?" Jon asked.

"You have a date with the officer you are withholding evidence from?"

"If you have to put it that way, yeah," Jon answered.

"You wonder why you get into messes all the time, huh?" George laughed.

"Good-bye George. But thanks again. I really mean that," Jon finished the call.

There was a sign advertising a Motel 6 just ahead. He pulled into the lobby parking and looked to the desk. There was a clerk. Jon secured a room and set the clock for 6:30AM in case he fell asleep. He stretched across the bed to rest his eyes a few minutes.

The ringing jolted him and he sat straight up.

"*Could it be 6:30 already?*" he thought. He swung his hand toward the clock to turn it off. He hit the "off" button but the ringing continued. Moving his hand to where he could see the numbers on the clock he saw it read 6:10AM. The ringing continued. It dawned on him it was his phone. Picking it up from the side table he flipped the phone open. "Ben calling" the screen said.

"*Oh, man,*" Jon moaned as he answered, "Hello?"

"Well, you made the news again," Ben announced.

Jon didn't like the sound of that. "What? That wasn't supposed to happen."

"But," Ben continued. "You have a new nickname."

"Ben, I don't have time for games. What's going on?" Jon was frustrated now.

"The headline is, "Missing Reporter Found in Charlotte." Then under that it says, "Unidentified Man finds Wounded Reporter Wandering Streets." Ben read to him.

"*Thank you, Marsha,*" Jon said to himself. Then he answered Ben, "Good. I'm glad they kept my name out of it. Any mention of Harley?"

"Not a bit. It just says Seay was found. No details of how he got there or any of it."

"Keep an eye and an ear on it, will you?" Jon asked him.

"Got it covered," Ben sounded very official. "You on your way home?"

"Later. I've got something I need to do this morning first."

"Ok, I'll be around here if you need me. Talk to you later."

"Thanks, Ben. See you soon." Jon hung up and lay back down across the bed. He did remember he had turned off the alarm and managed to not fall back to sleep.

An hour later he was cleaned up, dressed and in his car. It was raining in Charlotte that morning. The city was getting its day started and cars were everywhere. He worried he would be late getting back to the police station.

She stood at the front doors under her umbrella. Jon pulled the Lincoln to the curb and jumped out to get the car door for her. "Am I late?" he asked.

She slid into the seat and folded her umbrella. "Not really. Did you get some sleep?"

He caught her meaning as he stood there holding the car door. "Shows that much, huh?"

"A little." She smiled.

He closed the door and ran back to his side. They pulled away from the station and Jon asked her, "Where to?"

She pointed straight ahead out through the windshield. There, at the end of the block, was an IHOP. "There," she said.

Jon parked and went to get her door again. This time she got out on her own. "I'm not fragile," She pointed out. "I am a cop."

"Sorry," Jon backed off a bit. "I'm old school."

She smiled at him and they went inside the restaurant.

After they were seated and had placed their order, Jon looked over his coffee cup and asked, "How long have you been in police work?"

"When you put it that way, most all my life," she started. "My grandpa and my Dad were officers. Dad just retired last year."

"So, you joined right out of school?"

315

"College. Dad insisted I go to college first." She was proud of that, he could tell.

"And now you are a Lieutenant," he said.

"Eight years as a beat cop, three as a detective and two as a Sergeant. I just made Lieutenant last year. That's why I'm still on the overnight shift."

Jon was adding numbers in his head. He figured 21 to graduate college so the rest came to 35. He was close. A slight smile came across his face.

"I'm 34," She blurted out.

Jon was taken aback and tried to act surprised at her revelation.

"What?" he offered.

"I've been a cop for 14 years. I know what you were doing. You were probably off by a year. I graduated from high school early." Her look went from stern to a grin.

"Same here," he said. "Age I mean. I didn't get through school early. As you can tell."

"What's your story?" she asked. "What you're willing to tell me, anyway."

"High school, few years in the army and then college. Pharmacy School after that, which is why I have the gun permit," he explained.

"Not all pharmacists have gun permits," she noted.

"No, I never was a pharmacist really. I was a traveling representative to hospitals and specialists. Sometimes I carried controlled drugs as samples."

"Was?" She picked up on the verb. "And now?"

Jon was stuck. He thought a minute and then smiled at her.

"Good Samaritan?"

She laughed. That was better than he thought would happen. He tried to go a little further.

"I came into some money a while back. I try to help people. I can't go into it more than that right now. I hope you can trust me."

"I trust George Vincent," she answered. "I don't really know you yet."

"That works," he said. "How do you know George anyway?"

"He's an old friend of my Dad's. He had a case years ago that ended up with the perpetrator in North Georgia. George was a big help catching the guy and getting him back here for trial."

"Sounds like George," Jon agreed.

"That was the main deal. They stayed in touch through the years. Worked again on a few other cases. It's good to have people you can call on. George is a nice man."

She finished her explanation and then turned it back on him.

"And you?"

"Me, what?" he asked. Jon was letting her last comment settle in. That idea about having people you can call on. It struck a chord with him.

"How do you know George?" she restated her question.

"Oh, I'm the neighbor of his assistant. The one who got kidnapped last month."

"That's right," she remembered. "The first Gump story."

"Enough of that, Ok?" he asked her firmly.

They enjoyed their plates of "pigs in blankets" and each other's company.

Through two table-sized pots of coffee they learned they were each an only child.

Their parents were older than the norm when they were born and they had just recently realized how spoiled they were because of it.

Jon called it having acquired "good taste" through a good upbringing. She thought that was funny.

As it got past 9:00AM she looked at her watch and said it was time for her to go.

"I need to get some sleep, Jon," she told him. "This has been nice."

"I enjoyed getting arrested by you, very much," he quipped.

She held her thumb and forefinger close to each other.

"That close," she smiled at him. "I hope the point will come that you can tell me what's going on."

"Me too." Jon shook his head. "Maybe soon."

She thought to herself that maybe he was with the Government. She could ask. But if he were, he wouldn't tell her anyway. Whatever he was up to George Vincent approved of it. For now, that was good enough for her.

He drove her back the half block to the station where she was parked. As she walked away he remembered he had not called for a plane yet. He couldn't carry his stuff back in a commercial jet. He called Gordon Flight Service in Dalton and asked how long till they could send someone for him. They told him it would be about three hours.

He decided to spend the time looking back at the house and the warehouse once more. He drove past the house first. He was surprised to see no "crime scene" tape anywhere. There was an unmarked police car sitting on the location, but that was it. No other activity at all.

He drove to the industrial park and around the warehouse. It too was quiet. The trailers were still there. The roll-up door was closed. He parked right in front of the roll-up door and got out. Using his special stethoscope, he listened inside. Nothing. He supposed they had emptied it by now as well. He found his video scope in the bag and

318

walked around to the end of the building. The hole in the mortar was still there. Checking what he could see through the scope confirmed they had cleared out.

He had hoped to bust them and stop the operation. Now they would just reopen somewhere else, like they had here. He needed to hit them at the top. He needed to get back to his original plan. He still had a removal to accomplish.

He thought about going back by the hospital to check on Daniel. Lori would be there and he didn't want to disturb them. Besides, that could lead to another conversation he couldn't finish. He opted to go to the airport and wait for the charter plane.

The rental car people were nice about the stain on the back seat. They charged him a fee to get it out but Jon didn't mind. He double-checked everywhere to make sure he had not left anything in the car. He zipped the duffle bag closed and carried it to the waiting room. Four hours later, he was back at his Dalton warehouse. Ben helped to unpack the bag. There was nothing to add to the news about Daniel Seay. That was good. They said he would be going home to Pittsburgh in another day or two. Jon made a note to check on him by phone after that.

He pulled the camera from the bag and tossed it to Ben.

"Compare the three guys at the end of this to those from the warehouse pictures," he told him.

Ben opened the pictures and came back to Jon with a strange look on his face.

"Those guys are dead, Jon," he announced.

"Yeah, just a little," he responded. "You'd be surprised how quickly they got up and left there though," Jon quipped. Ben was still standing there with his mouth open.

Jon walked to put away his gear and said,

"Look, those are the guys that were going to kill the reporter and me if I'd let them. Understand?"

"Yeah." Ben really did understand. This wasn't just fun and games. It was life and death.

The man at the hospital was one thing. He knew Jon had handled him but he didn't see it.

Now there were pictures. Jon had gone up against three men, three killers would be more correct, and he won. Now here he was acting like it was no big deal. Ben understood before, but now it was different.

Now it was suddenly real.

52

Two of the three dead men matched pictures of those who had been in the Charlotte warehouse. There was no doubt. Jon had Argus people working with Charles Harley. The only problem was he couldn't prove it with empirical evidence. He saw the man there, he heard his voice but that was it. Daniel was so out of it in that house, he could never testify about who had held him. So it was back to the plan. He needed to get to Harley and take him out. The man would be in Washington for months now. Congress was in session and would stay there till the Thanksgiving break. He couldn't wait that long. In fact, Harley might still make another move on Daniel and his wife. He needed to get to this guy and fast. Jon planned a trip to Washington to look around. Planning was essential to success.

His second day home he got a call from George. A phone number had been relayed to George. They wanted him to get it to Jon. The caller asked for anonymity and security from being identified. The number was from Pittsburgh.

Jon dialed it and Daniel Seay answered.

"Well, hello." Jon was pleased to hear from the reporter. "I thought you were still in Charlotte."

"They figured they needed to move me quietly. I've been here since yesterday," Daniel told him.

"You're not at your home, are you?" Jon asked.

"No, no. They didn't think that would be a good idea. They have us hidden for right now."

"Good," Jon confirmed. "They are right. You listen to those people. Say, how are you feeling?"

"Better than you might think. The wound was clean and I was very lucky."

"That's great to hear." Jon was happy at the news.

"Look Jon, there's a reason I called you." Daniel was being timid.

"Ok," Jon replied. "What's up?"

"Don't take this the wrong way, please. But I've studied you for quite a while. I think I know some of how you operate."

"Really?" Jon was getting interested but skeptical.

"I said, please don't be offended. I have some information that may be of help to you," Daniel offered.

"I'm listening." Jon's voice held no emotion.

"There's a certain club in Arlington, Virginia that our mutual friend has a membership in."

"Go on," Jon prodded him.

"He goes there twice a week this time of year. He likes to sit over the golf course or in the Conservatory and read by himself," Daniel told him.

"Interesting information. Any certain two days in particular?" Jon asked.

"Tuesdays and Thursdays, like clockwork."

"I suppose you're going to tell me the name of this club, right?" Jon sensed this man truly wanted to assist. But the change in attitude was overwhelming. Daniel understood the danger he was in and that sort of thing can alter your perspective. But this much?

"Washington Golf and Country Club," Daniel stated.

Jon was quiet for a minute. Then he told Daniel, "That would be good information if anyone wanted to write a book about the guy. It might be helpful for other things as well."

Then Daniel quoted a man Jon respected highly, "I think the first duty of society is justice."

"You know your Alexander Hamilton, huh?" Jon asked rhetorically.

"I've studied some," Daniel told him.

"Do you know this one?" Jon asked him, "No man in his senses can hesitate in choosing to be free, rather than a slave."

"I do now."

"Daniel, it's been great talking to you my friend. I promise I will take your counsel under advisement. You will hear from me soon. Thank you."

"Thank you, and good luck," Daniel added.

"My best to your lovely wife." Jon hung up and sat quietly.

Was the reporter setting him up? This getting to know people was complicated. Trust was hard. Could what he had been through turn Daniel so completely? It was possible.

Daniel sounded sincere, but he had spent months tracking Jon. What to do?

He decided he would travel to the DC area. Those were his plans already. He would check out this country club on a Friday. If it felt right after that, it could be the answer to accessing Harley. He would keep this to himself. Not even Ben would know. If things went bad, he didn't want any hard feeling against Daniel from anyone.

His phone rang again. It was George.

"What was that all about?" the DA asked him.

"That was my reporter friend. He's back home but no one is supposed to know."

"I thought maybe that was it," George said. "How's he doing?"

"Says he feels pretty good. They got him under wraps for a while yet. Good "catch up" time for him and his wife, huh?" Jon laughed.

323

Doug Dahlgren

"There you go!" George had a chuckle. "Hey. Want to have some dinner tonight with us?"

"Who's us?" Jon asked.

"Doris, me and Ben. I'm getting Doris out of the hospital for the first time. Going to a real restaurant."

"I wouldn't miss it," Jon replied.

"Great. We're meeting at the Cellar on Walnut at 7:00PM."

Jon took a drive to the new house. Visits there seemed to help clear his mind. It wasn't long till he would bring Ben out here to see it. From what his builder said, maybe another week.

They had settled on the floor plan. With George and Doris' plans more public he was able to use the space as he wanted. The main first floor was wrapped in the plywood sheeting that gave it full shape.

Inside, the stud walls now defined the rooms. The electricians were running wires everywhere. Plumbers had red and blue tubes going to the baths and kitchen. He went to the closet in his suite and the shaft was nearly complete. The elevators would be ready to test next week, both of them.

Jon walked down the stairs to the basement areas. Only the first two levels were apparent to guests or anyone who wasn't supposed to know about the third. A hidden button opened a door to a set of stairs to that level. It would hardly be used once the elevators were working but a backup system was always good to have.

In that third level basement he walked to the rock wall he would later have removed. He listened and felt for vibrations, nothing so far. The other crew was working, coming this way closer every day. At some point there were bound to be questions. He'd deal with that as it happened. The garage area looked great. It should hold 6 or 7 vehicles.

Jon went back to the main level and found his builder. They walked outside to where the driveway would come off the street. Jon
324

asked about a flat area in front of the driveway but not in front of the house. "Was there dirt under that rock?" he asked. The answer was "Yes." He told the man he wanted to plant an elm tree there. He asked if that was feasible.

The builder took a few measurements and looked over the edge. He declared it quite possible if the tree wasn't too big to start with. Jon was pleased. He wanted that elm. He already had one picked out at the nursery in town.

Jon thanked his builder again and drove down to check on the tunnel. It was going great. The man in charge told him they were averaging 16 feet per 24 hours now. That was better. Jon looked at the hole in the back wall of the station. He measured it at 16' wide and 12' high. It was time to look into a hologram projector. One that could reproduce a picture of rock over an area that size. He'd put a sliding door there as well for security. But the hologram would allow quick, secretive access with the solid doors opened.

Things were coming along. He was pleased. Jon looked at his watch. It was time to get back and clean up for dinner.

~

The air in Washington, DC was hot and sticky. No ocean breeze like he had left in South Carolina. Charles Harley still felt pretty good about it all. Days after the big fiasco and there was no mention of him in connection to it. Juan Castrono would be coming in tomorrow. He was Harley's pick as his new right hand man. Castrono didn't know that yet, but the decision wasn't his anyway. The Representative's desk was piled high with papers he was to read. He passed them off to his staff and asked for a condensed version he could talk about. The House Whip had been looking for him. Harley sent word he was back but didn't wish to be bothered.

"*Leadership people think they are such hot stuff,*" he told himself.

As long as he got re-elected, he couldn't care less what those clowns thought. He didn't really need their money for that anymore. Like so many others in Congress, he had a sure thing. Once he got Juan working on a new location for the drug dump, they could get going again. The paint cans didn't appear to be exposed. The Charlotte plant had not been touched really. He just couldn't risk it after the house deal.

"*Damn that Dowd, anyway.*" He looked at his schedule for the next few days. There was time for him to get to the club. He had not been to the club in weeks. He could use some relaxing time there.

Maybe he'd go there Friday too, just to be different.

~

The Cellar restaurant was busy that night. Jon got there and could see Ben's Ford in the lot. He didn't remember what George was driving these days. He figured they were there.

The hostess took him to their table in the back. It was quiet there. Doris' walker was against the wall. She was getting around good but needed the helper till the cast came off.

George started to stand as Jon got to the table, Jon waved for him to stay seated and slid into his chair.

"Good evening." Jon said. "Doris, it's so great to see you away from that hospital room."

"It's terrific to be out, let me tell you, "she said. Her smile was wide.

He was tempted to ask how she felt, but that was obvious. She was beaming.

"So, what have you been up to?" George asked like he didn't know.

"Not much, I've got a trip planned for later in the week. What is this, Tuesday? I may leave on Thursday."

"Leave?" Ben piped in, "You just got back."

"I've got things to take care of, unfinished business. You know how that is." Jon stated.

George looked at him but didn't speak. He picked up his menu and asked, "The steaks still good here?"

Doris grabbed her menu and chimed in, "I think I want the fish."

So when the order went in, it was three steaks and grilled salmon. George brought up the arrangements they had told Jon about. Ben didn't seem too surprised. He liked George and knew his Mother did as well. That subject was approved rather quickly.

George then asked Jon what he was thinking about for a more normal residence.

"I've been working on an idea or two. I guess I need to get Ben in on it to see if they'll work," he announced.

Ben looked up from his salad, "What ideas?"

"We'll go see a couple things next week, Ok?" Jon smiled. "I hope you like what I have in mind."

"What? What do you have in mind?" Ben was like a kid being withheld from a secret.

"I'd rather show you what I'm thinking about than try to explain it. Next week, I promise."

Doris sat there and smiled. She picked at her salad but went after the salmon like a starving refugee. "All I've had is hospital food for weeks," she quipped.

"I'm glad you're enjoying it, dear," George said.

Ben looked up at that term. His eyes went from George to his Mother and then to Jon. He didn't say anything, but he heard it.

"Now," George said. "Here's the big news for tonight. I've got the room ready and the doctors said, 'Ok,' so Doris is not going back to the hospital. She's coming to my house."

Doris leaned over the edge of the table and hugged her friend.

"What about my things?"

"I know where they are," he told her. "We'll get what you want from the storage whenever you want."

Ben suddenly thought of something he had almost forgotten.

"What about Dad's tools?" he asked.

"They are packed up with your things, Ben," George told him. "Your mom says they are yours."

Ben looked down at the table and shook his head, slightly but firmly. He kept his head down till his eyes cleared up. It had just hit him. The garage his Dad had set up was no more. That garage was all he had left of him. He would have the tools, but not what his Father had created for them.

Jon picked up on what the boy was thinking. He had been in the garage and knew the detail of the organization that had been there. Jon realized that Ben was upset by the sudden, complete change. But he did not see it as a weakness in the young man, rather quite the opposite. He reached over the table and grabbed Ben's forearm.

"I believe we can duplicate that garage just like you want it. Ok?" he told him.

Ben looked at Jon and nodded his head "Yes."

"Thanks," he said.

When dinner was over, Ben went with George and Doris to help get her set up at George's. Jon offered to get the check but George refused him. Jon excused himself and went to the warehouse residence to check on things and to prepare for his next trip.

53

Juan Castrono was concerned. He had been called to Washington to meet with the man known as the "Bird". That was the top man in the country. The one who called the shots and directed the operation. He had only met the "Bird" once before, on the drive from the Atlanta airport to Dalton. Juan had overheard the conversation between his boss, Armando and the "Bird". Juan always did his best at his job. He had to. His life literally depended on it. He knew how the group managed their company, with violence. Juan wasn't about violence he was a thinker. Armando had brought him up because he could reason things out. He could remember facts and figures and help Armando keep up with the business. Now the "Bird" himself wanted to see him. Juan was very concerned.

They met at a Waffle House in Arlington, Virginia. That wasn't easy because it was Friday and everybody was out for breakfast. They had to wait for a table, standing along a wall waiting with people in work clothes and some in business suits. The "Bird" never said a word while they waited. That didn't help Juan's nerves. When they were finally directed to a table, his host led the way and sat at an angle with his back to the window. Juan slid into the booth and looked at the man.

"My name is Charles Harley," the "Bird" said. "I need you to come up here and work for me personally."

Juan's concerns now took over his facial expression. "Me?" he asked. "Why me?"

"I've lost some key employees recently. Had to let another one go kind of suddenly," the Congressman told him. "I've heard good things about you from several others. You're who I want."

"Sir, I'm honored, don't misunderstand me. But I don't know if I'm comfortable with this," Juan struggled to explain.

"You speak pretty good English. I like that, John. Can I call you John? Those Latin names bug me." The "Bird" raised his cup and drank half his cup of coffee.

"What? John? Sir, my name is Juan. I don't understand any of this."

"Ok, be that way. I'll learn to deal with Juan. But you work for me now, starting now. That's it. You understand that I hope." The "Bird's" face was very stern.

Juan shook his head and rubbed at the condensation on his water glass but he didn't say a word.

"Good," Harley said. "Meet me here tomorrow at 11:00AM." He handed Juan a note with an address.

"It's my club. It's big so you'll have to ask for me." He drank more of his coffee and waved the now empty cup at a waitress.

"So, you want a waffle or something?"

Juan wasn't hungry but he ordered some toast. Harley next handed him a bulging envelope and said,

"This should hold you over till we establish your pay."

Juan looked in the envelope. It was full of twenties, fifties and a few hundreds. He didn't know how much it was, but it was a lot.

The "Bird" ate a waffle and drank two more cups of coffee. He didn't say another word the whole time. When he was finished, he looked at Juan and nodded his head once. He then put a twenty-dollar bill on the table and left. Juan sat in the booth for a few more minutes, still staring at his toast. What could he do? He could try to run, but where? He had a new job. That was that.

~

Most of his morning was spent looking around the Capitol Grounds. It was too busy and fluid for any planned contact. By the afternoon Jon had checked out where he thought the man lived, his office building and the eating establishments the upper class appeared to frequent. Sitting and listening here didn't help. There was way too much going on.

He had dinner at a small diner and thought about what Daniel had told him. He didn't really know Daniel that well, or did he? What was it that drew him to go help this guy when he knew he was in trouble? Did he know somewhere deep inside who to trust? Was this like his sixth sense about those who were evil?

The more he thought about it the more questions he developed. He decided to do what he always had, trust his gut instincts. Right now, they were saying trust Daniel. He opened his notebook and looked at the address of the club. Arlington, Virginia. He would go there tomorrow and check it out.

~

From his hideout in Pennsylvania, Daniel Seay reached out to others he knew would be worried about him. He talked with Earl Johnstone of the Burlington Hawk Eye in Iowa. They didn't discuss Harley much, not over the phone. Daniel did hint enough to let Earl know the Congressman was involved in the mess, for sure. He told Earl that the experience, the entire experience from Texas to Charlotte, had caused him to rethink the man everyone called "the Son."

"Don't go and get 'Stockholm Syndrome' on us now." Earl cautioned him.

"Ok, I can tell what you're thinking." Daniel got frustrated with that comment. "We need to talk sometime. There's more to this than I ever thought and I'm not suffering from any syndrome. Stockholm or otherwise."

"Alright, don't get mad at me, man." Earl was trying to backtrack. "He does kill people, remember?"

"Yeah, you're right. But there are many others he could have killed, but he didn't."

"I don't understand," Earl said.

"Look, I just wanted to let you know I was fine. We'll get together when they tell me it's okay for me to get out again. Take care and," he paused for a second and almost didn't say it. "Look into things more yourself, will you?" Daniel finished and hung up.

Earl Johnstone looked at the quiet phone receiver and did his best to understand what he had just heard. Either the trauma had sent Daniel "around the bend" or it opened his eyes to another side of this story. He thought about the stories Daniel had told him. About his travels tracking this killer and the people he interviewed. The only ones hurt were, in fact, verifiably evil.

It took Daniel several hours to calm down after his call to Earl. It was hard enough facing his change of heart about the killer. But then having to defend himself to a friend over it was frustrating, even infuriating. He did feel he needed to call Matt Turlock in Shreveport, but decided to leave any of that discussion out for now.

Matt, the newspaper editor beat him to the punch. It was actually Phil Stone, Matt's good friend and Police Captain in Shreveport, who had thought things through.

Stone was a homicide officer and had been for many years. He understood killers and this guy did not fit the profile. He was an "avenger" or an "angel-vigilante," as Stone described him, but not a hardened killer.

"What he did actually saved lives in the long run. Those were the ones you wonder about," Stone had told Matt.

Stone had already figured it was that man who had saved Daniel in North Carolina.

"The guy does what he does as a last resort," Matt quoted his police Captain friend again. "Killing is very targeted and specific for him. When he sees an innocent in trouble, he has to help."

As Daniel verified that Stone was correct, the Louisiana newspaperman laughed out loud.

"They'll be no living with Stone now," he proclaimed. Then he apologized to Daniel for the laugh.

"Sorry, I know you went through hell, it's just that Phil nailed it and based only on what you had told him when you were down here. I don't even think I told him about your meeting the guy in Georgia."

Daniel thought about his next statement, but only for a moment.

"It the kind of thing we all think about doing, once in a while, but not seriously. We don't act it out," Daniel confessed. "I don't know what to do with what I know about him now."

"Well, be thankful he was there for you. There's a good starting point," Matt offered. "Phil Stone is the best judge of people I know. Sounds like your gut tells you to agree with him. I'd go with it, for now anyway."

"Thanks, Matt. I appreciate that." Daniel felt better now. "We'll get together and talk more about this soon, Ok?"

"That's a deal. You take care, buddy," Matt finished and hung up.

Daniel put his phone down gently, looking into blank space as he thought. He had received the acceptance of a peer for not moving against Jon with what he knows. But Daniel had already gone much further. Jon offered no commitment to using the information Daniel gave him, but the line had been crossed. Matt would not approve.

54

Late summer in Washington, DC could be downright uncomfortable. Maybe it was the moisture from the Chesapeake Bay without the breeze from the ocean. Whatever caused it, it was worse than Georgia after a rainstorm. Jon drove his rental car to Arlington, Virginia that Friday morning and found the Country Club with little trouble. He had bought some fairly expensive casual clothes for this visit. He hoped to project himself as a wealthy friend of a member, a member who had asked him to look around the facilities. He claimed he was considering getting on the waiting list to be a member himself. The Internet had provided him the name of a club member from the west coast, a man who was currently out of the country and couldn't be reached.

He signed in and was given a guest badge. It would allow him four hours to wander about and check out the place. He went for the bar first. Sitting at the end, he ordered a ginger ale and listened to the conversations.

Most were mundane until he heard a voice behind him state,

"Harley, what are you doing here?"

It was him, Charles Harley with a Latin man in tow. This was Friday. Daniel told him Harley was a Tuesday and Thursday visitor. Had Daniel set him up with all this? Whatever it was, this was not good. Jon was ready to leave when the other voice sounded off again.

"Don't look for your favorite chair, Charlie. I use it on Fridays." The man was smiling as a joke. Harley slapped the man on the arm and laughed back at him.

So this was out of the ordinary. The Congressman was being chided about being here today.

"*Ok, so Daniel was right,*" he thought.

He kept his seat and watched as the two men ordered drinks. The Latino fellow seemed uneasy. Harley was boisterous and talking to nearly everyone.

"Good to see you guys. It's a shame they won't let you in on the good week days," he teased them. "Don't worry Jones, I'll leave the chair for you, today."

The man he spoke to raised his glass toward Harley as in a toast. The Congressman and the uneasy Latino walked toward the area called the Conservatory. A beautiful but narrow Florida-room.

It had white rocking chairs and white wicker chair sets lining the 60-foot length of the room. The room was about seven feet wide and had glass walls along either side. One separated it from the dining room and the other looked over the golf course.

Jon stayed back but where he could see that Harley and his guest had stopped half way down and sat at a wicker set. Their conversation was one sided but that was all he could tell about it. Jon straightened himself and walked down the Conservatory, taking in the view of the golf course the whole way. He stopped a time or two, but not where he would be considered eavesdropping. As he passed the men, Harley gave him a quick glance and that was it.

The Latino squinted and looked at Jon very hard. Jon heard Harley ask his companion,

"What's wrong?"

"I don't think anything, Sir. He just looked familiar to me. I don't know from where."

Jon could hear them as he walked. The Latino was not familiar to him at all. It was weird but not that unusual, probably just a mistake. Jon got to the other end of the walkway and turned to the

335

stairs. He went down to the patio area and circled back to the other end of the building.

Jon noticed the staff. They were mostly men in short white jackets. They carried small round trays and wore white gloves. The trousers and shoes were black. He sat for a few minutes to study them. They were everywhere but didn't appear to have a certain area that was their responsibility. It seemed they would deal with whatever came up regardless of where it was.

Drinks were the main things they delivered. Each carried on those trays. A couple had the trays in the position, but no drink visible. He managed to see they were carrying notes, messages of some kind. He got up and walked back to the bar. It was nearing the noon hour and men, mostly, were gathering to go into the dining room. He counted only four women in all. Two of those were underage.

He looked back toward the Conservatory and noticed the lounge area. Huge wing-backed, leather chairs were spaced for privacy. He walked to the far corner and sat looking to the Conservatory entrance. It was then he noticed the man Harley had referred to as "Jones." He had been almost hidden in the chair. The chair was positioned with its back to the bar. The man was intently reading a book. He was in his own world. Jon also noticed a small side table with a drink sitting on it. That was Harley's regular chair he noted. An idea began to form in his mind.

He looked up to see Harley and the Latino walking from the Conservatory toward the dining room. The Latino was again staring at Jon. Instinctively Jon looked up and glared back. The other man ducked his head finally and followed his host. Jon had no idea what that was about. He could recall faces well. That one meant nothing to him. Who did that guy think he was looking at? Jon shook it off and continued his tour. He found several other places of interest to him, a small linen closet around the corner from the bar and a set of stairs that were not marked. They were intended for the service staff. He made mental notes and took pictures where he could. He found a member's sign-in book in the lobby and looked through it. Harley had not been there in a couple months, but when he came he usually signed in around 10:30 or 11:00AM. To Daniel's credit, those days were Tuesdays and Thursdays.

By mid-afternoon Jon had what he needed. He would go home and concoct and evaluate a plan. If satisfied with it, he would return on next Tuesday to visit the Country Club again.

Juan Castrono ate his lunch but his mind was elsewhere. He knew that face. He always remembered faces but he could not place that one. Harley kept breaking his concentration by introducing him to other men. Juan would have a permanent guest pass to the club so he needed to know certain people. When there wasn't an introduction, Harley was telling him details of his new job. Nothing untoward was mentioned here, that would come later.

They visited the tennis courts and the pool area after lunch. The club was spectacular and Harley was quite proud of what the good people of Iowa were paying for him to have. One thing Juan needed to remember was the parking. If he was bringing Harley here, he could park in the member's lot. If he was coming by himself, even to meet Harley, he had to park in the general lot. This was very important. The member's lot was a valuable asset. They coveted it like it was gold.

Juan would be glad to get away from there that day. He needed time to think. He really needed to remember who that guy was, for his own sake. It was like that song you get in your head and can't think of the title. Gets to you after a while.

Jon's return flight would not get to Atlanta until 4:45PM. That meant 6:00 or 6:15PM before he could get to the uniform supply shop in mid-town. Ownership can be a good thing. He called the shop from Ronald Reagan Airport and asked the manager to stay for him.

Overtime, even on a Friday night wasn't a bad deal for the employees. Jon paid well for overtime, especially when it was for him. He had further e-mailed pictures of what he needed and the manager had told him "no problem."

He requested the right arm to be bigger around than the left and he also needed a white golf glove in an extra large. Traffic was bad that afternoon and he didn't get to the shop until just before 7PM. He was still greeted with smiles and the full treatment. The white jackets were really throwbacks but they had several in stock. They had let out the sleeve for him and fitted two pairs of black trousers to his measurements.

The golf glove was the issue. No Extra Larges. He would need the additional room for what he had in mind. He told them he'd check with the local golf shop in Dalton. That would need to be in the morning now. They closed at 5PM. The outfit looked good and they even had shoes to match. Jon took two sets and signed timecards with nice bonuses for everyone who had stayed.

Traffic was still a nightmare so he stopped by the Varsity for a couple of chilidogs. That filled his hunger and an hour or so of time. It was after 11PM when he finally got back to the warehouse in Dalton. Ben was still up, going through e-mails.

"Should we tell the guy from Illinois what happened with his lead?" he asked Jon.

Jon realized he hadn't even sent a "thank you" to the man, the unknown assistant who had spotted the move of Argus to Springfield. Without him Jon would have never known about Charlotte, NC and Daniel Seay could well be dead.

"Yeah, just tell him his work was well received and appreciated." Jon was very official.

"Kind of formal for a thank you, isn't it?" Ben questioned.

"They expect that from me, Ben. They really do."

"Ok, how was the trip? You going to tell me where you went?"

"It went fine, Ben. This one is back to the old rules, Ok?" He looked right at him. "I'll tell you what you need to know, but nothing else. I want you to have deniability, got it?"

Tension momentarily filled the air. Jon was getting serious. There was only one thing to do.

"Yes, Sir," Ben responded. Then he changed accents to a deep tone and added. "Hey, let's just be careful out there."

Jon caught the reference. He knew Ben was making fun of him, but it was funny.

"Been watching television again, huh?" Jon laughed.

"Yep, 'Hill Street Blues' was on TV Land network again this week."

"Ok, Sarge." Jon shook his head smiling. "I'm going to bed. See you in the morning."

55

The knock on the frosted glass door didn't wake him. Jon had to open the door and holler into the room. "Hey, get up. I need your help with something."

Ben struggled to get his eyes to work. His clock said 7:15AM.

"Saturday doesn't have a 7:15," he thought, *"Saturday doesn't start till 11AM."*

"Come on, I'm serious. I need an idea on this and I don't have much time." It was Jon again.

Ben stood and threw on his pants and a shirt. Walking into the main area he could tell Jon had been busy. The "workshop" was lit up like a football stadium on a Friday night. Tools were strewn all over the workbench and he had one of the arms and several white gloves lying with them.

"I need to wear this white glove over the finger tips." Jon explained. "But the arm doesn't work when I do that."

Ben thought about what Jon said and asked, "Do you have to wear that glove or do you just need the tips to be white?"

Jon threw himself into a chair and rocked back. "See, that's why I got you up. What can you do?"

"Tell me what you need, exactly." Ben rubbed his not completely awake eyes.

Jon sat up and showed him the glove. "It has to be white. And I need this pocket in the palm to be rigid, like the leather allows," he explained.

Ben looked at the pocket. Jon had carefully sewn a 2" pocket into the palm. He had used leather from another white glove and added three rows of perforations. The pocket was sewn on three sides but open across the top, that being between his forefinger and thumb.

"What's the pocket for?" Ben wanted to know.

"Don't worry about that, Ok? I just need the arm to work with this glove."

"Can I cut the finger tips off the glove?" Ben asked.

"It needs to look like a complete white glove," Jon insisted.

Ben told him why the glove would not work over the fingertips control for the arm.

"The leather is too restrictive and tight. It shorts out the sensors and they won't work."

Jon said he had found that out. "But I can't have anyone notice the tips are different."

"Can you use a cloth glove?" Ben asked him.

"Cloth won't do for the pocket." Jon saw the look come over Ben's face so he added, "Don't ask. I just need the leather in the pocket."

"Alright," Ben was thinking. He walked to the blacked out windows and turned back to Jon. "If I can just cut out the areas where the fingerprints are in oblong circles and cover those with white cloth or maybe a gauze, you shouldn't be able to tell."

"Will the arm work?" Jon asked.

"Yeah, it should. The gauze would give you better grip but it might snag."

"Won't need it that long. Try the gauze, will you?" Jon smiled. He liked the idea.

Ben looked for his Exacto knives as Jon went into the chemical room. Ben was not allowed in the chemical room. He could see Jon through the frosted glass, taping up the seams around the door.

341

"What are you doing in there?" he asked.

"Just stay out there, whatever. Do you understand? If I ever go down in here, don't come in. That's an order." Jon was adamant. More so than Ben had ever heard before.

"Ok, ok." Ben responded. There wasn't much else he could say.

Jon unlocked a heavy steel cabinet and found what he was looking for, the vile of Saxitotoxin. Another drawer in the cabinet held capsules, empty capsules of various sizes and makeup. Some were heavy and some were quite brittle. He tested several for breakage and selected the ones he thought would do the job.

He found his supply of powder propellant, the type that reacted to air and carefully filled two of the capsules with it. Jon then took out a respirator that looked like something from NASA and put it on. He took out a gown made of a slick material and pulled that on. Then it was heavy rubber gloves and he was finally ready to work with the toxin.

He had used the Saxitotoxin before. It was quick and powerful. It also dissipated very fast. One capsule of the product should be plenty. He made sure that the two-sided capsule would twist at its joint. He carefully drilled a microscopic hole through the joint into the center of the capsule but not through it. Matching a syringe to the hole size, he withdrew several grams of the toxin and inserted the needle into the capsule. As he pulled the needle from the capsule he twisted the top half to misalign the holes and seal the capsule. Jon carefully wiped the edge of the joint and turned on a tester unit to check the air and the surface of the deadly capsule. All was clear. Placing all three capsules into a small transport box, he then locked the box back in the cabinet. He removed the respirator and the other protective coverings and checked the air again, before he opened the door.

"How are you doing?" he asked Ben. The prior tension was now gone.

"It's coming pretty good," Ben offered. "What do you think?" He handed the glove to Jon. Two of the fingers had been surgically altered and heavy gauze pads inserted to cover the holes. Jon slid the glove on and could immediately tell the difference.

"How long till you're done?" he asked the kid.

"Couple hours and we'll be ready to test it with the arm." Ben said with pride.

Jon smiled at him and tapped his head. "Good work," he said. "You're quite the boy wonder sometimes, you know?"

Ben didn't even look up, "Don't go there."

Jon laughed, "Ok."

The phone rang. Jon answered and George's voice said in jest, "I'm going to start charging you for my answering service."

"What now?" Jon asked.

"You need to get a number you give to people yourself. Marsha called. Said she didn't have a number for you and wanted to tell you something about the reporter. I didn't say anything. She doesn't seem to know you've talked with him already"

"Hey, thanks." Jon suddenly felt a bit lighter. "Did she leave a number?"

"Yeah, would you like me to get her on the line for you, Sir?" George quipped.

"Funny. Just give me the number, will you?"

As he wrote the number down he thought to ask, "How's Doris this morning?"

"I haven't bothered her yet," George reported. "The nurse said she was sleeping really good. I think she's comfortable and glad to be out of that hospital."

"Great. I know she must be." Jon thanked him for the number and they concluded the call.

"I'll be back in a minute," Jon told Ben and he went into his private room. Ben waved and kept working.

As he punched the numbers he could feel apprehension and excitement building. He wasn't used to it and he didn't care for it. When the voice on the other end answered he instantly felt better.

"Hello," she said. It really sounded nice. It was Marsha.

"Hey, what's up?" Jon was doing his best "I'm cool" routine.

She paused for a couple of seconds and then continued,

"I found out your reporter friend went home, a couple of days ago actually. Nobody knew except the higher ups."

He thought about not telling her but his mouth overrode him,

"Yeah, I talked to him yesterday."

"Oh, well," she stuttered. "Sorry to bother you."

"Bother who? You're not bothering me. I'm glad to hear from you. Really."

Words spewed from him in random order. Then he asked her, "You doing Ok?"

"Just got off work a few hours ago. Found out about the reporter and couldn't sleep. Just thought I'd give you a call."

Jon liked what he just heard. Once again his mouth overrode his mind,

"Say, can I come back up there to see you, sometime? I mean, I don't want to appear too forward but I'd like to see you again."

Marsha was quiet again. Jon waited, hoping he had not overplayed his hand.

"That would be nice," she finally answered. "You've got my number."

"Yeah," he nearly blurted. "Let me give you a number where you can reach me, Ok?"

"Sure," she said coyly.

He repeated the number for her and then wished her sweet dreams. She said she believed she could sleep now and Jon liked that.

When the call was over Jon leaned back in his chair. What was he doing? Friends everywhere and now these feelings he didn't even understand completely. He was supposed to be a loner. Loners worked alone. Or did they?

56

The glove was ready to test just before lunchtime. Jon slid into the arm and its controls and pulled the glove on over it. It felt better, much better. Jon could tell the pressure was released from the fingertip sensors. He activated the hydraulics and moved the arm about.

The grip tester showed he had complete control over the strength the system offered. The glove looked good enough to fool anybody and the gauze gave him some sense of feel for picking things up.

Jon nodded his head in approval and smiled at his young assistant.

"Great job, Ben. This will work," he told him.

"Still not going to tell me what this is all about?" Ben asked once more.

Jon ignored the question and made another suggestion. "Let's get lunch and take a ride. There's something I want you to see."

They had a burger at a Steak 'N Shake off Walnut Drive and headed north toward the mountain. Outside of town about two miles the road swept to the right and then straightened out. There it was. Ben saw the amazing structure and commented about it. He was confused when Jon turned into the drive and went up to the first level.

"Whose house is this?" Ben asked him.

"It's mine," he answered. "And yours as long you wish to stay here."

They walked around the main floor and Jon pointed out the rooms and features. He took Ben to the basement and then the second basement where Ben's workshop and "garage" would be located. The house's garage was a separate building near where they parked. It would hold four vehicles and a couple of bikes if needed. Jon suggested they go look at the second floor. "That's where our private rooms will be," he told him. Besides the private bedrooms there was a library where Jon's books would be kept. "Why not the first floor?" Ben asked.

"Those books are special," Jon answered. There's the parlor downstairs and we'll keep some books in there, but this is my library." He took Ben by the arm and led him to what would be his room. Since it was Saturday the workers had left at noon. Jon thought about waiting till next week to bring Ben out here but he needed to go out of town. Those trips were always dicey. There was no telling how they would go.

They walked through Ben's area and Jon pointed to the huge closet room. Inside Ben noticed the strange little room with the odd door. It was the elevator. There was a note on the wall. The builder put the note for Jon about the elevators. "The main unit needs a bit more work but the secondary unit is good to go," it read. "Just turn the power on at the main box and follow the instructions if you like."

Jon had asked that the power panel box, for the circuit breakers, be put in his room. That was a bit unusual, but not a big deal. He walked over to his room and found the panel. It would be mounted behind a mirror when all was completed. He opened the panel and threw the main breaker. A few lights came on and they could hear the pump for lifts building pressure. A light inside the elevator in Ben's room showed system not ready. After about a minute it switched to a green light indicating it was good to go. They stepped into the round container and Jon swung the door closed. He hit "1" on the controls and the unit fell, abruptly to the first floor and the door opened on its own.

"So far, so good," Jon smiled. He closed the door again and hit "B3" this time. Again the drop was attention getting, but not harmful. The stop at the bottom was soft and smooth and once again the door opened by itself. This was an area he had not mentioned to Ben before. Jon reached to a spot on the wall and found the lights.

The space was huge. It was as big as the other two levels plus the dugout area. Ben pointed at the dugout with a question in his eyes.

"That's where we'll keep the vehicles," He said. "The job vehicles."

Ben nodded his understanding while Jon walked to the far rock wall. He put his hand on the rock to see if he could feel anything yet.

"What's that about?" Ben asked.

"That's the big secret." He pointed at Ben and his head bobbed up and down. "When I built my first secure room I forgot a very important detail."

"Ok, what was that?"

"Escape," Jon proclaimed. "Escape or simply undetected exit and return."

Ben didn't say anything but his face clearly showed he needed more information.

"There's an old building a half mile down the road, an old gas station. A tunnel is being dug from that station to this wall."

He looked at Ben with all seriousness.

"That's the secret. Only you and I can know about this. No one else, no one." Jon walked back into the center of the third level basement and stretched out his arms.

"This space and how we get to it is our business and ours alone. Understood?"

"Not even Mom?" Ben asked him.

"Not even," Jon answered. "We will have our computers and monitors down here. All my special gear and the records you have organized so well for me. My cars and trucks with their special abilities, all that stays down here. All of it stays between us."

"When will it all be ready?" Ben asked him.

"They tell me about four more months. The two men in charge of the projects do not know about each other. I'd like to keep it that way."

"Sure," Ben agreed and then a thought hit him. "You're not giving up what you do, are you?"

"Give up?" Jon was puzzled. "I don't know what you mean."

"I didn't think so." Ben smiled at him and then asked, "When are you going back out?"

"Tomorrow."

They rode the elevator back to the main floor. Ben was quiet. Jon let him walk around on his own for a while. There was so much to take in. Ben was impressed but concerned. This house was amazing, no doubt about that. But it represented a huge change in lifestyle and direction. Ben had accepted the changes caused by his mother's kidnapping. But now, instead of winding down and getting back to normal, it was going further. The news from dinner last night, his mom moving in with George, realizing he could never go back to the only home he had known and now this. He had told Jon he was committed to what they were doing. These creeping doubts, should he talk them out with Jon or just work through them? He looked at his friend. Ben could tell Jon was thinking about his trip. He could see worry in his face.

"*Man up,*" Ben scolded himself. Jon had altered his game plan for him. They were a team now and he knew he was an asset to Jon.

"This is just amazing, Jon," Ben finally spoke. "How do you come up with this stuff?"

"Necessity is the mother of invention," he answered. "Not just in material things, but sometimes in philosophy." Jon turned the lights and the power off and they went outside.

He showed Ben the area in front of the drivewaythat was just below the ledge. It had been flattened out and the hole partially dug.

"This is for an elm tree I have picked out," Jon said.

"An elm?" Ben was curious. "Something special about an elm?"

Jon looked a touch disappointed in him. "The original tree in Boston was an elm."

Jon walked to the car but Ben stood there for a minute more.

"The Liberty Tree!" Ben finally exclaimed. He stepped back a couple of steps and shook his head.

"That's cool." He smiled wide at Jon, "That's so cool!"

When they got back to the warehouse hideout, Ben told Jon he wanted to go visit his mom.

"No talk of the house just yet, Ok?" Jon reminded him.

"No, Sir," he responded firmly. "That's our secret."

Jon spent the rest of the afternoon packing. The tools and devises he would need. This trip would require several disguises as well. He picked the Mercury for the ride. After packing, he sat down with his maps to plot the routes he would use. It had been a while since he sat alone and planned one of these trips. His latest work had been mostly reactive to the situation. This could not be reactive. It had to be planned right down to the last detail.

Jon left Dalton, Georgia at noon on Sunday. He headed south to Atlanta and then east toward Augusta. From there he would follow I-20 to Florence, SC. At Florence the highway connected with I-95. He would rest at Florence. The next day's drive to the DC area should take about 8 hours.

As he drove north that Monday morning Jon's cell phone rang. He didn't have it with him. He did not want to be disturbed on this job. The phone was left at the warehouse.

Ben answered it after it had rang three times in a row. The caller sounded stressed. He needed to talk to Jon.

"He's out and I don't know when to expect him." Ben explained. "If he calls in I'll tell him you called."

The caller was nearly frantic at this point. "Tell him its Daniel. I need to talk to him."

"Yes, Sir." Ben tried to be soothing. "I'll let him know as soon as I hear from him."

57

Jon didn't like to wear wigs. This Tuesday called for not only a wig but also a fake moustache.

He packed the black trousers, shoes and white coat in what looked like a tennis bag, a very full tennis bag. He had another coat in the bag, as well as his tools and yet another wig. He dressed in tennis shorts and even a pullover sweater tied around his shoulders.

The mercury was dressed in disguise as well. Virginia plates would help it blend into the other cars in the lot.

Arriving at the club parking lot, Jon took his time gathering the bag from his trunk. He watched for the right group to gain entrance with. It wasn't too long till they showed up.

Six of them, all dressed to play tennis were laughing and talking as they walked to the entrance. Jon approached them from an angle and blended in as they reached the doors.

As they signed in, he asked questions to different members of the group. Things like what court they preferred to play on or was it supposed to rain today? Mingling in, he simply walked in with the group after they had all signed the book.

Once past the lobby Jon went to his left and found the linen closet. The door was locked but only with a push-style lock like a bathroom door would have. He stuck a ballpoint pen into the hole and the door opened to him. Checking around, there were no witnesses, so he stepped inside and closed the door.

There wasn't much room, but it was enough. He changed into the black trousers, shoes and a blue pullover shirt. The wig came off, as did the lip hair. Unfolding the white jacket, he smoothed the wrinkles and hung it behind the door. Jon carefully arranged the other items in the bag. The next change would have to be quick, really quick. Once he was ready, he pulled the door open by a crack and checked. One group walked by the lobby and then it was clear. He stepped out from the closet and walked into the bar area. It was 11:35AM.

After doing a pass to see if Harley was there, he found a stool near the far end of the bar. Harley was indeed there. He was in the dining room seated with a party of five other men. They were talking loud and laughing. It was not difficult to pick them out. From the look of their plates they were almost through with lunch. Jon ordered a Sprite and settled in.

He noticed her pass by again. He had seen her before. She looked nervous and clutched her purse strap tight to her with both hands. Each pass across the front of the dining room doors she would pause and look inside. The last walk by, her fourth, put her at the lobby end of the bar. Jon got up and slowly stepped toward that end as well.

He found a seat several feet in front of her. He was between her and the dining room doors. He found her image in a mirror and sipped on his drink. She stayed where she was but kept looking around. Then the noise began and it got louder.

The commotion from inside the dining room was obvious. Harley's loud and obnoxious group was on its way out. As they emerged from the dining area into the bar Jon saw her move. She stuck her hand into the purse and started to walk forward. Jon swung around on his stool and stepped half way in front of her. He grabbed her arm at the wrist where her hand went into the purse and looked her in the eyes. Her nervousness went into panic. She looked like she was about to faint.

"Lori?" Jon whispered right in her face. The panic changed to shock in her eyes.

"Who are you? How do you know me?" she stuttered.

Jon looked down into the purse. As he had feared, her hand was on a small revolver. He kept pressure on her wrist. Not allowing her hand to move and pulled her toward the lobby and the front entrance.

He leaned in to her and whispered again, "I'm Jon."

Her resistance to his pulling eased as she looked up at him,

"You did come." She said.

Once outside and off to the side, Jon turned her to him and grabbed her by both arms.

"What are you doing here?" he demanded.

"He didn't think you would come," she said.

"What?" Jon shook his head.

"I heard you and Daniel on the phone. I heard what he told you and I saw the disappointment on his face when he hung up." She swallowed hard and continued.

"He didn't think you believed him. He didn't think you would come."

"So you're here to do just what?" Jon was angry.

"That bastard tried to kill my husband," Lori cried. "I was going to kill him."

Jon took several deep breaths. He looked to see if they had gathered any attention. No one seemed to have noticed.

"Lori," he said very clearly and firmly. "Go home."

"Why didn't you let Daniel know you believed him?" she asked.

"I don't like people knowing my business or my whereabouts," he said. Then he repeated himself.

"You need to go home. Call Daniel, I'm sure he's worried sick. Get some rest, what did you do, drive all night?"

She nodded yes.

"Don't touch that gun again till you are away from here." He pointed her to the parking lot. "Now go. And I'd be thankful if you didn't mention seeing me here."

Lori Seay shook her head and walked away. He watched her till she got well into the parking lot and then turned back to the entrance. Now what? He was outside and there was a guard at the sign-in book. He thought he could still see Harley at the bar but he couldn't just walk in. Not through here anyway. His tools were in there, in that linen closet and time was a big issue as well.

He took a deep breath and called on Silas for inspiration, but he realized that he was alone. He had broken nearly every self-imposed rule that he had. "The Son" was on his own.

This job had become a personal vendetta; it was more than a simple removal, there was payback involved this time. His tempered resolve now focused on the man, the target not the mission.

The feeling swept through him like a cold wind but there was no time for that now. Jon looked around and made his decision, his access to the building now was not here it was around back.

Half walking and half running around the side of the building, he got to the patio area and walked along the edge of the golf course.

No one challenged him.

The plan was intact. He got to the stairs under the parlor and went up. The parlor was where the leather wing backed chairs were. As he stepped into the parlor a quick glance caught Harley settling into his chair. Jon walked back to the bar to wait and watch for his opening.

As he sat and studied the bar area another ad lib came to mind. He prepared a note using the name of the reporter Harley had killed in Iowa.

"*This man should see that name once more before he dies,*" Jon thought in silence.

~

Juan Castrono had spent the weekend studying locations for the next receiving hub.

The east coast was where Harley wanted it and below the Mason Dixon line. Places north of there were out because of the weather. If a snowstorm closed the northern routes it would close off distribution to the south. While checking out locations by the Internet, he still tried to place that face he saw at the club. He realized it only meant anything when it was connected to Harley.

His mind started to unwind. He remembered the trip from the airport in Atlanta and back. He thought he had picked up a tail several times that night. He never told Armando or anyone, but he thought he saw it. A green Jeep would be there and then disappear. At the airport while dropping the "Bird" off, he saw it again. It drove right past them.

That was the face, the man driving the Jeep. That was him.

Juan tried to call Harley's office. He wasn't in they told him. He was at the club.

"Could you call him there?" he asked.

"No, he doesn't like being disturbed while at his club," they told him.

Juan jumped in his car. He didn't care for Harley, but if he got whacked, what would happen to him? His only choice was to tell him what he remembered, and quick.

~

Within ten minutes Jon saw what he was waiting for. Those leather chairs had small flags the member could raise when he wanted service. Harley raised his flag and a man with a white coat responded to him. Jon had timed their reactions and the average was 5 minutes.

From a drink being ordered to its delivery took about 5 minutes. Jon left the bar and went to the linen closet.

He changed in less than two minutes, including the arm, the gloves and the packet he kept in the jacket pocket for now. He moistened the white towel he would carry over his left arm and put it in place.

Jon left the closet and went down the stairs to the lower level. Across to the same stairs he had just used a few minutes earlier and back to the parlor. He stood at the door and waited till the server started back towards Harley's chair. Stepping in with his chest out, he walked up to the server and read his name from his badge.

"Adam?" He stopped the server. "You're Adam, right?"

"Yes. What's the problem?"

"No problem," Jon stated. "There's a big party down on the patio trying to order lunch. They asked for you and I said I would see if I could find you."

The thought of a large party meant a good tip. Adam looked at the drink on his tray.

Jon held up his tray and asked. "Who's that for? I'll take care of it for you."

Adam passed off the drink and pointed to Harley's chair.

"Thanks man, you're new here aren't you?"

"Very new." Jon smiled. Adam was on his way downstairs.

Jon took the packet from the jacket pocket and slid the capsules into the palm of his right glove. He took a note from another pocket and laid it on the tray with Harley's drink.

He then walked over to the man and sat the drink tray on the side table. Harley didn't look up from his book.

He simply said, "Put it on my tab."

Jon spoke to the man as he activated the arm unit.

357

"Its been taken care of for you, Sir." And pointed to the note on the tray. The note read, "Compliments of Peter Cass."

Harley turned his head with a start and tried to stand. Jon grabbed his face with the right hand and held him in place. Harley's effort to squirm did not match the power of the arm.

Jon leaned his head to Harley's ear and whispered,

"Daniel says Hello."

He then buried his face into the moist towel, behind the wing of the chair, and pushed the palm of his right hand into Harley's face.

It was over in half a minute. Jon slowly raised his head with the towel still pushed to his face. He had never been that close to a release before.

He lowered the towel and took a slight breath. The product had dissipated. The air was clear. He wiped Harley's face and sat him straight in the chair. Jon sat the glass directly on the table and took the tray and the note. Tucking the tray under his arm and the note in his pocket, Jon walked back through the bar area. He sat the tray on the bar and calmly ordered another drink. Then walking around the corner to the closet, he disappeared inside. He needed to change once more.

Adam came up by the stairs at the end of the Conservatory. He had not found any group looking for him and was pissed. He wouldn't say anything to anyone about it though. What he had done, leaving one guest for a more lucrative one, was strictly against the rules. If he found that new guy he'd give him a piece of his mind but that was all.

As Adam walked back toward the parlor he noticed the congressman in his chair. Something was strange about him. His feet. The congressman's feet were at odd angles. He eased up to the chair to check on him, and then sounded the alarm.

A tennis player with reddish brown hair and a moustache emerged from the closet off the lobby. He noticed that the guard was not at the sign-in book. He could hear a commotion coming from the other end of the bar and looked to see. A small group of lookers had gathered around the leather wing backed chair. A server came running to the bar.

"Call the paramedics," he proclaimed. "And where's the Secret Service that's on duty here?"

The agents of the Secret Service were all down at the tennis courts. A senator's young daughter was playing in a tournament and she was easier to watch than anything else going on. Their pagers and radios went off and they ran toward the main building.

The tennis player, with his oversized bag, walked out the front doors and to the parking lot. He noticed a Latino man running from the lot to the doors. It was that guy who had been staring at him last week. The tennis player looked right at the Latino but the man did not notice him.

"*Not a bad get up,*" Jon thought smugly to himself. The Mercury was waiting for him and he placed his bag into the trunk and pulled away. As he got onto the main street out front he could hear sirens. He eased the Mercury toward the interstate and kept going.

~

Within two hours it was breaking news throughout the country. Iowa Congressman Charles Harley was dead of an apparent stroke at his club in Arlington, Virginia.

Daniel saw the news on TV. He had heard from Lori so he knew she was all right. She should be asleep by now. Getting some rest before driving home.

Lori Seay was in fact sitting on the edge of her bed at a motel in Falls Church, Virginia. She stared at the TV with the report of Harley's death. Lori's hand cupped her mouth as she muttered to herself, "*Oh my God.*"

~

Jon had planned to leave the area traveling due west. The rules required it. He found he was going south on I-95. He would do so till just beyond Richmond where he would turn onto I-85 south. He was being drawn to Charlotte, NC. He told himself he shouldn't. The rules were in shambles, but he kept going.

58

The news stopped George Vincent in his tracks. He had not heard from Jon in a couple of days, but had no idea he was "out of town."

He called Ben and asked to speak with Jon.

"He's not here right now. I can have him call you when he gets here." Ben was quite formal.

"Yeah, Ben. Do that for me, will ya?" George didn't know if he was upset or relieved it was over. He put the phone down and turned the volume back up on the TV. There was no sign of foul play and no one claimed credit.

"Jon's MO for sure," he thought.

The media tried its best to make it a somber event but few people, even outside of Iowa, felt too bad. The House Leadership was not overly concerned. They could replace his vote and perhaps even get someone who was more engaged into what they were there for than Harley ever was. They didn't say that, not on camera anyway. But the "sad" looks on their faces were forced. That was obvious.

~

Juan had walked into the club far enough to tell what had happened. He went back to his car and sat there. The ambulance came. The police came. More Secret Service agents came. Many of the members and guests left. Juan did not know what to do. He didn't like what he was doing, but that was mainly due to his fear of Harley. That was over. What would his role be now, he wondered. The "Bird" was

361

gone. There would be a new leader and a new direction. Was this the time to make a break from these people? The thought of that scared him as much as Harley had. They would find him. So, what to do?

He had money. Most of what Harley had given him plus the money he had at his office.

"Discretionary funds," Harley called it. He decided there was no one here now to report to. He would go back to Atlanta. He knew Atlanta. He was comfortable there. He would send out a message that he was in Atlanta when he got there. They would then tell him what to do. The cartel would rebuild. There was no doubt in Juan's mind about that.

~

Charlotte looked different to him coming in from this direction. It was bigger than he thought. It took an hour to get through town at the rush hour and that's what it was. 5:00PM on Wednesday. She would be asleep he figured. He didn't want to disturb her because she had a full shift to cover overnight. He drove to her station and parked outside. Remembering the pancake house up the street, he walked to it. He didn't eat. He had coffee and stared at a paper.

Not far from there, Marsha lay on her bed staring at the ceiling. She had heard about Harley. Marsha knew the story and the connections. She lay there until around 8:30PM and then got dressed to start her evening. At 9:15 her phone rang. It was Jon.

Before her judgment could tell her no, she had given him her address. Thirty minutes later, he was there. Marsha opened the door and he stood there. He looked tired.

"Are you ok?" she asked, grabbing him by both arms.

"Yeah," he answered without moving. He just stared straight ahead.

"I've lost Silas," slipped from him as he just stood there, as in a trance.

What had happened could have gone bad in so many ways. Yet he got through it. He wasn't sure how he'd managed but by some form of providence he had. At this point, he was aware of but one thing. He knew he was mentally exhausted.

Marsha shook him slightly and softly asked,

"Who is Silas?"

"Nobody. I'm sorry," he managed to focus and look her in the eye. "I don't know where that came from, don't worry about it."

The look on her face assured him the discussion was not over though she would let it pass for now.

He had never spoken that name aloud before, not to anyone. But that wasn't the only change.

The missions, the removals as he called them, were supposed to be completely objective. The first four had gone smoothly, just as he planned. This one started out on the right path but suddenly became personal, to the point of vengeful. Jon never thought of himself as a vengeful person, not until Ben got hurt.

Then Doris' kidnapping added to it and things just snowballed. Had all that not been connected to his target, it might have been different. But Harley was connected to all of it, even Daniel's ordeal.

His target became an obsession. Not on just one, but several levels. He had gone so far as to torment that last removed evildoer with a remembrance of some of his acts. It had become way too personal. Not at all what he set out to do. He had thrown his own rules to the wayside at every turn, reacting rather than thinking and planning. And yet he succeeded. Or so it seemed. Was that "providence" working with him in spite of himself?

And now, in his stupor, this new person in his life was pulling him to her with some magical power. He was at her doorstep and he didn't know what to do. He wasn't sure why he was there. Marsha looked at him and stepped forward. She threw her arms around him and said softly,

"Come in, Jon."

She took his hand and led him inside. To her he appeared to be in shock or near it.

She stayed with him till time for her to go to work. She said not a word about Harley.

She knew. No one had to tell her, not even him. The minute she saw the news she knew it was Jon. But if he wanted to talk about it that was up to him. She would not press the issue with him. Jon had little to say about anything those first hours with her.

"I'll call you, here, in the morning and we'll get breakfast," she said. Then followed it with,

"You will be here then, won't you?"

Jon looked at her and said he would. After she had left he lay sideways across her bed and fell asleep.

He slept until the phone woke him at 6:20AM. It was Marsha.

"You up for some breakfast?" she asked.

"Sure, I could eat." Jon felt better after sleeping. Something about where he was had helped.

This wasn't home but it felt like home. He was comfortable here.

Marsha could hear it in his voice. She was happy for that, but she knew he still would not talk about what he had done.

"Do you want to meet at the IHOP?" she asked him.

Jon smiled at the suggestion. He had not eaten at an IHOP until last week. Now it was in his top five places to go.

"Since that's the only place I know so far, and I like it. That will be fine, he quipped.

"I'll be there in an hour," she said and hung up.

Jon washed his face and shook himself more awake. It was Thursday. He hadn't called Ben yet. The need to report in was also new but it was strong. He knew Ben would be worried. He picked up her phone and dialed.

Ben said nothing about the news from Washington. He did say he was glad to hear from him and had been worried a bit. He then told Jon that Daniel and George had called. Jon said he felt he knew what Daniel had called about. He told Ben that was taken care of, but Ben interrupted him.

"No, he called again just yesterday. It was something about Louisiana. He seemed less stressed than when he called the first time."

"Ok, I don't have that number with me. It's in my cell phone under Daniel Seay, would you get it?" Jon asked him.

"Sure, Oh...and, George called. I'm sure he heard something he wants to talk about."

That was as close as Ben let on that he knew anything.

"I'll call them later. I've got a couple things to deal with this morning. If they call back tell them I'll call today. Ok?" Jon was thinking clearer with each passing minute.

"Got it," Ben said in a very official tone. Then he asked, "When you coming home?"

"I'm not sure yet. But I'm fine. Don't worry about anything. I'm fine." Jon was assuring.

He hung up from Ben and immediately called George. It was still early, but he loved to call George early. The number rang several times before a sleepy voice answered.

When he realized who was calling George went off, "I knew you'd call at some ungodly hour. Where the hell are you, anyway?"

Jon laughed into the phone. "You going to arrest me, officer?" It was good to laugh.

George stopped and got serious. "I suppose you got your issues worked out?"

"Yeah, one or two."

"Are you all right?" George asked him sincerely.

Jon appreciated the question. The feelings of caring weren't just one-way.

"Yeah I am. It's good." Jon paused for a second. "Stuff keeps happening though. Getting in the way."

George didn't respond to that, he knew those things were out of his area. He was quiet for a bit and then changed the subject.

"I see you're calling from Marsha's phone. How's she doing?"

"She's great. We're meeting for breakfast in a few minutes."

"Go slow there, Jon. She's a good girl. I've known her most of her life," George cautioned him.

"Thanks. I like her too, you know," Jon said.

"I gathered that." George was flip.

They finished their call still having mutual respect for each other. They just chose not to say so, directly.

59

The IHOP looked better this morning. Jon and Marsha had a nice breakfast and talked. He was more talkative than last night. His wits were about him again. He still didn't go into what he had done or what had happened in its course. Just being around her made it better somehow. He was relaxing. Catching his breath.

When the meal was over they went back to her place. Jon explained that he had used her phone and offered to pay.

"Don't worry about it." She smiled. "I have a plan with my cell phone, it's no problem."

He said there was still another call he needed to make but didn't want her number to become involved. She asked had he never heard of *67? He had not. He could reprogram a cell phone with a straight pin but he had not heard of *67.

"You can hit that before you dial and the other end doesn't know where the call came from," she told him.

"Really? Can I use your phone, again?" Jon made a face.

"Go ahead," she laughed. "I'm going to the ladies room."

Jon dialed the *67 and then Daniel's number. The phone was answered on the second ring. The voice on the other end sounded stronger than the last time they had talked. Jon was glad to hear that.

"Daniel, it's Jon. You wanted to talk to me?"

"Yes, thanks for returning my call." Daniel gathered his thoughts. There was much he wanted to say. " I owe you a huge debt of thanks but that's not what I'm calling about this time."

Jon assumed from that that Lori had gotten home safely.

"Ok, what is it?" he asked the reporter.

"I met some friends in Louisiana while I was...." He paused for too long.

"Hunting me?" Jon offered wryly.

"That's not true Jon, or fair really. I was trying to verify you. You're a fog out there to most. Many don't even know you are real." He took a breath and continued, "others think you're a group or a mob."

"Too many know now, that's become obvious," Jon countered.

"But you're still an enigma, a mystery that no one can be sure about."

"An enigma with a fan club." Jon wasn't laughing.

Daniel stopped for a moment. His point wasn't getting through so he changed the topic.

"Look, the Lori thing. I had no idea she had gone till I got up Tuesday," he said.

"Well she about stepped in it." Jon was short and terse.

"I know, she told me. I'm glad you were there to stop her. I really am."

"Well, you have one brave lady on your hands, man," Jon told him.

"I know, sometimes I just wish she would think a minute before she acts."

"That's good advice. You mind if I use it sometime?" Jon joked.

There was no answer to that. Daniel didn't even try. He went back to his purpose for the call.

"Jon, these folks I met in Louisiana, Shreveport to be exact. Anyway, they are good people. You can trust them."

"Why would I need to trust them?" Jon asked.

"I want you to consider meeting them," came the reply.

He could hear Jon grunt before he spoke. When he did, he was again blunt.

"Daniel, I know too many people already. It's getting to be a problem."

"Again, I followed you, I studied you, Ok?" Daniel was trying to be convincing. "I know you and understand how you think and work."

"Then you know I would rather be left alone." Jon was being firm. "What I do can be jeopardized by having too many chiefs. Look what your wife got in to."

"There's only one chief, Jon. That's you." Daniel was emphatic. "But a support staff, fellow believers who help with information, cover stories, contacts. It could be very valuable to you."

There was quiet from the other end. He could tell Jon was thinking.

"Daniel that's all flattering, I assure you, but I need to work alone." Jon was adamant.

"Listen to me, please. I spent two hours on the phone to Shreveport having this idea drummed into me." Daniel was now being forceful himself. "It was the police captain's idea. Just listen will you?"

"Go ahead." Jon sounded calm but skeptical.

"You've been called a Son of Liberty." Daniel stated.

"I never said that." This was a sore subject with Jon. "I study those heroes and try to honor what they stood for. I never claimed to be one."

"Jon, hold on a minute. How many were there?" Daniel asked him.

"How many what?" His patience was being tested now.

"Was there just the one Son of Liberty back then?" the reporter pressed him.

"I'm not a...." Jon started but Daniel cut him off.

"Yes you are. You are standing up against evil that cannot be touched." Daniel could feel power growing in his words. He continued, "That type of unchecked evil causes people to give up on their beliefs."

Jon didn't speak but Daniel could hear him breathing.

"The Sons of Liberty were a group. If such a group was handled wrong, it would constitute evil in its own right. Some claimed they were wrong even then, but they paved the way for this country's freedom."

Daniel struggled to remember how Phil Stone had worded it.

"They handled what they did correctly, as I know you do." The reporter was going now, "A mockery of justice disheartens people. Stopping the mockery can be a powerful tool for right and freedom." Daniel paused to let Jon think about what he had said.

"Jon, are you still there, Jon?" he then asked.

"Yeah, Daniel. I'm here," Jon responded slowly.

"Think about it, will you. What Matt Turlock called me about was simple but impossible at the same time. Capt. Stone heard about the news from Washington and figured it was you right away. He said, 'I knew he wouldn't give up on getting that creep.' Then he started sharing with Matt about all the unsolved cases where they know who is responsible and can't get to them. The intimidation the gangs and the drug dealers use against regular people. The fear people live in, here in our country. There has to be something that can be done about it. Something that, while beyond the rule of law, reinforces that law."

"That's a nice speech, Daniel but you're setting me up way too high."

"I don't think so, Jon. I see the detail you go to. You have to be satisfied by over a hundred percent before you act on something. I've been behind you, every case you've handled."

"Removed," Jon interjected.

"What?"

"Removed, I call it removal," he said with a touch of pride in his voice.

Daniel took that as his opportunity to close the pitch. "The spirit of the Sons of Liberty can work again." He let that sink in a second, and then went on. "We have a foundation for it. Matt and Capt. Stone in Louisiana, there's another newspaper man in Iowa, myself and I know you have a DA in your town covering for you already."

"You've met George, huh?"

"Yeah, together we can identify and help clear information on cases that might need your type of expertise to correct." Daniel was winding up now.

"Who's in Iowa? I thought that editor got canned," Jon said.

"The editor did. I've been dealing with Earl Johnstone. He was a friend of Peter Cass'."

"Oh, I see," said Jon. "I may have seen him in the office that day."

"Jon look, just please consider it." He paused for several seconds this time and then said. "Thanks again for what you did this week." And then Daniel hung up. Jon sat there with the phone in his hand for some time after Daniel had hung up. Finally Jon pulled the phone from his ear. He looked at it, pushed the off button and laid it down.

Marsha had been in the room again for some time.

"Everything all right?" she asked.

"I don't know." Jon smiled at her. "I was just offered help by people in three states who don't really know me."

"I haven't known you long enough to 'know you,' but I feel like I do." She sat next to him and put her arm around him.

"You think you know me?" he asked her.

"I'm a cop. Of course I do." Marsha grinned.

They sat on her bed and talked. He asked if she really wanted to know what he did or maybe what he was? She had read Daniel's piece in the Post Gazette several months ago. She had followed the stories from Iowa and Georgia. She knew what he was doing before she ever met him. And then when she did meet him, she felt strangely comfortable with it all.

"I saw what you risked for a friend, a friend you hardly knew. The chances you took and how others were willing to stand up for you, especially George Vincent."

She leaned into him, "I've only known you a short while. But I know I want to know you more. You're no vigilante and you're certainly not a terrorist. Some will call you those things, but not me. You do what you do for the right reasons and only when there is no other way. I know you took care of that jerk in Washington on Tuesday. I knew when I heard about it that it was you."

"And you let me into your house?" Jon asked. "You still trust me?"

"I believe in you and Silas," she said coyly. "Silas is the Son, isn't he?" She paused with a deep breath. "And you are Silas."

Jon did not reply in words.

Marsha looked him in the eyes. His concern and question of her trust was still there. She leaned in to kiss him. Her answer was silent but strong. That first kiss led to another even more intense and their emotions took over from there.

60

Somewhat later that afternoon, he knew she needed to get some rest and he needed to return to Georgia. Jon asked if he could use her shower. As he got up to walk toward the bathroom, she could see the remnants of several bruises he had acquired. They were healing but still evident, four on his back and one on his left arm.

Round golf ball sized bruises that she recognized for what they were. Marsha covered her mouth with her hand but said nothing. He had been in a major gunfight, probably when Daniel got hurt. The police vests like she was familiar with would leave much bigger bruising, if they stopped the bullets at all. Whatever he had must be superior to the standard issue Kevlar. Her curiosity was strong. Not just on a personal but a professional level. Still, she asked no questions. He would talk about it with her when he was ready, if ever at all. She joined him in the shower and they stayed there until the hot water ran out.

It was nearly 3PM when he kissed her one more time and said he had to go.

"I'll call tomorrow," he told her as he pulled the door to. When he got to the Mercury, he had the strange sense that he was leaving something important behind. Another feeling he wasn't used to. He shook his head in wonder of himself and cranked the car to life. It would take several hours to get back to Dalton, but that was fine. There was much to think about and the drive would be a good time for it.

The house was coming along and they would need to move soon. He had not yet ordered Ben's surprise vehicle. The Ford 500 would stay upstairs in the main garage, as would his own private vehicle. The new car he planned for Ben would be part of the secret. Kept in the third level sub-basement and used for special occasions. The elm tree he had picked out should be ordered before someone else gets it. Figuring out how to coordinate the tunnel project into the sub-basement without wide spread knowledge. That would be a challenge in itself. There was work to do back home.

"*Home*" he thought. How that had changed in just a couple of short months. His ranch house with the safe room was gone. The neighborhood he loved, even the easy life style he had become accustomed to, all gone. He once did what he did in complete anonymity.

There were few complications, if any at all. Now it was difficult to keep up with who knew and how they might react. His focus had been blurred by relationships. The loner was now a member of a group, a group of friends who cared about him, and he them. The rules he had so carefully crafted would have to be revised, if kept at all. They served him well through four, no, four and a half missions.

Were all these changes because of mistakes he had made or just the natural course of things? He missed what he had had, but did not regret any action he had taken that led to the changes. He had a clear head with no pressing issues and time to think. Maybe he could have it figured out before he got home.

Then of course, there were the big things. Changes he could decide on, or could he?

The new considerations he needed to work out in his mind. Life-changing considerations. Another human being had become more special to him than he ever imagined, much more than any of the others. It was on a new level of caring, one that could get in the way.

She was now a part of him and that feeling would not leave. He didn't want it to.

And... he had the offer from Daniel, a chance to meet with and work with others. The plan was problematic at best.

Getting more people involved. More places where something could go wrong. But it also offered the possibility to accomplish more good. More than he could have ever thought of by himself. The drive would be a good time to think.

The Mercury turned toward Interstate 85 and Jonathan Crane was headed home.

~

In a small house on the north side of Atlanta, Georgia, Juan Castrono had received a message from Bogotá, Columbia. It was short but direct. "Contact Dewey Hanson in Pennsylvania for instructions." The cartel was alive and moving forward.

Those who expect to reap the blessings of freedom must, like men, undergo the fatigue of supporting it.

Thomas Paine